## STREET FIGHT

Ferris's face turned a mottled red. His sword scraped free, and Ferris drove the point at Jobber. Jobber sprang forward, both arms raised in a cross-handed block. He caught Ferris's sword arm just at the wrist, forcing the arm with the sword up over his head. Then he grasped the sword hand in his own hands and twisted around sharply. Jobber jerked Ferris's outstretched arm down hard and slammed the back of the elbow against his shoulder bone. Ferris screamed as the joint was pushed upward and smashed with a noisy crack. The sword fell, skittering across the street.

Jobber let go of the arm and rammed his elbow into Ferris's belly. Ferris doubled over groaning, and Jobber turned swiftly, catching him by the ears. His knee surged upward into Ferris's face. Ferris gave a final strangled moan as he collapsed to the ground in a messy heap, his nose and mouth bleeding.

Jobber smiled at his bloody handiwork...

# MIDORI SNYDER
# NEW MOON

ACE BOOKS, NEW YORK

This book is an Ace original edition,
and has never been previously published.

NEW MOON

An Ace Book / published by arrangement with
the author

PRINTING HISTORY
Ace edition / February 1989

ISBN: 0-441-57179-4

Ace Books are published by The Berkley Publishing Group,
200 Madison Avenue, New York, New York 10016.
The name "ACE" and the "A" logo
are trademarks belonging to Charter Communications, Inc.
PRINTED IN THE UNITED STATES OF AMERICA

10 9 8 7 6 5 4 3 2 1

*For Charles and Mary Ann, with affection*
*"There's many a dark and a cloudy morning,*
*turns out to be a sunshiny day."*

"A ragged colt may prove a good horse."

**A Cockney proverb**

# 1

"How about the one in green. Re Elman's daughter, isn't it?"

"No, she's too skinny."

"I like that. Something exciting about getting stabbed by a hip bone."

"Not me. I want breasts I can fall into. Now what about Alva, eh? Look, she's winking at me."

"Spoken for already."

"What difference does that make? It's Firefaire. You bed any who's willing."

"Not when the intended groom is a member of the Silean Merchant Guild. Casir's son, you know the one with the ugly scar—"

"And the big sword?—"

"The very same."

"Hmm, maybe you're right. My death would be such a disappointment to the ladies."

"Not to mention yourself."

"What's your opinion, Alwir?"

Alwir turned his head from the window, looking at his brothers Renn and Balder for the first time. He'd been standing next to them, staring out the window, not seeing them really, just hearing their conversation as it drifted with the usual stream.

"About what?" he asked absently.

"Where have you been?" Renn challenged. His cheeks were flushed red with wine. "All of Beldan's eligible women—"

"And not so eligible," Balder added with another wistful glance at Alva.

"All these women," Renn continued, "waiting to be noticed. And where is your mind at? Where are you looking? Out the window, like a village idiot waiting to howl at the moon."

Balder rapped his knuckles against Alwir's chest. "You should be howling at the women," he added, chuckling at his own humor.

"I was just thinking," Alwir said softly.

1

"Not allowed during Firefaire," Balder scolded.

"What is allowed then?"

"Drinking and whoring. What else is there that matters?" Balder answered, brushing the front of his velvet waistcoat. Alwir noticed his older brother had dyed the faint traces of gray hair black just for this occasion.

"What else indeed?" Alwir said dryly.

"So which one do you think I should reward with my manly graces?" Balder repeated the question, turning to face his younger brother.

Alwir looked out across the large room at the gathering of courtiers, Silean nobles and merchants and the few wealthy Orans permitted to attend such an august event. The room sparkled with the dazzle of wealth as shimmering silks and jewels competed for the light. Dotted among the bright clothing were the somber tones of Silean clergy, their dark blue robes sweeping the floor. And around the edges of the room, standing almost invisible against the walls, were the Silean Guard in uniforms of black and gray. Alwir recognized almost all of the Orans present, members of the Readers' Guild, his own family among them. He scowled to himself not liking what he saw. They were Orans casting themselves like foolish sheep to wander among Silean wolves. He felt the anger rise in his chest, his hand tighten on his wineglass.

"Well, Alwir?" Balder prodded him with the question.

"The one in blue and gold over by the wine bowl," he said and turned back to watch the window. He had hardly seen the woman and only mentioned her to satisfy his brother's question. He wasn't interested in the whoring. Worried thoughts occupied his mind. He looked up into the black night, the stars faint pinpricks. Where was it? Surely the moon should have risen by now?

"Zorah's tits!" Balder swore loudly and angrily.

"Shhh," hushed Renn annoyed. "Curb your tongue, man. The Queen will hear you."

"I'll give her permission to swear on my arse."

"Shut up, Balder, you'll get us into trouble," Renn snapped, looking over his shoulder to see if they had been overheard. A Guard stared back, his expression unreadable.

Balder quieted, venturing a glance across the room. The Fire Queen Zorah was surrounded by admirers wishing her tidings of the coming year and asking in return for the blessings of Firefaire. Alwir joined his brother in mute staring.

It was hard not to stare at her. He knew she was ancient, at

2

least two hundred years old, and yet she appeared no older than a young girl on the threshold of adulthood. Her face was a slim oval halved by a straight nose. Her eyes were deep green, flecked with sparks of yellow. Around her head a nimbus of copper-colored hair fell to her waist. She laughed at something whispered in her ear, and he marveled at how the strands of red-gold hair caught the light. She wore no jewels. She needed none, for the hair wreathed her head like a crown of fire.

Balder whispered furiously at him. "That choice of yours has a nose like a horse and a set of teeth to match. You've gone blind living in the countryside, Alwir."

"No wait a minute," Renn said suddenly, a finger rubbing across the stiff bristles of his mustache. "I know her. She's one of Re Navi's daughters. She snagged me yesterday with a very interesting proposal. Too bad I was already on my way to Ninen's chambers. I almost changed my mind."

"Tell me what she suggested," Balder said, growing more interested.

Renn motioned him closer, and as his brother leaned down to hear the whispered words, Renn made a quick gesture with his hands to illustrate the complexity of her suggestion.

Balder's eyes widened with surprise and he smiled hugely.

"The little fox!" he exclaimed. "Where do the ugly ones come up with such beautiful ideas? Oy, Alwir, have a listen to this."

Alwir held out a hand to silence him. "I know it already." He waited a moment, staring back at their baffled expressions. "You asked where she might have gotten the idea . . ." he let his voice trail off, deliberately leading them to the wrong conclusions. In truth Alwir had no idea what Renn had feverishly whispered into Balder's ear, but he didn't want them to know that. Better to play their game and keep them amused. Worry and anticipation had distracted him all evening. If he wasn't careful, he'd make a dangerous mistake. Ever since Alwir's return from the country, his brothers followed him, watched him closely. Alwir had worked hard to give the appearance of a changed man. He bantered with them, feigned interest in their affairs with women and drank to please them. Now they were relaxed, believing at last that Alwir was one of them. It wouldn't do to let his anger and disdain of them unravel that impression.

"You cur," Balder said admiringly. "Back one month from the country and already you've bewitched them. Can't say as I understand it either. You're hardly much to look at. If anything you've grown thinner and certainly more dour."

3

"It's his poet's soul that attracts them," said Renn. "They take one look at his pale, soulful face, instrument dangling in his hand—"

"I've seen his instrument," countered Balder, his glance straying beneath Alwir's belted waistcoat, "and I don't think there's much to it."

"Ah, but the music I make with it, brother," Alwir retorted. He took another swallow of wine to hide his impatience. How much longer was he going to have to stand here? How to get away from them?

"Spare me please the details of your musical prominence—"

"Hist! The Queen approaches." Renn shut them up.

As the Fire Queen Zorah crossed the room, the guests drew back, parting like a wave and bowing respectfully as she passed. Alwir stared at her and shivered. She was ice and fire, cool white skin surrounded by flaming hair.

"Alwir Re Aston," she said, acknowledging him. "It is good to see you in court again. I was afraid we had lost you to the countryside."

"It is good to be back, Madam," he lied.

"Did you bring your instrument with you?"

"Indeed, Madam, my brothers and I were discussing that this very moment."

"Are you still writing music?"

"When time permits."

"Will you play this evening? For me?" she added, and flecks of gold leaped in her eyes, inviting as a fire.

"I would be honored, Madam."

"I look forward to it. Some new songs perhaps."

"It would be my pleasure."

"I am sure the pleasure will be mine, Re Aston." She tipped back her head, and he felt her smile like a caress. He smiled back into her beautiful face and wondered if she would take pleasure in the songs they sang of her in the mountains. Of her betrayal and her tyranny. No, he thought angrily, she'd find no pleasure in those songs. Even though he'd written most of them, and they were his best work.

She turned away, and he watched her move through the crowd. They eddied around her like smoke, following her, clinging to her presence. Even the Silean clergy trailed close, their faces sour, Alwir guessed, at being subject to so beautiful and yet heretical a creature as Oran's Fire Queen. Only the Regent Silwa remained unaffected by Queen Zorah's presence. He stood hands clasped behind his back, legs apart. Alwir studied him for a moment and saw in turn that he was watched. The Regent's stare was appraising, almost challenging.

"Now you've done it, lad. Bewitched the Queen herself!" Renn was whispering.

"Not likely," Alwir frowned.

"Oh no, it would be *my* pleasure," Balder said in a falsetto voice that mocked the Queen.

"Can it be you're jealous, brother?" Alwir asked.

Balder snorted and finished off his glass of wine with a hasty draught. "I'd sooner a woman I could possess. Not one that owns me."

"An incendiary remark, Balder," Alwir said.

"It's true though, isn't it? A Reader can't piss without the Queen's permission," he said bitterly.

"That's what bothers you the most, isn't it? Not that the Sileans squeeze Oran of life's blood, not that the Queen permits it. But that you cannot do as you would wish. That even you, a noble at the court, a Reader, must await the Queen's pleasure, like any common Oran farmer." Alwir tried to heed the warning in his head, tried to stop himself before he betrayed the extent of his true feelings. With effort, he closed his mouth.

"Still the same Alwir," Balder said his eyes narrowing. "Spewing forth with sentimental bilge about the common man."

Alwir steadied himself, calmed his rushing pulse. "No," he answered carefully, "I'm not the same. I've changed."

Alwir turned back to the window, not wanting to see the hostility that masked fear in his brothers' faces, fear that his imprudence might cost them what little place they held at court. In the black sky, the tip of a new moon rose from behind the Keep's parapets like a dagger half-drawn from its sheath. *At last!* Excitement pressed against his spine, and his fist clenched the stem of his wineglass. They should be to the outer wall by now. It was time to go. It was fortunate that the Queen herself had provided an excuse for his absence.

"I'm going," he said, trying to sound less angry. "Only to return instrument in hand, tightened and tuned."

Balder caught the attempt at humor and responded in kind. "Hear how his poet's soul gloats!" he said to Renn. "Oy, Renn, introduce me then to that horse-faced girl with the delicious idea."

As they sauntered across the room, Alwir exhaled nervously and started for the entrance of the hall. He moved quickly, trying

5

to avoid people who might have engaged him in conversations and slowed his escape. At the entrance to the hall, Ener Re Aston stopped him, one hand clapped on his shoulder. Alwir turned sharply to stare into his father's face, obedience like an unwanted habit stopping him in midstride.

Ener Re Aston was an elegant man. His silver hair was combed back from a square cut face. His eyes were light blue, his jawline firm and unyielding even with age. At his throat he wore a simple gold chain that carried the emblem of the Readers Guild, a silver face surrounded by a wreath of fire.

"It's early yet, Alwir," he said.

"I'm not leaving," Alwir answered. "The Queen has requested I play tonight. I'm going for my lute."

"The Queen does us an honor."

"What honor is that, father?"

His father's hand tightened to a grip on his shoulder. Creases deepened in his face.

"Play well, son. Something that favors the Queen." It was a command.

"I shall play as I wish. I am not a servant." Alwir's anger flared. "I am my own man."

"Then act like one, and not a foolish child!" Ener answered. "This is not the place for insolence."

"Nor for justice, father. And all Oran men deserve justice."

"I forbid you to speak in that manner."

Alwir stared back at the ice-blue eyes. The warnings clamored again in his head. Hold your temper, Alwir. It's foolish to fight with the man now. Other things were more pressing, needed his attention. Nothing could be served by arguing. Besides, it was an old quarrel, one that had no end. Alwir let his shoulder sag beneath the weight of his father's hand.

"As you wish, father."

Ener released him, his hand drawing reluctantly away from Alwir's shoulder. "Three years in the country. I thought it would be enough to forgive and forget the old hatreds. Alwir, it's Firefaire. We should be celebrating the coming year and your return to Beldan. Can't there be any peace between us?"

Alwir held his gaze, wrenched by an old ache. If anything, after three years living in the country the gulf between them had widened. It was his father who had tried to mold him into an instrument of cruelty, as closed to the suffering of the Oran people as were his brothers. And now he pleaded to Alwir for peace. What could the man know of peace?

"It may happen, father. Though I expect not." Alwir shouldered past him, not wanting to remain any longer in his father's presence.

The sounds of the court ball followed him as he moved steadily through the corridors of the Keep. He could hear the murmur of their talk, broken by the sounds of laughter. Servants bustled past him, some enveloped by clouds of steam from cooked food, others laden with trays of dishes and glasses. Wine stewards traveled up and down from the cellars carrying dusty black bottles of Silean wine and Oran brandy in their arms. Gray uniformed Guardsmen stood in silent pairs at the entrance to many of the suites and smaller halls where others of the court held private Firefaire celebrations. All paid scant attention to the young man as he descended the stairs, moving quickly but without undue haste.

Alwir stared at the white marble steps streaked with veins of black and gold. All of it imported, he thought angrily, hewn from the quarries of Silea and transported to the Keep of Beldan at a great cost. A cost borne by the taxing of the Oran peasantry. It felt hard and cold beneath the soles of his soft leather boots.

At the base of the stairs he turned down a smaller corridor, one that led through the remnants of the old Keep. Here the stone changed abruptly to pink and gray granite. This was Oran stone that blushed a rosy color when the sunlight fell across it in the Avadares Mountains. He touched the walls lightly, finding reassurance in the ancient stone. There were fewer torches here and no Guards. The servants' sleeping quarters he knew lay off to the right, and the laundry rooms with their huge wooden tuns lay somewhere to the left.

At the end of the passageway Alwir found the door he was looking for and withdrew a ring of skeleton keys. The Mastersmith had promised him that at least one of them would work against the old door. The locks were old, from before the Burning, and there were only a few variations to the tumblers in the keyhold. Like the old sections of the Keep, these remaining locks were all that stood of a simpler time before the Burning and the Silean treaties when locks were not so important.

The old door was constructed of heavy wood, and though it was braced with rusted bands of iron, it had warped in a few places, its surface rippled with age. Few had reasons to come this way, and Alwir guessed that it had been more than a year since anyone had used the door. There was a Guard posted a little ways beyond the door along the walls of the parapets to keep the servants within and all others without. Inside, the door remained locked and bolted. Alwir glanced around quickly. He was alone. The door was sheathed in shadow, torches casting only faint circles of light farther down the passageway. Quickly he slid the bolt back and turned the first key. The lock refused to budge. Alwir tried a second key, pushing hard.

With a scrapping noise the lock responded, the mechanism shifting before clicking into place. He blew a grateful breath and then pushed gently against the door. It gave slightly and he stopped. If they got this far, they would have no trouble opening it for themselves. In the meantime he didn't want to draw attention to the door by leaving it open too far.

Alwir straightened and brushed his hands on the sides of his trousers. They were sweating, and he realized now that the muscles of his back ached with tension. He arched his neck and rolled his shoulders, forcing the muscles to relax. He'd not be able to play worth a cock's bones if he allowed himself to remain knotted up like this. He started back the way he had come, turning once to view the door. Dark and shadowy, it was hard to tell that the bolt had been drawn. Satisfied that it looked as before, he continued his way toward his chambers to retrieve his lute.

It seemed so simple an act. They had wanted proof of his commitment, proof of his willingness to seal his fate with theirs. He had given them maps of the Keep signed in his own hand and warned them of where Guards were stationed. They accepted the information gravely, knowing that they had little to lose if they were betrayed and he much if it were discovered that he had aided them. They were laborers most of them, poor Oran peasants. And he was Alwir Re Aston, a son in the Re Aston House, the wealthiest family in the Readers Guild. Zorah's blood, how he hated that honorific Re! No true Oran bore such a title. It was the Sileans who had brought it with them, just as they had brought oppression. And it was the Fire Queen herself who shackled Oran Readers to the Silean chain by insisting that they alone of all Oran people should be known by such a title. He was Oran, but all his life that small article, wielded like a knife, had cut him off from Oran society. That is until now, he thought with satisfaction.

In his chambers again, Alwir took his lute from its silk case and tuned the strings until they sounded sweet and mellow. He began to play, his hand moving swiftly up and down the neck of the lute, his fingers becoming more limber. Then he practiced two pieces, harmless melodies, until he felt himself prepared to face the Queen and the court. It'll do, he nodded to himself and calmly slipped the lute back into its case.

As he stood to leave, his eyes strayed to the window again. The crescent moon was high, suspended like a farmer's scythe above the window. They would be here soon now. He'd better hurry.

At the doorway of the Anvil, Jobber peered in through a haze of gray-green smoke at the noisy crowd. The Anvil was normally a quiet inn, serving the local guildsmen, ferriers and watermen. But tonight it was packed with the Firefaire crowds that filled Beldan's streets seeking refuge and entertainment in every inn and tavern in the city. Jobber's eyes carefully scanned the crowds, picking out likely targets. The guildsmen were settled in their usual seats along the edges of the soot-streaked walls. Ferriers and hammermen from the local stithies huddled together, their red neck scarves proclaiming their guild. They puffed away on long-stemmed pipes, smoke rising in a thick cloud over their heads and lending a sharp, pungent smell to the steam of cooked food and the sour odor of spilled ale. In one corner two whores jiggled their corsets for a group of admiring seamen. A line of watermen occupied the spaces along the bar like a row of tethered bulls. And in the middle of the inn, crammed elbow to elbow at the long wooden tables, countrymen and their wives, journeymen and peddlers, recently come to Firefaire for the Hiring and trading, scraped spoons to plates and washed down greasy stew with brown ale.

"Busy night, tonight," Jobber rubbed his chapped hands in glee as he watched the innkeeper, a rotund little man, wiping his sweating brow on a dirty apron while he filled jugs with ale. In the corner near the hearth, Jobber made out the dirty gray uniforms of three Silean Guardsmen. Piss drunk by the look of it, thought Jobber happily. They'd not give him any notice. They were shouting obscenities and slamming their tankards down on the wooden table. One Guard grabbed the serving girl, and she shrieked above the din as he pulled her down roughly on his lap. Brown ale from the tankards in her hands splashed like the tide over the struggling couple.

"Let go! Let go of me!" the girl shouted as she wrestled with the man who seemed oblivious to the beer soaking he'd just received and was intent on keeping the wriggling girl on his lap. The serving girl kicked him smartly, the heel of her wooden clog smacking into his shin. Howling, the Guard released her to clutch his bruised leg. The girl bolted from his lap and dashed behind the bar for safety. The other Guards roared with laughter and insults. An older Guard with a slab face and grizzled beard cuffed the injured man. Then he turned and shouted drunkenly to the innkeeper that more ale was required to pay an insult fine to the Guard.

Good, thought Jobber, as he slipped inside. The innkeeper has enough to keep him busy without noticing old Jobber helping himself to a copper or two. Actually Jobber wasn't particular. It didn't have to be money. Another roar from the hearth brought the innkeeper scuttling with the ale. A countryman eating near Jobber's elbow turned his head to gawk open-mouthed at the commotion. Jobber chose that moment to snitch the better part of the man's roast mutton and move away just before the man returned his attention to his plate. Standing near the bar and well hidden by the broad backs of two watermen, Jobber grinned as he watched the confused man turning his head this way and that searching vainly for the rest of his meal. Jobber's shoulders lifted with silent laughter when he saw the man venture a timid peek under the table.

At sixteen years of age Jobber was an old hand at the snitch. Rake thin, he wore the hungry look of all street poor. It was only the sleight of hand and odd jobbing which brought a few coppers his way that sustained him. His clothes were a collection of cast-offs: a man's linen shirt with the sleeves torn at the wrists, a leather vest tied on by frayed laces, and a pair of trousers so stained and faded it was hard to recall their original color. He had no hose, and his bony feet protruded from holes in the remains of a pair of too-small boots.

But he was not without distinction to those who knew him. He wore a cap of sewn leather scraps that covered his head down over his ears and was tied beneath his chin. It resembled a toad's back, and he wore it constantly, almost as if it were a second skin. It made his features seem narrow, the green eyes bright like an alley cat's.

"Oh no, not you again!" an angry voice disrupted Jobber's snatched meal. Jobber jumped, ready to bolt, but a hand grabbed him by the neck of his shirt and held him fast against the bar. The wood felt wet and sticky and very hard against Jobber's neck.

"I thought I told you not to come in here again, you pissing little thief," the innkeeper's voice hissed in his ear.

"Leave off," Jobber said, hurriedly swallowing the last of the mutton with noisy gulps. "I ain't done nothing wrong."

**10**

"Not yet, you haven't. But I won't take the chance that you will. Off with you. I've enough trouble already, and I don't want more from you." The innkeeper released him with a shove, and Jobber was pushed against one of the watermen, who growled threateningly at him.

Jobber twisted around, furious. His pale face pinked with anger, and he raised his voice. "Don't be so shitting pushing, man. I may not be flash enough for you, but at least I'm Oran, and you'll not have to kiss my arse like those frigging Silean bast—"

Jobber didn't finish, for the innkeeper lunged across the bar, snatched him up by the vest and clapped a beer-soaked hand over Jobber's mouth.

"Don't say it! It's talk like that nearly destroyed my place last time you was in here, you miserable bit of trash. I had to pay an insult fine to the Silean Guard, not to mention the damages done to my place. And then there was the business of the three Guards you managed to send to the infirmary. I had to pay the rutting fee for that! Had to take it right out of my death tax savings. I'll be lucky if I've enough left to be burned at Scroggles when I go!" The innkeeper's eyes were red and bulging in the fleshy face, and he wheezed as he spoke.

"Might have been more Guards down if you hadn't gotten in the way! I done you a favor tossing out the filth—"

"The only filth that's going out is you."

A hand in a black glove restrained the innkeeper. A woman stepped between Jobber and the innkeeper.

"Fighting with the Guard is a treasonous offense," she said.

Jobber looked at her, saw the black uniform with its fire emblem stitched on the chest and paled. Of all the fire's luck, he had to open his mouth in front of the Knackerman. He cursed himself and his temper.

"Three Guardsmen did you say?" she asked the innkeeper.

"Aye, and no small fortune to get them back on duty."

"And where were you when this—" she cast a cold, gray eye on Jobber, trying to summon the right word to describe him, "this boy was fighting?"

"Keeping alive," the innkeeper shot back and then abruptly shut up. Jobber felt the twitching of a smile. She'd caught him right enough. The innkeeper might sqawk about the insult fine, but he was just as glad to see someone else give the bastards a beating.

The woman looked over at Jobber again. "Impressive," she

**11**

murmured. "Let him go," she said to the innkeeper. The innkeeper hesitated. She repeated herself, her voice soft but commanding.

The innkeeper grumbled under his breath and released Jobber only after he shook him a few times. Jobber exploded with a string of obscenities that turned the heads of the watermen, who regarded him with curiosity.

"Stubble it!" the woman in black ordered, and Jobber to his own astonishment shut up. He stared at her, open-mouthed but silent. The watermen grunted and returned to their tankards.

"So you can fight?"

"I take care of myself," he answered sullenly.

She snorted disgustedly and shook her head. "You'd have to with that loose trap of yours. It's that temper that gets you into real trouble." Jobber flushed angrily but stopped himself from replying.

"With what did you fight the Guards?" she asked.

Jobber remained silent.

"Nothing to say for yourself now? Let me guess then." She cocked her head back the better to scrutinize him. "No sword. That's definitely illegal for an Oran such as you. And you don't stand like a swordsman. Bottles then? Tables and chairs tossed over your shoulders?"

Jobber fidgeted uneasily.

"Show me your hands," she ordered, and before he could refuse, she had grabbed him by the wrist.

"You've not been Named. No tattoo. So you've no working papers. Not even a permit to beg, I'll wager."

"I never beg," Jobber snapped in reply.

The woman tsked loudly, shaking her head as she turned over his clenched hand to look at the knuckles. The flesh was gray and thick with calluses where the skin swelled around the knuckles. "A follower of the old style, I see. Wooden hand or perhaps stonecutter. Also illegal," she said, letting his hand drop.

"Can't prove it," he said defiantly.

Without warning she swung at him, one tightly curled fist aimed for his jaw. Reflexes brought his hand up to block the blow, while the other hand spun forward in a counterattack. In the same instant she dropped her arm smoothly and deflected the attack to her stomach. Her free hand shot up, grabbed him lightly around the jugular and squeezed. Jobber gasped with the suddenness of the strike.

"Fast," she nodded. "But I'm faster." She released him, and he brought his hands to his throat, rubbing it.

"You going to arrest me?"

She shook her head. "Haven't got the authority anymore."

Jobber frowned, confused. "Ain't you the Knackerman?"

"Knackerman," she repeated, pursing her lips with disdain. "I have always hated that title, though I suppose from your point of view my occupation was nothing more than to kill the unwanted and remove the carcasses off the streets. Though you could have at least gotten the sex right," she grumbled.

Jobber wasn't so sure he was all that wrong. As a woman she wasn't what he'd call inviting. She was thin, and the bones of her frame stuck out at odd angles to her straight back. Her face was middle-aged, with short black hair graying at the temples and lines creasing the corners of slate-blue eyes that at the moment were red-rimmed. Drunk, he guessed, though her stance seemed steady enough.

She gave him a half-smile that for some reason made Jobber more nervous.

"Innkeeper, bring me two bottles of Oran brandy."

The innkeeper protested, but the woman turned to glare at him, and he backed up a step, hands held out in front of his paunch. In profile, Jobber could see the flattened bridge of her nose where it swelled in two bumps. Broken, he figured, and more than once. He shifted uneasily, glancing toward the door and hoping she would forget about him.

The woman reached into the money pouch at her hip and pulled out two strings of bright newly minted coppers. The innkeeper disappeared to fetch the brandy.

Jobber stared at the strings of copper. He licked his lips and could feel the tingle on his fingertips.

"What's your name, thief?"

"Jobber." He wrenched his eyes away from the coppers and found himself snared by the sharpness of her gaze. He felt naked for a moment, as if she had seen through him and knew his secrets.

"Only one name?"

"It's enough."

"Whose Flock?"

He shook his head. "None. I'm on my own."

She raised an eyebrow. "That takes courage. And probably explains why I never saw you before. I know most of the older Flocks." She inclined her head. "I'm Faul Verran. I was First-

13

watch—the Knackerman to you—but I have left that post nearly five seasons back." She stopped abruptly and her jaw clamped shut. Jobber watched fascinated as her skin flushed a rosy hue and a muscle twitched in her cheek. Angry enough on something, he guessed, though she wasn't about to share it. Then she inhaled deeply and smoothed her features with the exhale. Whatever it was, she had banished it. The same half-smile reappeared at the corner of her mouth.

The innkeeper returned with two bottles of brandy and sat them on the counter.

"No messing about in my place, do you understand?" he said shaking a warning finger at Jobber.

"Perhaps you should tell that to the Sileans," Faul said coolly, nodding in the direction of the drunken Guards.

The ale-soaked Guard was now bent over, trying to carve a woman's name into the tabletop. His knife dug deep ridges into the wooden surface. But he was having trouble spelling. The others were encouraging him, shouting out the letters. But the Guard grew increasingly confused and, abandoning the original name, decided to carve one that was easier to spell. The innkeeper cursed beneath his breath but made no move to approach the Sileans.

"Drink with me," Faul said to Jobber, grabbing a bottle by the neck in each hand. She nodded her head toward the great hearth and set off with the bottles through the crowded inn. Jobber's face brightened, a tongue wetting his dry lips, and eagerly he followed her.

Faul stopped suddenly, and Jobber, who had been pushing through the crowd behind her, nearly stepped on her heels. Faul thrust the bottles in his hands. "Hold these while I clear us a seat."

Jobber peered over her shoulder and groaned as he saw that Faul was standing beside the Sileans' table. Her hand rested lightly on the hilt of her sword. She was looking the Guard over, disgust clear on her face. Jobber didn't like the look of this one bit. He was in enough trouble as it was without this drunken woman adding to his worry. He looked in the direction of the door. Maybe he could just nick out with the bottles. Z'blood! he swore as a party of boisterous fair-goers burst through the door, packing the crowded inn tighter still and dashing his hopes for a quick escape.

"You've had enough. Get out," Faul was saying to the Guards.

"Oy, who's that?" a blond-headed Guard asked, squinting up as if trying to get the image of Faul into clearer focus. Ale stained his shoulders and chest.

"I said get out."

"Will you look at that, trousers and tits! What is it?"

Jobber stole a glance at Faul and felt the hairs lift on his neck. Tension coiled like a snake in her body. The slate-blue eyes had hardened, and her lips held a small humorless smile. He saw the subtle movement of her thumb as it pushed lightly against the guard of her sword releasing it from the scabbard.

Zorah's tits, Jobber swore again, he had to get out of there. She was gonna frigging get him killed. Though his fists clenched and his knees bent for flight, he didn't move. Instead he stared at Faul, mesmerized by the smoldering rage gathering in her nail-sharp figure. She was waiting.

The blond-headed Guard stood up unevenly, and his chair fell backward with a heavy clatter. The noisy inn quieted suddenly except for the scrapping sound of chairs and benches as patrons moved hastily away from the Guards. In a far corner a plaintive voice called for port but no one answered. The serving girl ducked behind a pillar. The innkeeper was watching Faul, a reddish-purple color spreading across his face like a bruise. He wiped his shining forehead again with the wet bar rag.

"You're talking to the Silean Guards," the man said thickly. In his hand he still held the short knife he had used to carve the table.

"I'm talking to shit, now get out."

The Guard lunged across the table at Faul, the knife cutting through the smoke. Faul stepped nimbly to the side, avoiding the clumsy attack. The man, off-balance, fell forward with a heavy thud on the table, his head cracking against the edge. A second Guard scrambled to his feet, reaching for the sword buckled at his hip. Faul stepped back, and the crowd squeezed farther out of her way. Jobber gasped as he saw the speed with which her sword left the scabbard with barely a whisper of sound. Before the second Guard could move, another hand gripped his sword arm, preventing him from drawing his sword.

"Leave it, Vargas," said the third Guard in a gruff voice.

"What are you saying?" the man asked, furious.

"I said leave it."

The third Guard stood, a hand still firmly gripped around Vargas. Jobber recognized him now as the older man. He was huge, shoulders rigged like a beam. His skin was a mottled red with drink, and sweat glistened on his forehead. He stared at Faul with a mixture of recognition and hatred. She held his gaze, the same humorless smile frozen on her lips.

"You're not Firstwatch anymore," he said.

"But I still scare you, Rubio."

"Another time—" Rubio said thickly.

"Anytime."

"You and me."

"Bring your friends, you'll need them to carry the pieces."

Shut up! Jobber was screaming to himself. Just shut up, you frigging raver, he wanted to shout at Faul. And she accused *him* of running off at the mouth! But he could see there was a difference. When he lost his temper, he never knew what he was going to say. It just happened, like a match dipped into the fire. But she wanted to fight. She was pushing, hoping they would get angry enough, stupid enough, to move against her.

Never taking his eyes from her, Rubio reached down and, using the fallen man's uniform as a handle, picked him off the table. The man groaned and continued to weave on his feet. His head rolled back, and Jobber could see the gap where there had been a tooth. Blood streamed down the sides of his face, darkening his hair at the temples. Rubio drew his arm around the man's waist and hoisted him as he stumbled, still groaning, to the door of the inn.

"You'll hear about this!" Rubio shouted to the innkeeper as he pushed his way through the crowd to the door. At his shoulder Vargas argued, protesting their leaving, but Rubio continued to shake his head. Jobber's gaze shifted back and forth between Faul and the departing Sileans. At the door he saw Rubio's angry face as he spoke words to his companion. Vargas's head swiveled around to stare resentfully at Faul just before he passed through the door.

Jobber let out his breath, only then realizing he had been holding it. Around them, the inn returned to life as chairs were pushed back to tables and loud conversations resumed. In one corner a seaman slipped his hands into the straps of his concertina and began playing a lively tune.

"Why'd you do that?" Jobber asked, his eyes narrowing.

Faul shrugged and returned the blade to its scabbard. She picked up the chair the Guard had toppled and sat down heavily. "They bothered me. Why do you do it?"

16

Jobber grinned. "Same reason, I guess. How come you ain't the Knackerman anymore?"

Faul didn't answer him, only stared with a cold, angry look. Her jaw clamped tightly again, and the muscles jumped in little twitches along her cheek.

"Yeah, well," Jobber laughed nervously, shifting in his seat, "none of my business, is it?" He looked up hopefully, but the face hadn't lost its hard edge. Zorah's tits! he swore to himself. Now you've gone and done it! She's sitting here with a face like a dried cod. You ain't gonna taste a drop of what's in them bottles. He stared forlornly at the black corked bottles resting just in front of him on the table. "Nice blade that," he tried again. "Oran steel, that's for sure, none of that brittle Silean trash. Foldover of fifteen judging by the pattern. Nice guard, too. An older one, ain't it?"

Her lips softened, and Jobber let out a quiet breath of relief.

"You've a discerning eye."

"Comes with good breeding."

She guffawed in sudden laughter, her mouth opened wide to release the deep, resonant sound. Still laughing, she tossed back her head, and the short black hair frizzed out around her head catching the red glow of firelight.

"Oy, no need to be insulting, you know," Jobber exclaimed in mock irritation, brushing away dirt from his vest. It was good to hear her laugh. Maybe there was hope for this evening after all.

"Go on, then. Open that bottle," Faul said, "and we'll drink to your breeding."

"And to yourself, Mistress."

"At least while I'm paying."

"In that case," Jobber grinned, "I'll toast your wealth, that it may last long enough to get us a bite to go with this. Don't fighting make you hungry?" he asked, squinting earnestly at her.

Faul shrugged and returned a dry smile. Jobber took this as sign of encouragement and, when the serving girl arrived with two glasses, promptly set about ordering plates of food and extra bread. He spoke quickly as if the luck he'd stumbled into would vanish in an instant. The serving girl cast Faul a tentative glance, waiting for Faul to object to this gutter rat making free with her coppers. But Faul, sprawled in her chair, was quiet.

"Right," Jobber said, turning back to Faul when the serving girl had left. "Now we can celebrate truly." He felt his spirits rise, the warmth of the fire heating the side of his body, a black bottle of Oran brandy sitting there so promising and food, hot

**17**

steaming food on its way. Nothing could have been more satisfying except a snitch of gold queenies from a Silean's pocket.

Jobber reached for a bottle. Faul grabbed him by the chin. He stopped, surprised, and tried to pull his head away, but she held him fast, studying his face in the light of the fire. She was staring again at him with that keen eye. She reached out her other hand as if to remove his cap.

"Give o'er, Jobber growled, and wrenched his head away. He averted his eyes, not wanting to meet her penetrating stare nor witness the sudden look of longing that filled the gray eyes. There were some things he'd never do for money, and if this nail of a woman had any thought that feeding him might lead to other arrangements, she could stick her sword in sideways. "Maybe this ain't so naffy an idea," he said as he started to rise.

"Sit down," Faul ordered, and he hesitated for a moment. "I said sit down." She leaned back, her shoulders slouched. "I meant no harm." Jobber looked over the inn and saw the serving girl approaching with a tray of steaming food and cut slabs of brown bread. That decided it. He sat down carefully, as if the stool might attack and claim him prisoner.

"I didn't mean to offend you," she was saying quietly. "For a moment you resembled someone . . ." she let her voice trail off.

"Don't get any ideas about me," Jobber said brusquely.

"Ideas?" Faul said frowning, confused.

"You know. Just because I'm drinking here and it's Firefaire and all. Well, that don't mean I'll be bedding with you."

Faul sat up straight, incredulity opening her narrow eyes wide. "Sex with you?" Faul said in an ugly voice. The serving girl standing by the table startled at Faul's words, spilling the gravy from the bowls as she set the tray down. Her eyes darted back and forth between the odd pair, waiting to hear what was said next. She pouted when Faul waved her away with an impatient hand. Faul leaned forward to face Jobber squarely. Jobber tensed seeing the steel glint in the eyes and the hard point of her chin. "Now listen here, little thief. You stink like a gutter, you look like a bundle of bones and you've probably got more fleas and lice than a dog. I'd sooner swallow my blade than let you lay a hand on me."

"Well," said Jobber, holding on to his bruised dignity, "I guess we're in agreement on that." Jobber quickly grabbed a bottle and uncorked it with his teeth. Vapors from the bottle tickled his nose invitingly. He poured himself a good measure and swallowed hastily. It was warm and smooth, washing away the sting of insult. She was fairly right about him. But not completely. He didn't have fleas or lice.

Faul ran a hand through her short black hair and gave the second bottle a sullen frown. She sighed, disappointment sobering her face. Then she pushed the tray of food aside with a quick decisive shove. "Can you drink as well as you fight?" Faul asked, her voice husky.

"Certainly," Jobber responded, wiping the brandy off his lips with the ragged end of his sleeve.

"Good," she said, ignoring her glass and lifting the opened bottle by the neck. "I'll wager you a string of coppers that you can't outdrink me. What do you say?"

Jobber grinned. "I drink better than I fight—especially when I'm not paying."

Faul said nothing but tilted the bottle back, the brandy pouring in an amber stream down her open mouth. Fire's luck, Jobber thought happily, as he watched her gulp the brandy down. She was already well in her cups. Before the end of watch he'd win the coppers easily and maybe relieve her of a few more in the process. If not, he shrugged, he'd still get free drink.

Faul brought the bottle down and handed it back to him, her lips pursed with an unswallowed mouthful. She gulped and gave a tiny shudder. "Go on then, the first one under the table loses," she said.

Jobber stared at Faul's face, seeing the grimace that lent her mouth a fierce bitterness. He'd seen that look on other drunks before; they caged their misery and anger until enough drink could free them of it. Jobber cautioned himself. Why she drank was her own business, he decided practically, and it was better not to know. He was drinking not out of sorrow, but to enjoy himself. As he lifted the bottle to his lips, he heard the shrill laughter of the whores and the sudden gusting of notes as someone fell on the sailor's concertina. But neither the laughter nor the stumbling music could turn his attention from the bottle.

# 2

The Firstwatch Gonmer pushed her chair back from her cluttered desk and sighed wearily. It had been a long day and now an even longer night. Her narrow face was drawn with fatigue, violet shadows ringed beneath her eyes in the glow of candlelight. Strands of black hair had worked themselves free of her braid and floated around her aching temples.

She pursed her lips in annoyance. "Z'blood," she exhaled noisily and absently raised a hand to restore the truant locks to their braid. She rubbed her tired face, and her hands felt cold on her cheeks. Her whole body was chilled from the hours spent hunched over her desk studying the maps and reading the dispatches that littered her desk, all of them pertinent details to planning this year's Firefaire. It was the largest festival of Oran; when the Fire Queen Zorah stepped into the Great Bonfire to burn away the old year and reemerged cleansed to welcome the new. But first there were three days of trading, hiring, drinking and any other kind of pastime the crowd could devise for itself. On the fourth day was the procession of dignitaries marching solemnly behind the Fire Queen. They would pass through nearly every section of Beldan, from the small cramped streets of the Guild to the broad avenues of High Street through Market Square, and finally, along with the gathered crowds, fill every inch of Fire Circle to attend the Great Bonfire. And following behind, but not too closely so as to offend the wealthy, were the children of the poor, coming forth to be Named before they received their working papers. And then after the fair, would be the grim task of overseeing the executions of the children who coming to be Named were found by the Readers to be tainted with Oran magic.

For most it was a time for celebration, a respite in a year's worth of constant toil. But to Gonmer, Firefaire was a pounding headache. As Firstwatch of Beldan she was responsible for the safety of the Queen and her retinue as they marched through the city. She was also responsible for the maintenance of order during the chaos that accompanied the festival. For at least five days Beldan's streets would be crammed with merrymakers, farmers and their livestock, traders and journeymen. Even the Ghazali acrobats and dancers come to perform for the crowds would think nothing of setting up their tents in the city squares and hobbling their horses to the nearest bush. There would be a thousand petty squabbles, murders and births, questionable trades and outright thieving before the festival ended. And there was always the threat of fire from the ubiquitous campfires smoking on every doorstep, effigies of the Queen waiting to be burned.

Gonmer exhaled heavily again and rubbed her eyes with her thumb and forefinger. In years past it had all been easier. The crowd was usually there to please itself, and fights were discouraged by the presence of the Silean Guard. The pickpockets might relieve some poor countryman of his purse, but in general they did little harm. And the prostitutes, ah well she mused, one got what one was willing to pay for.

But in the last six seasons the mood of the crowd had changed. Droughts and strange blights had brought on one bad harvest after another. Stomachs were tight with hunger in the countryside. The Silean gentry continued to prosper, but the small Oran farms were becoming worthless, the soil blowing away in clouds of dust. Many Oran families had already lost their farms and more hired out as labor for the wealthier Silean farms that could afford to build the irrigation canals. Oran farmers came to Firefaire no longer to celebrate, but to seek work in the Hiring Field and to contract their children for a seven-year service to the Keep.

And some came for yet another reason, Gonmer thought sourly. The last six seasons had also brought the New Moon to Beldan. Vengeful peasants she had thought of them when she read the first reports of violence to come in from the countryside. They fought skirmishes over water rights, vented their anger by attacking Silean farms and fleeing with livestock and grain. Recently they had become bolder and more organized as they attacked traveling merchants, relieving them of gold, metals and cloth. And now Gonmer could see from the reports of scattered violence that littered her desk, the New Moon had brought its discontent to the city.

Gonmer picked up several reports and shook her head disgustedly. Three men killed in Hammer Alley fighting Sileans, two more killed on the riverfront trying to sink cargo barges and this one, a boy, killed while painting the crescent moon on a wealthy home in the Silean district of the city. They were Oran farmers, more suited to toiling the soil with a plow and rake than wielding weapons against the Silean Guard. It was rumored that the New Moon sought the support of the city Guilds. The hostility between the Guilds and the Fire Queen was well known. Gonmer wondered briefly if the Guilds would support these farmers, using them perhaps to gain a foothold for themselves against the Queen and the Silean Guard. She shrugged the thought away for now, returning her attention to the problems of the fair. The New Moon might be no more than a poorly armed nuisance, but they could still be trouble, and Gonmer didn't want them making their reputation by disrupting Firefaire.

In the grate, the hearth fire had been reduced to powdery gray coals that cast a faint light and only a little warmth onto the room. Gonmer shivered once and then stretched her body catlike, the long arms reaching high above her head and her back arching with a fluid motion. "Ah!" she sighed as she felt the blood moving through her cramped muscles again. She winced suddenly as a needle of pain dug sharply at her side. She pressed a hand firmly against the angry ache in her lower rib and scowled.

"Gonmer," she scolded herself, "if you don't move faster in sparring, those shitheads are going to do more than clip your side." Sparring this afternoon had been a mistake, she decided. Her sparring partner, a Silean from the Thirdwatch, had managed to land a solid punch to her lower rib before she had countered with a blow that broke his jaw. It shouldn't have happened. Their sparring should have been controlled. At her chair, Gonmer shrugged and then winced as the stitch in her side complained at the movement. The man was a Silean and like all the Silean Guard resented her. The fight was a personal attack. "Stupid bastards," she muttered, "when will they learn? In Oran the Firstwatch will always be a woman." The Sileans may cling to their low opinion of women, Gonmer thought archly, but while they served duty in Oran they will submit to the command of the Firstwatch. For two hundred years, since the first treaties brought the Silean Guard into the country, it had been so. And for nearly two hundred years, Gonmer frowned, the Firstwatch has had to prove her mettle against the stupidity and narrow-mindedness of her adopted troops.

She stood and pushed away the chair. "Lais," she called out, as she picked up the writing quill and tapped it absently on the table.

Across the room a bundle of makeshift bedding sighed, shifted

22

slightly at the voice and then settled back into formless bulk.

"Lais!" Gonmer called more sharply and rapped her knuckles against the desk. This time the blankets rustled to life and a face peered out from beneath, eyes blinking at the candlelight. For a moment the eyes stared, dazed, and then widened as they took in the stern face and stiff figure standing by the candles. With alarm, a young girl threw off the covers and brought her sluggish body to stand at attention.

She was tall, and her lanky frame seemed an immature version of the Firstwatch. Her dark hair cropped close to her scalp accentuated the high cheekbones of the heart-shaped face and pointed chin. She stood erect, silently staring ahead out of dark eyes and tried not shiver as the room's chill settled on her sleep-warm skin.

Gonmer scowled angrily and crossed to stand in front of the desk, hands held behind her back.

"Lais," she warned, "if you value your life, you won't forget the stupidity of falling asleep while on duty. The Firstwatch sleeps soundly only in death, and had I been any other tonight, you might have slept for the final time. Have I made myself clear?"

"Yes, Firstwatch," came the clipped reply, "I regret the breach of duty." Lais lifted her chin higher and pulled her bony shoulders back further, trying to stand even more erect.

"Perhaps a few nights sharing quarters with the Second or Thirdwatch might awaken you to the dangers of heavy sleep."

The girl's face paled at the suggestion.

"Firstwatch," she stammered, her tongue tripping over the words, "You wouldn't . . . I'm not ready yet—"

"I said 'perhaps,'" snapped Gonmer. "But sooner or later you will have to face it. You will have to learn that you cannot fight, Lais, if you are either afraid or asleep." She paused, staring into the young face that was trying to look bravely back. "After watch there will be extra training for you, and then I will decide whether or not you are ready to pit yourself against the Second or Thirdwatch."

"Yes, Firstwatch," Lais responded obediently.

Lais continued to stand stiffly at attention, and Gonmer noticed in the flickering yellow light how the last few harried days hung badly on the child as well. Though the eyes glittered brightly now with a charged sense of duty and silent apprehension, dark smudges beneath her eyes contrasted against her pale skin. Too little rest for both of us, Gonmer thought, as she considered the child. But it would be wrong to relax her training or show special favor. Lais must inherit the position of Firstwatch, and it was Gonmer's duty to train her successor, train her hard for the position. I'd only do her a disservice if I allow her a weakness now, she thought.

For a moment, Gonmer remembered her own teacher, a woman sharp like the crack of a whip. The Firstwatch Faul had selected her from the ranks of Oran children indentured to the Keep after their Naming Rite. Gonmer had been a skinny farmer's child, too tall and bony to be a successful prostitute and too hostile to make a good servant. Faul had seen that look of defiance in her eyes, just as Gonmer had looked for and found the same in Lais. For ten years Faul trained Gonmer, pushing the limits of her endurance. Those, too, had been long days and nights. Faul had been a demanding teacher, even savage sometimes. But it was a training that served her well, Gonmer thought proudly. Faul had given her the strength to survive, the skill to be Firstwatch and command the Silean Guard. It was nothing less than she would give to Lais.

A lock of Gonmer's hair fell forward, disturbing her peripheral vision. She turned suddenly from Lais and crossed to where a small mirror was mounted on the wall. She yanked free the knotted leather that bound her hair and began to retwist the fraying braid. As she worked, undoing the long braid and smoothing back the hair from her temples into a new twist, she spoke to Lais.

"Tell the servants to prepare a meal that I may eat here in my rooms. No meat or wine, but something hot, and a pot of strong tea. My work is far from over tonight, and I must continue until I have certain details worked out to show the Queen in the morning."

She finished braiding the black hair, patting it lightly over her scalp and securing the ends with a leather cord. She turned back to Lais, who stood waiting to be dismissed. "Tell the servant you're to eat, too. We've too much work to do, and now your extra training will not enable you to take the time to eat after the watch."

Gonmer leaned down gracefully to retrieve her sword where it rested by her chair. She buckled the sword belt over her slim hips. With a practiced gesture, she pulled the sword slightly from its scabbard to inspect the blade. The candle's small flame ignited a spark of light along the polished steel. With a soft grunt of

24

satisfaction, she returned the blade, listening for the click as it locked into place.

"I'm going for a walk to inspect the watch. I need the fresh air—and a stupid face to yell at." The lips twisted into a grin. "That should clear my head."

Lais relaxed, the bent back shoulders drooping more naturally. The Thirdwatch was Dario's charge, guarding the city during the sleepy hours of the late night. It was notorious for its lack of discipline. Gambling by the Guards was overlooked as were the whores that came to the gates of the Keep, provided Dario received his share of the night's earnings. Gonmer would have no trouble finding an outlet for her tension.

Gonmer settled a small black cape about her shoulders and pinned it in place with a silver brooch that was shaped like a circle with a flame in its center. "Go on," she ordered Lais, "and see that you return by the fourth hour with my meal. Be a hair's breadth late and you may be assured of spending the night with the Secondwatch."

Lais gave a curt nod of her head and left the room quickly before Gonmer. Gonmer paused in the doorway, watching Lais as she hurried down the dark corridors of the Keep. Gonmer noticed how she moved, smoothly but alert, her body readied against surprise. Satisfied, Gonmer turned the other way and headed down the corridor for the open parapets of the Keep.

As she walked down the corridor of the Keep, Gonmer kept her head erect, her mind fixed on the image of the maps spread out on her desk. She could almost see a pattern in the winding city streets and began to sense where she would deploy the Guard to the best advantage. At her hip the sword bounced lightly, a familiar and comfortable companion in the dimly lit hall. Gonmer passed through the main hall, stopping for a moment to listen to the sounds of a lute being played in the state room upstairs. Pretty, she thought, wishing she could remain to hear more.

She made for the main entrance of the Keep and suddenly changed her mind. Better to take a different route, through the old Keep, and enter from at the back of the Keep. It would give her the element of surprise against the watch, who would normally expect her to appear first at the front gate and the sentry tower. She turned and, passing through white marble corridors, headed for the old halls. Guards stationed in the hallways saluted her as she passed, and she smiled, seeing the brief look of surprise on their faces.

Gonmer felt as if she had stepped into Oran's past when she

moved from the brightness of the white marbled halls into the old section of the Keep. Almost without thought, her step slowed and her gait grew more relaxed. The walls, though ancient and crumbling, exuded a sorrowful grace. She stopped briefly to look at the remains of a frescoe once painted on the plaster. It was chipped and peeling, exposing the ancient stone and crumbling mortar of the old Keep. In the flickering light of a smoky torch she saw the arch of a dancing figure, arms outstretched to meet the grasp of another dancer who had long since peeled away from the wall. She felt a sharp jab beneath her foot and winced as she stepped on the fallen remains of mortar. Cursing softly to herself, she made a mental note to assign workmen to repair the corridor before it became too dangerous.

Gonmer approached the ancient wooden door and stretched a hand to the bolt. She stopped and frowned. Someone had pulled the bolt already. A servant perhaps? She took a ring of keys from her belt and sorted through them until she found the right one. She inserted it and turned. It locked. So, she thought, growing more puzzled, it had been unlocked. She turned the key again and unlocked the door. Besides herself only the matron had a complete set of keys to the old Keep. She'd have to talk to the woman when she returned. It wasn't wise to leave these doors unlocked.

Gonmer pushed open the door, and it creaked tiredly. She frowned at the noise, not wanting to be discovered. But as she stepped into the cool night, she saw no one about. Above her the new moon rose in the dark sky and the stars glowed with their distant blue and green light. A breeze plucked at the edges of her cape and carried the smell of the sea up from the harbor. Gonmer hesitated in the dark, weighing the silence and stillness of the night around her.

Where was the Guard? she thought angrily. She should have been able to hear them from here. At least, she thought suspiciously, she should have been able to spot the light from their fire somewhere down the open walkway that snaked along the parapets. But there was no one and no sound, just a silence that might have been soothing, might have been peaceful, had it been another time or place.

Gonmer eased away from the door, hugging the shadowy walls of the Keep and crept slowly, silently down the walkway, her eyes searching for signs of movement. In her dark clothes she merged with the shadows. As she passed an opening in the stone wall, she turned her head and glanced down toward the city.

From here she could see the tiny bonfires that lit the city streets and made it seem a haven of fireflies buzzing with excitement. A muffled sound snagged her ear and turned her head sharply. She froze, expectant. There were no more sounds, only the wind as it brushed against the stones of the walkway.

Gonmer continued to creep along the walkway, appreciative that the new moon didn't cast enough light to betray her approach. She squinted in the near darkness and spied the lumpy figures that ringed a gutted fire. She approached them cautiously, hand resting on the hilt of her sword. She nudged one with a toe and nimbly stepped back as the heavy weight fell to one side, lifeless. She bent and touched him and then brought her hand away quickly, wet and sticky. She knew by the rusty smell it was blood. Gonmer wiped her hand clean on the jacket of the dead Guard. The body was still warm, she noted, the attack was recent. Very recent. "Z'blood!" she swore softly, and moved to the second figure. He was lying face down, and she turned him gingerly. His face peered up at her, and she saw the gaping slash across his throat, worse than the shocked smile still on his lips. She didn't bother to check the third man. The assailants had been swift; caught by surprise, the Guards had not even drawn their weapons.

She stood slowly and loosened her sword from its scabbard. She stepped across the gutted campfire and started at the loud crunch as her foot crushed something lying on the ground. She crouched, waiting to see if the noise alerted anyone else. Never taking her eyes from the darkened walkway, she bent lower and fetched the thing from beneath her foot. She held it in her hand, and it rolled in her palm, smooth except for a crack down its spine. Dice, she thought disgustedly, and she set the shattered piece back down on the ground. She heard a rustle in the deep shadow and stood quickly, hand tightening on her sword.

A form separated itself from the shadows and confronted her from the other side of the campfire. She kept her blade in its scabbard, waiting, and inched her feet to one side of the closed circle of bodies. At worst she could jump the dead man between them, but she didn't like presenting herself as a target. The shadow remained still, waiting for her to move. A feint then, she thought, and make it good.

She let loose a loud battle cry that exploded on the silence and flung herself across the circle to the right of the shadow. It jumped to life and swung a sword high overhead. Gonmer stopped just under the arch of the falling blade and shifted quickly to the left as the sword came down in a wobbly arc over her head. It hissed

**27**

in the air but missed her, and while its point was down, Gonmer leapt over the corpse between them. She lunged to the shadow's left side withdrawing her sword from its scabbard as she passed so that the blade's edge cut deep into the shadow's side as she pulled it free. She heard the startled cry as she flowed past the shadow, slashing deeper as she went. Then she stopped, feeling the shadow hanging on the trailing tip of her blade. An upward jerk twisted the blade free of the body, and the shadow fell behind her. She brought the sword up slowly, hilt level with her shoulders, both hands on the handle.

She stood, panting lightly, exalted by the sudden thrill of fighting. She waited, still tensed and poised. Not over, her senses warned. The shadow wasn't a skilled swordsman. He had been clumsy, slow in his handling of the sword. He couldn't have killed the Sileans alone. There had to be others. She turned her body evenly, shifting side to side, keeping her weight balanced on the balls of her feet. Z'blood, it was dark; impossible to see anyone in the blackened spaces along the wall. She peered into the darkness and then stopped, remembering. Night training with Faul. Gonmer standing in the center of a dark room, waiting for the swift attacks. Gonmer peering then, too, trying desperately to defend herself against the sudden strikes. Then Faul's harsh laughter echoing from every corner of the room. "Forget your eyes," she commanded. "They're useless here. Feel the attack on your skin, feel it in the air."

On the walkway, Gonmer breathed deeply, calming herself. She stood very still, listening, feeling the cool moist breeze blow across her cheeks. She could hear the shadow behind her dying, the blood as it dripped in a light, steady patter on the stone walk. Something moved against the wall, and she felt it as a stirring of the air. She turned to face it, sensing its presence. She brought her sword down to her left hip, in a ready position, held in a two-handed grip.

Sword and attacker moved as one, bursting from the shadow in a single arc that swept toward her head. Reflex brought her sword up as a block, and the two blades clashed with a shower of blue sparks as steel scraped against steel. The attacker pulled back and then lunged again, swinging the blade across Gonmer's midsection. Gonmer shifted, but not fast enough, and she felt the tip of the blade open a shallow furrow across her ribs. She gasped as the burning sting spread across her flesh. "Z'blood!" she growled and swung her sword up in a deadly fury. One-handed she launched the blade upward. It caught the wrist of her attacker's sword hand and cut it cleanly off. The sword clattered to the stones and blood spewed from the severed limb. Her attacker stumbled back, holding out the bleeding arm defensively. Gonmer's sword continued to swing upward until it peaked. She turned the blade earthward, and with two hands on the hilt, drove it down across the neck of her attacker. The blade tugged as it met the flesh and then whistled as it broke free at the shoulder and continued through the air. The severed head was tossed against the far wall of the walk and landed with a dull thud. The body stood wobbling, its arms held up in supplication. Gonmer watched unblinking as it fell.

Gonmer waited, breathing hard, hands clenched tightly on the hilt of her sword. Adrenaline coursed in her blood and she swallowed, her mouth dry. Her heart drummed in her chest, beating loudly, but she forced herself to remain still until she was certain there were no more attackers. Around her the breezes eddied, lifting the short sides of her cape. Slowly and deliberately, Gonmer lowered her sword. There was no one else, she could sense it. She wiped the blade on the corner of her cape and, using her thumb as a guide, returned the blade to its scabbard. She listened for the sharp click and then exhaled a long ragged breath. She inhaled through her nose, taking in a cleansing breath to calm her racing heart. Pain flared from her torso, and she placed a tentative hand over the open wound and pressed. Not deep, she scowled, but a wound on the belly was a damnable place. She'd be stiff and sore for a long time until it healed.

Hands still pressed protectively around her middle, Gonmer walked down the walkway until she found a lit torch, smoking greasily in its iron sconce. Grunting against the pain, she lifted it out and continued down the walk in search of the other Guards. She heard voices below and knew she was above the next station. Leaning her head over the side between two parapets, she shouted down to them.

"Who's on duty?"

They didn't hear her, though she could hear them guffawing loudly and quarreling noisily among themselves.

"Who's on duty?" she yelled again, more loudly.

They stopped talking and faces turned to peer up at her. Someone shouted. "Oy, who's up there? Come down here where we can see you."

"This is Firstwatch, you piece of whore's shit. There are five dead up here, and if you aren't quick about your business, I'll see to it you join them."

The Guards scrambled to their feet, grabbing their swords and cursing. Gonmer leaned her forehead against the damp stones trying to cool the hot anger that burned on her cheeks. There'd be no yelling at them, she told herself. They'd only think her a raving bitch. But there would be disciplining, extra hours on duty and extra training until they choked on it. She'd make the living pay for the incompetence of their dead compatriots. She'd make sure they'd not forget themselves on duty again. They'd hate her, but she'd be saving their lives.

Gonmer returned, carrying the torch. She wanted a closer look at her attackers. She wanted to know how they had gotten so far into the Keep without being seen. She wondered, too, about the door. It had to have been someone from inside the Keep.

She approached the first attacker and turned him over with her foot. The torch cast a flickering orange light over a slack face. The eyes were rolled back and only the whites showed, a milky yellow beneath a heavy brow. Gonmer bent down on one knee and looked closer at the man. She opened his cloak and tsked, annoyed as she saw the small crescent moon stitched on his shirt. Well, she thought, shaking her head, she should have guessed. She took one of his hands and saw the gnarled calluses of a farmer. She shook her head again and let the hand drop.

She stood and crossed over to the second body. She couldn't tell much from it except that it was smaller and swaddled in black clothing. No wonder she hadn't seen him in the shadows. Her eye caught on the silvery gleam of the sword, the hand still clenched around its handle. She stooped to examine it and was surprised by its beauty. Surprised and alarmed. Since when did Oran farmers have swords like this? She was impressed by the pattern of waves glimmering on the edge of the blade made by steel alternated with a ribbon of iron. No one forged blades like that anymore. It was illegal. She straightened and went to look at the head laying near the wall.

She held her torch aloft and saw the head, too, was muffled in black fabric. She bent down and peeled back the fabric. Nestled in the cloth the head appeared like a face amidst the petals of a black rose. The eyes were shut tight and the mouth was drawn to a small frown. When Gonmer saw it she drew back her hand and felt herself become sick with sudden anguish and horror.

A woman's face lay there, brown hair matted with blood at the temples. A face like her own; good Oran stock with high cheekbones and almond-shaped eyes. Gonmer stared at the face, confusion and anger warring within her. She looked away and shivered. She had killed in fights before. She thought of death as a common face. But she had never once killed a woman. Gonmer struggled to detach herself emotionally from the face. She turned back and looked at it again. She forced herself to study it, to grow used to the idea, but something in the face forbade it. It wasn't a woman's face exactly, she saw now, noting the fullness in the cheeks; it was a girl's. Gonmer squeezed her eyes shut and stood brusquely, ignoring the pain in her belly. She drew a hand across her mouth. "Shitting bastards!" she spat, uncertain whether she was angry at the Guards for having failed in their duty or at herself for having succeeded at hers.

# 3

In a private booth at the Boneman, Ratcatcher waited for the Upright Man, trying not to let his nervousness show to the child sitting across from him. The boy was about eight, and like all members of the Waterlings Flock, he smelled rank of the sewers and sea. His pale skin and wide-set eyes made Ratcatcher think of a goggle-eyed carp. Squat they called him, and it seemed the right sort of name to Ratcatcher, as the boy was short, with a bowl belly. Squat had been eager enough to come with Ratcatcher, but the waiting was wearing on him, making him less sure. He was swinging his feet, kicking the table legs, and the steady thump of it set Ratcatcher's teeth on edge. He reached across and cuffed the boy.

"Stop kicking, Squat, or I'll cut your pegs off," he said irritably.

The child quieted his legs but couldn't stop fidgeting in his seat.

"Sit still, you frigging pin."

"I can't," Squat whined. "When's he gonna get here anyway? Maybe this ain't so good an idea."

"Just because the Upright Man's late don't mean he ain't coming. He'll be here soon enough." Ratcatcher softened his voice, trying to calm the worried child. "Look it's gonna be naffy, I tell you. The Upright Man is gonna be real pleased with you. Just tell him the truth, that you got the old stuff in you, and he'll be good to you. Real good. 'Member that dell in Tippenny's Flock, the one with the black hair?"

"Yeah," Squat answered. "Don't see her 'round no more."

Ratcatcher smiled smugly. "On account she's working the hill. Silean houses."

Squat looked skeptical.

"It's true I tell you. She was an earth element. Had the touch for metals she did. Knew how to pick out the queens from the sillers, even hidden away in a pocket. The Upright Man has her working all decked out like a flash dell, snitching in the big

**32**

houses. Great life, she has. Great. Eats whenever she wants to," he finished and saw the effect it produced on the boy, who if lucky ate every other day.

"What about my tattoo, my papers? I can't be facing the Readers, now can I?"

"Trust him. He's got it all worked out."

"Really?" Squat asked hopefully, his usual sly gaze unguarded.

"Yeah sure," Ratcatcher answered and then turned away. You really are a shitter, he told himself. But the gold coins weighed nicely in his pocket, and there'd be five more if the boy was delivered alive and unharmed. With all that gold he could eat and drink away any sour taste of betrayal. He just hoped that Squat hadn't told anyone where he was going. It had been a stroke of luck that the boy had squealed his secret to Ratcatcher in a boast ful moment after Ratcatcher had caught him snitching in his corner of Market Square. The Upright Man was gonna be pleased. It had been a long while since Ratcatcher had snagged a brat with the old stuff. Maybe there'd even be a bit of extra in it for him, Ratcatcher thought, humming to himself.

The latticed door to their booth swung open, the noise from the commons room was suddenly loud. A figure wrapped in a long cloak filled the doorway, blocking the light of the room beyond. The Upright Man entered and took a seat beside Squat, the silk lining of his cloak rustling. Ratcatcher stood and quickly shut the door. The tiny booth was filled with the musky perfume of incense and candle wax. Squat stared wide eyed with fright and awe at the partially masked face of the Upright Man, his black eyes half-closed.

"Gentlemen," he said in a smooth quiet voice.

"Sir," Ratcatcher said quickly, pulling off the battered cap he wore on his head. His tongue flicked out over his dried lips as he tried to close them over his long front teeth.

"You must be Squat," the Upright Man said to the child sitting anxiously at his side.

"Yessir."

"Good. Let me see your hands, Squat."

"Sir?" Squat asked, casting a confused glance at Ratcatcher.

"Your hands, boy," the Upright Man ordered a little more sharply.

Squat thrust his dirty hands before him. The Upright Man's clean, tapered fingers gripped them tightly and the carefully trimmed nails dug small crescents into the boy's skin. He turned

Squat's hands over, studying the knuckles and then the palms, lingering to touch a half-healed scratch on the palm.

Satisfied by what he saw, he released Squat's hands and turned to Ratcatcher. "Leave us, but wait in the commons until I call you."

Ratcatcher nodded briskly and stood to leave. At the lattice door he cast one last look back at Squat. Then he pushed through to the light and noise of the commons room, drawing in a deep breath of smoke. He'd have a drink while he waited for the Upright Man to finish his business.

In the booth the Upright Man slowly unwound the silk scarf that had covered the lower part of his face. Squat tried not to stare but he was curious, for at that moment he was the only one he knew who had ever seen the Upright Man full face. It wasn't as spectacular as he imagined it should be. Seeing all the features together, Squat thought the man looked more Silean than Oran. Only in the almost almond shape of the eyes had he seemed Oran. But his nose was prominent, and his square chin was covered with a neatly trimmed black beard in the fashion of a Silean merchant. The Upright Man leaned back, hands together on his lap and smiled at Squat.

"Who were your parents?" he asked.

Squat shook his head. "Dunno. Sometimes I think I remember a woman holding me, but then . . ." he gave a shrug.

"Do you have the old power?" The Upright Man leaned forward again, the black eyes suddenly piercing.

"Yessir," Squat answered softly.

"What element?"

"Water, sir."

The Upright Man exhaled heavily and leaned back, a look of disappointment crossing his face.

"Can't you use my element, sir?" Squat started talking quickly, afraid that the Upright Man would not want him and all those images of wealth and food would disappear before he'd even a chance at them. "I can call mist, sir. Works well on the snitch to give a little cover. And, and . . ." he was grasping for other uses to which he could sell his talent, though calling the mist was the only one he'd ever done. "And I'm sure there's other ways, too, sir. I know I can be of service to you."

The Upright Man leaned forward again and held out a hand. "So, you want to be of service. Give me your hands, Squat."

Without hesitation Squat thrust out his hands. He flinched as the Upright Man clamped his fingers tightly around Squat's wrist.

34

Squat squirmed a little, not liking the position, feeling the polished nails dig into the veins of his wrist.

"Ow!" he cried as a nail bit the surface of the skin and cut it.

"Are you ready to join me, Squat?" the Upright Man asked, pushing back his chair to stand over the boy. Squat looked up and shivered with sudden fear. The Upright Man loomed above him, a tall, menacing black shadow, his lips parted in expectation. Squat felt a thin trickle of warm blood from the cut on his wrist ooze down his forearm.

"Sir . . . ?" Squat said, thinking to ask a question, trying to find a way to push back the cold rub of fear that tightened in his belly. He tugged on his trapped arms, wanting to free them.

But the Upright Man didn't answer. Lifting Squat's injured arm high above Squat's head, he laid his lips to the wound and began to suck at the trickle of blood. Squat felt the warm lips on his skin and the brush of the Upright Man's mustache. He tried to jerk his arm free, but the Upright Man clutched him and sucked harder, drawing blood in a fast and furious stream to the open wound. The skin burned as if scorched with coals. A searing pain shot down Squat's arm and lodged like an arrow in his chest.

Squat opened his mouth to scream but no sound occurred. He gasped, choking on small cries as he struggled to fill his lungs with air. His head rolled back and he stared at the ceiling, the beams swirling violently, turning like the spokes of a wheel. There was a roaring in his ears, a bellowing of distant thunder that he realized was the wild pounding of his own heart. He tried to shake off the mouth that clamped more fiercely against his skin, but his gestures were feeble. Water, he thought, as he felt for a moment the touch of magic. Not his magic, but another's calling the water in his blood. Blood flowed, bubbled away from his flesh, as it was drawn to the cut. A shudder racked his body, and his legs kicked out convulsively. He couldn't stand and was dimly aware that the Upright Man had laid him out on his back against the table, one hand squeezing the faintly pulsing artery of his throat, the other still holding his wrist. The mouth on the wound drew blood with needle sharpness, pricking and burning as it sucked away his life's fluid. Squat blinked his eyes with infinite slowness as darkness crowded the corner of his vision. Then he closed his eyes and let the darkness whirl him down into a cold emptiness, hearing only the dull thumping of his leg as it kicked vainly against the table.

• • •

A scant hour before the lighterman made his rounds and gutted the street torches, the Upright Man reeled drunkenly out of the Boneman. His cloak shielded him in the darkness, and the silk scarf partially covered his face. He stumbled down the street, lurching from side to side, shaking his head and moaning. On Carrion Street he staggered to a stop and leaned heavily against a cold brick wall. Near his feet a dying bonfire smoked and the acrid scent of burnt rags crowded in his nostrils.

In his stomach a different fire raged, erupting with violent waves of nausea that sent bursts of light and pain stabbing into his skull. His heart beat furiously, wild erratic pulses that seemed to bang it against the brittle hardness of his ribs. He waited a moment and then tried to take another step.

A wave of light attacked him, exploding in a shower of brilliant blue stars, lancing his head with needles of pain. The sparks fell and he cried out as they seemed to scorch his skin. He groaned, a rusty metallic taste filling his mouth. He tore off his scarf moments before he pitched forward, one hand clutching the wall for support, and vomited over the bonfire. It hissed furiously, sending fresh plumes of smoke into his face. He turned away from the wall and vomited again into the street.

"Frigging sod!" screeched a whore who was unfortunate enough to be near him. His vomit splattered across the hem of her dress, and she shook the skirts angrily. "Hope you choke on the stuff!" He paid her no attention, for his ears were deafened with a booming sound, the harsh roaring of his own retching. The few people still on the street at that hour avoided the Upright Man, drawing wide circles around him as he groaned, doubled over and swaying in the street.

With effort, the Upright Man straightened slowly and squeezed his eyes shut. The pain rippled, spread outward like the concentric circles of a pond. It flared white hot in his skull, blinding him before it rushed down through his chest and stomach. His heart bucked wildly. He gasped as the searing pain continued churning through his torso, snapping every nerve in his spine until his back arched. Heat flushed his skin, and he felt the sudden painful tightness as blood swelled in his groin. He was stretched rigid with the pain, arms jerked outward and fingers splayed. His legs trembled and then buckled, folding beneath him as he fell.

Lying on the cobblestones, the Upright Man rolled to his back and stared upward at the pinpoints of distant stars. Each prick of light lanced him, pinning him to the hard stones of the street. In agony, he groaned and his chest heaved with a long ragged cry. He waited, staring at the sky.

Then slowly the searing waves of pain subsided, ebbing outward through his legs and arms. His frantic heartbeat calmed and his limbs relaxed onto the cold unyielding ground. He closed his hands into fists, as if to squeeze the last drops of pain from his flesh.

And then it ebbed, the violence of pain gave way to a warm rush of pleasure. The Upright Man shivered and sucked in grateful breaths of cold air. Sweat glistened on his forehead and exposed cheeks. Tears swam in his eyes and he blinked to clear them. He rolled his body to the side and lifted himself unsteadily. His legs still trembled so he waited, his hand pressed against the wall for support. Then he took his hand from the wall and tried a tentative step.

Released from the pain, the Upright Man smiled. There might be one more seizure, but he knew from experience that the worst was over. Like little jewels, condensation clung to his shoulders in a fine mist.

The Upright Man spat into the street. He wiped his mouth with a linen cloth and then carefully retied his black silk scarf over his face. Though things had changed much since the day he had first arrived in Beldan, it wouldn't do to be recognized here. Ratcatcher would see to disposing the body. There would be no one who would connect him with this murder. Save Ratcatcher and he was too greedy to kill off a patron who paid in gold. The Upright Man settled his cloak more firmly around his shoulders, touched lightly the sword at his side and satisfied that all was well, he began walking, his frame growing more steady with each step. The mist followed him, trailing his footsteps with whispered sighs.

From the alley, pairs of feral eyes had watched the Upright Man hungrily. A drunk, they thought, coming home and not likely to make it. They were waiting for the man to tumble and kiss the stones. Then they would take him, rob him of whatever he'd left in his pockets. But now the watching eyes retreated to think. Unexpectedly, the man had risen. And what's more, he didn't look so drunk. The mist made it hard to see him clearly, but there had been no mistaking the sword at his side. What seemed easy a moment ago now seemed too much trouble. One of them touched the other in the dark, giving the signal to leave. They'd try another place.

"Wait!" another hand stalled. "Follow!"

"No," answered the first, slapping it away. "What are you on about, Mole?" came the furious whisper. "I tell you that steel is good and sharp."

"Something ain't right."

"Yeah, your head. Come on, this ain't the pigeon for us."

"Finch, I need to follow."

"Let him go," said another whisper. Trap, Mole's sister, laid a hand on Finch's arm.

Finch groaned and shrugged it off. "I hate being out with you two. You got to inwit everything. Can't you leave others' lives well enough alone? We're interested in their queenies and sillers. I don't give a frigging pin about their thoughts."

"Man's dangerous," insisted Mole.

"So don't go. We got to find Squat anyhow and we're late."

"Can't," Mole said. "Need to follow him. Hear that noise?"

"What noise?" Finch àsked angrily. "Ain't nothing but the wind."

"And it's talking to us."

"Let him go," Trap pleaded.

"Zorah's blood. Go on then, if you must. But keep your nose well tucked and don't be out after light. Trap, you come with me. I've already lost Squat for the night. If I come back without any of you, Kai will peel me. 'Member," she warned, "Kai wants us to meet her at Market Square, main tunnel, after Firstwatch. Don't hold out on us or I'll squill to Kai that you was cheating."

"Yeah. I'm off."

"That's the truth of it," Finch muttered to the dark.

There was a quiet scurrying noise like owls beating through the night forest as feet started running lightly down the dark alley, splitting at the corner to follow different paths.

The Upright Man was walking quickly now, his boot heels clicking impatiently on the cobblestone streets. He passed from the dark alleys into the broader streets of the Pleasure quarters. Tired whores, their faces pallid in the lifting dawn, moved with a slow, weary gait into the shuttered doorways. A drunk lay slumped at the entrance of an inn, his arms cradling a bottle, a dog curled at his feet. The Upright Man walked with increasing speed through the streets, turning from Blessing Street to enter High Street, which led straight up away from the heart of Beldan and toward the Keep. As he watched the Keep's high walls rise on the horizon, he could smell the salty tang of the ocean, the fresh clean breeze washing away the smoky odor of the Boneman and the sour taste of his own vomit. Torchlights wavered on the parapets of the Keep, and windows high up in the towers glimmered with light.

He walked steadily toward the high wall and the entrance gate. On either side of the gate the white sentry towers shone like fangs. He could see the Silean Guards already gathering for the next watch. They scuffled as they came to the gate, talking quietly in low murmurs or taking the last puffs of their pipes before their duty began. The sky was growing lighter with each passing moment, and in the sky over the Keep's shoulder a faint smudge of orange streaked against the night's blue.

The Upright Man relaxed and loosened his scarf, freeing it from around his face. He had no fear of being recognized here. Only to the Flocks was it important that his identity not be known. He thought on the night's catch, pleased by the kill. He smiled at the faint cloud of mist, all that remained of Squat's power, crouched at his heels. Have a care, he cautioned himself.

The Upright Man looked up quickly, taking in the faces of the Guards that made up the Firstwatch. Most of them were sons of wealthy Sileans, forced to do their duty in the Guard. But among them he saw one or two faces that he recognized as sons from Reader families. He knew none of them would think to Read him as he passed, so familiar was he to them. But Readers were always Reading, sometimes when they were not even conscious of it, and if he let himself be discovered for so foolish a reason . . . the Upright Man concentrated focusing his mind on the white sentry towers through which he would pass. The mist disappeared and he walked calmly through the gates and into the main hall of Beldan's Keep.

Stepping cautiously from the shadow of a building, a boy stood and watched the man in the black cloak strolling through the gates of the Keep. He blinked at the light of the rising sun as it cast a gold shimmering light across the sentry towers. His own face was yellow in the reflected light, for it was so pale that it bore no color of its own. His hair was nearly white and his eyes a crystal blue. The thin ridges of his collarbones tented the sides of a ragged shirt. He shivered in the cold, his trousers too short and his legs bare of hose.

Mole stared at the man disappearing into the Keep. He had seen a Guard salute him, had seen the man in the black cloak return the salute. And it bothered him. He knew of no good reason why he should have followed the man in black. Except for the inwit, as he called it, a compelling intuition that kept him dogging the heels of a perfect stranger.

Yet there had been something familiar about the man. Not in his shape nor his walk, but in the sound of the air, the mist that played around his feet. Mole could almost hear words, ghostly cries of another in the mist. He could sense confusion in the swirling air.

And there were the images, brilliant visions boiling in the air where the man passed—all of them terrifying—a white face, mouth opened in a rictus of terror that bled into the semblance of a gaping wound, blood pulsing, trailing in a stream, turning clear water to rust. He saw the sun speckling the water, lighting a dark patch; the patch rolled over, and in the harsh glare, Mole saw the flat white of a skull gleaming through a blasted tear of skin. Mole wanted to flee, but the inwit urged him forward, made him follow the trail of images, look where he was afraid to look. If only the bugger would have turned around, Mole thought angrily, to have been able to see the man's face, his eyes. The dark dreams of the silk scarf gave no answers to Mole, only a palpable sense of fear.

Then as the man entered the Keep, Mole gasped at the sudden stillness. The visions stopped and the air, which moments before had been so agitated and tormented, became utterly quiet. Mole tensed, every muscle poised for flight. He cast his mind, opened his senses to the light and noise of the street. But there was nothing that held even the faintest touch of the man's mind. The ghostly cries had vanished. Mole watched the morning winds lift off the water driving the ocean current ashore. He saw the currents as floating patterns, watched them drift and eddy around his body as if avoiding touching him with their cool fingers.

The Firstwatch Gonmer barked out orders, and the Silean Guard arranged themselves smartly. Mole jumped at the sound of boots marching and the shrill caw of the Guard's whistle. Quickly he slipped into the shadows and began running quietly down the streets. There was a tunnel entrance not far away, and he made directly for it. He found it at the end of a street of shops, covered over with strips of wood. It was easy enough to pry off a loose board and slip inside the tunnel's darkness. He fell a short drop and landed in a crouch. Water splashed around his ankles but he paid it no notice. He was a Waterling, used to traveling the abandoned tunnels that crisscrossed beneath the city. It was safer down here, safer than traveling above in the light of day where

Readers sometimes turned their gaze on gutter rats. He ran down the night black tunnels, water splashing as he fled. He trusted the smell and taste of the water to guide him through the maze to the main tunnel beneath Market Square.

And as he ran he caught the image of a man's face, the lines hazy and blurred, as if the face floated just beneath the surface of water. He could see only the eyes clearly, a shining black except for small pinpricks of red. Inwit told Mole it was the face of the silk scarf he'd followed. Mole sobbed in terror, imagining a hand reaching from the blackness of the tunnel to grasp him about the throat, the fingers long and tapered, the nails a polished silver. He ducked his head and covered his face with his hands to shut out the vision. Breathing hard and fast, he sped through the dark tunnels as if pursued.

# 4

The sun rose over the edge of the harbor casting a pink and gray glow across the water. Ships crowded the docks, the clutter of spars and masts like a forest of leafless trees. Smaller coastal packets, with blue and green sails, bartered for space between the high-walled hulls of the black Silean merchant ships. The ships creaked as they bobbed gently in the rolling tide that nudged them closer to the piers. Dockworkers unloaded and loaded cargo, their breath a cold steam in the brisk spring air. Above, the gulls wheeled and screeched, fighting over the scraps that floated between the piers and littered the water's edge. The tang of brine mixed with the smoke of fires, as fishwives scaled the morning's catch and hawked their wares.

At the doorstep of the Hungry Owl, a serving girl in a mended apron and stained skirt swept at the dirt and dried mud of the doorway. Her face was puffy and her nose stuffed so that she was breathing through her mouth. From time to time she raised watery eyes to the dawn and sighed audibly.

"Get a move on, Maise," came a sharp order from behind, and Talia Rousen, mistress of the Hungry Owl struck her head out of the doorway to hurry the servant. She had a shrew's face, with small squinting eyes and a long pointed nose that twitched in the direction of the serving girl. Talia twisted a greasy hank of brown hair into a tight little bun at the base of her neck and thrust two hairpins to hold it in place. "There's four beds that need making, ale that needs pouring and a sink of dishes that needs washing. Don't be standing here like a dullard sweeping your feet!"

Maise sighed again and redoubled her efforts with the broom. A flurry of brown dust gathered about her feet and she started coughing.

Talia stuck her head out of the door again. "Dolt! How many times do I have to tell you, throw water down before you sweep!" She drew her head back in the window and stormed angrily through the inn. "That's it! That's it!" she cried exasperated, raising her skinny arms in the air. "See if I hire out another country wretch at Firefaire. Not to be trusted with washing their own faces!" She reached the door to the cellar and screamed down the darkened stairs. "Fran! Fran! Do you hear me?"

"Yes, my love," came a muffled reply.

"That's it, I say! I'll not hire out at Firefaire this year! I've had enough of sniveling, lazy, good-for-nothing country girls! Do you hear me?" she screeched again.

"Yes, my love."

In the cellar, Fran Rousen, innkeeper of the Hungry Owl, rolled his eyes as he tapped the ale keg, watching the brown beer form a thick head in his tankard. He took a long draft of the beer, habit closing his ears to the continual complaining of his wife upstairs. The tankard came down and he smiled at it, foam clinging to his mustache. He frowned again as her voice penetrated his peace, asking him a question.

"Yes, my love," he responded automatically, knowing that no matter what she asked it would do for an answer. Her heels banged as she stomped away across the wooden floorboards. He took another draft of beer. She wasn't a bad wife, he thought, just a bit high-strung. She did have her good points. She might scream like a crushed cat, but she could cook like pure cream. Talia was the reason the Hungry Owl was a success. Many a wealthy countryman stayed at the Owl during Firefaire because of its excellent food and clean beds. He had to give her that; she'd made the Owl a richer place than it had been in his father's time. In the darkened cellar, Fran raised his tankard to her in a silent salute. He drained his tankard and turned to go upstairs. Hand on the wall, he heard the shrieking of her voice and the metal clash of kitchen pots as they were flung off the walls onto the tiled floors. But, Z'blood, she could be a curse sometimes, he muttered, and he steadied himself before he took the stairs.

In the alley behind the Hungry Owl, Talia's shrill voice woke Jobber where he slept buried deep beneath scraps of paper, rags and mouldy straw. His hand poked out of the heap and swept away the trash that covered his sleepy face.

Jobber sat up, eyes blinking, and a small groan issued from his lips. He dropped his head into his hands waiting until the pain at the base of his neck stopped throbbing. "Z'blood," he exhaled and felt his tongue thick as old leather. His stomach gave a lurch, and he tasted bile even as he swallowed hard. He didn't want to be sick but knew from the rocking in his head and the saliva in his mouth that it was inevitable. Best get it over with. He hauled himself up, standing on shaky limbs and retched noisily on the

**43**

trash. When he was done, he spat to clear his mouth of the foul taste and lifted his head, squinting at the new light.

"Welcome Firefaire!" he said to the sky, and stepped away from his vomit.

A vague thought entered his storming head. Did he win last night? He slapped his chest pockets but felt no string of coppers. Ah well, he thought, he hadn't lost entirely. Managed to get this frigging hangover. Z'blood, he swore softly, as he rubbed the base of his stiff neck, Faul was a strange dell. Scary, Jobber thought, remembering Faul's silent anger that would surface abruptly as a violent twitch on her otherwise smooth face. And that near brangle with the Guards, Jobber shuddered to think what might have happened to them, to himself. Yet the more they drank together, the less her strangeness mattered, and after awhile he discovered he liked her. Huh, he snorted, you'd kiss a Silean's arse after that much brandy. But no, that wasn't it. He was attracted to her. Despite her anger, and despite the huge quantity of brandy Faul consumed, Jobber sensed a solid core, an undeniable vein of strength that pulsed with the same intensity as her fury. She picked her own fights, never the other way round. Growler had been like that, Jobber thought.

In the alley, Jobber shrugged, wincing at the pain it brought to his head. Faul said she was leaving; she'd had enough Firefaires to last her a lifetime. She was taking a packet ship up the coast —and what was the name of the thing? Stupid name it had. Completely unlike her. Some kind of flower or something. As Jobber tried to recall the name, he remembered instead, with a sudden flush of embarrassment, that he had begged her to stay in Beldan. Even promised somewhat rashly to sneak her into Crier's Forge. It was illegal for women to be in the forges, but Jobber knew that Mastersmith Donal didn't hold with too many of the Queen's laws. It had seemed an easy promise to make at the time, and Faul had seemed pleased enough by the offer.

Now why had he done that? he wondered, shaking his head, getting himself tangled with such a strange dell? Maybe because she reminded him of how much he missed Growler. And for a moment in the alley, Jobber pictured Growler's face, its sternness overcome by a flash of smile. Then Jobber shook his head and resigned the memory to a distant past. Growler's dead, he told himself brushing away the creeping sadness, you do fine on your own. Still, Faul had helped drag him back here and covered him up with paper so he'd be warm. Not bad for a Knackerman. She must have been drunk, he thought; she'd certainly drained more of the bottle than he. But his last memory of her was her leaving the alley on steady legs, a hand raised in farewell.

"Oy! You there! Where you been?" Talia's shrill voice rattled his ears, and his head began to howl in protest. He grimaced at the pain but turned to answer.

"I've been here, haven't I? Just waiting for you."

Talia's balled fists rested on her hips. "Huh, you look like a corpse and stink like one, too."

He didn't answer, just prayed that he wouldn't vomit in front of her.

"Well, I suppose you'll be expecting me to feed you first, and me with my hands full and a gimp of a serving girl for help," she fumed.

The thought of food turned his shifting stomach, and he shook his head.

"Nah, Mistress, no food. I can see you're in a hurry. But I wouldn't mind a bit of drink," he added hopefully. More of the beast that bit you, he thought to himself, hoping the ale might ease his aching head.

Talia's thin lips pressed tightly together and he instantly regretted his request. To his surprise and relief, she shouted over her shoulder, her toe tapping impatiently. "Maise! Maise! Bring out a tankard for Jobber and be quick about it." Looking back at Jobber, she wagged a finger at him. "Now look, I want ten loaves, all new bread, don't let that cheat of a baker sell you day old. I want thirty firebuns and make sure there's enough sugar icing on them. The last batch was shamefully naked. And last I'll take six loaves of black bread. And mind, lift them first and see if they're heavy. I'm paying for the nuts and fruit in them, and I don't want those airy things they've been passing off lately. You'll have him charge it to the Hungry Owl and tell him I'll settle up after Firefaire. Have I made myself clear then?"

Maise had just appeared at the back door carrying a wooden tankard of ale and an empty basket for the bread. Jobber licked his lips and took the cup.

"Yeah," he answered, "very clear, Mistress."

"Good, and be quick about it. There's food here if you return in time." She turned and stormed back into the kitchens leaving Maise waiting for Jobber to finish his drink and hand her back the tankard.

He peered at her over the rim. She reminded him of a tired cow, her bleary eyes gentle enough but with no great intelligence. The ale cleaned his mouth of the taste of vomit and improved his spirits. He smiled at her as he handed back the cup.

"Been rough with the mistress?"

She grunted in agreement and then sniffed hard. "It 'ud be less awful to bash my head against a wall."

"Will you hire on again?"

She looked at him as if he had suddenly sprouted horns. "Nah, I'll go home. Work's just as hard and food's scarcer, but at least I'll be away from that screaming wretch. And another thing," she wiped at her damp nose with the back of her sleeve. "I'll be out in the fresh air away from this awful smoke and dust. I've been sick ever since the day I hired on here."

Talia's voice screeched out the door. "Maise, where are you, dolt? I need you here!"

Maise lifted her shoulders and frowned. "Raving bitch," she muttered and headed back to the door.

"Fire's luck," Jobber called after her as he picked up the bread basket, but she had already disappeared inside.

Jobber turned and sauntered out of the alley into the twisting dockside streets. He knew he should hurry, but he didn't trust his head to stay on his shoulders if he moved too quickly. The ale in his empty stomach sloshed, and Jobber waited to feel the warm flush as the alcohol in Fran's good brown ale made its way in his body. In the meantime he'd do what he liked best: just stroll and keep an eye out on the street.

Jobber had lived all his life on the streets of Beldan. It was home to him. There was no place that he had not touched or seen; Market Square and its crowded streets of shops and stalls, the jutting piers of dockside webbed with nets and rigged masts, the dark alleys of the Guilds and Hamader River spanned by skeletal wooden bridges. He knew even the wealthy homes of the Sileans with their elaborate gardens that bloomed on the hill in the shadow of the Queen's Keep. Throughout the twisting turning of the city, Jobber counted every street and alley as another might count the rooms in a house. Beldan, beloved Beldan.

Jobber breathed in deeply the smell of the dockside neighborhood; salt and fish from the ocean mixed with the slops pooling in the open gutters. Above, the sky turned a pale blue and the sun lit the faces of the plaster and wood houses. Long and thin, the houses were squeezed together, their upper balconies leaning dangerously over the narrow streets. From every balcony red and orange flags snapped in the breeze, brightening the pewter gray of the weather-beaten wood. The streets were quiet now, but Jobber knew that before the day was out High Street would be crammed with fair-goers, their numbers spilling over into every small sidestreet. He paused briefly to breathe in the smoke and peace of the early morning.

Jobber turned up from the dock streets into the winding streets that led him past the spice shops, apothecaries and teahouses. In the tiny windows strange plants grew, their vines clinging around brightly colored bottles of tonics and cure-alls. In the teahouses steam clung in a warm mist to the windows, and Jobber could just catch the scent of rolls and savories. Hanging standards of green and red stripes announced the services of skilled leechers and smokehealers that would for a few coppers either smoke or bleed the illness from the body. Jobber stepped over a puddle that surrounded a broken bottle and wrinkled his nose at the sharp smell. His eyes watered, reminding him of why he never sought cures here. "Sooner kill you as heal you," he grumbled. There were no stray cats to be seen on the street, no dogs and only a few sparrows brave enough to perch on the sills of the teahouses. To Jobber, that the animals themselves kept their distance was proof enough that in a street devoted to health one could die from scrounging in the trash.

On Twopenny Street he stopped for a moment in front of a teashop, its doorway decorated with bright blue tiles and a grinning bird, its painted wings spread over the lintel of the door. He often wondered how the artist had gotten the bird to smile so ecstatically, but then knowing the owner of the shop he thought it made sense. Zeenia was crazy, just like the grinning bird, closing the shop down sometimes to fly off around the country. Then she'd come back and keep the shop open all night for days at a time even though it was illegal. They would shut her down, she'd pay the fine and then open the shop again. She'd heat up the great brass tea urns and talk about her travels to any and all with the time to listen. It was a good place to come when the days were wet and cold, for she didn't mind the stray Flock member or even the vaggers that sought shelter there, staying all night sometimes. One did pay for it though, Jobber reflected, by having to listen to Zeenia's rambling lectures.

Someone rapped on the window, and Jobber saw Zeenia's smiling face staring back at him. Jobber waved and Zeenia suddenly disappeared, steam condensing on the window where her face had been. The door banged opened, and Zeenia stood out on the shop stoop with a mug of tea in each hand.

"Oy, Jobber, the blessing of Firefaire on you."

"Same to you, Zeenia."

"Come in. I'm only back this last two days, and I have news of the world."

"I'm on an errand for the Hungry Owl," Jobber answered, relieved that he could refuse her offer without offending her. With his throbbing headache he didn't think he could listen to much of her chatter.

"Have the tea then," and she stretched out a hand with the mug.

"All right," Jobber shrugged and put down his basket to join her on the stoop. "I can only stay a few moments."

"Ah, the wickedness of work, to draw a man away from the true path," Zeenia said.

"And what's the true path?"

"Travel. Study. Contemplation. All the old ways of the Oran vaggers."

"And who feeds the vaggers so they can keep on traveling?" Jobber teased.

"Don't tell me you've taken up farming since I last left?"

"Nah."

"Then don't argue with me. I've known for a long time, Jobbernowl, that you would as soon sit on your arse and be fed than twirl a stick in the ground for your meal."

"So what, then? That's a fair description of most of Beldan."

"My point. If we are to embrace a life freed from labor, then we should at least fill it with knowledge to recompense those that toil."

"Sounds like a vagger," Jobber said.

"I wish I was. But I find their discipline too harsh. I need a bit of fun now and then."

Jobber glanced up at her and smiled. Her dress was gaudy, a strange mix of Silean corsets to which orange ribbons had been added over an Islander's skirt of red and black wool. In odd contrast to the bright skirts, she had tied a drab scarf over her head, the two ends meeting the top of her head to form a tight little bow. Jobber thought it made the heart-shaped face seem sad, accentuating her pale complexion and freckled skin.

"What's that on your head?" Jobber asked, taking a sip of the tea. It was hot and fragrantly spiced. Zeenia may be crazy, he thought, but she could make tea.

"Oh this," she snapped, annoyed. "Stupid, ignorant, lazy know-nothing . . ." she started shouting at a shop across the street. Zeenia shook her fist at the herbal shop, its door festooned with straw effigies of the Fire Queen.

**48**

"What are you on about?" Jobber asked, puzzled and a little concerned. He drank his tea hurriedly, planning a hasty retreat. When Zeenia wanted to vent her spleen, few were safe in her vicinity.

"What do they know of henna? What do they know of hair dyeing? I ask you," Zeenia looked down at Jobber imploringly. "For hundreds of years the Ghazalis have known how to do it. Whores on Blessing Street know how to do it. But a herbalist on Twopenny Street can't dye a dead man's teeth black! Look what his henna did to my hair!" Zeenia snatched the scarf from her head, and Jobber choked on his tea as her hair tumbled out in marbled shades of blonde, orange and green. "I wanted it to be beautiful for Firefaire. I wanted to be a Fire Queen in my own shop. Now I look like the fringe of some demented rug. Frigging bastard!" Zeenia was shouting across the street. She threw her mug of tea into the street, where it crashed, shards of porcelain scattering everywhere.

Jobber gave his tea a final swallow and, setting the cup down on the stoop, tipped his head in a quick farewell. "I'm off. Thanks for the tea."

But Zeenia didn't hear him, for she was shouting now in full voice, announcing to the nearly empty street that the herbalist was selling poison to anyone foolish enough to trust him. Doors opened with a slam, and other voices called down to Zeenia to shut up.

As he reached the corner, Jobber saw a lighterman, his face grimy with soot beneath the battered black hat he wore to save his head from the showering sparks of the torches. On his shoulder, he hoisted an iron pole, capped with a bell for gutting the torch fires.

"Not again . . ." he was muttering, his eyes staring over Jobber's head to the scene developing on the street.

"Zeenia's back," Jobber said with a smile.

"I ain't going down there. Last time she grabbed my gutter and started swinging at someone. Nah, I'll come round later and do the torches. If their shops burn down, it's no frigging business of mine." And he turned quickly and headed down another street. Jobber heard his hoarse voice as he called the hour of the First-watch, gutting the night's torches along the street. And behind Jobber on Twopenny Street other voices raised in an angry chorus, replacing his fading cry.

Past Twopenny Street Jobber wound his way up along a gentle slope. The smell changed and Jobber gave a half-smile. Tobacco, beer and something else underneath, cloying and sweet. Blessing Street marked the entrance to the Pleasure district. Drink, smoke and women, whatever a paying man could want. Along the street Jobber noted the hanging standards of the inns he knew; the Anvil, in which he was now considered a welcome guest after last night; the Rose, a place in which one could easily get killed despite the delicacy of its name; the Raven's Claw, a dour little place with yellow glass in its windows and a smoking hearth; last and favorite with Jobber, the Maidenhead, where all the whores went to drink in peace when they weren't working. Jobber chuckled to himself suddenly, remembering the night a drunkard had decided to badger a woman in the inn. Bell, a large, ham-fisted woman and owner of the Maidenhead, picked up the hapless fool by the scruff and chucked him into the street. As he lay there floundering in his drunken stupor, she had lifted her skirts daintily and pissed on him.

Jobber passed the Maidenhead, and a woman's voice called down to him from the balcony.

"Jobber, that you?"

"In the flesh!" he answered quickly, stepping out into the street and looking up.

"Ooh, now wouldn't that be lovely?" He flushed and saw Trina, her henna-red braids hanging in a messy tousle around her broad face. Jobber thought of Zeenia's green and orange hair and gave a chuckle. Trina leaned way out the window and smiled at him, seductively. Her bodice was opened completely, and the tops of white breasts pressed invitingly against the sill.

"You're up early, dearie," she called down.

He shrugged and stared back, trying to look nonchalant at the generous display of flesh.

"Can you do me an errand this morning?"

"Be glad to, once I finish another."

"Good. I'm needing some pennyroyal from the herb shop. These pains is fixing me something terrible. Can you get it for me?"

He nodded, wondering if "pains" was something that came with whoring.

"Here, wait a minute," and she ducked her head inside the window and reemerged a moment later, throwing down a string of coppers for the herbs and a big piece of barley bread and dried cheese wrapped in a cloth as payment for his troubles. "Sorry, it ain't much, but if you come by later, maybe I can give you

50

something more interesting," and she smiled coyly at him from behind half-closed lids.

"Might do that," he replied smiling and turned to go. She stopped him again.

"Here, something for your vest." She took off one of her earrings and tossed it down to him. He caught it before it hit the ground. "So you'll remember me," she said.

"Thanks." He turned over the earring in his palm. It was a little heart carved in ivory and strung on a gold hook. "Pretty," he murmured to himself and poked it through the leather of his vest. He turned up the street, trying to hurry feet that insisted on going slow.

Not far from the baker's shop Jobber saw a small figure sitting hunched on the steps of the Naked Man, raking patterns in the dirt with a stick. He recognized the thatch of blond hair that stood on end like the spikes of a hedgehog.

"Oy, Dogsbody!"

The child stood up and squinted. Jobber waved his hand and hurried up the street.

"Jobber, where you been?" Dogsbody asked, giving him a broad smile full of crooked teeth. He was a boy about ten and like Jobber wore tattered clothes.

"I've been about," he smiled and ruffled the younger boy's blond hair. "Pickings have been good. Even managed to get drunk already."

"That's the fire's luck on you, Jobber. Must be nice." Dogsbody shook his head admiringly and sat back down on the stoop of the inn, his bare knobby knees poking through tears in his trousers. "Me now, I ain't had it so good. I had my pigeon right in my hand when a Guard noticed me and set up the alarm. I had a shitting time getting myself out of there. Ratcatcher chewed me out good."

Jobber slapped him on the shoulder consolingly. "It's only the beginning. Firefaire's tomorrow and by that time streets'll be too busy for anyone to notice. Next time I see you, your pockets will be stuffed."

Dogsbody shook his head. "Nah, you won't be seeing much of me, I'm afraid. I've decided to be Named this Firefaire. I'm giving myself to the Keep."

Jobber drew back, surprised. "Nah, you ain't hardly old enough," he argued.

"I am, too," the boy insisted. "'Sides, I'm sick of the street,

51

I'm sick of being cold and always having to scramble for a bite to eat."

Jobber frowned. "It's not the first time you've been cold or hungry. Go on then, what's so bad as to make you sell your freedom doing hard time at the Keep?"

"We all have to sell our freedom some time, Jobber. You know that."

"But why now, why not later?"

Dogsbody said nothing, just rested his chin on his knees. Jobber noticed a bruise, pale green and yellow along the side of his cheek. Dogsbody sighed and scratched his head.

"It's that shitting Ratcatcher. He's been on at me like he does all the little ones. Z'blood, I won't be buggered by him or anyone. If I'm Named and sent into the Keep, he can't get me there."

Jobber's face flushed an angry red. "I'll beat the frigging dog if he lays a hand to you."

"Nah, won't do any good," Dogsbody replied, shrugging thin shoulders. "You may be good in a brangle, but I'm not in your Flock, Jobber. Remember, you won't have one."

"I can't, I told you. I'm on my own," Jobber answered sharply.

The boy gave him a searching look, as if trying to understand Jobber's reluctance. "So who's to offer me protection then? Even if you beat Ratcatcher square, sooner or later Ratcatcher 'ud catch up to me. So I'm off then to be Named and join the ranks of men."

"And slave in the Keep for seven years of service," Jobber answered grimly.

"Well, I expect I'll bear it like a man," said Dogsbody. "Doubt it's worse than life out here."

Jobber sighed. It was hard to argue with that. At least the boy would eat regularly. Then he looked at Dogsbody and tugged on his cap strings. "You're sure you've none of the old power in you? I mean it wouldn't do to go up against the Readers only to be plucked out for the noddynoose."

"Nah. I'm clean there."

"Right then," Jobber said, nodding his head. "If it's to be, then don't go hungry." He reached into the basket and pulled out the bread and cheese from Trina, handing it to Dogsbody. "Here, eat! You'll need your strength for the Naming. The way I see it, you'll be standing about for hours before it's over and done with."

Dogsbody's eyes sparkled at the food, and he tore into the bread like a starving wolf.

"Oh yeah, one thing more," added Jobber, unhooking Trina's earring from his vest. "You'll need a bit of flash to take with you. Here now, stand up and let me pin it on you."

The boy stood up still stuffing the food into his mouth. Jobber pinned the heart earring on the front of Dogsbody's tattered shirt. "A man needs a heart in a place like the Keep."

"Thank's Jobber. How do I look?" Dogsbody stuck out his chest in what he imagined was a mature pose.

"Just fine," Jobber lied, trying not to notice Dogsbody's boyish face and thin arms. He felt a new pain in his chest that had nothing to do with the hangover. "What'll you call yourself when you're a man?" he asked, hoping to distract the pain.

"Not Dogsbody, that's for sure. Damn shitting name." He cocked his head to one side, thoughtful. "Dunno yet, I guess. I ain't given it much thought. I'd take my dad's, if I knew it."

"Well look, I've got to go now, but meet me at the Hungry Owl before the end of Secondwatch. I'll see if I can wriggle us a couple of tankards. Time like this needs a little celebrating." Jobber stood up to leave, and Dogsbody stopped him with a hand on his arm.

"Thanks again, Jobber. I'll see you there."

Jobber stared at the small hand, and the pain squeezed tighter in his chest.

"Yeah, later," he said thickly. "I've got to run now. Don't forget, the Hungry Owl."

"I won't," Dogsbody called after him.

Jobber hustled up the street, glancing at the sun that told him he had wasted too much time. If he was late arriving at the baker's and there wasn't enough bread to fill his order, Talia would probably take after him with a kitchen knife. He'd seen it happen before, though she'd never actually cut anybody, just waved it about. Her bark was bad enough, Jobber decided, no point in making her so mad she'd bite. Jobber hurried himself, his feet kicking up a fine dust as he walked.

From the parapets, Alwir watched Gonmer dismiss the First-watch for their duty. The lines of gray and black Guardsmen threaded through the streets away from the Keep to their assigned tasks. Alwir rubbed his eyes tiredly. Irritated by lack of sleep, they itched and burned. But how could he have slept? The New Moon had failed last night.

He had been playing for the Queen when the Firstwatch's page brought the news. His hands had trembled where they rested across the lute, the fingers suddenly cold. The attackers were both killed, the page announced. Laborers, she had answered, when the Regent Silwa asked who they were.

Alwir wondered for a moment if they had carried the maps with them. Maps that contained his signature. He had stared at the entrance of the state room, expecting the Silean Guards to come and arrest him. But no one came. In fact he was forgotten as the Fire Queen and her Regent left hurriedly with the page.

After their departure, the room came alive with talk. More than once he had heard a voice raised in anger, insisting that Oran peasants must be made to pay for the attack. An offense against the Silean Guard should not go unpunished. Retaliation, that was the answer. Peasants needed to learn their proper place, and if it took a hard blow, perhaps that was all peasants understood. Alwir grew angry, sickened by their hate. He had left as quickly as he could, unwilling to listen any longer to their outrage. Even his own brothers were gathered close to other nobles, their faces red with indignation as they clamored for retribution and punishment.

But Alwir had found no relief in his chambers. Each time he closed his eyes, he saw them as they had been at the last meeting. Dabin was a big man, with more strength than grace. And though he would have preferred to remain in the west country, plowing the fields for spring, he had felt he had no choice but come when the New Moon issued its call. Sahira had been younger than Alwir when she joined the New Moon. Fast and light on her feet, she was naturally gifted with the sword. She had smiled at him and tugged his hair when he expressed his concerns about the whole plan.

"If I fail," she said, her smile broad, "I know there will be others to come after me. That gives me courage. I can't hope that it will end with me, but I know that it will begin with me. And that gives me pride."

On the parapet Alwir stared angrily at the disappearing lines of Guardsmen. There were other things he could do; he would use his Reader's talents to help fill the ranks of the New Moon.

He lifted his gaze, looking out over the maze of Beldan's streets until he found the square patch of green. He drew a deep breath and let his senses open. He focused on the Hiring Field and smiled as here and there he saw flashes of color, greens, blues and silver all shimmering like morning stars in the dawn's gray light. He imagined the auras like crowns of light worn by Oran peasants, invisible to all but the Reader's eye. They were down there, the Orans born with the ancient gifts of power. And though the Fire Queen had passed an edict two hundred years ago condemning those born with such power, power that might threaten the peace of Beldan, they were still there, like the hardy scrub roses that continued to bloom amid stones. The Silean clergy could denounce Oran beliefs as heresy, starve vaggers who clung to the old spiritual life, but neither they nor the Queen could rob the Oran people of the heritage of blood and magic. The Fire Queen might bleed her people, but the magic endured despite her. Alwir took a deep breath and calmed his senses. He would find them, those children not yet discovered, and urge them to flee north to the safety of the New Moon. That much he could do before his brothers and the other Readers began their own shifting and winnowing through the Firefaire crowds.

Kai sat in her flat-bottomed boat, feeling the gentle rocking of Hamader River beneath and hearing the creaking boards of Grap's Bridge over her head. In the shadow of the bridge, she shivered slightly with the damp of the morning river mist. Thin and bony, she wrapped her red skirts about her thighs for extra warmth. But she was too pleased to be annoyed with the cold. Firefaire had been good to the Waterlings this year, chance netting them a wide assortment of badly needed things. More than one drunken fair-goer had tumbled into the river, the current freeing a scarf, a coat, even a fan. Without a trace of squeamishness, Kai had picked the pockets and stolen the clothes of one hapless fool that had fallen in and drowned. Relieved of the weight of his clothes, she sent the corpse on his way again downriver. Horsedrawn carts chanced crossing the narrow bridges that swayed over the river. All it took was a jostle, a slight jarring of the wagon, and into the Hamader fell providence of all kinds. Recently it had been a bag of apples, bobbing merrily through a litter of floating paper and a dead cat. And just yesterday Slipper had pulled out a brace of cocks floundering in their wooden cage as the Hamader dragged the soggy birds through the city on their way to the Ribbons and the open sea beyond. Then, too, the barges were doing a brisk business now in seed grain and livestock, heading up river to the Silean estates. Kai herself had provided the diversion while Slipper and Stickit scuttled aboard unseen from the riverside and relieved the barge of a few sacks. Oh yes, there was much to celebrate this Fire-faire.

Kai smiled, contented. As Flock leader of the Waterlings, she took her responsibility seriously. Intelligence and enough stolen coins had enabled her to strike a good bargain with Perce and the river pirates, earning her Flock protection and a beggar's charter, provided she kept her Flock along the waterways and the Rib-bons, the marshy islands along the mouth of Hamader River. She looked older than her twenty-odd years. She was a plain woman, her chin almost disappearing into a scrawny neck. But her eyes were large and dark, and the stare commanding beneath arched brows.

Kai twisted her black hair into a knot and tied her shawl tighter around her shoulders. She glanced up quickly at the sky, the pink sunlight fading to a morning blue. Soon it would be too light to keep this perch unnoticed. She bent and covered the sto-len goods with a blanket, her hand lingering long enough to pat the humped back of a sack of wheat. There'd be bread on the Ribbons for her Flock. White bread, just like the Sileans ate.

"Oy, Slipper, Stickit, take an oar. We're away to the Rib-bons," she called softly over her shoulder to her companions.

"Yeah. Day's up," Slipper answered and bent forward to grab his oar. "Not a bad night," he smiled at Kai, a row of mismatched yellow teeth fanning out from one corner of his face to the other side.

Kai smiled back at him. "There'll be something extra for the two of you. I'll see to it," she promised.

"Be nice, seeing how it's Firefaire and we've been working our arses off in this here skiff," grumbled Stickit.

Kai glared at the round-faced girl, her double chins hiding her neck. It was a mystery to Kai how the girl stayed so fat while the rest of them lived so lean. Kai presumed Stickit cheated. Maybe worked two Flocks without the other knowing, doubling her share of the take. Maybe she whored on the side for food she ate alone. Kai once kept her down at the Ribbons for a month just to see if she'd lose the weight and grow thin like the rest of the Flock. But it never happened. Instead Stickit whined and com-plained so much that Kai was obliged to bring her riverside be-fore the rest of the Flock mutinied. Since then Kai had given up the notion of discovering Stickit's secret. As long as she did her share of the work and pulled her quarter for the Flock, Kai let it go.

"Oy, Kai," Slipper called, his voice suddenly urgent.

"What?"

"A Floater. Coming down, just there," Slipper said, pointing to a blacken shape bouncing along the tide. It hit against the wall of the river and twirled slowly, heavily toward the center of the river again.

"Frigging shit, not another," moaned Stickit. "Give me the uglies, they do."

"Can you hook it fast, Slipper?" Kai answered, trying to judge the distance between them and it. She glanced up at the sky again. It was growing light quickly now. She could hear the movement of carts over the bridges, the lighterman calling the hour, the banging of shutters thrown open. She looked at the black shape again, frowning at the small size.

Slipper reached into the bottom of the skiff and pulled out a long pole with a sharp hook at the end. He leaned over the edge of the boat, reaching out to snag the floating shape and drag it toward the boat.

"Easy now," Kai warned, helping him drag the body in. "Nice and slow. We only got one try on this 'un. It's nearly daybreak."

Kai reached hand over hand, carefully dragging the soggy shape to the boat. She wondered for a moment if Slipper had been wrong about it being a Floater. It felt small and too light. Usually Floaters were heavy, rolling ponderously, as if eager to be on their way and objecting to this final insult.

"Quick," Kai barked as the dark-clothed body floated alongside the boat. "Get it in."

She and Stickit leaned over the side, the boat dipping gently to the water's edge. Kai grabbed the body and hauled it in, grunting as she felt the weight slam over the side and land wetly in the bottom of the boat on top of the grain sacks. She turned it over and gave a harsh cry when she saw the face.

Squat stared up at her with blue-blind eyes as watery as fish on a monger's stall. Something had nibbled a hole in the skin of his cheek.

"Frigging shit, frigging shit," Slipper whispered over and over, looking with disbelief at the cold, wet face.

"Who was he on with?" Kai asked in a low voice.

"Finch," Stickit answered. "They was to work the Pleasure district. Z'blood, what happened to him?"

Kai opened Squat's coat, her hands trembling as she peeled back his ragged shirt. The tail of an eel wriggled in the sleeve, and with a shudder of disgust, Kai plucked it out and tossed it back into the river. On Squat's chest the ribs rose like a cage

**57**

beneath the stretched skin. The skin was bleached white, without a mark, without a bruise, as if the child had been encased in a fine white alabaster powder from which there were not even streaks to suggest veins. "Like the others," she murmured in a frightened voice and her eyes lifted to Slipper.

"What others?" Stickit said suddenly, her eyes narrowing.

"Shut up," said Kai.

"What others?" the dour girl said, her lower lip jutting out.

"Just row, damn you. Row the frigging boat."

Stickit stared at her a moment longer as if to protest, but Kai held her gaze, and swearing under her breath, Stickit took up the oar with Slipper.

Kai folded the soggy ends of Squat's coat over his body again. She stared over the prow of the boat, willing it to travel faster. She tried to steady herself, but each time she caught the panicked look in Slipper's eyes her heart galloped with fear. She was Flock leader, she reminded herself angrily. She couldn't afford the fear. She glanced down at Squat, the white face rebuking her. Should have keep him closer to the Ribbons, she told herself harshly. He trusted her and she'd failed her. Somehow she'd failed in her duty to him and he'd been killed. Like the others. Rage and misery constricted her throat, strangling her. She forced a cough, the air huffing from her mouth in a muffled sob. Wrenching the shawl from her head, Kai covered Squat's dead face, shielding herself from its cold, relentless stare.

Jobber rushed down Baker's Lane and turned onto High Street, his arms wrapped tightly around the full basket of bread, his thoughts elsewhere. He hadn't been able to stop thinking of Dogsbody and the Naming. It nagged him, itched like an old sore he couldn't reach to scratch.

Jobber shifted the heavy basket up higher in his arms, his head barely able to see over the rim. It was the law that all Oran citizens be Named. Each child once Named was tattooed in the fleshy space between the thumb and index finger. Only those Named received working papers that allowed Oran citizens to hold land and to be hired as laborers. Even living on the street wasn't safe for very long. The Guards made regular sweeps of the city, checking papers and checking hands. For the Sileans it provided an opportunity to tax the poor and contract cheap labor. But Jobber knew with a chill that went deep into his bones that the Naming had a more insidious purpose: to find those who still carried the curse of Oran magic and to send them swinging on the noddynoose. Though it was Sileans that herded them to the Naming, it was the Readers, casting their keen gaze in search of the magic aura, that signed the death sentences. Without wanting it, Jobber's heart rattled, hearing the hammers pounding nails into the scaffolds.

Damn the Readers, he cursed vehemently. And damn the magic that tainted his blood. He lived alone, because he could trust no one with his secrets. Only Growler had known that Jobber carried the old magic. And along with fighting, Growler had taught him a vagger trick: how to mentally shield the blaze of his aura from the Reader's eye. But it required a steady mind and concentration to hold the shield. Jobber's temper betrayed him, and the last time it happened, Growler had died fighting to give Jobber the time to escape. Jobber sighed, the smooth strands of wicker pressing into his cheek. Growler's death had been his fault.

And that was the other reason Jobber wouldn't have a Flock. He knew he'd never be able to concentrate hard enough to pass in front of the Readers at Fire Circle. He had no future—only the time left before the Sileans and Readers found him. He didn't want to care for anyone or feel the pain and sorrow of losing them. Once had been enough. Loneliness closed like a fist around him, but he was resolved to live alone. I am a Beldan street snitch, he said defiantly. That's all I've ever been. And before the Sileans catch up to me I'll please myself by giving the bastards trouble, he thought with a twisted smile.

Jobber rushed down the street, his gangly legs lengthening their stride in an effort to hurry. His foot caught on someone's heel and Jobber tripped, shoving his basket into the person's back directly in front of him. Then Jobber's head jerked forward, and his face crashed into the wickerwork of the basket.

"Oy, get off," came an angry shout and someone shoved back. The basket was knocked from Jobber's arms and went tumbling to the street. Jobber lost his footing and fell sprawled on his backside in the street. He shook his head, stunned for a moment, but the sight of the firebuns rolling out of the basket, dirt smudging the white icing, ignited his temper.

"Frigging oaf, why don't you look where you're going? Did your mother fuck a stump? What are you doing standing in the way like that? I oughta call a Guard—"

Jobber stopped with a squeak as he looked up and saw the angry faces of Silean Guards staring back at him, their hands moving to their swords.

He looked down again at the spilled bread. "Z'blood," he cursed his temper.

The Guards moved closer to him. Coldness replaced the hot fury of anger. Not looking at them, he stood up slowly, brushing himself off casually. How many had there been? he thought quickly. Five, his memory answered. Too many at once. He settled his breathing, drawing the shield protectively around his aura.

Jobber looked up and coughed, embarrassed. "Ah, excuse me, sirs, I'm sorry about this." Inwardly he was relieved. Sileans, but no Readers. He could see by the shoulder marks on their gray and black uniforms they were Firsts, probably on their way to start duty. Firsts were culled from the sons of wealthy Sileans to do their part in the Guard. They were easier to placate than the louts hired for Seconds and Thirds, scraped up from the dregs of Silean society. "I hope I haven't hurt anyone?" Jobber smiled deferentially and hunched his shoulders.

"Take it back," one of them said. A man, not much older than himself, Jobber thought, looking very red in the face and gripping his sword with a bit too much passion for Jobber's comfort.

"I'm sorry, sir, take what?" Jobber asked innocently.

"Take back the insult about my mother."

"It was your foot then I stomped on. Oh, I am sorry." Jobber bent and started to pick up the buns, blowing the dirt off them.

"Come on, Ferris, forget it. We're going to be late," another Guard spoke, glancing nervously in the direction of the Keep.

"You go ahead, I'll catch up."

Jobber watched them out of the corner of his eye as he picked up buns, returning them carefully to the basket.

"Ferris, it isn't worth it. If you're late for duty, Firstwatch will have your balls."

"Let her try. Go on if you're scared of the bitch. I mean to educate this street scum to the stupidity of insulting Sileans."

The Guard shrugged and turned to the others. "Let's go." Jobber saw one of them hesitate and then decide with the rest. They turned, leaving Ferris standing, hand clenched on his sword and a nasty smile spreading on his face.

Good, thought Jobber. Better odds. This might even be fun. He checked the street. No one was about, only a few shopkeepers opening their doors.

Jobber straightened his shoulders, meeting Ferris's spiteful stare with one of his own.

"Take it back, street scum. Take back the insult."

"Street scum, is it?" Jobber answered, moving closer to Ferris but staying just out of reach of the sword arm. "I needn't take anything back. You're a piece of Silean shit flung out of your own country to stink up Oran. Just the sight of you is an insult to me."

Ferris's face turned a mottled red. His sword scraped free, and Ferris drove the point at Jobber. Jobber sprang forward, both arms raised in a cross-handed block. He caught Ferris's sword arm just at the wrist, forcing the arm with the sword up over his head. Then he grasped the sword hand in his own hands and twisted around sharply. Jobber jerked Ferris's outstretched arm down hard and slammed the back of the elbow against his shoulder bone. Ferris screamed as the joint was pushed upward and smashed with a noisy crack. The sword fell, skittering across the street.

Jobber let go of the arm and rammed his elbow into Ferris's belly. Ferris doubled over groaning, and Jobber turned swiftly catching him by the ears. His knee surged upward into Ferris's face. Ferris gave a final strangled moan as he collapsed to the ground in a messy heap, his nose and mouth bleeding. Jobber checked the street. No one saw them. He dragged the unconscious Ferris into a doorway and propped him up against the locked door. Jobber smiled at his bloody handiwork. It was going to be something of a shock for the tradesman when it came opening time. He retrieved the sword and laid it across Ferris's knees. A Silean sword, he noted, and with a poor grain. Useless bit of steel that, he thought contemptuously.

Jobber's eye caught on the fat purse hanging on Ferris's belt. He untied it quickly and weighed it in his palm. "That'll do very nicely, Master Ferris. Glad to see you Sileans know when to pay your insult fine."

Jobber moved away from the slumped Guard and gathered up the last of the firebuns quickly. The stolen purse he tied beneath his vest for safekeeping. Hoisting the basket up, he hurried off again down the street. He felt revived by the fight, and his eyes sparkled at thought of the extra money he had just acquired. Fire's luck, that's what Dogsbody had said. Well maybe he was right. Jobber grinned delightedly. After Trina's bit, he'd leave off doing any more jobs for the day and give himself a real holiday visiting Crier's Forge. Maybe he'd even ask Master Donal about Faul, he thought with sudden good humor. There could be no better way to celebrate Firefaire than to breathe in the smoke and steel dust of the swordmaker's forge, feel his face grow hot from the fire and hear the hammer's clang against the anvil. Then he began to run, the basket bouncing awkwardly. "Welcome Fire-faire," he shouted to the street. "Same to you," a startled shop-keeper answered back as Jobber sped past.

# 5

The Regent Silwa Re Familia stood rocking back and forth lightly on the balls of his feet, his hands clasped behind his back as he tried to settle his annoyance. Fire Queen Zorah gave him a side-long glance and smiled to herself. She had interrupted his morning routines, summoned him like a common servant and now she would make him wait. He glared at her with the bright blue eyes of an indignant child. He was easy to understand, she thought, sometimes too easy, she sighed. He could never appreciate the subtlety of games. . . . Too caught up with his own arrogance and, she thought, her smile widening, desire.

"Give me the sword," Zorah said to her Firstwatch and held out her hand. Gonmer handed it to her, the hilt placed in her hand. Zorah raised the sword, testing its weight and balance. Though it had been a long time to feel such a sword, it was instantly familiar, like a numb limb awakened after sleep. She tensed with the sharp edge of fear at the recognition of its touch, but it was fear that altered to relief when she felt the inert slowness of the metal. It had no life, no piercing song to call forth fire from her touch. She brought the sword down, the point facing the floor, and the sunlight from the open window sparkled on the wavy pattern of the blade. "It's a fake," she said, her voice soft with a light husky tone. "A good one, but a fake nonetheless."

"A fake what?" asked Regent Silwa. Zorah remained silent, staring at the light bouncing off the blade. "Madam, explain this."

Zorah's angry thoughts flared. He thinks he is important. He thinks he rules Oran, but he doesn't, she told herself. I do, and so he will be made to wait. "The blade is too short, there are flaws in the patterns—see?—there," she pointed with a finger, "where the swordmaker cooled the iron too quickly. And of course the blade carries no life of its own. But it's still a good copy of the original." Zorah spoke to the Firstwatch, ignoring her Regent's growing impatience.

"What original are you talking about?" Silwa asked.

"Show him the sword, Firstwatch," Zorah said, tossing the sword to Gonmer, who caught it neatly by its handle, only the sudden lift of her eyebrow betraying her surprise. Silwa took it from the Firstwatch, scowling angrily. Zorah saw his expression change, admiration replacing annoyance as he held the sword in an awkward grip. For all its length, it was light weight and supple, unlike the heavier Silean swords.

"Look at the guard," Zorah prompted Silwa, enjoying his confusion.

Silwa's brow drew together as he studied the sword. It was an oval guard, cut with a pattern of two mountains. Between the mountains a crescent moon was rising over the edge of one peak. She could see that it meant nothing to him.

"Well?" she asked, a smile lifting the corner of her mouth.

"I'm not familiar with Oran swords, Madam."

"More's the pity, Regent Silwa. Describe the guard."

"Two mountains with a moon between them."

"Ah, a moon. What kind of moon?"

Regent Silwa's anger burst out. "Madam, I must protest, this riddling game is wasting our time."

"Time is your problem, Regent Silwa, not mine. I have an infinite amount of time." She tossed back the red-gold mane of hair, her green eyes flashing.

Silwa opened his mouth to reply, but a hand on his arm stayed the words.

"Please, Madam, you must understand how the events of last night have troubled us. We wish of course only to serve you more effectively. Perhaps you could enlighten us." Adviser to the Regent, Antoni Re Desturo, bowed his head and gave the Queen a pleasant smile.

"I thought Adviser Antoni that enlightening the Regent was your responsibility, not mine."

"Indeed, Madam is correct. However, by your own decree much in the way of Oran history has been suppressed. Thus you must forgive our ignorance."

Zorah regarded him with distaste. She hated him far worse than she disliked the Regent Silwa. Silwa at least was handsome; all the Silean Regents had been handsome men. He was square-shouldered and dark-haired, the deep blue of his uniform highlighting the blue of his eyes. She thought Silwa an honest man, if not a little narrow-minded. His solutions to problems, like his world, were military. But Antoni Re Desturo had the smoothness of a snake clothed in green Silean silk. He hid his expression beneath a dark beard, and his eyes were as black as a crow's and always searching. Antoni was a dangerous combination—intelligent as well as ambitious—and more than once Zorah had heard the undertones of contempt in his diplomatic speech. But he was Adviser to the Regent, chosen by Silwa, and she could no more dismiss him than Silwa could dismiss her choice of Firstwatch. It had been a condition of the treaty, a pretense at keeping the balance of power even.

Zorah turned to Silwa, a pout forming on the perfect lips. "It's a copy of a Fire Sword. The guard depicts the crest of my sister Huld, the new moon rising between two peaks. A new moon, does that suggest anything to you?"

"The rebel farmers?" he asked.

"Exactly."

"Might it come from Huld?"

Zorah shook her head. "I told you the sword has no life. And in any event, Huld is long dead."

"There are some who claim she still lives."

Zorah stopped him impatiently. "She is dead like the rest of my sisters. Destroyed in the Burning."

Silwa's brow drew together across his face in puzzled concern. "I had heard—"

"Foolish tales. Vagger talk stirring up old hatreds that should have died with the Burning. Though Huld plotted against my other sisters and me, I loved her. And when she died, destroyed by the forces she unleashed, I felt the pain of her death as if it had been my own." Across Zorah's cheeks the pale skin flushed a rosy hue. The air grew sharp with the metallic scent of copper. Around her shoulders the fire-colored hair crackled and snapped with electricity.

"The Guilds then," suggested Silwa, eyeing the Fire Queen's angry hair cautiously. "A Swordmaster could make the sword and claim it comes from Huld."

Zorah remained silent, distracted by memory; the harsh grating of stone like granite teeth, the razor stench of charred wood; Huld's wintry face like gray ash.

"What was the New Moon doing in the Keep?" Silwa asked, and Zorah realized that he had asked his question twice.

She blinked slowly, to clear away the shadows of the past. She saw again the sunlit room. "Assassination, I expect," she said quietly.

"Was it you they were after?" Silwa asked.

Zorah shook her head. "No. They would never attack me. I am the Fire Queen. I cannot be killed."

"So it is also rumored," Silwa said quietly.

"But not believed, Regent Silwa?"

"If I am not to believe the tales of Huld's continued existence, explain to me, Madam, how it would be easier to believe the tales of your immortality. It is a difficult idea for a Silean to accept."

Zorah laughed and shrugged her shoulders. "So I understand. Silean religion grants immortality only to the dead. And you yourself know well that I am not dead," she added coyly. Silwa frowned, embarrassed. "The fact that I am still here after all these years and will be long after you are dust and bone should be proof enough. Were it not true I would have been killed a long time ago, perhaps even by your forebearers in those first months when Silea came to my aid." She moved to stand before him, her face lifting to his, an intimate smile closing the distance between them. "But let me offer more convincing proof."

Before Silwa could object, Zorah drew her wrist down across the sword's blade edge.

She gasped in sudden pain, her eyes half-closed. Silwa reeled back in horror, the Queen's blood staining the edge of the sword. From her wrist a thin stream of blood trailed across the white skin onto her dress.

"Madam—" Silwa said hoarsely, but she brushed him away with one hand, holding the injured arm up high.

"Watch," she whispered.

Silwa stared at the slash on her wrist, shocked as the blood ceased to flow and the skin closed. There appeared a brown line of scab, and then it, too, faded, replaced by a pink scar. The blood had not yet dried on her arm when the scar vanished and her skin was as before.

"I am Oran," Zorah said. "Understand what it means, Silwa. I am not like those children the Readers find. Those are the remnants of Orans once gifted with the use of power. A gift too dangerous now in the hands of children. It nearly destroyed Oran once. I *am* the source of Oran's power. Oran exists because of *me*. You cannot kill the land or the water or the sky, nor extinguish forever the fire. And for the same reason, you cannot kill me."

Silwa said nothing, only stared at her wrist. Little men, Zorah thought, studying him. Their reaction was always the same. They thought of her as a child, a woman like their own wives and daughters pampered into dullness and obedience. It pained them to learn the truth, to measure the smallness of their mortality against her power to endure.

Silwa's eyes met hers, and he spoke in measured tones as if to belie the grim effect of her act. "It wasn't me they were after."

Zorah nodded in agreement. "They would have paid too dearly for that loss. Silean honor would never allow such a crime to pass without severe and brutal punishment. The retaliation might be more than the New Moon would wish for."

"You are correct, Madam. Silean honor would require nothing less for one of my position," Silwa answered coolly.

Zorah smiled at him. There, she thought, now he feels better, not so naked. He's cloaked himself again in his pride.

"Who do you think then? One of the guests?"

"If it were me," she said slowly, "I'd attack the Firstwatch."

Gonmer looked up, startled.

"They didn't just send a hapless farmer. They sent a skilled and trained swordsman."

"Woman," Gonmer corrected.

Zorah nodded, understanding. "Yes. More appropriate still. I didn't think there were vaggers left who would train women. And yet I can see the advantage of surprise in it," she mused privately, "and the poetry. You said the fighter was good, didn't you?" Zorah looked at Gonmer, fine gold eyebrows raised.

"Yes. Very good," Gonmer answered, reflecting for an instant on the flash of steel, the quick arc of the blade.

"To disrupt Firefaire, the easiest way would be to kill its chief organizer," Zorah continued. "Your apprentice is too young to assume the responsibilities of Firstwatch. Putting a Silean in such a position of power, no matter how temporary, could very easily encourage even the most placid of Orans to protest violently. Stir up the Firefaire crowds. Create friction into which the New Moon would draw up sides and raise the call for blood."

"Can peasants really conceive of so intricate a plan?" Antoni asked with a measure of sarcasm.

"Not alone," Zorah agreed. "But there are others. Vaggers perhaps, who could impress such simple people into such daring acts."

"Or the Guilds?" Antoni asked again.

"Yes, of course the Guilds, but I don't think so. Their quarrel belongs in Beldan. They wouldn't waste their time with country folk."

"Perhaps they supplied only the weapons?"

"Possibly," Zorah added.

"Who could make such a weapon?" Silwa asked. He placed the sword carefully on the table, eyeing the blade that still carried traces of Zorah's blood with deep mistrust.

"There are few smiths left with the skill to make such a sword as this," Zorah said. "It could not have been made in the country. The steel is too pure and the work, even though flawed, too skilled for the likes of a country forge. It was made right here in Beldan." She turned to Gonmer. "Go to the Guildmaster Donal at Crier's Forge. I doubt that the Elder Donal would have consented to making it, but he has a son Named not five years ago who also works at the forge. Though why he should want to become involved with the New Moon is unthinkable to me."

"A Guildsman no doubt wanting to revive some former glory to Oran," Antoni said speaking quietly to the Regent, but loud enough that the Queen might hear.

"I was not aware that Oran had lost its former glory," Zorah snapped. "Oran smiths are without peer, even in Silea. The steel you wear was forged and shaped here, as are most of the swords now worn by Sileans."

"I meant no insult, Madam," Antoni bowed his head apologetically. "I was merely commenting on the hostility of Guild members who claim you have denied their right to practice certain ancient skills. As the Regent suggested earlier, they may have in mind a plan to force you to restore those rights."

"I am well aware of your own interests in those rights, Adviser," Zorah said sharply. Antoni's face gave a look of mild surprise. "Though Sileans consider Oran magic akin to evil, they would avail themselves quite happily to the power of a Fire Sword."

"We are easily impressed by the tales, Madam," Antoni answered.

"But more so by the truth. You have been in Oran long enough, Adviser, to know that Oran magic was not built upon tales, but reality. But know this as well: I will never permit the Guilds the rights they once enjoyed. It was the Guild of Smiths that aided my sister Huld, and their Fire Swords created the Burning that tore our country apart with civil war. I cannot be persuaded, even by violence, to grant them the power to do so again. They would threaten the peace of Oran," she answered angrily.

"Of course, Madam," Antoni murmured smoothly, "peace is what we all want."

And profits, you thief, Zorah thought snidely. That's all the

Sileans ever wanted from Oran. And there was little she could do to change that. Two hundred years of meddling in Oran society had not softened Sileans to the Oran way of life. Rather they had forced the landscape, the people, to submit to Silean culture. Some of it she had permitted, Zorah admitted to herself. But she had only done it so that there might be peace in Oran, freedom from the nightmare of the Burning. And peace in her own undying soul.

The Firstwatch Gonmer bowed smartly before Zorah. "With your permission, Madam, I shall go to Crier's Forge immediately."

Zorah nodded. Gonmer took the sword and left quickly, her boots tapping a staccato rhythm down the corridor. Adviser to the Regent, Antoni Re Desturo, bowed deeply, first at Zorah and then Silwa, before leaving. Zorah bristled with irritation and turned away.

Regent Silwa remained, standing by the table. Now that they were alone, Zorah regretted her sharpness and wished she had not belittled him. He might be her servant but she needed him. He couldn't know how the sight of Huld's sword, even a fake, ignited old terrors. The world in chaos and herself lost in its center. She needed warmth, comfort, something to push back the lingering coldness of fear. He caught her gaze and turned to go.

"Silwa, wait," she called, "I'm sorry. Forgive me."

He stopped, one hand lightly tapping his thigh as he hesitated. "What do you want from me, Zorah?"

"Companionship," she answered softly.

"You humiliate me with your arrogance and your power. For this I should give you companionship?"

"Silwa, I ask your forgiveness." She crossed the room to him and placed her hands on his chest. "I am two hundred years old, and I have the manners of a bad-tempered child. Please, Silwa, stay."

"Zorah . . ." he started to say, but she placed her fingers lightly over his mouth.

"Silwa, I know you are busy. I know I have no right to ask you, but I will ask. Stay with me a little while. After all, it is Firefaire," and she smiled at him to soften the angry expression of his face. She arched her back slightly, her hips and thighs resting against him, her head tilted back in surrender. Beneath her hand on his chest she felt his pulse quicken.

Silwa sighed and bent his head to kiss the warm flesh of her neck. His arms circled her waist, and Zorah felt the lingering

69

shadow of fear withdraw beneath his embrace. She closed her eyes, the sunlight on her face and Silwa's hands stroking her breast. She twined her arms around his neck, her fingers playing with his hair. He pulled his head back to stare at her, his gaze penetrating. She knew that look, had seen its like in every one of her Regents. It was love corrupted by ambition. They were not content to be her lover. They wanted to possess her, much as they believed they possessed Oran. They wanted, she thought, to be the only one out of all the others she would remember for an eternity. She met his stare full face. Her eyes held his, and she soothed him with a smile. She could do this honestly, with no sense of betrayal. Each new Regent was no different from the man before, and so to her they merged into one person, one living entity that struggled to keep pace with her immortality. To each one of them she might have been unique, but to her they were all the same man.

Silwa bent his head again, his mouth covering hers, the stiff bristles of his mustache prickling her soft skin. Zorah clung to him, yielding to passion. It's Firefaire, she thought, her heart beating faster, a joyous celebration. Huld's coldness can't touch me here. Death has no place in this sun-filled room. The red-gold firehair crackled with pleasure, and Zorah smelled the sweet fragrance of copper and rosewater. Zorah pulled away from Silwa's kiss and burst out in happy laughter. "Come," she whispered, eagerly tugging at the laces on his uniform, "let us celebrate Firefaire as is expected."

With a shout, Silwa lifted her high in the air, his arms clasped tight around her thighs, his face pressed between the soft curve of her breasts. She bent over him, her arms resting on his shoulders, the red-gold hair forming a shimmering curtain of fire around his head. "Lighterman, is your torch ready?" Zorah asked him, grinning.

He grinned back. "I have it here, Madam. It needs but the touch of your hand to ignite it."

"Oh," she answered coyly, wrapping her legs around his waist. "That will be my pleasure."

"So I would hope, Madam."

"Let me have it then," Zorah giggled.

"I intend to, Madam," Silwa answered, carrying Zorah to a small couch and laying her down on her back. "Indeed, I intend to."

# 6

Alwir gazed across the Hiring Field, weariness settling into his bones and hunger growling in his stomach. He would have liked to ignore the hunger but he could not. Reading drained the body, left it weak, and only food could restore his strength. He picked his way between the small groups of laborers hunkered around their smoking fires and makeshift camps in expectation of tomorrow's hiring. He caught the fragments of conversations, worried murmurings filled with anxiety; would there be another drought, would there be work for this season, would a child survive the Reading.

Alwir passed a woman looking as weary as himself, sitting on the damp grass her eyes half-closed as she nursed an infant. At her side a farmer in a dun-colored smock instructed a smaller child to mind the fire. A horse nickered near the wagon, and absently Alwir followed the sound. Then he noticed another, older boy sitting in the shade of the wagon, his legs drawn up tight and his eyes staring out nervously across the Hiring Field. He chewed his nails, not bothering to brush away the black hair that covered much of his thin face. Alwir felt the chill on his spine as the boy's dark eyes suddenly met his own. Scared, Alwir thought, and haunted. Though he was tired, Alwir Read him, instinct answering him even before he saw the aura of white light spreading in a faint corona around the boy's head. An air element, Alwir thought, now seeing again the boy's frightened face.

"What do you want?" the farmer's gruff voice made Alwir jump. Alwir faced the man and saw the younger child scoot behind the man's smock. Alwir smiled as the child peeked out. The farmer's broad callused hand rested reassuringly on the child's shoulder. Alwir looked at the man, his shoulders stooped and his legs bowed from years of hauling heavy sacks. His leathered skin was brown from the sun, his hair greying. But two bright blue eyes stared back at Alwir like a warning.

"Have you come for the Naming or the Hiring?" Alwir asked, smiling comfortably.

71

The farmer continued to eye him suspiciously before answering. Alwir had dressed carefully, to appear as neither wealthy nor destitute. His trousers were of plain but good wool tucked into smooth leather boots. His shirt was without embroidery, but the linen was finely woven. Alwir could sense the man judging whether this well-dressed youngster was a prospective employer or simply trouble looking for a meal.

"Both," he answered at last. Then, rubbing his hand over the stubble of a new beard, he asked, "And yourself?"

"Neither. May I sit awhile?"

Again the peasant hesitated, scratching the skin of his cheek. He glanced quickly at his wife and she shrugged her answer. Alwir unslung a bag from his shoulder and pulled out a small Oran fiddle with a scrolled neck. He tuned it lightly, waiting for the man to make up his mind to invite him. Alwir then let his fingers pluck a familiar tune, the muted sound sweet.

The farmer smiled, showing the gaps in his yellowed teeth. "There'd be no harm in it," he said.

Alwir joined them, sitting on the ground, the fiddle tucked beneath his shoulder. He played them a dance tune, his fingers tapping lightly over the neck, the bow drawing smartly over the strings. The woman smiled, and even the baby at her breast stopped sucking long enough to give him a round-eyed stare. The younger child leaned against his father's shoulder, the small face wrinkled with delight.

"Go on then, goodman, give the man some bread," the woman said when Alwir had finished playing. "He do look as if he could use a bite to eat."

Alwir held up his hand and nodded his head. "Thank you, Mistress," he answered respectfully and the woman beamed. Alwir would have preferred to refuse the bread, imagining how meager the family's supplies might be, but to have done so would have insulted them deeply. Instead he reached again into his bag and pulled out a roll of finely cut tobacco and offered it to the man. The farmer sucked his lower lip approvingly. He quickly brought out a long-stemmed pipe and proceeded to pack the bowl with the light-colored tobacco.

Alwir ate his bread, chewing slowly. From the corner of his eye he watched the older boy, still sitting alone by the wagon. He had hoped the music might have brought the boy closer so that Alwir could talk to him as well as the father. But he stayed by the wagon, lost in his own worried thoughts, as he nervously ripped off fragments of his fingernails.

72

Alwir quickly swallowed the crust of bread. "You mustn't go to the Naming," he said quickly.

"What are you saying?" the man asked, suspicion returning to his face.

"Don't send your son to the Naming," Alwir repeated.

"If he don't go, he won't get his working papers. Then how will he be hired?"

"If you send him to the Naming, he's as good as dead," Alwir answered harshly.

The woman clutched her baby tighter to her breast. The farmer leaned back slowly on his heels and squinted through the pipe smoke at Alwir.

"Who are you to say such a thing?" the farmer asked.

"A Reader."

He heard the woman gasp and saw the color drain from the farmer's face, his ruddy cheeks ashen as the smoke. But the blue eyes sparkled with defiance. Gently he pushed the younger child away from his side to stand with his mother.

"You're lying," the man said softly. "You know now't. Trying to rob us, that's all." Beneath the scornful tone, Alwir heard the unease in the man's voice.

"I wish that was all it was. But it's not and you know it as well as I." Alwir turned his head toward the boy waiting near the wagon. "Your son. He's a child of the old power. An air element. If you send him tomorrow to the Naming, the Readers will pick him out like chaff from the wheat."

The farmer gripped the thin stem of the pipe so tightly it snapped. He threw the pipe down and spoke as if the taste had turned to acid in his throat.

"What do you want?"

"Not to see him dead," Alwir answered simply.

"What price?"

"None asked."

The man's eyes opened wide with surprise. It was not the answer he had expected. He stared at Alwir uncertainly, and then Alwir saw the wooden look of resignation. When he spoke, it was with difficulty. "I bribed the village Reader with the last parcel of land we had left. Now we've now't but our hands to hire out. The Reader gave us a medal for him to wear 'round his neck, said it would shield the child's magic from Beldan's Readers. But it didn't, did it?"

"No."

"It was land worked by my father, and his father before him, back to before the Burning. It's Silean land now," the farmer said, his head slouching deeper between his shoulders. "It weren't so hard to leave it thinking that at least my son would be spared. And now I've not even that."

Alwir swore, as rage burned fiercer than the hunger in his belly. How many Oran farmers were cheated of their land, he wondered. This man who sacrificed all for his son would have lost him the moment the child stepped before the Readers of Fire Circle.

"I would offer you another course," Alwir said.

"What then?" the man whispered to the fire.

"I have friends that will get him to safety. To the Avadares Mountains."

"So far north? And how will he live?" the man asked, stirring the fire. The wood crackled and a burning spark lifted into the air.

"The New Moon."

The farmer scoffed angrily. "Exchange one treasonous death for another."

"Perhaps, perhaps not. At least with the New Moon your son has a better chance at staying alive."

"Until he's caught."

"A certainty if you stay in Beldan and send him to the Naming." Alwir reached out and urgently grabbed the man by the arm. "Ask him, ask your son. Let him make his own choice. He may rather die fighting than swinging from the noddynoose like a common thief."

The man shook off Alwir's grasp and sat back silently. Alwir turned to the woman, but she looked away refusing to meet his eyes. Finally Alwir looked at the boy, his arms tightly hugging his drawn-up legs and his chin resting on the tops of his knees. The downcast eyes stared at the grass. Alwir sighed heavily, accepting their silence as refusal. He repacked his instrument, storing it away carefully in its bag. He stood up and slung it again over his shoulder. The man stopped him.

"How does he get out of the city?"

Alwir gave a small smile. "Go to Iron Alley, behind the forges in the Guild district. Ask for Crier's Forge. People there will help him."

The man nodded and stood stiffly. "We'll think on it."

"Fire's luck to you," Alwir said, hoisting the bag higher on his shoulder. "And to him."

Alwir left quickly, striding across the grassy field in the direction of Market Square. His head buzzed with the sound of angry bees, and he felt faint. He had to eat something substantial before he became too exhausted to stand. As he approached the entrance to Market Square, he was struck by the sudden odors of frying fat, smoked fish and overripe fruit. Saliva pooled beneath his tongue and his stomach grumbled more loudly. Alwir shoved his way into the milling crowd of fair-goers, sidestepping the small herds of livestock being led to the Hiring Fields for grazing. He squeezed through the tightly packed crowd and aimed for the food stalls on the edges of Market Square.

Stumbling through the crowd, Alwir's boots scuffled through the debris of fruit rinds, lost ribbons, crushed paper cones that once held sweets, and animal excrement left behind by frightened livestock. He followed his nose until he came to a rickety stall with a grease-stained counter that had been painted bright red. The stall was tended by a heavyset woman, wearing a dingy apron tucked up beneath her large breasts. She skewered a pink and white sausage on a stick and, after wiping her hand on the apron, joined the sausage with others over a fire.

"Oy, hot and spicy!" she shouted as she picked up another sausage and spitted it. "Very hot! Three coppers an' all!" she cried.

"I'll have two," Alwir said, fishing for the coins.

"Right," she said, and wiped her greasy hair out of her face with the back of a shiny hand. She grabbed two sticks and laid the sizzling brown sausages on a bit of paper. Oil soaked through the paper as she sprinkled salt on the sausages before wrapping them up.

Alwir gave her the coins, and she tucked them away in a pocket before handing him the sausages. "Lovely bit of meat that," she added proudly.

Alwir tore open the paper and began stuffing one of the sausages in his mouth. As he bit down, the hot spicy fat squirted in his mouth burning his tongue. But Alwir didn't care. He chewed rapidly and just enough to keep from choking on the meat before he swallowed it. The woman gaped at him and then, slowly shaking her head, went back to her task of spitting sausages.

Still eating, Alwir threaded his way through the crowd again, passing other stalls that offered tempting foods for the fair-goers. He was finishing the second sausage when he stopped in front of a baker's stall and bought a loaf of bread and a small bag of iced firebuns. Continuing through the square, he bought three pears from a barrowboy's cart, a small box of berries from a black-haired girl in green-painted clogs and several apples from an old man who hauled the fruit on the back of a cart pulled by an even older-looking goat. The pears were juicy and sweet, and he ate two of them, just standing amid the flowing crowd.

It was as he was standing, shoulders leaning forward and chin out to keep the juice from dripping down his shirt, that he felt the light patting of a hand near his pocket. The hand slipped in softly and searched for the string of coins he had stored there. Alwir flushed, feeling foolish as a stranger's hand groped intimately in his pocket while he stood there, pear juice dripping from his beard and a bag of food clutched awkwardly beneath his elbow. He coughed noisily and straightened, dropping the pear core into the street. The hand withdrew swiftly, without his coins. Relieved, Alwir wiped his face with the edge of his shirt cuff. He hadn't wanted to face the pickpocket while looking so ridiculous, but now composed and a little cleaner Alwir cast a curious eye about him, wondering who it might have been.

He studied the faces of the crowd as they milled past: Sileans in dark blue silk, feathered hats and riding crops to flick at the cattle and beggars that strayed too close to them; a group of journeymen, happily drunk, their voices raised in song; a Silean clergyman with an outraged expression, who walked through the crowd as if besieged by demons on all sides. Alwir watched in amused curiosity as the clergyman passed a vagger standing quietly beside a stall that sold little straw effigies of the Queen. They stared at one another mistrustfully, the vagger's hand wrapped around his tall staff, the clergyman reaching down to touch the string of prayer beads at his waist. The clergyman scowled with disgust at the tattooed symbols on the vagger's face. The vagger laughed at the clergyman and strolled away, the nob of his staff just visible over the heads of the crowd.

Alwir sighed. It was impossible to guess who among this crowd would pick his pocket. It could have been anybody. Even that vagger over there, he thought ruefully. Fire knows, they didn't eat often enough, and petty thieving to them was acceptable since it went to support them in their higher calling. If caught, they always explained it as a prayer tax, which considering that everything else in Oran life was taxed always seemed to Alwir a reasonable argument.

*There!* There is was again, the light feathery touch that rustled his pocket. Alwir stood still and hummed, feigning indifference. His face blushed as the hand dug deeper into his pocket in search of the coins. He felt the string of coins slide out. Without another thought, Alwir whirled around and clamped his fist over the wrist of the exiting hand.

He had expected someone older. At least someone taller. He was prepared to meet face to face the thief whose hand he clutched. Instead his gaze was jerked downward to a struggling girl in a tattered blue dress who was kicking him in the shins and swearing. He stared fascinated by the contradiction of the verbal threats issued in a bold voice and the spareness of her frame, her face half-hidden by a tangle of blond hair that fluffed around her head like a seeding dandelion.

"I ain't done nothing to you, bastard!" she shouted, glaring up at him.

Alwir laughed and that made her more angry. She started kicking him again, this time catching him painfully on the leg-bone. His laughter was cut short by a yelp, but he didn't let go of her.

"Z'blood, stop it," he ordered.

"Let go then!"

"Not 'til you stop! Look, you robbed me! Give me back the string of coppers you took and I'll let you go."

"I ain't nabbed nothing of yours, so let me be or I'll scaffer you. Cut you quick, I will, dump you downside so's the Ribbon crabs can feast. There won't be nothing left of you even the Bonecruncher would backsell at the Racket."

Alwir shook his head, understanding more the intent of her words than the actual meaning. With his one hand still tightly wrapped about her wrist, he held out the other bag with the food in front of her.

"Hungry?" he asked.

She stopped her kicking and stared at the proffered bag of food, the apples gleaming over the top of the bag. She darted a glance at Alwir, uncertain.

"What's your lay?"

"Go on," he said and gave the bag a little shake.

She snatched the bag from his hand. Alwir watched as the girl quickly discovered her dilemma. In one hand she held the bag, but Alwir held her other arm, preventing her from being able to set the bag on the ground. With neither hand free, she couldn't reach into the bag. Twice she held the bag up to her nose, smelling the bread, catching glimpses of the sweet firebuns squished in the bottom of the bag, and twice she lowered the bag, with an expression of angry disappointment.

"You're a bastard, ain't you? Want to see me grovel? Eat with

**77**

my nog stuck in this here bag like the Ragman's nag at her oats. Well, shit on your plate," she said to Alwir, her eyes downcast.

Alwir winced. "All right," he answered quickly. "I didn't mean to tease you. I just wanted you to stop kicking me. Now give me my money back and the food is yours."

"Gimme my hand back first."

"The money first!" Alwir shouted.

"My hand," she answered, sticking out a determined chin.

"Well, well, Alwir, what sport is this? Need any help?"

Alwir jerked around, at the sound of his brother's smug voice. Balder stood there with Renn, both of them dressed in the black and gray uniforms of the Firstwatch. Each man escorted a young woman elegantly dressed in Silean silk and now tittering behind gloved hands. Alwir's face flushed red and then white.

"Leave off, Balder, this is a private matter."

"Really, Alwir, she's not much to look at. Couldn't you have selected someone a little cleaner?" Balder held a linen cloth over his nose.

"A little older, too, I'd say," Renn added, looking the girl up and down.

The girl wrenched away her hand violently, and with a sudden desperation renewed her struggle to free herself. She twisted her body so as to hide behind Alwir. Alwir glowered at her, holding her tighter and wondering at her panic. She had dropped the bag of food, the apples spilling out on the cobblestones as she bent her head to bite his hand.

"Ow! Zorah's tits," Alwir shouted at her as her teeth sunk into his hand.

"Give her the back of your hand, Alwir," suggested Balder. "That always works. The bitches love it."

Alwir turned back to his brother, annoyed at his interruption and confused by the girl's panic. And then he saw the reason for it. Balder and Renn had worn their Readers emblems proudly pinned on their chests. The dull silver blinked like a third eye in the sunlight. Surely the girl now struggling to free herself had seen them, and if that were the reason, then she had greater fears than his calling the Guards. Alwir swore at himself for his own stupidity.

"I can handle my own business," Alwir snarled at his brothers. Picking the kicking girl up, he tucked her under his arm and dragged her away through the crowds, his one thought to get her away from Balder's and Renn's curious gaze. She screamed obscenities at him, her arms flailing. But Alwir kept moving through the crowds, his jaw set in a determined scowl, his eyes searching for a quiet corner. He could feel the eyes of the crowd on him, heard the jibes and shouted curses from people kicked in passing by the wriggling girl. Those didn't bother him half as much as the concern that his brothers might follow him.

He turned down a sidestreet, only once stealing a glance over his shoulders. His brothers were nowhere to be seen, and Alwir breathed a thanks for that. He tried not to look at the girl tucked under his arm, her skirts and petticoats billowing over her waist to reveal her pale, skinny legs that scissored with fury. Her head bobbed like a flower at the end of a broken stalk. He kept moving down the street lined with shops that sold rugs and draperies. The doors were opened wide to reveal the crimson-patterned rugs hung from racks. Apprentices sitting cross-legged on small cushions tied the knotted fringes and kept a sharp eye to the street. Smaller rugs and bolts of cloth were stacked on carts beside the doors. A group of shopkeepers sitting at table while they shared a meal gawked and then called out obscene suggestions to Alwir as he strode past with the girl still struggling beneath his arm.

Alwir found an alley and turned gratefully into its quiet darkness. He stepped through puddles of gray filmed water, tossed out from the morning's cleaning. Empty crates and garbage lined the walls of the narrow alley and muffled the girl's cries. Above, a shutter slammed shut, while another opened and a curious child peered out. A scrawny yellow cat, interrupted in its cleaning by Alwir's passing, hissed before returning to his paw.

Alwir dropped the girl from under his arm but kept a firm grasp on her shoulders. She tried to twist away, so he shoved her roughly into the wall and pinned her shoulders against the cracked plaster.

"Frigging bastard," she hissed at him, staring back at him from beneath the fringe of yellow hair.

Alwir didn't answer her with words. He let his eyes unfocus and stared back at her, searching for the light that he knew would shine forth from within in her face. He almost sighed with pleasure when he saw the beautiful aura of light green wrapped around the girl's head like ivy. "An earth element," he whispered. And beneath his hands he felt the thin shoulders sag with defeat.

"Frigging Reader bastard," she repeated hatefully.

Alwir dimmed his Reader's sight and saw the lines of her face shift into hard-edged clarity. Staring at her closely now, Alwir realized she was older than he had first thought. Her skin was white, pulled tight across the small frame of bones, and her eyes, which he now saw clearly beneath her crown of fine hair, were blue. They stared back at him with cold malice.

"I mean you no harm," he said quickly.

"Then let go of me."

"Only if you promise not to run."

She didn't answer, her face sullen.

"What a fool I've been," Alwir said as much to himself as to her. "All this while I've been going 'round Reading farmers' children, trying to warn them, and meanwhile in my own city of Beldan there are those like you. Right here, that I could have helped. What's your name?"

The girl cocked her head up proudly. "Finch."

Alwir nodded, easing his grip slowly on her shoulders. "Right then, Finch. Listen to me, and listen hard. I know you've the old power. Won't be long before other Readers learn it, too. So I'll give you a bit of advice."

"Don't want it from the likes of you!" she spat.

"Even if it will save your life?"

"Huh," she snorted angrily. "Feeling shame, ain't you? Squilling on us turns your food, does it? So you go round and pretend to save us, all so's you can sleep at night feeling all good like." She shook her head disgustedly. "Meanwhile it don't change a thing for me."

"Shut up and listen," Alwir snapped, shaking her a little. "There's a risk here for both of us in telling you this."

"Oy, get off my toes," she groaned. "Your Reader's arse might get a slap, but I'll be swinging off a noddynoose."

"I have never sent anyone to execution for having the old power!" Alwir replied hotly.

"So few?" she said skeptically.

"I refused. It's wrong . . ."

"You're right there," she interrupted and cocked a half-smile.

"In Iron Alley behind Crier's Forge there are people that can help get you away from the city."

"There ain't no other place besides Beldan," Finch said lightly.

"They'll send you north, to Avadares," Alwir continued. "There the New Moon will protect you."

Finch gave a scoffing laugh. "Daft, dearie. Me with the likes of farmers. I'm a city girl. Beldan born, Beldan bred. I'd die in fresh air. And to join up with dirt-twirlers? Z'blood, it don't bear thinking."

Brusquely Alwir let her go. "Keep your Beldan arrogance

then. Lot of good it will be to you when the butcherboys sweep the city and take you in."

Finch flared up angrily. "My arrogance is all I got. Ain't no one can take that off me. It's you who don't understand. You think those northern clods would welcome me, a Beldanite, in their midst? I'm trash to them. They'd bury me in a week."

"No," answered Alwir. "They'd greet you like lost family returned home. There are others already there like you, having the old power. Join them."

Finch stared at him, hesitating.

"Here," said Alwir digging in his pocket. "Take it as a measure of good faith." He handed her a gold coin stamped with the profile of the Fire Queen. "Maybe you know of others in the city like yourself. Tell them of my offer."

Solemnly, Finch turned the coin over in her hand, as if considering. She looked up at Alwir, her expression not so sharp. "I'll go then," she said and then darted away from the wall.

Alwir stumbled back to let her pass. "Fire's luck, Finch," he called after her as she ran down the alley.

Alone again and exhausted, Alwir walked slowly. The yellow cat jumped down from a crate and followed him, winding between his legs and calling in a soft meow. Alwir bent down and picked him up. The cat rubbed his bony head beneath his chin. Alwir felt the little bumps of scars in the dry rough fur. "Strays," Alwir mumbled to it. "I never thought of the strays." Then setting the cat down again, he left the quiet alley for the crowds of Market Square.

# 7

"First we eat," Kai said, handing out the crushed apples and hard crusty rolls to the Flock, "and then we'll outwit the answer." The apples were too ripe, and Kai knew with an inward shrug that later they'd all complain of rumbling guts. But for now the fruit would give strength and a taste of Firefaire sweetness.

They gathered in the tunnels beneath Market Square, the stone and earth walls corrugated with chiseled marks from ancient axes. Once a mine, early Beldanites had dug the basalt beneath the city to make plaster for the buildings. But during the Burning many of the mines had caved in, exposing the honeycombed weakness of the ground beneath the city. Though the Queen had banned further mining, there were still places where the tunnels held. And beneath the city the maze of passageways served as a hidey-hole to Kai and her Waterlings.

In the flickering light of a campfire, Kai looked her Flock over as she handed them the fruit and bread. These were the inner circle of the Waterlings, the ones who carried Oran magic in their blood. These four (five when Squat was still alive) were special to her, and Kai guarded them like a crow does its young. Slipper, a boy a few years younger than herself, took his share of the bread with a scowl. Their gaze met and she saw the worry that clouded the green eyes. He wore a lighterman's old hat, the brim pinned back with a sprig of Firefaire straw. Kai guessed he wore it to hide his huge ears that flared out on the sides of his long face. It didn't help much since the other features of his face were just as awkward. His nose was a beak between wide-set eyes and his chin a knobby point. Water was his element, and of the Flock he best knew the way through the underground tunnels, the constant dripping of water revealing to him the locations above ground. On the other side of the fire sat the twins, Mole and Trap, both of them air elements. Equally pale and slight, they always seemed to Kai as if they were two shards of fallen crockery that she had picked up from the street. So much alike, Kai mused, watching the similar bland expressions in their rounded faces, and yet growing different daily. Mole never dressed warm enough. He told her once he didn't want the weight of cloth to his back in case it should happen that the wind might carry him aloft and he should fly. Trap, his sister, always complained of the cold even in summer and wore a heavy black jacket she'd stolen off a drunken waterman. With her head of white hair like a moon rising above her black shoulders, she preferred to settle down in the sheltered doorways. One ear cocked to the street, she would listen to the hurried thoughts of passersby. Brother and sister sat close together, not quite touching, but Kai knew that the space between them was quickly closed by the unity of their thoughts.

And lying farther off, wrapped in a dirty white sheet, was Squat. Kai felt a sharp jab between her shoulder blades as she looked at the bundled shape. Then she looked away, nervously twisting her limp hair into a knot at the nape of her neck.

"Anyone seen Finch?" Kai asked, annoyed. "She's late again."

"Yeah," answered Trap. "She said she'd come down soon as she'd made a pigeon. He was too good to miss."

"And too damn dangerous!" Kai snapped, letting her hair go. The knot unraveled, falling in a single black curl down her back. "Nothing but butcherboys and Readers out today. I warned her to wait until after the Naming. There'd be less chance of getting caught, what with all the Readers figuring they're done for the year and getting themselves chinup drunk. No one would give a crossed-eye for her then." Kai bit down hard on her lower lip and then released it. She gazed upward at the roof of the tunnel, as if to hear far above her the noise of the crowded square. "Z'blood, she's on for trouble, I tell you."

"She'll make out," Slipper said gruffly. "Don't she always?"

Kai turned a sharp eye at him. "Who's Flock leader here?"

"You are, Kai."

"But she forgets it. Run into trouble, she will. If not with them," she jerked her thumb upward, "then with me. I said First-watch down here, and she ain't here yet." Kai leaned forward and blew on the little fire. Into the flames she fed the broken legs of a stool that she had collected earlier from the trash. Smoke billowed thickly before rising in a thin stream to catch the draft higher up. Their shadows wavered against the walls, stretched upward into the darkness of the caverned roof. A draft brought cool moist air, heavily ladened with the musty scent of earth. Kai hunched impatiently over the fire, tucking her skirts around her thighs. She stole another glance at the waiting shroud and made up her mind.

She took a burning chair leg, using it as a torch and walked over to where the body lay. Z'blood, she swore, she didn't want to look, but she had to see for herself. She had to know if Squat had died like the others she and Slipper had fished out from the Ribbons.

She pulled back the shroud and shivered. Squat's eyes caught the torch light and stared back like two dull coins. His neck had stiffened, and his head was twisted to a sharp angle, as if he searched for something just behind him. A row of teeth showed in the gouge on his cheek where the eels had nibbled, the edges of the gash ragged with their teeth marks. Kai undid the coat and stared at the leathery white skin. She wrinkled her nose at the sweetish smell of the body. Her heart quickened and her stomach squeezed. The ripe taste of apples stuck in her throat. She ran her hand lightly over his chest, flinching at the coldness. Nothing. Not a bruise to show he had struggled. Not a mark to show where a blade had caught him unawares. She lifted one stiffened arm, the fingers curled in a taloned grip. She saw it then, the thin line cut across the wrist. White skin puckered in lacy folds, opened to reveal the stamens of emptied veins. She shook her head, muttering under her breath and let the hand drop. Z'blood. Like the others. The same mark.

Mole came close to her and scratched his head. "How'd he die?"

"I don't know," Kai answered and quickly covered the shroud over the flat, lifeless face.

"You're lying," the boy said softly.

Kai was silent, trying not to think her frightened thoughts. She cast a glance over to Slipper, but he was staring at the fire.

Mole grabbed her by the sleeve. "What is it, then?" He was shouting, his face knotted with fear, his eyes leaning into her as if to catch the images that scattered with her thoughts.

"Shut up now!" Kai said firmly. She averted her eyes from his demanding stare. "I don't know nothing yet." She pushed and Mole fell back, intimidated by the smoldering rage that raised her shoulders and made her sharp features grow more predatory. "Who saw Squat last?" she asked.

"Someone's coming!" Trap whispered, her head cocked to one side.

"Who?"

"Finch," answered Mole.

Kai waited, not even bothering to hear the sound for herself. She knew that the twins could sense someone's approach before any of the rest of them. On more than one occasion it had saved their lives when the tunnels had been invaded by the Guards and another time by Ratcatcher and his bullyboys. She lifted her head, finally hearing the faint scuffle of feet down the dark tunnel, then the soft sound of someone breathing heavily as if from a run. Finch broke through the darkness and into the circle of light, a grin on her face.

"Kai! Kai! I got us a queenie!" Finch called excitedly.

"And we got us a corpse," Kai answered coldly.

"Z'blood!" Finch stopped in midstride, her eyes darting from one to the other. She brushed the wayward hair from her face, holding it back off her forehead. "Squat?" she asked, realizing his missing presence.

"Yeah."

"Who done it?"

Kai shrugged her shoulders. "That's what we're trying to outwit. Squat was on with you last night. You tell me. What happened?"

Finch slumped down beside the fire.

"Let's have it," Kai demanded.

When Finch looked up, Kai saw the hard glimmer of light in her eyes. She read anger and perhaps guilt, but not grief. The streets made grief meaningless. None of them cried anymore, only felt the slight twinge, the burning of a tear welling up before it was wiped away.

"We had a brangle," she said in a low voice. "Nothing serious," she amended quickly. "He wanted to work down near Greave Alley. I said no, it was too close to Ratcatcher's burrow. I didn't want him messing around with that Flock."

"And then?"

Finch shrugged. "He told me to piss off. So I . . . I gave him one. A clip over the ear. Weren't much, but it cut his pride."

"Is that true?" Kai looked pointedly over to Mole and Trap. They nodded quietly.

"Think he had something else in mind already," Mole said.

"What do you mean?" Kai asked sharply.

"Almost as if he wanted the fight," Trap agreed.

"He was hiding something," Mole continued. "I could tell. He was all jumpy, scared but excited."

"You think he started the fight so as to get away from the lot of you?"

"Could of been that way," Trap said. A small hand appeared from the folds of her coat to scratch her cheek thoughtfully. "At

**85**

the time, it's hard to know. Could have been anything, just wanting to be clear of us for the sake of being an only for awhile. It's Firefaire. The streets are busy."

"Maybe someone made him an offer?" Kai suggested.

Finch scoffed. "For what? He was a little 'un, barely able to keep from ringing the tattlebells. Not many who'd want him for their Flock."

"I did," Kai said pointedly. "What happened after you cuffed him?"

Finch combed a hand through her tangled hair, her fingers catching on a snarl. She yanked her fingers through it angrily before answering. "He hit me back. So I told him he could go get himself buggered at Ratcatcher's if he thought he was such a naffy prig." She rested her chin on the tops of her knees. "He took off. I figured he'd cool off, come back to us after he'd been out on his own." She shrugged. "That was the last of him we saw."

Kai folded her skinny arms across her chest. "Where were you when you fought?"

"Near Carrion Street—" Trap answered. She drew her big black cloak around her feet and inched closer to the small, spluttering fire.

"In the alley," Mole finished.

Kai walked over to Slipper and touched him on the shoulder. He looked up startled, as if he had been caught napping. Kai knew what he was thinking. It was Slipper that had found Little Mag nestled among the reeds of the Ribbons, her tawny hair covered with crabs.

"What's around there, anyway?" she asked softly.

"Ah," he started, swallowing thickly, "there's the Packet."

Kai pursed her lips. "River pirates? He was a water element." She shook her head. "Nah, I've already squared a deal with Perce for protection along the river from the Ribbons to Last Penny Bridge. He wouldn't take much notice of Squat. So what else?"

"The Boneman," Mole said suddenly. "That's—"

"Ratcatcher's hidey-hole," Trap finished. "He was there, too, last night. Heard Nicker yapping about it to a dell. They didn't see me," she said quickly to Kai, "I was crouched up in the dark, and he was shooting his mouth off. Said the Upright Man was coming to give them a load of chinkers. I figured it was all talk to tip the dell back on her heels."

"Is that what you think, Mole?" Kai asked.

"I wasn't there."

"Why not?"

"Frigging shit," Finch hissed under her breath.

"I was following a silk scarf we spotted on Carrion Street."

"Zorah's tits!" Kai exploded. She reached around and grabbed Finch, yanking her up by the shoulder. Her fingers dug into Finch's arm, and Finch cried out. "What were you doing out there?" she snapped. "You're supposed to be on watch. You're supposed to be looking out after them." Kai drew a hand back to slap the girl, but Finch twisted away.

Mole jumped up and shoved himself between Kai and Finch. "Nah, it wasn't her fault. Kai, listen," he shouted pushing her back. "Listen!" Mole ducked his head, a cheek pressed against Kai's waist as she ignored his pleas and swung her arm out trying to hit Finch. He pushed harder, knocking her back a few steps.

"Let go," she snarled between clenched teeth and clamped her hands on his shoulders to wrench him away. He clung tighter. "I said let go!"

"Not until you back off of Finch," he answered, his voice muffled by the folds of her skirts.

Kai growled in frustration and raised her arms straight up in the air. "All right. All right, then. Just bugger off me," she said irritably.

Slowly Mole released her and warily stepped back. "It weren't Finch's fault. We told you already that Squat wanted out. Maybe no matter what, he would have found a way to shake us. What happened to him was of his own choice."

"Harsh words," said Kai.

"Harsh life," he shrugged.

"And what about you, eh? Suppose you'd met the same fate as Squat. And all 'cause Finch doesn't follow Flock rules and let's you ramble on your own? What's the point of a Flock then if you can't be protected?"

"I wasn't scaffered. I'm here 'cause you gave me good sense, Kai. I knew when to come home, didn't I? Squat's death ain't your fault neither, Kai."

Kai stared at him, his chin lifted, the white hair shoved off his forehead. His thin shoulders were stretched back, the posture proud. She felt the burst of anger bleed away into a sorrowful ache. Grief flowed silently in her like the turning of a slow tide, drawing away her strength in its undertow.

Kai twisted her hair into another knot, yanking it back so tightly it hurt.

Finch spoke up. "Look, Kai, I didn't think there'd be a harm to it."

Kai sighed and let her hair fall. Her arms dangled wearily at her sides. "Tell me about the silk scarf. Why him?"

Mole looked uncomfortable. "I don't know why exactly. Something about him called to me. It was as if I knew him."

"Did you wink him?"

"Nah," Mole answered, shaking his head slowly. "I tried to, but he wore this mask across his face and then there was a mist."

"The night was clear," Kai said suddenly. "You sure it was mist and not smoke off a fire?"

"Yeah, it was mist. I passed through it. Wet and cold it was. Followed him 'til he reached the Keep. Strange now that I think on it. Maybe it wasn't the silk scarf that called me. Maybe it was the mist. Like dream walking, it was," the boy screwed up his face, remembering. "Times I almost knew him, and then it 'ud slip away and grow all strange." Trap whimpered softly, and Kai knew that she was sharing in her brother's thoughts. Mole went to sit beside her. He took her hand and held it in his.

"Did the silk scarf go into the Keep?" Kai asked, surprised.

"Yeah," Mole nodded.

"And the mist?"

"Gone. Just like that."

"Just like that," Kai repeated softly.

"What's it mean, Kai?" Slipper asked.

"I ain't sure," Kai answered. Thoughts fluttered in her head, random stalks that seemed to gather into sheaves, possibilities binding them together into explanations. "Squat could call the mist," she said. "Could it have been Squat you sensed?"

Mole's eyes widened with surprise. "I don't know. It was queer, Kai. Scary. I kept seeing bad things happen, like someone bleeding and then someone drowning. Ghost faces on the water."

"How did the silk scarf get into the Keep?" Kai wondered aloud. "How did he pass the Readers?" Kai chewed on her lower lip, an idea taking solid shape in her head. Three of her Flock dead. And she had found others like them floating in the Ribbons. At first she thought it was the same old grief: a mother or father killing off one of their own rather than have them face the Naming. But when Slipper found Little Mag, Kai knew it was something different. Little Mag was one of hers, a Waterling and not some other's child. Later it was Tip and then Falin. Kai had noticed the slash on the wrist, their bleached white faces. They were being murdered. But by whom?

"Trap," Kai said sharply, "you said the Upright Man was coming to pay a visit to Ratcatcher?"

"Nicker said that, but I don't know as it was true."

"What are you thinking, Kai?" Finch asked, moving closer to the fire again.

"Have any of you seen the Upright Man before?"

They shook their heads, peering back at her with confused expressions.

Kai took a deep breath. "Well I have, just once at the Beggar's Hand. He's a tall man, carries an Oran sword, flash cloak, good leather boots. And he wears a mask, a black scarf tied round his face."

"My silk scarf?" Mole said, astonished.

"The Upright Man plies his trade in the big houses, probably lives on the hill, maybe he's even a Silean merchant, no one knows for sure, do they? That's how he manages it all. Fences goods for Ratcatcher and Bonesnip. Takes his cut and sees to it that the Guards don't bully the Flocks. As long as they do their job, that is. Two years ago Sparrow screwed up, and the Upright Man had him scaffered."

"Why the mask? He's one of ours, ain't he?" Finch asked.

Kai gave a short laugh. "Not half. He's his own. Makes his living playing both sides. The Upright Man don't trust no one. There'd be a fine screw for turning in the Upright Man to the butcherboys. So he keeps his own identity secret even to the Flocks."

"What's that all got to do with Squat?" Slipper asked, frowning.

"I ain't sure yet. Call it a wild hunch," and she gave a small smile at Mole and Trap. "More your skill than mine, I know. But outwit it with me and see if it don't have a pattern. Squat gets himself lost around Ratcatcher's burrow. Rumor also has it the Upright Man's there, too. Mole follows home a silk scarf, masked and touched by a mist, that has the feel of Squat. And Squat, well he turns up dead in the river." The Kai stole a quick glance at Slipper and then back to the others. It was time for honesty. "And something else. Squat ain't the first Waterling to get himself scaffered. Two years ago, I lost Little Mag, and after her, Tip and Falin. Each one rolled home on the currents to the Ribbons, all of 'em scaffered like Squat." Kai paused to settle the racing of her heart. Her breath caught in her throat as it tightened around the words.

"I remember," said Finch. "You said they'd drowned."

Kai shook her head. "I lied." She reached up nervously to the hank of hair that hung limply down her back. She twisted it. "I

**89**

was afraid if you knew the truth of it, you'd cut out of the Flock. It's my responsibility as Flock leader to keep you safe. Maybe I've not done the best job of that." She looked back at them, but they made no reply.

"Where else would we go, Kai?" Trap asked after a moment. "There's no one else we'd trust not to sell us out to the Readers."

Trust, Kai thought. A precious coin on the street. She heaved a sigh, determined now to make a clean tale of it. "They weren't drowned. They was white, bled clean but with no mark on 'em except a gash across their arm and what the river fish managed to take off before we found 'em. It's the same with Squat here," and she jerked her head in the direction of the shrouded corpse.

"Why would someone want to kill Waterlings?" Trap asked.

"Not just Waterlings. I've seen others scaffered the same," Kai answered.

"Were the others like us?" Mole said hesitantly.

"Yeah, all little 'uns."

"Nah, I mean like *us*."

"You mean with Oran magic?" Kai asked. Mole nodded solemnly. The arched line of her brows drew together in a deep furrow over her black eyes. Another possibility bloomed to life in a brilliant flash of red.

"Zorah's blood!" Finch swore.

"That's it, ain't it?" Kai said simply. "Zorah's blood, your blood, blood of the Oran magic."

"I don't understand," Slipper growled uneasily.

"They was white, white like they didn't have a drop of blood left to them. Maybe someone thinks it's a way to get magic. Steal it from those that got it." She looked at Slipper, her mouth hardening to a thin line.

"Nah, it ain't so," said Slipper, horror showing on his face. "You can't get magic that way, can you?"

"It doesn't matter much whether or not it's true, so long as someone thinks it is. And maybe it can be done at that. Squat gets scaffered. And Mole here follows a silk scarf surrounded by a mist that calls to Mole. Squat's farewell, or maybe a warning."

"You think it's the Upright Man doing it?" Slipper asked angrily. He took off his hat and punched a fist in its center. The folds of his ears caught the light and glowed a pale pink.

Kai sat down near the fire, squatting on her haunches. She tucked the folds of her skirt around her thighs, stared at the crackling flames. "I don't know," she shook her head. "I don't know." She cocked her head to the side, trying to guess the reason the Upright Man could need magic. "It wouldn't be of much use in the Keep. He couldn't use it without getting noticed."

"And what about on the street?"

Kai shook her head more vehemently. "He certainly don't need it there, neither. He don't do the work himself, he gets others to do it for him. If they had magic, well, you'd think it 'ud be to his advantage . . . like Finch here, with good taste in jewels." Kai gave a slight smile. Finch answered with a nod of her head.

"Ain't it more important to know who's fingering us?" Slipper asked anxiously. "I mean, if it is the Upright Man, how'd he find out about Squat? Maybe he knows about the rest of us?"

"Ratcatcher," Finch spit into the fire. Her fine yellow hair floated around her head, contrasting with the raw edge of her cheek. "Ratcatcher's the Upright Man's bullyboy. I'd lay odds on it."

"But he ain't a Reader," Slipper argued. "How'd he know, anyway?"

"Nah, he ain't a Reader," Kai answered, "but like I said, maybe Ratcatcher made an offer too good to refuse." She looked at them, her eyes glittering. "What would it take to get you to sell that knowledge to someone on the street? Money? Food, maybe? Squat was a little 'un, not long on good sense. Maybe he squealed on himself."

"Maybe he squealed on the rest of us," Finch said sourly.

"There's a chance of that."

"What about Little Mag?" Slipper asked quietly. "Ratcatcher wasn't Flock leader when she got it."

"Nah. Sparrow was. He was a flash sort, wasn't he?" she said evenly. "Mag was a pretty thing herself. Specially in that blue silk dress. Like the color of the sky, like her eyes. She never told me where she'd gotten it. I should have seen it as a sign something was off." Her mouth softened as the current of grief returned, tugging away her resolve. "They were all of them little 'uns. Easy enough I expect to trick into telling on themselves."

"Think he's got himself a Reader?"

"Nah, I'd know it," she answered with certainty. "There's only one street Reader, and that's me."

"That ain't true anymore," said Finch. "I got caught today by a pigeon who turned out to be a Reader."

"What?" Kai roared. She bolted upright, her thin face like a sword's point aimed at Finch.

"I didn't know," Finch shrilled. "He looked like a laborer,

standing stupid in the crowd. Z'blood, he seemed such an easy pigeon."

"What happened? What did you tell him?" Kai balled her hands into fists.

"Nothing. Nothing," Finch insisted. "Look, he caught me fair enough, hauled me off to an alley and before I knew it, Read me. I thought I was finished. Then he give me this queenie," and she held out the gold coin. "Told me if I was to go to Iron Alley near Crier's Forge, there'd be people to get me and others like me with magic out to safety in the countryside."

"What people?" Kai asked.

"New Moon," Finch answered softly.

"New Moon," Kai repeated sarcastically. "Now what would they want with us? How'd you know he wasn't working for the Upright Man?

"That's just it, ain't it? If he was working for the Upright Man, he'd have given out a better story than that, wouldn't he? I mean I don't see Squat getting himself all hot for the New Moon. There ain't no money in it," Finch argued, scrambling to her feet. She kicked a stone and sent it skipping against the earthen walls. She swung her arms in frustration. "I tell you, Kai," and she turned to face the piercing eyes, "he was telling me truth. He wasn't the sly sort."

"Odds ends, it's queer," Kai said, shaking her head. "I don't know what to make of it. Crier's Forge, though, that ain't the sort of place for Flocks. The Guilds don't hold with snitches in their district. New Moon, huh?" she shook her head again, sucking in her lower lip as she thought. "What do they want with magic?"

"A weapon against the Sileans," Slipper said.

"Or the Queen," Kai said, suddenly gaining another insight. "The Upright Man, maybe he thinks to take the Queen, too." She shivered at the idea, wondering anew how he managed it. How did he hide the magic from the Readers. From the Fire Queen. To possess such knowledge might save her Flock's skins in the future; perhaps give them a chance to grow old.

"All right," Kai nodded, calming the rapid beating of her heart. "Good work, all," she said encouraging them. "You, too, Finch. I got no quarrel with you. We need each other. And maybe Mole is right. Squat made his own choice and nothing could have prevented it. But look, we don't know what's known now about us. So far none of the other Flocks have guessed the truth about the Waterlings. But it's just a matter of time before they put it together. So for now, no one even so much as looks sideways,

**92**

understand?" They nodded solemnly. "You keep your hands in your pockets and you say nothing to anyone, not even to the other Waterlings. It's possible that someone squealed from inside," and Kai thought of Stickit and her expanding girth. "So until we know what's going on and who's to trust, we stay low."

"What about Squat?" Slipper asked.

"Take him to Scroggles," Kai ordered.

"Money?"

"Finch, give Slipper your queen."

"That's a lot of money for a corpse, ain't it?" Finch said, hesitating.

"Give it to him, Finch. It'll ease your mind in the long run."

Reluctantly, Finch handed over the gold coin into Slipper's waiting hand. He pocketed it and turned quickly to the shrouded body. Hoisting it over his shoulder, he started down the tunnel, his feet splashing in the small stagnant puddles.

"What about us?" Finch asked.

"The three of you head off to the Ribbons."

Finch groaned. "But it's Firefaire, Kai. You can't send us away to the shacks."

"I want you all out of here for now," she answered firmly. "I need room to sort this out without worrying about all of you bumping into trouble."

"And yourself?" Finch asked sullenly.

"I'm going to pay a visit to Ratcatcher."

"Is that smart?" Trap asked. She stood up, the huge coat hanging below her knees. She tucked her hands into its pockets.

Kai shrugged. "It's what's needed," she answered grimly.

"And the Reader's offer?" Mole asked, coming to stand by his sister. He shivered in the cool air.

Kai nodded. "I'll mosey over there, too. Go on now," she said with an impatient toss of her head. "Out with you."

They left, with Trap casting a worried look over her shoulder just before disappearing down the dark tunnel. Kai exhaled noisily and rested her face in her hands. Responsibility weighted her shoulders, collapsing them around her chest. She whispered their names, a litany of her dead: Little Mag, Tip, Falin and now Squat. Kai saw their faces, red and muddied with dirt when they were alive, then white as sheets in death, their lips the color of slate. She breathed in deeply, clutched by a dizzying sense of panic. Her cheeks flushed hot in her hands. Sweat prickled her scalp, raising the hairs on the nape of her neck. She felt the anguish boil in her heart, force itself through the veneer of control. She choked on the cries that burned her throat until the pain grew so great she had no choice but to release them. Sobs burst into the stillness of the empty tunnels, and her keening echoed from chamber to chamber as it traveled through the underground.

And then the sobs subsided, and the tunnels grew quiet again. Kai's hands dropped away from her ravaged face, and she fumbled in her pocket for a cloth to wipe away the tear stains. Sniffing hard, Kai cursed herself for this moment of weakness. Not again. She'd not cry again for them. The dead didn't need her sorrow. They needed vengeance. And the living needed the power of her cold rage. She started walking down the tunnels, following the faint odor of salt air that would lead her to an opening near the docks. Arms swinging at her sides, her back straight and rigid, Kai settled on nothing less than scaffering Ratcatcher for his part in the crime. For she was certain it was he who had fingered Squat. And then she'd take on the Upright Man himself. Kai's hands twisted like talons around the folds of her skirt. Choke him with his own silk scarf I will, she thought. Cut him 'til he bleeds like a stuck pig and gives back what he stole from us. In the dark tunnels, her lips pressed into a cruel smile.

# 8

The stone walls of Crier's Forge echoed with the clang of hammers and the hiss of steam. The air was thick with the gritty smoke from the forges. Dark as an underground cave, the hot metal glowed brilliant white and blue, while the coal bed cast a warm red light.

Beneath the bricked sides of the coal bed, Jobber knelt, hands on the bellows, and his face beaded with sweat. Eagerly he pumped the bellows, the air sucking noisily through its wings before whoosing over the coals.

"Harder, lad. Put your back into it!" Master Donal called out to Jobber, as he studied the coal bed, waiting for it to reach the right temperature. In his huge fist he held a waiting bar of cold dull iron. Beneath the peppering of black ash, the coals bloomed a bright orange. Master Donal dug the ironbar in, shoving it deep into the heart of the coal bed. Then he waited, a frown of concentration on his soot-streaked face. "Don't stop now, Jobber, keep the heat even!"

Jobber pumped harder, his wiry arms aching with the effort. A trickle of sweat dripped from beneath his cap and scored a track on his forehead before it stung his eye.

The Mastersmith pulled the bar out with tongs and laid it across a flat, shiny anvil. The bar gleamed blue-white against the black. "Now to, lads," the Mastersmith shouted, and the Hammermen began to beat the bar, lengthening it with each stroke of the hammer. Jobber blinked as the hammers clanged shrilly against the sword and small specks of powdery black carbon broke away. "Good, that's right, even strokes. Don't rush now," the Mastersmith nodded, keeping a sharp eye on the stretched bar of cooling iron. "Now fold it back and we'll give her to the fire again."

Jobber watched fascinated as Wyer, Master Donal's son, carefully folded back the stretched iron with his hammer and gently tapped it into place. Donal took up the bar and returned it to the coal bed, burying it once more beneath the red embers. Jobber pumped the bellows, leaning his head closer to the scorching heat. He stared expectantly as the fire transformed the hard dark iron into a supple gleaming metal. That's what he liked best about the fire: a magic of its own that willed anything within its grasp to be transformed.

Wyer smiled down at Jobber, his white teeth bright against the soot-stained face.

"If you stick your nose any closer to that fire, Jobber, you'll be burning it off!"

"Nah," Jobber scoffed, "the fire an' me are friends. It won't burn me. I know it too well."

"That may be," replied Master Donal in his gruff voice, "but fire makes a queer mistress, and I've enough burns to prove she can be nasty when she's of a mind. So back up a bit before my best bellowlad is burned to cinders."

Reluctantly, Jobber pulled back from the coal bed.

Master Donal withdrew the newly heated bar and laid it on the anvil. Wyer and the other Hammermen swung their hammers, stretching the bar and working in the carbon to produce the steel blade. Jobber sighed, watching the long smooth shape of the sword evolve beneath the constant beating. Twice more they folded, then heated it, and twice more they hammered until the carbon and steel rippled in a light wavy pattern on the newly formed edge.

"That's enough." Master Donal called them to a halt and returned the elegant length of steel to the coal bed for a final time. "Wyer, you'll do the tempering on the edge. Go and get the clay pot to wrap the blade."

"A new skill for him?" Jobber asked, one eyebrow lifted in surprise.

"And about time, too. It's a delicate touch as needed to wrap the blade. To know how to keep the core flexible and strong but the edge sharp and keen. Makes for a better sword."

Jobber watched Wyer as he went to fetch the clay pot. He was built like his father, medium height and stocky. Beneath the length of his leather apron, Jobber could see the flexing of Wyer's strongly muscled thighs and calves. He wore his hair short and pulled back from his square face, and though Jobber knew that it was light brown, in the forge everything was covered with fine soot making it appear near black. Wyer returned with the pot swinging from one hand, his sleeves rolled back to expose his thick forearms. Jobber studied him as he approached, something habit had taught him to do. Wyer walked with a steady gait, hips over his heels, and his body weighted solidly toward the ground. Not a man to unbalance in a fight, Jobber thought.

"Where's Master Donal?" a voice called out, and Jobber looked to the voice, his eyes squinting at the light of the doorway.

"Who calls me?" the Mastersmith answered.

A troop of Silean Guards entered the forge, and Jobber saw the Firstwatch Gonmer stop and look around slowly in the dark interior of her forge. At her side was her apprentice standing stiffly at attention, but blinking, Jobber thought, like an owl. Jobber's eyes returned again to Gonmer. The new Knackerman, no less. Very flash company for the Master indeed. And either very stupid or very bold, Jobber thought with amusement, to be standing here in Crier's Forge uninvited. Jobber sniffed after a moment's study. Faul carried herself better than this one.

"Master Donal," the Firstwatch called out again.

Donal's head reared up like a bull, and he bellowed at the Firstwatch. "Out of here!" He charged, pushing her back forcefully with his huge hands. The Guards behind her tripped over their feet, bumping into one another as they hurried to get out of the way. They all fell back like seven pins before the ball.

Stupid, Jobber decided, watching the Firstwatch's clumsy retreat from Crier's Forge.

Gonmer sputtered angrily as Master Donal continued to push her roughly into the street. Jobber sidled closer to the doorway to watch, amused as the indignant woman tried to regain her composure. Master Donal stood with his hands on his hips, coal dust rimming his lips and smeared across his forehead. He pointed one admonishing finger at the Firstwatch.

"You of all people, Firstwatch, should know the law. No women allowed in the forge!"

Z'blood, thought Jobber ruefully. It was going to be harder than he thought to convince Master Donal to let Faul in the back door for a look 'round once this was over.

"I'll not have my forge closed because of your carelessness. It was your own Fire Queen, Firstwatch, who made the law."

"She's your Queen, too, Master Donal," Gonmer answered in a flat tone of annoyance, brushing soot from her uniform.

"My Queen perhaps, but not my Guildmaster."

"Meaning?"

"I don't agree with the law, though I am forced to comply with it, even if it means tossing out someone as important as yourself." Gonmer stopped brushing and gave him a sour look. Master Donal answered it. "It was the Queen imposed this law and without the sanction of the Guilds," Master Donal finished, and Jobber could see that in spite of the stern set of his mouth, the eyes twinkled merrily. Knowing Master Donal, Jobber could well imagine that throwing out the Fire Queen's own Firstwatch had given him great satisfaction.

"It is the Queen who rules Oran, not the Guilds. She is not required to seek the permission of the Guilds," Gonmer argued.

"Not while she has the Silean Guard to bark at her heels."

The Guards stiffened, and Jobber saw the restless look that passed between them. He wondered whether Gonmer was good enough to control them should they get ugly. The girl at Gonmer's side shifted nervously, her hand opening and closing around the hilt of her sword.

"Careful of your words, Master Donal," Gonmer said evenly. "They approach treason."

"Has the truth become treason, Firstwatch?" Master Donal asked.

"I didn't come to argue politics, Master Donal."

"It's not tax time, though Z'blood, it seems we pay more often each year." Donal looked out at the small crowd clustered around the sides of the forge, just watching. At the mention of taxes, there came an angry hiss, and someone cried out "thieves!"

Jobber kept his eyes to the Firstwatch, as her face became more severe. She wasn't going to answer the Mastersmith's taunts. Jobber was impressed, thinking he'd never be able to manage his temper in a crowd like this. Not too many people, it seemed, were on her side. But she stayed whatever harsh words she might have had, stilled her Guard with a sharp look and went to the business at hand. She unwrapped a sword from a black cloth and handed it to the smith. An interested murmur rippled through crowd as the sun flashed on the blade.

"What do you know of this?"

Master Donal raised the sword, his eyes studying the sun's reflection on the grain of the blade's edge. Jobber pressed closer to the open door, attracted by the beauty of the sword. He'd never seen one like it. It was similar to the ones made here in Crier's Forge, and yet something in the design of the oval guard, the ribboned patterning of its blade edge, made it seem ancient.

"It's poor workmanship," Donal said and Jobber gasped, surprised.

"I would have thought differently," Gonmer replied.

"Do you doubt my skill?"

"Of course not. But I have had the opportunity to see this sword at work. It was my impression that it was well made."

"Well made perhaps by the day's standards. But poorly conceived, considering what the smith intended it to be," Donal finished.

"And what was that?"

"A Fire Sword, from the looks of it."

"Who made it?" Gonmer asked.

"None that I know of, Firstwatch," Master Donal answered, meeting her gaze. "The making of Fire Swords is proscribed. The skill required has long since passed from our hands."

"Am I to understand that this is an old blade then? Not newly made?"

"Hard to say," Donal answered. Taking a small hammer from a belt at his waist, he knocked the blade from its guard and examined the tang. "Unsigned," he said. "Could have been anybody." He looked up at the Firstwatch. "Since the Fire Queen changed the guild laws, it is impossible for the Guilds to regulate the making of swords. Even a country stithy could have turned out this piece and sold it without the local Guildmaster knowing it. For this one, Firstwatch, you can not blame the Guilds, but rather the foolishness of the Queen's laws."

"A convenient argument, Mastersmith?"

"Are you suggesting I need one?"

"Have you been approached by the New Moon, Mastersmith?" Gonmer asked pointedly. Jobber leaned forward to hear his answer.

"Oy! That's him!" shouted a Guard. "That's the thief that robbed Ferris this morning!"

Intent on the confrontation between the Firstwatch and Master Donal, Jobber hadn't bothered to closely study the Guards. But at the Guard's shout, Jobber's head jerked up, alarmed, and he recognized two of the faces from the morning's fight.

"Z'blood," Jobber swore and ducked back into the darkened recesses of Crier's Forge. Wyer moved up quickly in front of him, his wide girth shielding him from the Guards.

"You there," Gonmer called irritably, "come out and show yourself."

"I'll get the little bastard," the Guard growled and made a move to enter the forge. Wyer's hand shot out and caught the Guard on the sword arm.

"You'll not enter Crier's Forge without permission of the Master. That, too, is the law, Silean."

Peering from behind Wyer's back, Jobber saw the Guard glare at Wyer, but the smith remained resolute.

"Take your position," the Firstwatch barked. "Master Donal, we shall respect the law, and expect the same of you. Send the boy out that he may be questioned in regards to an assault on a member of the Silean Guard."

"I find the charge hard to believe. A boy against an armed Guard." Master Donal crossed his arms over his chest.

"Frigging shit," Jobber moaned. Jobber tried to rid himself of the coin purse, but his nervous fingers failed him, and he only succeeded in tightening the knot from which the purse hung. He looked frantically for an escape, jumping over the piles of iron scrap that had been delivered that morning and dumped at the alley entrance to the forge. As he thrust his head from the doorway, he stopped quickly, catching himself. Three Guards appeared in the alley blocking his escape. Glancing right, Jobber saw two more.

Jobber ducked back into the forge and saw that the other smiths and apprentices had left their work to stand shoulder to shoulder behind Wyer. In their hands they carried their hammers and bars of cold iron. Jobber groaned again. Crier's Forge was ready to use him as an excuse to fight the Silean Guard. Even if they won the skirmish, Jobber knew they'd lose in the long run. The forge would be shut down, and perhaps Master Donal stripped of his rights to practice the craft. It didn't make sense to Jobber why the Master should have chosen himself as an excuse for a brangle. But Jobber knew that he couldn't let Master Donal do this. He decided to surrender before things got any worse.

Jobber cut the strings of the purse on a half-finished blade and left it behind the bellows. If the Master found it, he'd know it was from Jobber. And maybe it would help to pay the insult fine that Master Donal was sure to get for harboring him. Jobber shouldered his way through the smiths, stopping at the entrance to the forge.

The crowd had grown, attracted by the promise of a scuffle. Jobber's eyes darted over them, sizing up their mood. Would they be sympathetic, or just as ready to see him caught and bound? Their expressions varied, some looking on him with mild curiosity, others with gleeful anticipation. He looked back at the Firstwatch and felt the nobility of his resolve shrivel.

"Jobber," Master Donal said in a soft voice to call him back.

Jobber shook his head. "Nah," he answered quickly, afraid he'd change his mind again if given the chance. "Ain't no good.

I'll handle my own brangles with the butcherboys."

"Jobber," the smith insisted and moved to stop him, but Jobber edged away from him and stepped into the light outside the forge.

Jobber's heart clanged like the smith's hammers, stretching his fear into a long cool terror. He concentrated on shaping the fear mentally into the keen edge of blade. They wouldn't take him. Not without a fight. The Firstwatch Gonmer's hand strayed near the hilt of her sword. She was frowning impatiently at Jobber. He wondered briefly if she was as fast as Faul. He hoped not.

Jobber stepped farther out into the street, squinting up at the bright sun. He tried to appear harmless, his hands held up to shield his face from the light. Beneath his hands, he glanced at the streets, trying to spot the clearest path through the tangle of Guards. If only the frigging Firstwatch weren't there. He didn't like the idea of ducking her sword.

"Come here!" the Firstwatch ordered, and Jobber shuffled forward, head down watching the loose dirt of the street swirl around his feet. It wasn't much, he thought, but it would have to do.

Jobber collapsed to his knees and began bawling loudly. "I ain't done nothing. I swear it! I swear it."

"Shut up," Gonmer commmanded.

Jobber groveled even lower and continued bawling, arms wrapped around his head.

"Get him up," he heard Gonmer order. Jobber waited until he saw the black boots of the Guard standing near his knee. As the Guard reached down, Jobber shot up, butting the man's face with the top of his head. The Guard lurched backward, groaning and clutching his face. Quickly, Jobber tossed a handful of loose dirt into the faces of the other Guards. He crouched as around him the Guards cursed and spat, blinded by the dirt. An open space presented itself between their legs, and Jobber leapt, hearing as he flew the swish of a sword.

Jobber was not quite through the gap when a hand reached out and grabbed him by the top of his leather cap. The hand held him, arms flailing wildly as he tried to free himself.

"No you don't, you shitting bastard," a Guard snarled. "I've got you." Jobber struggled against the grip, but the more he struggled, the tighter the strings of the cap choked his neck. Jobber held the Guard's wrist for balance and threw a kick backward into the Guard's knee. The kneecap wrenched to the side with a popping sound, and the howling Guard collapsed forward, still holding on to Jobber's cap in a clenched fist. Jobber strained to free himself of the falling weight. The strings of the cap suddenly snapped, and Jobber's head jerked roughly as the cap slid off his head and fell to the ground with the Guard. Jobber continued his movement and then stopped stunned as he realized the cap was no longer on his head . . .

The crowd gasped as the whirling dust settled and the Guards drew back in confusion. Jobber turned, staring wide eyed as a cloud of long hair, red as the coal beds of Crier's Forge, billowed and crackled with new found freedom. Jobber felt the wind lift the wild hair and hold it up to the sun where it glittered like a newly minted penny. . .

"Oy, it's a dell," someone looking at Jobber yelled, and the crowd shoved closer. "Frigging looks like the Queen!"

Jobber stopped turning and faced the naked sword of the Firstwatch. Without the cap she felt light-headed, exposed to the brilliance of the morning sun. She could smell the metallic reek of copper, feel the flush of heat color her cheeks. She heard as if distantly the roaring of the crowd like the wind gusting through the Great Bonfire. But her eyes were trained on the shocked face of the Firstwatch.

Gonmer's sword was steady, the shining length of blade holding Jobber at bay. "The Fire Queen," Gonmer whispered hoarsely. The sword's point dipped, as Gonmer stared hard at Jobber's dirty face surrounded by a gout of flame-colored hair.

Jobber stole the moment. Swiftly, she sidestepped the sword and plunged into the cheering crowd. They parted in a terrified scramble as Jobber's blazing hair sparked like an angry fire.

Behind her, Jobber heard the Firstwatch yell, "After her, shitheads!" followed by the shrill cawing of a Guard's whistle.

Don't think, Jobbernowl, she cried to herself, just run. There was no Growler this time to fight the Guard. At the corner of her eye, she saw the red strands of coarse hair. Z'blood, she groaned, the Guards would take her for a purse, but the Readers would hang her for this hair. Frigging magic, she spat. What good was it, except to place the rope around her neck? So as not to slow her flight with deeper terrors, Jobber pounded her feet on the streets, repeating over and over like a charm, "I'm a snitch, only a Beldan snitch."

# 9

The noise of the crowd thundered in Jobber's ears, faces and colors blurring as she ran. Above the din, she heard the Guards shouting, the rough stamp of their boots and the shrill caw of their alarm as they pursued her through the streets. Jobber fled like a hare in the brambles, spotting the openings in the tangle of people and darting through just before they closed again. The Silean Guard however used no such finesse. Collecting themselves like the point of a stake, the Guards wedged their way through the throngs of journeymen and tradesmen that filled the streets of the Guild district. Behind her, Jobber sensed the crowd split apart like wood beneath an ax, and she sped faster to stay ahead of the charge.

As she ran, Jobber tried to think. She could hide in the Guild district. They'd never find her in Dyers Alley or behind the Tanneries. She ducked into a darkened doorway and looked around quickly, getting her bearings among the shopfronts and trade houses. Through the wooden door she could feel the steady rhythmic thumping, and over the low voiced beat, a whirling noise. She nodded, recognizing the thump of treadles and tossing of shuttles. She was on Treadle Row. Above her head hung the blue standard that identified the Weavers Guild. Right, she decided. She'd take a shortcut through the weaving house and double back up the alleys. The door behind her was locked, and her knock went unheard over the thumping of the treadles. She glanced up, the windows too high and too narrow to be reached from the street. Jobber pushed off from the wall and began running again, grabbing a look over her shoulder. More Guards had joined the chase. They spread across the street, two men to each side, ducking their heads into doorways. Two more continued straight down the street, hoping, she knew, to catch sight of her red hair.

Jobber saw a gap between two carts piled high with bolts of cloth ready for Market Square. She swerved, intending to sprint through the ground floor workrooms, then out behind to the tiny alley used by stockboys and traders bringing supplies. Her foot slipped suddenly on the remains of a rotted pear, and she gasped as the edge of the cart collided with her hip. The shock sent her spinning back into the street, doubled with pain. The cart wobbled and tilted, unwinding a bolt of blue cloth down the side of the cart. A hand reached out to hold her steady.

"Here, now. What's the rush?" someone said, gripping her arm. She looked up, and a man's face stared back in concern. He wore a smock and a blue scarf tied around his neck. A weaver, she thought, instantly relieved. His grip was strong, the blue veins thick on the back of his chapped hands. Limping from the pain in her hip and blinded by the tears that filled her eyes, Jobber tried to pry the hand off her arm.

"Let me go. Z'blood! Let me go!"

Behind her came the shouting of the Guard.

"Oy, hold that red-headed girl, she's wanted by the Guard!"

Jobber swiveled around and saw the grey uniforms bearing down on her, pushing aside those too slow to move out of their way. The two middle Guards had drawn their swords.

Jobber turned back to the weaver and saw his face darken. The grip on her arm tightened. Jobber drove her knee into the weaver's groin. The hand opened as a scream was torn from the man's lips. He doubled over, shouting obscenities at her in a hoarse shriek. She took off again, pushing through the crowded street, arms pumping the air for more speed. Along the row of weaving houses journeymen stepped out to stare curiously. Some of them hearing the shouts of the Guard reached to catch her as she ran by. Others stepped nimbly out of her way and cheered her on. But none allowed her passage through their workrooms.

Frigging bastards, Jobber cursed, as she kept running, shifting this way and that to avoid obstacles in the street. She leaped over a watering trough, then swerved to avoid a team and wagon. They were too afraid to help her. Too afraid of the Silean Guard. If they were seen letting a fugitive escape, they'd be closed down and their Guild charters revoked. And it wasn't like she could slip in unnoticed. Her red hair spun around her in a flaming cloud. Who could mistake the sight of her?

She tore past the weaving houses, with their double doors and narrow windows, and came to a row of buildings where fullers finished woolen cloth. The air was pungent with the smell of wet wool, acid and soap. Soapy water washed the streets, and huge tuns filled with steaming water squatted near the doorways. A woman, wiping her red swollen hands on a wet apron, came to stand at the door and stare as Jobber ran past.

Past the fullers were stockingeers and hosiers. A group of scraggle-faced boys had left their stocking frames to gather on the crumbling stoop. They shouted gleeful obscenities at her and waved to the Guards farther up the street. Before Jobber could shout back her own retort, an older journeyman hauled them in, cuffing one or two before slamming shut the doors.

No good. No good, Jobber cried frantically to herself. None were willing to give her passage. She ducked into the doorway of a Wig-maker, body bent double over her knees as she tried to catch her breath. Her legs ached and her hip throbbed where it had struck the edge of the cart. She pressed a hand to it, trying to force away the sensation of pain. Through her heavy breathing she heard the alarm whistles of the Guard. Three short blasts. Damn. Damn, damn the fire. Had to be three squads at least searching for her. Spread out, they'd be hard to escape from. Damn again. Whose purse did she steal, anyway? Z'blood, probably the son of some shitting wealthy Silean. Why'd they care so much? It was only money. But then there was his manly pride she'd robbed him of. Sileans took that seriously. She felt a sudden tug on the back of her hair. Whirling around, hands in ready fists, she came face to face with the Wig-maker.

He jumped, startled by her ferocity. He was a plump man with watery blue eyes set in a doughy face. He wore a light gray jacket, expensive lace stitched to the points of his collar. His soft white hands were held out harmlessly in front of him.

"Don't take offense, pretty-pretty," he said petulantly. "I only wondered if you'd like to sell it?"

Jobber frowned at him. "Sell what?"

"Your hair, pretty-pretty. Fashionable color, that. I'll give you a good price."

He moved closer, as if to touch her hair. Jobber drew back rapidly, out of the shadowy doorway and into the sunlit street again.

"Frigging bastard," she screamed at him. "None of me's for sale."

"Only your hair's worth anything, gutter trash," he sniped.

"Oy! Over here!" Jobber glanced up the street and saw the Guard that had spotted her. She swore loudly and started running again. The Guards following after her rushed past the surprised Wig-maker.

Jobber realized with alarm that the Guard was taking no

chances of losing her in the Guild district. At every turn and alley she saw them in the streets searching. It seemed like most of the Firstwatch had been called up just to ferret her out. It was no good hiding out up here. The riverfront was too wide open, not enough places to slip through unseen in daylight, and she didn't trust not getting lost in the tunnels. That left the Pleasure district and Market Square. She could always duck into the Maidenhead. Bell would hide her. Or would she? Bell was such a stick for honesty. She'd short shrift for any cheater, and worse yet, she'd always something of a sweet spot for Jobber. She'd not take kindly to the idea of having been deceived. Jobber shook her head. Market Square then. She might yet be able to lose herself in the crowds of fair-goers. At least it would be harder for the Guard to pass through the throngs of people and animals. There she could snitch something from a stall to cover this damnable red hair of hers.

Jobber crisscrossed the narrow streets, fleeing from doorway to doorway, crouched behind slow moving wagons and barrows loaded with wares as they lumbered toward Market Square. The farther down through the city she moved, the more congested and chaotic the traffic became. She squeezed through a group of farmers and their dogs, and then waded clumsily through a flock of frightened sheep. The sharp musk of the animals clung in her nostrils making her sneeze. She was relieved when she reached Spice Street, and the air was suddenly filled with rich aromatic smells of sweet fragrant smoke and heavy perfumes. Little bells over the shopkeepers' doors jangled gaily as customers entered and left, the scents blowing into the street through the opened doors.

At Players Square she was surrounded suddenly by a drunken crowd of fair-goers singing bawdy songs. A heavy man with a paunch that threatened to undo the laces of his vest clapped Jobber on the shoulder and pulled her roughly in to join their singing. Jobber struggled to free herself, her head darting around keeping a sharp eye out for the Guard. But the man was big and he leaned on Jobber companionably. He passed a nearly full tankard of ale under Jobber's nose and she grabbed it. Head tipped back, she poured a long swallow of the warm ale down her dry throat. It washed away the dust of the street and the sour taste of her own fear. As she brought the cup down she noticed that two of the women in the party had red hair. Well, almost red. The henna they had used to produce this fashionable color left odd streaks of gray-brown at the scalp. They were regarding Jobber's bright copper-colored hair with obvious envy.

Must go, she thought. Swiftly she elbowed the man under his outstretched arm. The hard point of her elbow poked him sharply in the soft floating rib. Not hard enough to break it but enough to inflict pain. The man drew his arm away, grunting in surprise.

"Thanks for the drink," Jobber called, sprinting across Players Square. There was a burst of gold light as the afternoon sun reappeared from behind a cloud. It ignited the fiery color of Jobber's hair as she ran. People turned to stare, awed by the shield of burning bright hair.

"Welcome Firefaire!" someone shouted in a slurry voice. "Burn the Queen!" shouted another after her. Jobber scowled furiously. Frigging hair, she swore. Nothing but an invitation to my hanging.

Three short blasts and Jobber knew the Guard had spotted her. Jobber reached the other side of the square, intending to run the short length of Finna's Arm. She wanted to get to High Street that joined up just at the end of the Arm. At this hour of the day High Street would be thick with people coming into the fair from the Western Gate.

At the corner where the square met Finna's Arm, a Guard emerged from a small inn, answering the cawing alarm. He spotted her running at full tilt and didn't have to ask if she was the quarry. He threw his body at her as she tried to swerve past and knocked her down in the cobbled street, his arms wrapped tightly around her legs.

Jobber landed on her bruised hip, and pain shot through her pelvis, wrenching her back along her spine to her skull. She lay stunned, shaking her head to clear the burst of yellow stars that darted to and fro, pulsing with the rhythm of the pain in her hip and leg. She raised herself on her hands, pushing up from the ground as she gathered her scattered wits. Her legs were pinned to the ground.

"Frigging shithead, let go of me!" she screamed and kicked out. But the Guard held her legs trapped, and all she could do was flail her arms and try to twist herself free.

The Guard stood up, breathing hard, holding Jobber around the legs. She hung upside down, writhing like a snake. She looked across the square and saw the others coming to join her captor. They had slowed their step and were now grinning. Never, she thought furiously. They'd never take her. A new wave of fury and desperation surged through her, and she began twisting and kicking, trying to break the Guard's hold on her legs.

"Nice catch, Estavo," said a Guard, and Jobber saw his captain's rank pinned on his uniform.

The man holding Jobber answered between short pants of air. "Thank you, sir. Scrappy thing, isn't it?"

"Whore's shit!" Jobber screamed up at them. "Silean scum. The dogs wouldn't piss on you!" Jobber's face was livid, with red splotches on her cheeks where the blood flooded beneath the surface.

"Nasty, too," Estavo grunted. He held Jobber out by the ankles and shook her roughly. "Shut up, street trash!" he commanded. Jobber's head waggled to and fro, the copper-colored hair cascading to the dirty ground like a shower of coins. But she refused to stop screaming obscenities.

"Put her down," the Captain ordered. Estavo complied, dropping her roughly on the ground. The other two Guards hustled around her, dragging her up to a standing position, hands clamped firmly on her shoulders. The street spun dizzily in Jobber's head, tilting in all directions as she struggled to regain her rightside-up balance. Her pulse pounded in her ears, and she gasped as the blood rushed down to her feet again. She wanted to be sick, to vomit over the polished black boots of the Captain, but there was nothing in her stomach to oblige.

She looked up defiantly at the Captain, an insult ready on her lips. His eyes flared angrily, his mouth screwed in a thin-lipped frown.

"She does look like the Fire Queen," he said to the others.

Before Jobber could utter a word, the Captain backhanded her, her head snapping cruelly to one side with the force. She felt the skin on her cheek split, and she only just stopped herself from crying out. Stars blazed bright yellow in the corners of her eyes. She shook her head to chase them away. She saw the Captain raise his arm and rotate his body to strike her again.

Reflex, spurred by rage, lifted her knee up. Her leg extended, snapping like a whip as she drove the ball of her foot into a soft spot on he inside of his thigh. She struck a nerve point, and his leg buckled with the shock. She kicked out again, this time driving her foot forward into his unprotected groin.

One Guard released her to catch the falling Captain, and she turned to attack the remaining Guard holding her. Her fist cocked and she launched it toward his throat. He jerked his head back but not fast enough as her hard bony knuckles penetrated his throat.

He fell back coughing and choking, air whistling in a thin stream through the collapsed windpipe.

Estavo growled and heaved his body at her, attempting to tackle her again.

"Not this time, whore's shit!" she snarled back at him and blocked the tackle by stepping neatly to the side. She grabbed his arm for support as he stumbled past her and jackknifed her knee into his gut. As he hunched over with the blow, she dropped her leg and hooked her heel behind his. With a twist of her hips and a sharp upward tug of her heel, she swept the unbalanced Guard off his feet and pushed him sprawling into the street. Her fist followed him as he went down and landed squarely on his face.

The remaining Guard, one arm weighted by the sagging body of his Captain, used his free hand to lift his alarm whistle to his lips. Jobber turned to flee, seeing the gray uniforms filling the square from the sidestreets.

Jobber streaked down Finna's Arm, the sound of the cawing whistle blasting in her ears. Damn, she swore, she should've taken him out before he'd used that thing! Too late now, Jobber, just run, she commanded her body.

Up ahead Jobber saw the stream of people traveling toe to heel down High Street.

Suddenly, where the mouth of Finna's Arm emptied into High Street, a gray draft horse pulling a cart nearly blocked the entrance. The huge beast had only to take another step before the entrance to High Street was blocked completely.

"Get out of the way!" Jobber screamed at the beast. "Get out of the way, you frigging lump!" Immediately another head peered around the horse, and Jobber saw a laborer, his coarse hair like straw sticking out of a black woolen hat. His mouth gaped and the eyes gazed bewildered. The horse raised his head, annoyed at being held back and rolled an eye toward Jobber. Can hardly tell which one's the beast, Jobber thought, as she continued shouting at the man.

"Let me through!" she cried, sensing the Guard gaining on her from behind. Her hip was screaming with pain at every step, and she knew that she wouldn't be able to keep this pace for long.

Jobber saw the laborer's eyes narrow, taking in the sight of the Guards. He jerked the halter down, pulling sharply on the cheek strap. The horse's nose was forced down, his chin pushed back to touch his chest. The horse snorted, surprised and angry, but hobbled to a stop, a huge hoof clopping on the cobblestones.

Jobber leapt past, just fitting through the opening. She felt the warm breath of the gray horse on her neck. Then she careened into High Street, stumbling into people. There were angry shouts of protest as she shoved her way through the crowd. Jobber turned once and saw the laborer who had held the space open for her now urge the horse forward. The horse reared its head annoyed and pranced forward, jostling the cart and pitching the occupants into the wooden sides. On the buckboard an Overseer holding the reins shouted at the laborer and flicked a little whip. The laborer ignored the man, and Jobber saw him search the crowd. When he saw her, he merely nodded. On the other side of the huge gray horse, trapped on Finna's Arm, the Guards shouted at the Overseer and blew shrilly on their whistles, unable to do anything else.

Jobber touched the cut on her cheek and winced angrily at the pain. Frigging bastards. Her hand dropped to her side again and she breathed heavily. What in Zorah's name was going on? This morning she'd nothing but the fire's luck and now she was barely ahead of the scorching flames. She shrugged and rolled her eyes.

One hand clamping the fiery hair to the nape of her neck, she continued moving with the steady stream of people all traveling down to Market Square. She had to get something to hide her hair. Another hat or a scarf like the one that hid Zeenia's green and orange hair. Maybe she should go in for a dress? Change her appearance altogether. Jobber snorted at the ground. She wasn't sure if she remembered how to wear one, it had been so long. Her gaze snagged on the sight of a troupe of Ghazali women just ahead of her. Covered from head to foot in black silk, it was hard to tell them apart. Tiny mirrors stitched to their head scarves winked like stars against the night-black fabric. Bells on their ankles jingled, and when a dancer lifted her hand to adjust her head scarf, Jobber saw the many silver and gold bangles that circled her wrist. As the woman retied the scarf on her head, Jobber noted, too, the hennaed hair. It was nowhere near as red as hers, for the hair of the Ghazali woman was originally black. But near the scalp, where the hair had been gray, the henna had dyed it a flaming carrot color.

Why not? Jobber decided. She'd follow the troupe to their camp and then snitch some of the dark clothes. The Guards wouldn't think to look for a Ghazali woman. Jobber grimaced, suddenly uncertain as she watched the women swaying gracefully, the dancers' art visible in every step. She'd never be able to move like that. The pain in her hip was spreading down her leg, and she was beginning to limp badly. She shrugged, turning a wary head to search the crowd. Well, she'd just have to hope no one would ask to see her dance.

# 10

Jobber tagged behind the Ghazali women as they sauntered down High Street. As they neared the center of the city, High Street broadened into a wide avenue lined with expensive shops and inns. The upper floors of the buildings were branched with stone balconies. Gargoyles, jutting out beneath the struts, rolled their baleful eyes and stuck out their tongues at the throng below. Near the mouth of Market Square, High Street became even more congested as smaller avenues directed the flow of people onto its wide cobbled street. On either side of the broad avenue shopkeepers set up stalls filled with shining, promising trinkets, hoping to catch the eyes of the crowd as they streamed past. Hawkers and barrowboys rolled heavy wooden carts laden with all nature of goods, their hoarse cries loud and strident above the noise of the crowd and livestock. A fruit vendor strolled upstream against the crowd, singing in high clear notes as she sought to tempt the fair-goers with strawberries.

Normally the heavy crowd would have delighted Jobber. She would have had her hand in nearly every pocket, jingling their coins for them with no one the wiser. In a crowd like this the snitch was as easy as plucking fruit off a tree. She spotted several of Ratcatcher's Flock darting in and out like fish as they helped themselves to the contents of others' purses. She watched Nicker, his red woolen cap set at an angle, snip the strings of a purse without jostling his pigeon. Jobber nodded in professional appreciation. Not too far from him was a younger boy with a runny nose. They called him Dew Drop because his nose always ran whether the weather was warm or cold. He'd a cough that went with it, too, one that racked his chest and stole away his breath at times. As Jobber watched, one hand wiped across his upper lip with a loud sniff, while the other dug stealthily into an unsuspecting pocket. Jobber looked around, searching the fringes of the crowd. Ratcatcher had to be here somewhere. He'd never let his Flock work this crowd without keeping an eye on them. They might get to thinking they didn't need him.

She saw him standing in the shade of an overhanging balcony. By comparison to Jobber he wasn't tall, but his barrel chest gave the illusion of strength and size. Beneath the brim of a brown wool cap two deep lines creased over thick black eyebrows. His front teeth were large, sticking out over his lower lip even when his mouth was closed. He was cleaning his nails, digging at the dirt with the tip of a rusty blade. Every now and then his eyes would lift and his gaze flicker watchfully over his Flock. Behind him Jobber saw the ropes and loops of sausages that proclaimed a butcher's shop. A brace of geese hung upside down, their heads dangling forlornly. A dirty white dog with a blunt muzzle circled his ankles. As Jobber watched, Pug, a girl with matted yellow hair and a snub nose, sidled up beside Ratcatcher, taking care not to come too close to the dog. Ratcatcher nodded and held out his hand without looking directly at her. Jobber saw the little pouch of coins that disappeared quickly into his palm and then into his pocket. Pug looked up, hopeful, but Ratcatcher ignored her and continued to clean his nails. The dirty face screwed up in disappointment as the child turned and dove into the crowd again.

Wouldn't do to run into Ratcatcher now, Jobber decided. He might get stupid ideas if he knew she was a dell. And on the fly, too. Jobber turned her attention back to the troupe of Ghazali dancers and swore when she saw that they had nearly disappeared farther down the street while she had been watching Ratcatcher. She hurried her step, wincing at the pain stabbing her hip. Ahead of her the black heads of the Ghazali bobbed like markers on a fisherman's net.

"Ribbons! Silks!" Jobber heard the booming of a hawker nearby, but she scarce noticed it as she saw the troupe turn off on a sidestreet. Damn the fire, she cursed, she was going to lose them. She started pushing her way through the crowd, using her skills as a fighter to jab and poke in sensitive spots and force a straight path where none existed. Jobber ignored the angry shouts that accompanied her rude jabs and craned her head to keep her sights on the entranceway of the street the women had taken.

"Ribbons! Fine Silks!" the hawker's voice was louder, almost in her ear. His hand reached out and grabbed her. "Oy, a ribbon, girlie, for all that hair! What d'you say, then?"

Jobber shrugged the hand off, her eyes searching the street.

"Come on, pretty dell, make you a flash sort for Firefaire."

"Leave off," Jobber growled at the hawker and then stopped with a whistle of surprise.

Two Ghazali women stood by the stall and stared at her with

amused smiles. In their hands they held several strands of blue and green ribbons.

"You really should you know," one of them said. "Maybe the green," she said holding it up near Jobber's head. "It would look nice with the red of your hair."

Jobber's face grew hot with embarrassment. "Ah well," she started coughing awkwardly. Why hadn't she seen these two before? Jobber looked up again at the woman who spoke to her.

She was pretty, with a smooth round face the color of polished oak. Brown eyes sparkled merrily, regarding her speculatively. The tip of a pink tongue protruded from between white teeth as if the woman held back a laugh.

"Yeah, it's nice. Nice," Jobber said lamely, nodding her head. This day was going nowhere right.

"How about the blue?" the woman insisted, and Jobber saw again the look of hidden amusement.

"Nah," she answered gruffly, "don't like blue." Z'tits! what was she doing talking about ribbons when half the Silean Guard was out for her? Jobber glanced around worriedly. No, she'd have to find another way out of this. She couldn't waste any more time chasing the Ghazali.

As if sensing her eagerness to flee, the second woman spoke up. "Come, Zia, we must be off. They'll be waiting for us to start the performance."

Jobber stopped, startled by the low pitch of her voice. The hollow tone was gentle and soothing as if she had sung the words.

"In a moment, Lirrel. I haven't found the ribbon I want."

Jobber couldn't help but stare at the other woman, Lirrel. She was short, her waist slender. The face was delicate, her skin light brown. Beneath the black head scarf Jobber saw the faint red tinge of black hair dyed with henna. But it was her eyes that held Jobber's attention, for they were as milky as opals, catching the light and reflecting it like small jewels.

Blind, thought Jobber, and she stared openly, fascinated as the world was reflected back in the silvery blue eyes. The Ghazali woman stared straight ahead silently, her arms resting at her sides.

"Zia, come, we must not stay here longer," a slim tapered hand flew up and tugged with irritation at the other woman's sleeve.

"Oh, all right. I'll take the blue then," and she paid the hawker a two-copper piece. Zia smiled over at Jobber once more.

**114**

"Come and see our show. We'll be dancing at the Breaking Fish, down at the docks. Innkeeper's bought our services for the day, hoping we'll pack his tavern. You won't even have to pay."

Jobber frowned suspiciously. "Why not?"

Zia laughed. "Your hair, that color, we call it *baraki*, or good luck. Come and share yours with us, would you?"

Jobber shrugged, irritably. "Yeah, well maybe if I'm not too busy." She looked out at the crowd again, wishing she had somewhere to hide. She caught sight of the laborer leading the big gray horse through the crowd. He didn't look too happy. But then the grim-faced man sitting on the buckboard looked about ready to scaffer someone himself. That's probably my fault, Jobber thought, and then straightened up, alarmed. If the laborer and the gray horse had come this far, the Guards wouldn't be far behind.

"Zia, now we really must leave." Lirrel insisted.

"Good-bye, hope to see you later. Remember, we're at the Breaking Fish," Zia called to Jobber as they turned and headed out into the crowd.

Jobber scarcely noticed their departure, her eyes trained on the crowd, half-expecting the Guard to come forcing their way through at any moment. Ought she to try and double back to the Guild district? How wide a net had the Guard cast? Then there was Ratcatcher. She'd have to hope she could pass by him and his Flock as well. Given her luck today, it didn't seem too hopeful. She turned and saw the two dancers as they turned the corner onto the sidestreet. There was still that, and now she knew where to find them. Jobber made up her mind.

She plunged into the crowd as if into water, allowing the stream of people to take her down the avenue. Glancing up, Jobber saw the bright orange and red Firefaire pennants waving from the balconies. A Silean nobleman in a feathered hat leaned drunkenly over a balcony and shouted to a group of gaily dressed prostitutes. They laughed in response and screamed back, thumbing their noses at him. Not to be outdone by Beldan's whores, the man leaned farther out, shouting all the while. He might have tumbled head first into the street were it not for a second man, who caught him by the back of his waistcoat. But the hat with the white plumed feather floated down to the crowd below and was snatched up by one of the whores.

Jobber circled like an autumn leaf caught in the current until she saw the street marker nailed to the side of the corner inn. It was decorated with three gold cups, signifying the gold merchants. Jobber edged her way sideways through the crowds and into the little sidestreet.

There was brisk business being conducted on both sides of the narrow road. Tight knots of customers clustered around the stalls and shopfronts. Jobber half-listened to the energetic voices arguing as they bargained for better deals. This was Guilders Row, or the Yellowman's Street. Here gold and silver merchants sat hunched near displays of hanging bracelets and earrings like dragons guarding their hoards as they beckoned and argued with customers. Jobber could hear the tinny clinks of weights chiming against the pans of the scales. In spite of herself she slowed her pace, admiring as she always did the way the sunlight flashed and sparkled off the precious metal. Her eye snagged on the soft moonlight gleam of a pair of silver earrings. She drew close, attracted by the way the crescent moons twirled and glimmered. Her fingers itched and she felt a familiar tingling along her arms. She knew what that meant. It wasn't an easy snitch, the merchant was sitting close by. But that didn't matter, she had to have them. Not to sell later, not to pay for a meal or ale, but just to keep for herself.

"Get off with you," snarled the merchant. He was waving her away with a chubby hand weighted down with a heavy gold rings.

"I'm only looking."

"You're only trouble, now move on."

Jobber mumbled a nasty insult. Her fingers were ready to snitch the earrings when she stopped, hearing the shrill caw of the Guard's alarm. The noisy shouting and arguing quieted as people stared up the street in wonder. A troop of Guards was turning into the street, the alarm blasting louder.

"Frigging bastards," Jobber spat. Before she ran, she reached out angrily and grabbed the earrings while the merchant peered up the street at the approaching Guards. The stall shook slightly, and he turned back just in time to see Jobber's hand retreating with the earrings.

He rose awkwardly from his chair and made a grab for Jobber. She jumped back out of reach and turned to run. "Stop, you thief!" he cried out. "Guards, Guards. Over here! Stop that thief!"

Jobber sprinted through the streets, running as hard as her injured hip allowed. Hands reached out to grab her, but she swerved out of reach, twisting like a fish through a torn net.

You're full of naffy ideas today, ain't you, Jobber? she said to herself crossly. Why'd you have to go and do that for? Why didn't you just stand out in the road and scream "over here" to the butcherboys? Z'blood, she snorted, leaping over the ashy remains of a festival campfire. What difference did it make anyway? She was a Beldan snitch, cursed with Oran magic. How much worse could it be? Snitch a purse, snitch earrings and burn the Reader's eyes out with her aura. Might as well get taken in for all as one. And they still had to catch her.

Outside the doorway to the Ringing Hammer, Faul Verran leaned back in her chair and drained her tankard. She set it down on the little table and scowled at the passing fair-goers. How long have you been waiting, Faul, she asked herself with growing impatience. A gutter thief promises to meet you and you believe it. She tapped her fingers irritably on the table. You haven't been so easily deceived since the night Shefek stole your gold chain . . .

"Shut up, Faul," she muttered out loud to herself. That was a memory that didn't bear thinking on. She snorted angrily. Most of her life was a memory that didn't bear thinking on. It was just as well to forget all of it. Only the moment mattered. And the moment, she thought sourly, looking at the empty tankard, was entirely too dry.

She hailed the serving girl, who was standing near the door to the inn, her attention completely occupied by a young Silean gentleman tugging at the strings of her apron.

"Oy, girl, bring me another!" Faul yelled, holding up her empty tankard. The serving girl came toward Faul, her face flushed.

The worst of it is, thought Faul glumly, the ale was terrible here. You could drink and drink and never get truly knackered. And for the hundredth time since she had discovered herself waiting for Jobber, Faul wondered why she had agreed to come in the first place.

There was of course Jobber's promise of getting her into Crier's Forge. Faul wanted that very much. Perhaps out of sheer perversity on her part; because the forges were a place denied her, and after so many years of abiding and upholding the laws, Faul now felt inclined to break a few.

But no, Faul thought shaking her head, that wasn't entirely the reason. It was Jobber himself that had her sitting here. For some reason it hadn't mattered to her that he was ignorant of anything besides Beldan, that he was arrogant and that he stank of the gutters. Above all those dreadful qualities, it was his face that held Faul captive. At first she was attracted by its feral sharpness and the quickness in his eyes. His nose was a straight, unbroken line, all of his teeth still in his mouth, both rare for a street fighter. But then, she thought, he was good at the old style, his hands swift and responsive when she had struck him. And she was intrigued that he managed to stay alive, even clear of the Flocks.

But when he had turned to face her, his profile limned by the glow of firelight, Faul knew with a twisting of her heart why she had asked him to join her. His eyes were as green as Silean jade but flecked with yellow flames. The hairs of his eyebrows, that had first appeared white, glimmered like fine strands of gold. This child dragged from the street wore the face of the Fire Queen like an image seen through a tarnished mirror. Faul took a sip of her ale, the taste bitter in her mouth. She hadn't been able to stop herself from reaching out for his cap. She had wanted to take it from his head, to see his hair, whatever color, so as to prove to herself that he was only as he seemed, a street thief.

Twenty years a Knackerman, Faul thought sourly. Twenty years of service and it ends in a moment. One day Zorah had looked up to notice the faint strands of gray, the lines that edged Faul's eyes and suddenly it was over. Faul had always known that day would come when Zorah would see her as too old and replace Faul with Gonmer. Faul herself had replaced Serefina at the same age. The Fire Queen would allow no one in her retinue to wear the mask of age. It was as if she kept her immortality by changing her servants so that they never stayed in her service beyond a certain age. She wanted only to be surrounded by youth. And where does that leave me? Faul thought again. The Fire Queen could dismiss her, strip her of all former rank and privileges, but Faul would always be duty bound. It was a part of the training, part of the life of Firstwatch, and it didn't disappear when she was turned out.

But without her rank, what was she now? Faul stared morosely at the crowd. All of Beldan and those from the countryside strolling the city streets, each one it seemed with reason to celebrate or to grieve. But all Faul wanted to feel was numbed. She stood up, angrily. She'd waited long enough for Jobber. He wasn't coming, and she certainly wasn't going to wait any longer.

She strode away from the inn, moving quickly between the throng. With effort, she slowed her pace. Where the frigging shit are you rushing to, Faul? she asked herself. You've nowhere that you're needed. Faul stopped in the street. A woman close on her heels, her arms ladened with cloth-wrapped packages, crashed into Faul.

"Oy, you, what are you stuck for?" the woman snapped and bent down to retrieve her packages before they were crushed beneath the feet of other fair-goers. Faul stooped to help her pick them up. The woman was fat, with smooth olive cheeks and shining black hair pulled neatly back. A housemaid, Faul thought, feeling the shape of a child's toy in the wrapped package. Probably a wet nurse for a Silean house, she guessed, looking at the generous cut of the starched white apron and the new wooden clogs. The woman hurried away without another word to Faul.

Faul watched her go, set on her determined course. She sighed, smoothing the rustle of a tic across her cheek. She continued walking, more slowly now, drifting with the crowd. She spied a vagger hunched over his staff as he talked to another vagger, this one a woman. Standing together in their straight brown robes and knobbed staffs, Faul thought them like a strange breed of trees growing in the cobbled streets. For a moment she envied their spartan life, their acceptance of a harsh fate for reasons of pure faith. Faul had none. Not in the old religions of Oran, and even less in the cold, cheerless rituals of the Sileans.

The cawing of a Guard's whistle caught her ear and she spun on her heel in the street, searching for the sound. Her blood quickened in response and without thinking she reached for her sword. Her hand clutched the hilt, and she took three fast steps toward the sound of the alarm.

She could see them, the black and gray of their uniforms streaking through the fair-goers. "What's the call for?" she shouted to a Guard rushing past her.

"A red-haired thief," he hollered back not even stopping to look at her.

"Wait!" Faul called, beginning to run after him. And then suddenly, Faul stopped herself and swore loudly. "Frigging idiot," she hissed. "Not your affair, is it?" The tic rippled up the side of her face, closing one eye as she forced her hand away from her sword. Stiffly she turned from the shouting and noise of the alarm and began walking the way she had come. She forced her thudding heart to be still. The vaggers were gone, no doubt having wisely slipped away at the first sound of the alarm, Faul

**119**

guessed. Faul trained her eyes narrowly forward, not wanting to acknowledge what was happening behind her. It was then that she realized a whole section of the crowd had fled at the sound. Beggars and snitches that had been in the crowd, as common as the dull dirt between the cobbled stones, were no longer to be seen.

Take that as a lesson, Faul, she said to herself. Get lost.

Faul turned down the street and headed for the harbor. She'd board the *Marigold* and set sail tomorrow for the west country. She wanted to leave now, *right now*, she thought savagely, but she knew the crew would insist upon celebrating the last day of Firefaire. And she owed them that. Tomorrow then on the first available tide, Faul consoled herself. And until then she could always drink away her bitterness.

# 11

Jobber hurried through the alleys of Beldan's dockside streets. Gulls screeched as they passed overhead, and Jobber ducked at the sound, thinking it was another blast of the Guard's alarm. She felt for the earrings in her pocket, both pleased and furious with herself for having made such a daring gesture. Now more than ever she needed a good disguise. Just until things quieted down. Firefaire was on tomorrow, and the Guard would be too busy with the day's events to worry about a street snitch. Even one like her, with red hair.

Jobber touched her hair, held a strand of it before her eyes. It was strange to think of it as a part of her. She had hidden it so long beneath the leather cap that it seemed almost as if it didn't belong to her body. She shook her head, surprised by the wind on her bare head and the flowing movement of hair on her cheeks and shoulders. The hair wasn't soft, but wiry and coarse like spun threads of copper. It had never held a braid nor a ribbon. It took no dye, not even the coal tar with which Growler had once tried to color it black. Jobber had tried to cut it, but it resisted even the knife.

Jobber sighed deeply, thinking again of the question she had asked Growler. What am I? Beldan's Fire, he had answered without further explanation. "Beldan's Fire," she whispered aloud to the hair. Even now Jobber didn't understand the words.

It seemed to her that there were very few things about her that did make any sense. She was composed of different parts thrown together and as mismatched as her cast-off clothing. Jobber looked again at the earrings in her hand, remembering slowly the truth about herself. She was female, a fact that grated against her male identity on the street. She was possessed with a power for which she had no use, but one that Readers were ready to see her hanged for having. She was a common street snitch, but one with a head of fiery hair that rivaled that of the Queen herself. Jobber shook her head, confused. It didn't help to think of these things, she warned herself. Staying alive was accomplished by simplify-

ing everything to its smallest portion. She cleared her mind of all
else and tightened her concentration on the shield around her
aura. That settled, she walked quickly, one eye out for the Breaking Fish.

At the sign of the anchor she turned down an alley. The stench
of rotting fish smacked her in the face. Her nose wrinkled at the
smell, and tears welled up in the corners of her eyes. Clouds of
flies buzzed happily around the barrels of discarded innards
stashed behind the kitchens of the Breaking Fish. Skinny cats
crouching over their pilfered meals hissed and arched their backs
as Jobber slipped through the alley. When she passed too close to
a barrel, a silver gray tabby swiped her ankle, the sharp claws
raking across her exposed skin.

"Z'blood," she shrieked in surprise. "You miserable beastie,
take that!" and she delivered a swift kick to the stray's side. The
cat yeowled as it landed against a barrel, scattering the other cats
perched on the rim.

"Worse yet," glowered Jobber, examining the bloody stripes
on her ankle. She daubed at the blood with an old stiff rag she
found amidst the alley trash and then gave up as it did nothing but
smear the blood around and make the wound hurt more.

Jobber crept near the alley entrance to the Breaking Fish and
then stopped, arrested by the sound of a flute playing a melan-
choly tune. She listened closely, the noise of the street hushed.
The music circled her like a warm breeze drawn from the ocean,
salty tasting on the lips and smelling of brine. Memories Jobber
had long denied reappeared in her mind, and sorrow mingled
with an almost forgotten happiness. Jobber closed her eyes, feeling the burn of tears.

"No, no, Lirrel, this is Firefaire. You can't play that song," a
voice said angrily. The music stopped and Jobber gasped, surprised at being released from the sound. Other, more ordinary
sounds penetrated once more: the screeching of gulls, a cat routing in garbage. The thickness of memory evaporated like a cloud.
"We need something gay and happy, something to make people
forget their troubles. That old tune will have them weeping."

"People don't want to forget their troubles. They want an end
to them." Jobber recognized the voice of the woman Lirrel. It
resonated with the same alto pitch as the flute.

"They don't pay us to remind them how miserable they are!"
another voice snapped.

Jobber heard Lirrel sigh. "Sometimes it's important to let them know we understand the hardness of their life. How can we move them if we give them false happiness?"

"Stop being political for once! This is Firefaire, Lirrel. People want to have a good time. The innkeeper wants happy customers."

"We are Ghazali, not prostitutes. It's our duty, our obligation, to speak the truth, reflect the heart even when that heart is troubled."

There was a long silence, and Jobber strained to hear more.

"*Ahal,*" a voice murmured, this one older, more resigned. "You are right, Lirrel. But neither is this the past when Ghazali music once brought peace to discord. We are no longer witnesses and peacekeepers. And for that reason we must compromise. Can we not in good faith, Lirrel, offer the promise of joy to make the sadness endurable?"

"Yes," Lirrel answered softly, and Jobber inched closer to hear her. "Yes, Ama. As always, I am too strict."

The older voice chuckled warmly. "A witness must be. Though we have strayed from the past, it is because of you, Lirrel, that the Ghazali will not lose the old ways altogether."

"This reminds me of a riddle." Lirrel's voice suddenly brightened.

"Oh, not now!" someone groaned.

"No, really. It's suitable," Lirrel insisted.

"Let's have it then and be quick."

"In the dark night, the weary cry out to me, but in the day am I extinguished, only to be reborn in every heart."

In her hiding place, Jobber frowned, a finger pressed against her lips as she tried to guess the answer. She heard the older woman's chuckle once more.

"Hope. The answer is hope."

"*Ahal,*" Lirrel said, "you have guessed right. My flute will play then of hope."

"Good, now please let's go before we're any later. Pirmi is going to wonder where we have been. He's been drumming long enough to hurry his thirst."

"I'm coming! I'm coming," Lirrel said briskly.

Jobber crouched in the shadow of the doorway as the dancers bustled out of the back room and through the kitchens of the inn. She could hear the soft swish of their skirts as they passed and the jingling of little silver bells tied around their ankles. Then all was quiet again except for the hissing of two cats quarreling over a fishhead in the alley and orders shouted out to the cook working

**123**

in the kitchen. Jobber waited a few moments more until she heard the faint strains of music that announced the beginning of the dance performance.

Jobber peered around the opened door and could see only the backs of the cook and the serving girl. They were squeezed together, leaning their heads and shoulders as far as they could through a small window that opened from the kitchen behind the bar out to the main room. They were watching the dancers and paying no attention to the boiling pots and open back door. Jobber slipped in quietly, hugging the greasy wall, and went silently into the room the Ghazali dancers had used as their dressing room.

It was a storage room and the grimy plaster walls were lined with heavy sacks of flour and grain. Barrels of salted meat squatted side by side with crocks of carrots and potatoes stored in sand. Hanging on wooden pegs were strings of garlic, dried tomatoes and peppers. In the sooty rafters overhead hung sausages and hard, flattened rectangles of dried fish.

Jobber smiled to herself as she saw the black garments and dresses of the Ghazali dancers scattered about the room, some lying atop the sacks of grain, others draped over the barrels. Here and there were other odds and ends: a string of unused ankle bells, a long-necked lute with a broken string, braid tassels in bright magenta and blue and a wooden box containing little pots and jars. The room smelled faintly of dried fish and the wood-scented perfume of the dancers. Untidy dells, Jobber thought happily, they'd never notice anything was missing from this mess. She stole another glance over her shoulder, and when she was certain none had seen her, she shut the door quietly.

She rubbed her hands together as she started for the first pile of black clothing.

"Let's see now," she said as she held up a long stretch of fabric. The little shards of mirror that had been sewn into it reflected back a hundred tiny portraits of Jobber's puzzled face. "Right, this goes on the nobbin'," and she swung the shawl over her head. The smooth silky fabric slipped off her head immediately and settled on her shoulders. Jobber tried again, fussing with the fabric to keep it on her head. Now how in Zorah's name did they get it to stay up there? she wondered peevishly. She gave up trying for the moment and looked over the other garments that remained.

Jobber picked up a black skirt, surprised by how heavy it felt, and fumbled through the folds to find the waistband. It was

**124**

thickly pleated at the waist, designed to widen in a full circle when the wearer danced. Jobber pulled it up over her trousers, tied it around her waist and then groaned as she looked down and saw that the skirt was not quite long enough to cover her bony ankles and the old boots she wore. She was struggling with the skirt, trying to tie it lower on her hips so that it would disguise her legs, when she heard the door squeak softly and felt the faint rush of air as it was opened.

Jobber whirled around, nearly tripping as the skirts caught between her legs. "Z'blood," she swore, arms thrown out to regain her balance, "frigging dress," and she looked up angrily at the door.

"I forgot something." Lirrel stood there, an amused expression spreading across the delicate face. One dark eyebrow lifted over an opalescent eye. She closed the door quickly behind her. "What are you doing?" she asked and then shook her head, as if to say she didn't need to be told the answer. "It doesn't matter, really. I'm glad you came. I felt certain you would."

"Eh?" said Jobber, fighting to get out of the skirt that had developed a life of its own and was determined to stay tangled around her knees.

"I saw you following us—"

"Nah," said Jobber, genuinely shocked. "How could you? You're blind."

Lirrel gave a throaty laugh. "Everyone thinks that. And it's true I do nothing to persuade them otherwise. But I'm not. In fact I see very well—even at night. It's only the odd color that confuses people. Like your hair."

Jobber stiffened. "Ain't nothing wrong with my hair."

"Not wrong, but decidedly distinct," she ventured carefully. "Or else why are you here, trying to hide it with one of my head scarves."

Jobber stared back at Lirrel, silent.

"You could just cut it." Lirrel tipped her head to one side as if listening. "But it won't cut will it?" she said, her eyes widening in surprise. "Nor take a dye."

"How did you know that?" Jobber started to yell and then quickly lowered her voice. Fear tapped a warning in her veins. "Nobody knows that 'bout me."

Lirrel gave a nonchalant shrug, but Jobber read excitement in her face. When she spoke her voice was calm and reasonable. "I know things. I knew you were following us long before I saw you. I could 'hear' you coming. I made Zia wait with me by the

**125**

ribbon seller to be certain." She laughed lightly at the memory. "I didn't really know what to expect. The sense of your approach was so . . . so loud and angry. When I saw the red of your hair, I knew it had to be you. Are the Readers after you?" Lirrel took a step forward, and Jobber shifted to the side cautiously. The way the silver eyes followed her was unnerving.

"Not yet."

Lirrel paused. "The Guards, then," she answered as if she had stolen the thoughts from Jobber's mind.

"It ain't nothing I can't handle," Jobber answered. She wanted desperately to get away from that steely stare.

"Let me help you."

"Why should you?" Jobber asked suspiciously. "You don't even know me."

"I feel as if I do."

"Just let me take some of these black things and I'll be on my way," said Jobber, scooping up a handful of fabric and inching toward the shut door. Why didn't she just knacker the woman and take off? It would be easy enough. But curiosity held Jobber back. How had the woman known about her hair?

"Oh no, I couldn't let you do that," Lirrel insisted. "You would invite worse trouble. Ghazali women never go anywhere alone. It's for our own protection, you see. If the Silean Guards saw you alone, they would assume the worst and no doubt solicit your attentions."

"Do what?" Jobber squinted at Lirrel, uncertain of her words.

"Try to hire you as a prostitute."

Jobber grimaced in disgust.

"Yes. And anyway," Lirrel continued with a smile, "you're a bit tall for a Ghazali woman, not to mention pale, and I doubt you've much experience wearing our dress."

"Any dress," mumbled Jobber, scowling at the puddle of black skirt that she had just fought to get off her legs.

"Let me help you," Lirrel repeated.

"What's your lay?" asked Jobber gruffly.

Lirrel blinked. "My what?"

"What's in it for you?"

Lirrel smiled again. "*Baraki*, the presence of good luck. The old power present in the color of your hair. To the Sileans, it's blasphemy. But to the Ghazali, you are blessed with luck."

Jobber snorted. "Queer sort of folk, ain't you?"

Lirrel laughed. "To some. But to ourselves, we are perfectly reasonable."

**126**

"Well, I can't say as I've had any luck today," Jobber answered sourly. "Fact is, I don't remember when it's been worse." That wasn't true, she reflected suddenly. Nothing was worse than the day Growler was killed. Jobber lifted her chin. "How do I know I can trust you?"

Lirrel stepped forward, her expression serious as she considered Jobber's remark. "*Ahal*," she murmured, "you are right. I shall tell you then. I am like you, possessed of Oran's magic. My aura no doubt, as white as the dove, for I am an air element."

"Prove it," Jobber said.

"I knew about your hair, didn't I? I know that you hide your aura behind a vagger's shield. That you mourn the death of someone—"

"That's enough," Jobber said, interrupting her. The hairs prickled on her neck. The woman saw too much. "All right then, I believe you. I'll pay you to help me."

"It's not necessary."

"Yeah, it is. I don't want to owe anything to anyone."

"It must be hard to live alone," Lirrel said.

"Not your business, is it?"

"No, I expect you're right," Lirrel answered softly. "*Ahal*, if you wish to pay me, I will accept whatever you think is fair."

"Here, will these do?" Jobber pulled out the stolen earrings from her pocket. She thrust them quickly into Lirrel's hand.

Lirrel stared at the earrings in her hands and then back at Jobber, her expression sober. "They're beautiful."

"Yeah, well, it's a flash bit of metal that," Jobber answered proudly. At least she knew to snitch things of value.

Lirrel put the earrings on, running the thin hook through her pierced ears. The crescent moons seemed to float amidst the dark waves of Lirrel's black hair, the reddish tinge of henna like the last rays of a sunset. Jobber swallowed at a thickness in her throat when she saw how the earrings gleamed with the same soft brilliance as Lirrel's odd eyes. The earrings belonged rightfully on a woman like Lirrel. Silly pin, Jobber said to herself, how'd you have worn those earrings, you don't even have pierced ears?

Lirrel smiled back at her. "Come, I'll turn you into a Ghazali and you can spend the watch here with us."

"What? Here?"

"It would be the safest. We're performing most of the day here, so you won't have to be seen outside, where your, ah, differences might be more obvious."

"All right. I'll leave when it starts getting dark."

"As you wish. Can you sing?"

"Yeah, like a farting duck."

"Hmm, not much need for that sound in our songs, I'm afraid. Just sit on the stage with the other musicians and look like you're a part of the group."

"But everyone will see me," Jobber argued.

"The best hiding place is often right beneath their nose. They won't think to look for you there."

"'Less, they sneeze. Supposing someone notices I ain't playing anything."

"Here, take my flute and hold it to your mouth. I'll sit next to you and play on another. The way I play will make it hard for anyone to tell that there is really only one player and not two." Lirrel handed Jobber a slim flute about the length of her forearm. It was a dusky gray color with a grain unfamiliar to Jobber. Along the shaft were scratched thin black spirals in a scroll pattern.

Jobber put her lips to the opening and tried to blow a note, wondering if she could produce the same hollow sound she had heard in the alley. The flute only gave a breathy squeak.

"What's this made of?" she asked, brows drawn together in a puzzled frown.

"Bone. From my grandmother."

Jobber paled and dropped the flute from her lips instantly. She wiped her mouth with a dirty hand. "Z'blood, that's awful. I ain't going to play any flute that was your granny's leg."

"Arm actually, and I doubt you could play it even if it was wood," Lirrel said sharply. "Here, if it offends you, take this one."

"What's this made from? Your ma?"

"Tcha," Lirrel answered. "No, it's wood, made from the ash. It has a sweet sound but not the soul that this one does."

"Then why don't you play the legbone?"

"Arm," Lirrel repeated. "Because it's too powerful a flute for this crowd. It would have them weeping."

Jobber believed that, remembering the music she had heard in the alley. "Yeah, well," she said shrugging her shoulders, "I just don't want nothing on my mouth that was once kicking about." She held up the second flute to the light inspecting it. Satisfied that it was wood, she blew a few shrill notes on it. Lirrel winced at the painful sound.

"Just hold it, don't try to play it or we'll all be in trouble. Now come on. I don't have much time to dress you properly."

Lirrel bustled over to the box of jars and pots. Her hand hovered over them until at last she found the jar she was looking for. Unscrewing the lid, she motioned with her head for Jobber to come close. Uneasily Jobber stood beside her, and Lirrel began smearing the contents of the jar on Jobber's cheeks. Jobber flinched as Lirrel's hand brushed the cut on her cheek.

"Ah, sorry," Lirrel apologized and continued spreading the cream more gently.

"What is this stuff?" Jobber wrinkled her nose at its sweet smell.

"Bark cream. We use it to color the skin a darker color. Your face is a little too pale to pass for a Ghazali. Don't worry, you can wash it off later with no ill effects."

"Hmm," Jobber said, "don't know if I like it." She twitched her nose, the cream itching her skin. She brought up a hand to scratch but Lirrel slapped it away.

"Remember, don't touch or it will rub off. Here now, I will color your eyebrows with charcoal."

Lirrel whistled a soft tune beneath her teeth as she worked swiftly to transform Jobber's face into the near likeness of a Ghazali dancer. Jobber stared back at her while she worked, fascinated by the eerie color of Lirrel's eyes.

Lirrel pulled a black cotton scarf from a pile and tied it tightly around Jobber's head, taking care to tuck all the shining red hair inside.

"Here now, take off your clothes and get into this shift." She held out a long black dress cut wide in the body. It had full-length sleeves that ended in bell-shaped cuffs. Small gold coins had been stitched along the cuffs of the sleeves. Across the collar and down the front of the dress was an embroidered panel worked in gold and silver thread, and this was outlined by more bits of mirror.

Jobber shook her head. "Nah. I never take off my clothes. They stays on."

"Must be difficult when you wash your body."

Jobber looked astonished. "You get sick doing that! I take care only to wash my face. The rest stays fine as it is."

"Now that's truly awful," exclaimed Lirrel frowning with distaste. "Do you mean to tell me that you've never seen yourself naked?"

"What for?"

"Indeed," Lirrel answered lightly. "Well how about just taking off your vest?"

"All right," said Jobber looking down at the vest. "But I don't want it getting snitched."

"No one will take it."

"Yeah, well they better not. I need that vest," Jobber said belligerently as she took it off and folded it into a small package. The man's shirt she wore beneath slipped down off one shoulder and she roughly pulled it on again.

"The dress is wide enough to go over the rest of your clothes and I think should be long enough on you. We would usually wear it belted, to take up the extra length, but on you it will fall just right."

Her arms held aloft, Jobber wriggled into the dress and pulled her covered head through the neck. It felt strange to wear a dress. Especially one cut from such fine fabric. She ran a hand over the glossy embroidery on the front. "Flash this. I look like a real dell."

"A what?"

"A woman." Jobber looked down at her front, the fabric falling in a smooth flat plain, rumpled only in spots by the garments beneath. "Well, sort of. No tits. Just as well, I guess."

"Why?" Lirrel asked, puzzled.

"Get in the way, wouldn't they? Bad enough I have to hide my hair, but to have to hide those as well, it 'ud be one thing more to worry about. I used to think that if I never touched women's things, maybe I'd not be one."

"Why don't you want to be female?"

"The street."

"I don't understand."

"Think on it. You said yourself what happens when one of your own kind goes out alone. You'd wind up scaffered or brangled by some shit of a Guard."

"Yes, but surely there are women—" Lirrel started to say, but Jobber was getting angry and she wasn't willing to listen. What did this Ghazali woman know about the street, anyway?

"I got a reputation for being nasty and a good fighter. But look here," and she tapped a finger in the other palm for emphasis, "if word got out I was a dell, I'd be cocking up my toes in no time. Ratcatcher, Bonesnip and Tinpenny, as much as they hate each other, would probably kick in together to scaffer me just to save their ratty pride."

Lirrel stared at Jobber's angry face. Silently she spread the bark cream on Jobber's hands.

"A solitary life is lonely," she answered.

"Yeah, well, it's safer."

"How will you escape from the Readers?" Lirrel asked. "Is your shield good enough?"

"Who cares?" Jobber answered bluntly.

"But the Naming? How will you face—"

"I don't plan on going." Jobber gritted her teeth not wanting to talk about it anymore.

Lirrel's eyebrow shot upward in amazement. "Can you survive on the edge of a knife?" she asked.

Jobber shrugged, a thin smile. "Better than most," she said with a bravery she did not feel. Today had been disaster enough. But what point was there in dwelling on it?

"*Ahal*," Lirrel murmured as if accepting Jobber's thought as a final argument. She turned to take up a large head scarf with tiny mirrors. She tossed it over Jobber's head and tucked it expertly behind Jobber's ears. "The scarf beneath keeps the silk from slipping off your head," she told Jobber. Then she brought the sides forward, close to Jobber's cheeks. She couldn't help but smile at Jobber's disgruntled face. "Your eyes are very beautiful," she said. "I hope no one notices that they are so bright a green. Ghazali eyes are usually brown."

"Yeah? What about yours then, eh?"

"I shall tell you a secret," Lirrel said quietly.

"Is that wise?" Jobber asked.

"I trust you."

"Very unwise."

"Ghazali are never Named, though many are tattooed."

It was Jobber's turn to be surprised. "How'd you do it?" she asked. Even in Beldan with its creative black markets none had been able to reproduce a convincing forgery of the Queen's tattoo. The color of the ink was too unique, the pattern too complex and intricate. And each tattoo carried just enough magic to glimmer in the Reader's eyes.

Lirrel was about to answer when the door flew open and an angry Zia stormed into the room.

"Lirrel, what's taking so long! Amer has had to keep singing the same verse over and over waiting for you to come back so she can finish the piece. It's starting to sound ridiculous. And *who* is that?"

Zia glared at Jobber, her hands balled into fists on her hips.

Lirrel snatched another flute from its bag and took Jobber by the arm.

'I'll tell you later," she said hurriedly. "Let's go," and she

131

dragged Jobber past Zia and out through the door.

"Lirrel!" whispered Zia furiously. "What's going on?"

Lirrel hissed impatiently over her shoulder, "She's *ghazat*."

"But this is madness—"

"And she's *baraki*."

Zia grabbed Jobber by the shoulders and swung her around in the doorway, peering into her face. She broke into a dimpled smile, and Jobber saw the pink tongue reappear between Zia's white teeth. "Tcha! You were right, Lirrel. She came."

"And if we don't go now, Amer will disgrace us all by starting to laugh at her own song. Come on," Lirrel urged, hurrying them through the kitchen.

The cook and the serving girl turned to stare as they passed through the kitchen with a soft rustle of their skirts. The cook eyed Jobber quizzically, and Jobber could see the woman sizing up her tall frame. But before she could say anything they were through the door and settled onto a small stage.

Immediately Lirrel began to play, the sound of her flute rising like a gentle wave beneath the singer's voice, caressing it, holding it aloft. The singer's voice faded as the flute played stronger, spreading the melody like a benediction of joy over the room.

"Z'blood, that sure were a long song, wannit?" Jobber heard the serving girl whisper behind her in the window.

"Sshh," hushed the cook, "just listen to that noise now. Naffy, ain't it?"

The music had quickened its tempo, the flute spinning out a rapid dance rhythm. Lirrel's foot began to tap lightly as the beat grew more insistent. It was soon accompanied by the soft slapping of barefeet and jingling of bells as Zia started to dance a quick series of light steps, tracing a small circle. Three other women joined her, their feet adding to the steady tapping of the beat. They linked arms, each woman holding the other around the waist until they formed a tight circle of dancers, spinning around and around. Beneath their black skirts multicolored petticoats appeared like streaks of whirling paint. As the dancers moved their feet faster, the dust on theold stage lifted and swirled until it formed a hazy cloud around their ankles.

Then with a stamp, two women released their hold and the circle of dancers flattened into a straight line across the stage. The audience began to shout and clap its approval as the dancers zigzagged across the old stage with increasingly faster and more intricate steps. Behind them, hunched in the unfamiliar black garments, Jobber stared nervously and tried not to scratch her itchy face or sneeze at the dust that settled lightly on her shoulders.

# 12

Gonmer pushed opened the heavy door of the state room and entered quickly. Behind her Lais struggled with an armload of maps. The rolled papers refused to stay tidily bunched, but slipped and separated from each other despite Lais's best efforts to keep them together. She pitched her body forward and lifted one knee awkwardly to hoist the rolls higher in her arms. Hunched over her bundle, she employed her chin as an extra hand clamping it down over the top of the bundle. She managed to secure a tighter hold on the wayward maps but at the cost of her dignity. In front of her the straight back and rigid shoulders of the Firstwatch scolded her for being clumsy.

Lais sighed quietly to herself. Z'blood, it had been an awful night and an even worse morning. The New Moon's attack last night had redoubled the Firstwatch's foul humor, and the ineffectiveness of the Guard to capture a common street thief had added fuel to her considerable temper. Lais had done ten extra turns at the training, fighting until she dripped with sweat and her tired arms could scarcely raise the sword. But still the Firstwatch attacked as if Lais herself had been responsible for the incompetence of the Guard. Now all Lais wanted was to stay out of the Firstwatch's way and not make any mistakes.

Lais reached the long wooden table that served as a desk and with relief set down the bundle of papers. She stacked them neatly and arranged them in order, knowing which ones the Firstwatch would show first to the Queen. That done she stepped away from the table and stood at attention, hands clasped lightly behind her back. She waited silently until the Firstwatch noticed her. Gonmer nodded and gave her a look that meant, listen hard and don't fall asleep. Lais pulled her shoulders erect.

First to approach the table was the Regent Silwa. Lais studied the way he moved with approval. He had the grace and confidence of a fighting man, his step even and slightly rolling. His dark beard was neatly trimmed, and his hair, unlike the elaborate style of most of the Sileans at court, was short in the front and tied back to a small single curl over his collar. At his side followed the Adviser Antoni. Lais disliked him. He was too well dressed, the cut of his clothes extravagant. He wore heavy rings on his fingers and his nails were polished. A crafty bugger, Lais thought, glancing at his composed face. His black eyes hooded. Sly and smart, he is. He'd been a long time at the Keep, and Lais figured he knew all the court games of power. Probably invented them in his spare time. Adviser Antoni rifled through the rolled papers. Lais bridled as he lifted one, examined it and set it down again out of its proper order. She went to replace it, but their hands met as he took it first, smiling thinly at her and returned it to its proper place. Lais twitched uncomfortably, wondering if he had played a game with her.

"Madam," began the Firstwatch, "I have brought the plans for your final approval."

The Fire Queen was sitting on a window seat, gazing out the window at the harbor. She stood gracefully, a dress of light blue silk rustling crisply as she moved. Lais's stomach contracted uneasily as the Fire Queen turned to face them. Like the thief at Crier's Forge. Cut from the same cloth they were. And her hair, fiery red and shimmering in the sun. How could there be two so alike?

"It's looking very festive out there, don't you think, Firstwatch? I don't recall having seen so many bonfires before," Zorah was saying, smiling at the open window.

"Not unusual, really," answered the Regent Silwa, unrolling another map and studying it. "Festivals become crowded when the populace has less. They give the illusion of prosperity when times are hard."

"A grim sentiment, Regent Silwa," Zorah replied, annoyed.

"Grim perhaps but accurate. There have been at least five years of bad harvests."

"Then all the more reason they should celebrate Firefaire. It's a festival of hope for the coming year."

"It's a hiring fair where labor is bought and sold."

"It's a spiritual event," Zorah insisted.

Silwa gave a short laugh. "It is an excuse to be drunk and disorderly for at least five days. Though I suppose a drunk enough man seeing you emerge from the Great Bonfire will swear to having been touched by divine grace."

"And so he will be, Regent Silwa," Zorah said evenly.

"Yes, I expect so," Silwa said softly. "But when he returns home to the country, he won't care about that. He'll care about

**135**

his stomach and whether or not he has work for the coming year."

Zorah reached the wooden table and looked over the papers. She picked up a map and spread it open without really seeing it.

"And what are you suggesting, Regent?"

"Put an end to Firefaire."

"Never," Zorah snapped at him. "I would not think of denying my people the right of the festival."

"Oran peasants will betray you one day, my Queen, and the festival is the perfect place for it to happen."

"If you're referring to the attack last night—"

"Not only last night. I suspect that is just the beginning. I, too, have studied the reports. There has been a steady increase in violence throughout the city. It's worse this year than any year past."

"A painted moon, a fight in an alley? They hardly constitute much of a threat."

"You don't you see my point, Madam. When you have a festival like this people come together from all over. They talk, they discover their mutual miseries. The New Moon doesn't have to travel for its recruits. It has only to come here."

"They're illiterate peasants," Zorah countered.

"You said yourself the woman that attacked the Firstwatch wasn't a peasant wielding a sword. Where are they learning to fight? Possession of weapons is illegal for Orans. Where are they getting the swords? It is at Firefaire your illiterate peasants drink in the company of Guildmasters who are only too willing to help them."

"Then we must find a way to increase the peasants' loyalties to the regime."

"Peasants think with their stomachs."

"Then ease the taxes and increase the use of common lands."

"Ah, that would not be advisable, Madam, as they are too profitable to our Silean interests. The Silean Guard must be paid for, after all, as well as those who serve to administer your state. The condition of the treaty is quite precise on the question of Silean compensation. It is an expensive necessity. You could ease the regulations on the more powerful Guilds, integrate a few into the court, thereby attaining their loyalty," Silwa suggested in return.

"That would be foolhardy," Zorah answered, frowning. "The Guildmasters are ambitious. They have never understood the sacrifices I made to keep Oran from destruction after the Burning. They would try to undo everything I have fought to save."

"So, it would seem, Madam, that neither of us are willing to change our present course of action."

"You are forgetting the Naming, Regent Silwa," Antoni broke in suddenly, and Lais jumped at the unexpected sound of his voice. "That, too, is a crucial part of Firefaire, and a lucrative one, I might add. There is the Naming tax and indentured servants for the Keep. And there is the procession to guard against the children born with the old power. It would not be in our interest to lose these important benefits of Firefaire."

"Perhaps," Silwa answered, tugging at his beard. "But there must be a better way. The Naming ceremony is to provide working papers. Surely we don't need such an elaborate ceremony for distributing those papers?"

"On the contrary. The Naming ceremony carries the weight of tradition. The Fire Queen," Antoni nodded graciously at Zorah, "is the symbol of divinity to the Oran people. Her presence makes the Naming ceremony a spiritual one, unsullied by economic realities. Rob them of that and they will grumble about the tax."

"The clergy will argue that Oran peasants should convert to the Silean faith anyway in order to purge their wretched souls."

"A commendable argument, Silwa. But the clergy also expect the peasants to accept their poverty as a penance. And that they will not do. Not while the clergy lives in a grand style. The Oran faith remains attractive not only for the beautiful presence of the Queen herself, but the commonness of vaggers who sympathize with the lot of the peasants. We must allow the peasants a fleeting celebration in order to keep them at their yoke the rest of the year."

Zorah stood quietly, her face clouding with annoyance, her eyes a brittle green. Lais knew that the Fire Queen had nothing but contempt for the Adviser. But what about him, she mused, casting another glance at Antoni. He was watching the Queen, his eyes playing over her face like a hungry man before a meal, as he smoothed the edges of his mustache. The Queen turned away from him, a slight shudder tensing her shoulders.

"I understand, Antoni, what you are saying," Silwa was arguing, "but surely you can see my point. Life has grown more uncertain these last few years. The Oran peasants are no longer to be trusted or mollified by so simple a holiday as Firefaire. Silean farmers have been threatened in the countryside, robbed of stores. Brigands have raided Silean merchants traveling along what used to be safe roads. And now there's violence here in

137

Beldan. I must advise against anything that would make that violence more handy."

"Spoken like a soldier," Antoni added, smiling.

"But that's what I am. I protect Silean interests in Oran. I am personally responsible for every Silean living in Oran."

"Even at the expense of the Oran people?" Zorah demanded angrily.

"At whose expense do you live, Madam?" Silwa asked dryly. "You retain Sileans to provide a service. A service that protects you from the treasonous factions of your own society. They must be paid for somehow," he shrugged.

"What I have done, I have done for the sake of my country's survival, for the good of all my countrymen that they may live in peace."

"Then it is your countrymen that must shoulder the burden for that peace."

Zorah fell silent and stared moodily at the wall. Silwa tapped a finger on the edge of the table. He waited for her to speak. She didn't, and only the restless movement of her hair and the acrid scent of copper betrayed the depth of her anger. Silwa sighed and looked back at the map.

"Perhaps this is the wrong time to discuss this matter. I am merely expressing concern at what I perceive to be a dangerous situation for all of us. I don't wish to be caught napping if the New Moon decides to risk an open attack. Last night was close enough."

"Firstwatch," Zorah turned to Gonmer, "Show us the final plans you have worked out for tomorrow's procession. The Regent Silwa seems to doubt your ability to manage an event such as Firefaire. That it has been held in Beldan for over two hundred years since the first year after the Burning, and that in all that time there has not been a single incident, seems to have escaped his knowledge."

Silwa turned to Gonmer, his expression resentful. Lais chewed the inside of her lip and looked to the Firstwatch. Gonmer's expression was troubled. But it was nothing to do with Silwa, Lais guessed. It was that girl she was thinking about. Lais knew Gonmer was going to have to explain why most of the Firstwatch was occupied in chasing a common street thief. Gonmer blinked and lifted her chin. That's it, thought Lais, here it comes, and she wondered how Gonmer was going to break the odd news to the Queen.

"Madam, before I begin, I feel I should inform you of a street girl I encountered today."

"Why should that be of interest to me?"

Gonmer cleared her throat. "She is a common thief—a pickpocket, though my sources tell me she doesn't belong to any one of the known Flocks of thieves. She is also a good fighter, well trained in the old style. Stonecutter, I believe. She managed to disable four Guards today in her escape."

"I thought the practice had been outlawed." Silwa's tone was accusing. "You don't mean to tell me that despite your best efforts the schools still exist?"

Gonmer pursed her lips. "We may outlaw it, but it is a different thing altogether to suppress the knowledge. All it takes is a single teacher and single student."

"What is this to me?" asked Zorah impatiently.

"What is most notable about the girl is that she resembles you, Madam, almost as if she were a sister. Her hair is the same red—"

"That doesn't flatter me much, Firstwatch," Zorah said. "Anyone can dye their hair.

"Excuse me, Madam, but I am certain the color is natural."

"How can you be so sure?"

"The quality of the hair was most unusual. Like strands of metal. Also, the girl hid her hair under a leather cap. Why go to the trouble of dyeing it, only to hide it?"

"Was she Named?" Zorah asked, becoming interested.

"I think not, Madam. She couldn't have been older than sixteen or seventeen. I would have recognized that face if I had seen it in a recent ceremony."

"Maybe she was Named elsewhere?"

Gonmer shook her head. "She knew the city much too well to come from somewhere else. She managed to elude the Guard fairly quickly. We lost track of her in Market Square and are still searching for her."

"Where did you meet her?" Zorah asked.

"Crier's Forge."

"Females are not allowed in the forge," Zorah said angrily. "Guildmaster Donal has defied me. I'll have him proscribed and his whole forge shut down once and for all!"

"He didn't know she was female. Even I was misled, for when I met her dressed in trousers and the cap, it was hard to tell that she wasn't a boy."

"I want her caught immediately. And I want her brought here.

Is that clear?" Zorah commanded in a steady voice that failed to match the fists at her sides that opened and closed with each word.

"But Firefaire—"

"I don't care about that. Enough is already planned as it is. It will do no harm if some merchant has to sit on his backside and wait tomorrow until these final details are worked out. I am more concerned that this girl be found."

"I shall see to it immediately," Gonmer replied. She bowed her head to the Fire Queen and then turned on her heel.

Whore's shit! Lais swore to herself, seeing the spark of fury in the Firstwatch's eyes. Lais knew that look well. No rest for any of us, Lais mourned, and no pleasure either if the girl couldn't be found by tomorrow. Why was she important enough to muddle up all the preparations? Lais wondered angrily.

"Wait!" Silwa stopped them from leaving. "Why should this red-haired girl be so important?" Silwa asked, repeating Lais's thought.

Zorah hesitated before answering. One hand smoothed the wrinkles from the front of her dress as if she needed to compose herself before answering. When she looked up at them, the Fire Queen stared through them as though they were ghosts.

"Since the Burning there have been no children with red hair. None born who might have carried a fire element. I am the last. That much I was able to do, even as Beldan was torn open by flames and Huld's armies razed the city to stones. If this girl has the old power, she not only threatens peace, but she could be the opportunity for a new Burning. And that you found her first in the forges only increases my concern."

"Have her killed then and be done with it," Silwa said roughly.

"No. Not yet. I must see her first. I must be sure that she is a fire element." Zorah stepped away from the table littered with the maps of Firefaire. "She shouldn't have happened," Zorah whispered vehemently. "I would have known. I would have felt it." Her voice trembled slightly. "Find her," she said to Gonmer. "I must see her and Read the truth for myself."

Antoni stepped away from the table and bowed quickly. "Perhaps you will excuse me as well, Madam? If I am no longer needed, there are other matters requiring my attention." The room was cool, so Lais wondered why the Adviser's forehead was suddenly shiny with sweat. Zorah nodded impatiently, dismissing him without a glance.

Gonmer motioned to Lais, and she barely had the time to gather the rolls of maps from the table before Gonmer had turned on her heel and was making for the door. Z'blood, Lais swore miserably under her breath. She crumpled the maps in a tight embrace as she hurried to follow after the Firstwatch.

# 13

As he hurried down Blessing Street, the Upright Man heard the hoarse cries of the lighterman announcing the hour of the second watch. His silk scarf was firmly tied over his face, a broad-brimmed hat pulled low over his brow, and his black cloak snapped behind him. It was late afternoon and his shadow lengthened behind him. Several taverns had trimmed their window lamps or started small bonfires outside the doors over which were roasting sausages and soft-shelled nuts. From the open windows above, whores called down invitations to the rushing figure of the Upright Man. One woman stepped forward from the doorway of the Bawd's Rest and blocked his path, her hips thrust forward and her smile leering.

"Oy, dearie, what's the hurry? Celebrate with me, then."

"Leave off," he growled in reply, stepping around her.

She clutched his arm, and he caught the pungent smell of her body, smoke and sweat mingled with a heavy perfume. He turned angrily, pausing long enough to look her over first. She had red hennaed hair that earlier might have been curled and dressed but by the late afternoon had become stringy. Her face was powdered white, but the powder stopped at her jawline, and her neck showed rings of grime in the folds.

"That's it, dearie, get an eyeful," she encouraged him and bent over just enough so that he could see her breasts. The partially opened corset revealed the rounded curves, her brown nipples like small buds amidst the lace. She inched closer. "You can keep your scarf on," she breathed. "I like a bit o' mystery." Her breath smelled of ale and cheap brandy, and he saw that she'd only a few good teeth remaining in her mouth.

He reeled back, rudely knocking her arm away. "Fuck off, you old cow."

"Shithead," she spat, as if he were something unpleasant scuffing her boot. "It's probably bent anyway," she yelled after him.

The Upright Man continued, not bothering to answer the

142

whore's charge. Another time and he might have had her scaffered for that insult. But not now. There was too much at stake and time was short. The whole Keep had hummed excitedly with the news of the red-haired thief that resembled the Queen. And the promise of a handsome reward for her capture had spurred many a young, ambitious noble into the streets of Beldan. Ugly rumors were already circulating, even among the most dignified of Sileans about the Queen's secret life in Beldan's streets as a petty snitch. Though it was a malicious story to them, a chance to insult the Queen, the Upright Man was familiar with the tale. He smiled behind the black silk scarf. If only those arrogant Sileans had known to whom they nattered their gossip. He had a hand in every one of their coffers, all their precious trinkets he had stolen away and they never knew, never suspected him. Upright he was to them, noble society. And neither the Readers nor the Fire Queen herself had ever sensed the Oran magic that laced his blood and fueled his ambitions. Ambitions which the fire-haired thief would realize for him, he thought, seized by the sudden urgency of his desires.

The Queen might have the Silean Guard to do her searching, but the Upright Man was not without his own little army to command. The girl was a street snitch. A coin or two in the hand of Ratcatcher and a promise of double the reward offered by the Queen would prick him and his Flock into action. They wouldn't mind in the least that it was one of their own kind they were betraying. That greedy little bastard Ratcatcher would sell his own mother to the Upright Man if he hadn't already done so to someone else.

The Upright Man turned down Blindman's Row draped in the darkness of the narrow street. Overhead, on either side of the alley, rickety balconies leaned so far out as to almost touch. A canopy of sagging wood permitted only tiny shafts of light, which were quickly swallowed by the deep shadows of the recessed walls. From between stacked barrels filled with cloth rags a stray dog growled, stiff legged, at the Upright Man. The Upright Man didn't turn at the sound but tapped his slender hand along his thigh. The ground rumbled slightly, and the barrels collapsed on the dog, burying it. The Upright Man smiled without stopping, as behind him the growls had changed into piercing yelps.

Out of Blindman's Row he turned into Knacker Alley. The kitchen door to a tavern opened briefly, the light describing a rectangle on the muddy ground. The Upright Man instantly slowed his step. A serving girl tossed a bucket of kitchen scraps into the alley before she quickly shut the door again. The Upright Man continued, picking his way carefully around the stinking garbage, aware of the animal eyes that suddenly blinked above in the tavern's eaves. With a boastful squeaking and clicking of yellow teeth, rats crept down the walls of the tavern and shambled over to the garbage. Farther down the alley, the Upright Man dodged the outstretched legs of a beggar, the wrapped feet splayed out in opposite directions. His back leaned against the wall, and his head was muffled in rags. Only the raspy snoring told the Upright Man that the skeletal creature was even alive. His boot kicked away a bottle of brandy, the glass tinkling as it smashed against a loose cobblestone. In his sleep the beggar whimpered and curled into a tight ball.

Almost there, the Upright Man whispered to himself. He hated coming here before dusk. But it was his only chance, and he didn't want to risk losing the girl to some bastard of a Guardsman. Ratcatcher should be in his burrow. The Flocks had been out all morning, but with the extra Guard searching for the red-haired girl, Ratcatcher would have brought them back here to wait it out. If he was smart.

The alley came to a dead end, blocked by a crumbling brick wall. Along the wall was leaning a broken barrow cart. Beneath the peeling boards was a nest of rags, a bed for the lookout. The Upright Man now slowed his step as he approached the wall. A small rat-faced boy with pocked skin poked his head out, relief evident in his squinty stare.

"Oy, Cully, is he in?" the Upright Man asked.

"Aye," Cully answered. "Flock's in, too, sir. Too many butcherboys to do any serious snitching. We come away from Market Square 'afore any wuz snagged."

"Sensible," said the Upright Man and turned to the building just on the left that leaned its tired face against the brick wall. In the upper reaches, broken shutters dangled from rusted hinges. They creaked lightly, miserable with age. The Upright Man opened a wooden door, scarred and pitted with a thousand cuts from the game of knife toss. He stepped inside the empty hall and turned right, ducking his head as he passed through a low-ceilinged hallway that smelled of urine and wood rot. Turning again to the right he reached for the latch of yet another door, this one opening out onto a small central courtyard that was located on the other side of the brick wall.

The Upright Man stepped into the courtyard, his gaze darting quickly to see who among the Flocks was present. He touched his scarf lightly, to reassure himself that it concealed his features.

The courtyard was bordered on two sides by identical brick walls and on the other two sides by the ramshackled facades of two decrepit buildings. They were little more than husks, many of the interior walls having crumbled or been torn down. In winter and in rain the abandoned buildings served as a warren for Ratcatcher and his Flock, where they bedded down amid the broken beams and rotting wood. But for the most they preferred to sleep outside, huddled around the small fire that Ratcatcher let them keep burning. There was more safety and fewer parasites in the open air than in the close, damp quarters of the ancient buildings.

The Upright Man smiled to himself to see the Flock gathered now around the fire, their faces glum and bored. Not a way to spend Firefaire, he mused. They'd jump at his offer. Nicker sat cross-legged and poked the fire, his red hat pushed back and a scowl on his face. Next to him Pug picked her nose and wiped it on the hem of her skirt. Dew Drop rested, his chin cupped in his hands. A cough lifted his scrawny shoulders. Except for Pug none of the dells were here. Off whoring for the day, the Upright Man guessed. In one corner, beneath an overhang decorated with the hanging cages of rats skittering at each other, Twofingers and Slake played a game of Knucklebones, shouting and cursing when the dice fell the wrong way. Only Dogsbody sat alone, his arms wrapped around his knees, his eyes watchful. The Upright Man noted it and wondered how long before Ratcatcher culled him from the Flock.

Nicker saw him approach and scrambled to his feet. "Oy!" he shouted over to Twofingers. "Get Ratcatcher."

"Get 'im yerself," the boy snarled back and then looked up to see the Upright Man warming his hands over the fire. "Frigging shit," he swore softly and grabbed his winnings before leaving the game. He slipped into a door, calling loudly as he went.

A moment later Ratcatcher came out, and the Upright Man understood why Twofingers had yelled on entering. No doubt the bastard didn't want to be disturbed in his sport. Ratcatcher's trousers were still half-buttoned, his face flushed and beaded with sweat. He looked annoyed. Behind him a boy not older than ten crept out, clutching at the tears in his shirt and holding what remained of his own trousers. His skin was chalk white, and his eyes stark with fear and pain. There was blood at the corners of his mouth. He slunk along the wall and tried to hide himself amid the clutter of accumulated trash. A new one, the Upright Man

**145**

thought without feeling, paying his dues to the Flock leader.

As Ratcatcher approached him, his pitdog jogged over on its stubby legs to join him, whining expectantly at his master. Ratcatcher swore and kicked the dog away.

"There ain't much to show you," Ratcatcher said, tucking in his shirt. "Ain't been able to prig much this day."

"I didn't come here for that," the Upright Man started.

Ratcatcher gave him a sly look. "Something else, then. Maybe more tasty?"

"That depends on whether you know where to find it. I want a certain dell—"

"They're working now, trying to make up the tally for our rotten scores."

"Not one of your dells," the Upright Man said harshly. Ratcatcher looked offended.

"The Guards have been chasing after a red-haired dell."

Dew Drop sniggered. "These days that's about every other 'un, ain't it?"

"This one's a snitch."

"My Flock?" demanded Ratcatcher. His glance roved along the building, trying to find the corner where the new boy crouched.

"No. No one's Flock. She's a queer chinker. Loner. Until recently, most figured she was a boy. Disguised herself with a leather cap. Settled often at Crier's Forge."

Ratcatcher's eyes snapped back to the Upright Man, a look of surprise visible on his face. "Jobber?"

"Know her?"

"Know him, anyway. Frigging little shithead. Raised with a vagger, I hear. Considered himself too naffy to join up with a Flock. Good with the clubbers though, gives a decent brangle. Lost more than one of my Flock trying to convince him to join up."

"Sounds like the dell I want. There's a reward out for her capture."

"Don't say," Ratcatcher's eyes twinkled with greed. Nicker straightened his stance and leaned in to hear. Pug gave her nose a final wipe and looked up. Even Slake ignored the dice, letting Twofingers snitch a copper from off the betting pile.

"Two strings of gold queens."

The Flock whistled and clapped its approval.

"Find her for me and I'll double the reward," the Upright Man said and stunned them into silence again. "But I want her alive. Do you understand?"

Ratcatcher shook his head and sucked on his long front teeth. "Can't bring Jobber in without a brangle you know. He—she," he corrected himself with a giggle, "ain't going to come along without a fuss."

"I don't care how you do it, but the dell must be alive." The Upright Man stepped up close to Ratcatcher, his crow-black eyes glaring over the scarf. He spoke in a low throaty whisper. "And if you kill her or bleed her too much so's she's no good to me, I'll peel you, like rotten fruit, piece by piece and feed it to your rats. Am I clear?"

"I got it," Ratcatcher replied steadily. "I ain't never let you down before."

The Upright Man eased back. "And the day you do will be your last." The Upright Man waited, allowing the threat to penetrate Ratcatcher's private thoughts. Oh yes, he reminded himself as he watched fear pinch Ratcatcher's face, you saw how Sparrow cocked up his toes at the end, didn't you? Beneath the mask the Upright Man smiled and let a suggestion of it reach his eyes. His voice was pleasant when he spoke. "Before I'm gone, let's see what you've managed to pull in today."

Ratcatcher motioned to Nicker to bring out the bag of stolen goods. As he did Ratcatcher saw Dogsbody ease away from the wall and slip through the door. He grabbed Nicker by the collar. "Go on after Dogsbody. He's scampered without my permission. Figure he's gone to warn Jobber, seeing how's they've been palsy of late." Nicker nodded gravely and pulling the red cap down over his brow followed after Dogsbody.

"Oh, she's ours," Ratcatcher said smacking his lips and then grinning with relief. "No doubt to it. I'll have her 'afore end of second watch."

"A fine boast," said the Upright Man softly, but beneath his mask he could taste the warm salt flavor of blood and imagine the fierce bounty of power threading in his veins. Just this final meal, he thought to himself, and even the Fire Queen would be vulnerable to him.

Kai entered the alley cautiously like a soldier venturing into enemy terrain. It had taken most of the morning to work up her courage to face Ratcatcher, despite her brave words to the Waterlings. But face him she would, to protect her Flock.

They were only children. It was bad enough they were perse-

**147**

cuted by the Readers. It was a queer twist of fate, Kai thought, that she had been born a Reader. Her mother had been a scullery maid at a big house. A Reader lad got her pregnant, and fearing to remain there, she had returned to the streets to have her child. The Reading had come naturally, the same as breathing. Kai stared, awed by the auras that glowed with the brilliance of stars: the deep blue of the water elements, green for the earth elements, and the air elements shimmering like a diamond's sparkle. And Kai had learned that of all the Orans possessed of magic, only Readers cast no aura. They could see, but not be seen. But in Oran's children the light always shone even when the children struggled to die at the end of the noose. Those were the times when Kai cursed the Fire Queen and cursed her gift. Cursed the sight that, while it didn't betray her to other Readers, enabled her to see the judgment of death that waited for others.

Kai tried to stop Reading. But it was impossible. Knowing that she could only tempted her to search the faces of those she met, surprised by the light that flared with such beauty even in the wretched, dirty faces of the street poor. She had grown up among the streets of Beldan, sullen and miserable, trapped between the commonness of public executions and the burden of being able to Read that fate in a child's future. You never swung the rope, she told herself, but then you never cut it either, she would argue back.

It was one night, rowing her skiff down river just letting the current carry her to the Ribbons, that she heard a baby crying in the dark tunnels that opened into the riverwall. She tied her skiff to a ring in the riverwall and climbed into the dark reaches of the tunnels, following the infant's cries. That was Little Mag. The mother must have known and had abandoned her in the tunnels. In the pitch dark maze of the tunnels, Kai found her by Reading the shadows until she was startled by the piercing blue shimmer of her aura. She carried the girl home to the Ribbons and set her mind on a new course. She'd find them, pluck them right out of the streets like the shells cast up after a storm. And she would gather them into a Flock.

That's how the Waterlings had grown. Child after child, her Reading them, taking them under her wing and leading them down to the relative safety of the tunnels. She knew enough to keep the special nature of her Flock a secret. And thinking on it realized she would have less trouble were she to acquire children without magic as well. Those who get into places that would not cause them any extra danger. So she joined the others, Stickit,

Digger and Terridown, to her Flock for appearance' sake.

None so far, she thought, knew the truth about the Waterlings. But children were unpredictable, and Kai wondered whether or not she had been able to impress them with the need for silence. Had Squat told on himself? Had he squealed on the others as well? Perhaps all of them had been charmed with tales into squealing on themselves. What promises, she wondered, could separate the Waterlings from their secrets? Almost anything, she spat disgustedly. The promise of more food, of a life above ground, money even. Already Slipper was growing restive, unhappy beneath the city streets, chaffing at the tight reins Kai held on all of them. And Finch, after him, defying her orders. What was she to do with her Flock as they grew older, less willing to have her protection and more at risk than before. And for a long awful moment Kai wondered whether she had done her Flock a disservice after all, had raised them only until such time as another unknown predator could trick them into death. Kai ground her teeth. One problem at a time, she thought. First, there's Ratcatcher to deal with.

Kai checked her pockets for the dagger she carried. It was a small weapon to wear into Ratcatcher's burrow. She hesitated, but the memory of Squat's white, bloodless face forced her to press forward. She wiped her sweating palms on her skirts, her heart beating furiously.

With an easy gait, she strolled to the wall and waited for Cully to poke out his head from under the broken barrow.

"Oy, I want to see Ratcatcher," she said.

"Who's to call?"

"Kai, from the Waterlings."

His face disappeared a moment, and she knew he bent to look through the spyhole in the wall.

"He's busy. Come back after he's through."

"Getting buggered again, is he?" she sneered.

"Jealous?" Cully answered, spitting into the alley.

"Depends. Who's the stick giving it to him?"

Cully laughed. "Go on, be rude if you like. But it's no less than the Upright Man himself, come down to give our boy Rat a thump on the back for a job well done."

"Don't say?" Kai answered calmly. Her hair untwisted from its knot and rolled down her back.

"I do say. So bugger off now 'til he's done his business."

"Do us a trick, Cully, and let me have a wink at the Upright Man."

"Nah, can't do that."

"Just a peep. Through yer spyhole there."

"You'd come under here with me?" Cully asked, leering slightly.

Kai kept her face smooth, though her stomach did a little dance of disgust.

"Sure, dearie. Just give us a wink."

Cully hesitated and then shrugged. "Come on down," he said and motioned with his hand for her to join him.

Kai bent down on all fours and crawled under the broken barrow. Cully's nest stank, the smell worse to her than the rank odors of the tunnels. He snuggled close to her, his lips pressed against her ear.

"Go on, dearie," he breathed in her ear. "Have a look."

Kai gritted her teeth again as Cully's hand slid along her back and came to rest on her upturned bottom. He squeezed, his fingers digging into her flesh. Her skin prickled, crawled at his touch, but she tried to ignore it as she put her eye to the spyhole.

She saw Ratcatcher talking to a well-dressed man, his black cape draped to the tops of his glossy black boots. And she saw the scarf tied around his face hiding all but his eyes. No wonder Mole had been frightened, she thought. Those eyes... smoldering like a coal fire, black and red. He leaned his head down, to hear some whispered message from Ratcatcher. Kai settled her mind and concentrated. He was hard to see through the narrow chink of the spyhole, but she trained her gaze forward to view the shadowy figure of the Upright Man. Her eyes unfocused, and she could feel the humming of power in her chest, rising with a fluttering touch to the backs of her eyes. The edges of his body rippled, the light oddly diffused. She held her breath waiting for the Reader's vision to show her. At the same moment Cully, taking advantage of her prone posture, slid his grubby hand under her skirt and grabbed her roughly high up on the inside of her thigh.

Kai roared with anger as her concentration was abruptly shattered. Pain lanced through her skull, the Reader's vision breaking like splinters of flying glass. She wheeled around and tried to slap Cully hard on the side of his head. But the quarters were tight beneath the barrow, and all she succeeded in hitting was her head on the roof of the barrow. Pain blossomed anew, blinding her, and she shrieked, drawing her legs up to shut out the groping hand. She kicked him and her hands clawed at his head.

"Frigging little shit . . ." she shouted, and he laughed as he ducked her blows and made another lunge for her.

The door to the alley creaked opened and they both stopped, suddenly frozen in mute fear. Cully slapped a hand over her mouth, though she wouldn't have let her presence be known at any cost. Stones cut into her back where Cully's weight pressed down on her. Kai heard the scrunching of boots, and turning her head slightly, she peeked out from beneath the barrow and saw the black heels of the Upright Man's boots as he headed out of the alley. They didn't speak as the Upright Man departed but held themselves quiet and motionless as the cobblestones. Not until she saw the Upright Man turn into Blindman's Row did Kai fling Cully's hand from her mouth and punch him hard in the face, drawing blood from his nose. He rolled off her groaning, and she climbed out from under the barrow, shaking her skirts as if they harbored a spider. She had Read something in the Upright Man; she had almost seen it before Cully had wrenched her away. Now Kai had one thought only, and she stormed off to follow the Upright Man, leaving Cully behind cursing his bloodied nose.

# 14

"That's it, I'm off," said Jobber with finality as she folded the black dress and laid it across a barrel of potatoes stored in sand. She leaned down and picked up her vest, slipping her arms into it and tying the lacings in the front.

"Ah no, not yet," Lirrel protested.

"I must. I've got to see someone," Jobber answered.

"I'm coming with you, then," Lirrel insisted and started taking off her black Ghazali skirts.

"No, you ain't."

"Yes, I am."

"No."

"Yes."

Jobber eyes narrowed. "Now look here. I don't want nobody with me on the street, have you got that? I may need to make some fast moves, and I don't want someone dragging behind me."

"I can assure you I won't be dragging. And what's more I probably see a lot better in the dark than you do. It's in my eyes, you know," Lirrel answered primly, tossing back her black hair.

They were alone in the small dressing room, the rest of the Ghazali dancers still finishing their meal in the commons room. After the last performance Lirrel had suggested quietly that they slip out before anyone took too careful notice of Jobber. A brown smudge under her eye had worn away, revealing the pale skin underneath. As it was, Jobber had nearly leapt off the stage when a squad of Silean Guards entered the Breaking Fish and sat down to drink. They had tried to appear as if it were their custom to drink here, as if they intended only to receive refreshments and entertainment. But Jobber had seen how they had questioned the inn keeper and how they watched the doorway and the crowd, scanning carefully for signs of Jobber's red hair. Jobber had started to slide away from the stage, but Lirrel had held her fast by the hem of her dress. "Sit still!" she whispered in her ear. "If you go now the whole room will know it." Jobber stayed on the stage but every muscle and nerve was tensed, ready to spring away at the first sign of trouble. As soon as the song ended and Lirrel had whispered to Zia that they were leaving, Jobber moved quickly off the stage and into the kitchens. There she realized she had been clenching her teeth. Her jaw ached and she felt the vague stirrings of a headache. Ale would help chase it away.

"Look, I don't need any more of your help," Jobber argued.

"Oh, I'm sure you're right," Lirrel said as she stood in her black sleeveless shift, hands resting on her slim hips. "I'm not suggesting I help. What about your hair?"

"What about it? It'll be dark soon. No one'll notice."

"And tomorrow?"

"I don't think that far ahead."

"No, I can see that. Just wait, Jobber, before you go until I get this on." Lirrel reached into a large sack and pulled out a light blue wool skirt with green felt bands running along the hem. She shook it out and put it on.

"Look more like a Beldan housemaid in that, except for your eyes that is," Jobber said, watching Lirrel dress.

"That's the idea," Lirrel answered, tucking in a white blouse. She put on the matching blue bodice, lacing it up in front with green ribbons. "I told you Ghazali women do not go out alone dressed as Ghazali. But there's nothing wrong with going out as someone else. And as you say, it'll be dark soon. No one will notice the color of my eyes."

"I don't get it."

"We're performers. Sometimes it's important to get a feel of the crowd in order to know what people want to hear. Best way to do that is to become part of the crowd. And sometimes a person needs a disguise if they are *ghazat*.

"Yeah, I heard you say that word before, but I don't know what it means." Jobber was watching Lirrel, fascinated. The rituals of female dressing were unknown to her, and she couldn't take her eyes off Lirrel drawing up the dark stockings, combing out her long black hair and tying it into a single long braid twisted with blue ribbons and settling an embroidered shawl over her shoulders, crisscrossing the ends over her waist in front and then knotting it in the back. Every movement was supple, the graceful bend in her waist, the slim arms reaching up to comb the silky black hair. Jobber felt the stirrings of envy, thinking of her own ragged frame. She had no female grace. Not like Lirrel, who made even dressing seem like a dance.

"*Ghazat*," Lirrel was saying, "is an old word. It used to mean

**153**

pilgrim. Before the Burning every Ghazali went on a journey throughout Oran to study at the sites of power and to compose stories, poetry and collect local histories. Recitation and singing at one time were the second most important part of our performances."

"What was the first?" asked Jobber, scratching her temple. Brown bark cream stuck under her fingernails, and she wiped it off on her trousers.

Lirrel looked up at Jobber momentarily shocked. "The Ghazali were peacekeepers. Witnesses to disputes. Ghazalis were expected, based on their collected knowledge of the past, to offer a judgment and settle those disputes. The songs and dances that came afterward were to inspire a return to harmony. Didn't you know that?"

"Why should I?" replied Jobber, nettled by Lirrel's academic tone.

"Well, the Ghazali people were very important in Oran."

"Once. But now they play a tavern show. And ain't nobody asks their opinion on the price of cloth."

"That's true," Lirrel agreed. "Though we witness misery and deceit, we have little opportunities to practice as peacekeepers."

Jobber shrugged. "Look, I don't mean to speak ill of you and yours, it's just that . . . well times are different, ain't they? Sileans pass judgments now. Hard ones, I might add, and the only music done afterward is the singing of gold and silver chinkers falling into Silean coffers."

"But the time will come again when Orans will need Ghazali peacekeepers, and when that happens there must be some among us who have not forgotten what it is to be Ghazali and who will carry on our traditions."

"I'd rather carry the chinkers," Jobber snorted and then felt embarrassed being so rude. She could see from the serious expression on Lirrel's face that it was important to Lirrel. And after having spent the day listening to the haunting voice of Lirrel's flute, Jobber thought it possible that the Ghazalis once might have accomplished so difficult a task as bringing peace to quarrels. "Oy, what do I know," she said softly and shrugged her shoulders. "I'm a Beldan street snitch. I run around ducking and hiding and never going anywhere." She laughed at herself and saw Lirrel begin to smile. "Like a clapperhead with one foot nailed to the ground running about in a circle."

Lirrel laughed and Jobber was pleased to hear the sound. "It's hard to imagine someone as resourceful as yourself nailed down.

**154**

But I haven't finished my explanation of *ghazat*."

Jobber winced inwardly, not really caring to hear the rest. Too much like talking to a vagger, with their long, windy sentences and gloomy tattooed faces. Growler was the only vagger she'd ever known who held his tongue.

"The Fire Queen has forbidden pilgrimages," Lirrel continued. "And then, too, the Sileans don't like our nomadic life. It makes it hard for them to keep us under their thumb where they can count us like so many goats. So *ghazat* now means someone who is escaping persecution, running away from the Readers or the Silean Guard. I would say, in your present situation, that you illustrate both possibilities." Lirrel searched the floor until she found an old pair of clogs. Slipping them on she said, "There, I'm ready."

"Why do you want to come with me?" Jobber asked.

"I like you."

Jobber snorted. "You don't know me at all."

"Really?" From the pocket of her skirt Lirrel pulled out a string of coppers. "I've two more strings in here. My share for playing today. Help me spend them."

Jobber smiled back at Lirrel. "I guess you do know me. I'd never say no to an offer like that. All right then you can come. But not in those," and she pointed to Lirrel's wooden clogs.

"What's the matter with these?" Lirrel asked, peering at her feet.

"Can't run in them."

"Hmm, I suppose you're right." She slipped them off and put on a pair of soft-soled black shoes. "Better?" she asked as she tied the laces.

"Much."

"And what about your hair?"

Jobber threw her arms in the air. "Frigging hair," she cursed.

"Here, I've just the thing." Lirrel rummaged through another bag, at last drawing out a heavy wool Islander's cap. The turned-up brim was knitted with a pattern of intertwining fish. Jobber took it uncertainly and pulled it on over her head. Without the glowing nimbus of hair, her face transformed, becoming long and thin and without a distinct sex.

"Better?" Jobber asked, tucking the last of the red-gold hair into the black cap.

"Much," answered Lirrel. "Here's a riddle for you," she said suddenly. "When she goes out, she wears a red cloak and when she comes back, she wears a black one."

"Well that's easy," Jobber said frowning. "It's me, ain't it? My hair under this black hat."

"You're half-right. The real answer is a spark from the fire, though it would seem to describe you as well." She smiled once more and then added, murmuring half to herself, "Beldan's fire."

"Why'd you say that?" Jobber snapped, chilled by the familiar words.

Lirrel looked confused, and then apologetic. "I'm sorry. I don't know. It was just there . . . hanging in the air, so I said it. I didn't mean anything by it."

Jobber faced Lirrel squarely, searching the pearl-colored eyes.

"It's the truth, Jobber. Perhaps it's from an old song that seemed appropriate."

"Yeah, yeah, sure," Jobber said, willing to be convinced. "Someone I used to know. . ." she started but didn't finish. Lirrel didn't ask her to and for that Jobber was grateful.

Lirrel still held the strings of coppers in her small brown hands. Jobber shrugged the tension from her shoulders and grinned.

"Oy, I've got a riddle for you, then."

"All right," Lirrel said, looking relieved.

"No fair using your whatever." Jobber circled a finger near her temple to indicate Lirrel's skill at picking thoughts from the air.

"Agreed," Lirrel laughed and covered her ears as if it would help.

"What is it that Silean lords keep in their pockets and Oran beggars throw away?"

Lirrel frowned, puzzled.

"Do you know?" Jobber asked excitedly.

"No, what's the answer?"

"Snot from their noses. Sileans always got those bits of cloth they're sneezing into—"

"*Tcha*, Jobber, you're disgusting."

"Yeah, I'm also thirsty. Come on then, let's get a drink. But not here," she added quickly, giving a little shudder. "Frigging butcherboys are too thick out there."

Lirrel picked up her flute and slipped in into the long pocket of her skirt. They left by the back door of the Breaking Fish, stepping quietly into the alley. Jobber peered through the darkness, but there was no one; not even the cats remained.

As they sauntered out of the alley and turned into HurryDown Road, they were greeted by the festival madness. Music and laughter drifted from the open doors of taverns. Small bands of musicians gathered on street corners, playing dance music for crowds of celebrating fair-goers. And everywhere the bonfires crackled, burning with bright orange flames and thick smoke, lighting the faces of the throng and casting frenzied shadows along the buildings. Twilight was falling into night, and the tops of the buildings made a jagged line against the fading blue sky.

Lirrel caught Jobber by the arm and tugged. Jobber never took her eyes from the street, the green pupils illuminated with the reflections of flickering flames. "Show me the city," Lirrel shouted in Jobber's ear, trying to be heard over a loud concertina and a strident fiddle. "Show me Beldan."

Jobber looked down at her, her face alive with pleasure. "Got the time?"

Lirrel bobbed her head. *"Aha!*. They expect me when they see me."

"What do you want to see?"

"You choose."

Jobber motioned with her head and veered sharply to the other side of the street. "This way," Jobber shouted, cutting a path through a party of dancers that were having trouble keeping to the complicated pattern of their dance. A couple turned the wrong way and collided with another pair of dancers. An argument erupted immediately, the men shouting first at each other and then at the musicians. Other couples prepared to join in the confrontation. The fiddler kept on playing, his mouth opened wide as he laughed showing teeth yellowed from tobacco. The concertina player set down his instrument and rolled up his sleeves.

Jobber cast a quick glance behind, pleased to see Lirrel following easily, slipping deftly in between the arguing couples. And in that glance Jobber noted the difference between them. Jobber had applied force, nudging and prodding along the way to make her path through the crowds. But Lirrel had brushed past them with no more force than a breeze blowing its way through the trees. People seemed to bend away from her almost without seeing her or sensing the disruption. Jobber clicked her tongue in admiration before slowing down to wait for Lirrel on the other side of the street. She'd do all right for herself. Z'blood, Jobber swore happily, thinking of Lirrel's bright coppers, she might even be fun to have around, as long as she didn't lecture.

"Frigging bastards. Couldn't find their arses in the dark!" Gonmer railed at the reports on her desk. The Guard was still out searching and still coming up empty handed. Beside the reports, the remains of Gonmer's untouched meal congealed with gray fat. A cup of tea had cooled and the surface shone slick and oily. Lais stood a respectful distance away, trying her best, Gonmer knew, to remain unnoticed. Gonmer had been furious all day. And when she wasn't lashing out at the Guard or snapping orders to Lais, she found herself brooding. Gonmer stared moodily at the floor, a hand wrapped around the hilt of her sword.

"One child with hair red enough to light the Great Bonfire, and they can't find her." Gonmer shook her head. The thief would be caught eventually and then hanged. So why did it bother her? she thought with annoyance. It bothered her like the stinging wound on her belly. She pressed a hand to it, wincing slightly. The muscles were stiff and every movement caused her to suck in her breath at the suddenness of the pain. Gonmer argued with herself. The girl was a street thief and with the old power. And with that hair, probably a fire element. That made her dangerous far beyond the pettiness of pickpocketing.

Gonmer looked up and saw Lais standing at attention. The thief was close in age to Lais. Gonmer saw the street girl again surrounded by the burning hair and her face as animated as a fox. She was smart, fast-thinking on her feet. Gonmer studied Lais and experienced disappointment. With her cropped hair and blank expression, Lais resembled a puppet; a wooden face carved to reveal nothing.

But that was the training, wasn't it? Gonmer reminded herself. To keep one's mind like calm water, smooth without a ripple, ready to reflect any danger and react swiftly. But had training turned her spirit to wood as well, Gonmer wondered. No, she thought, martial training didn't do that. After all it was clear that the street thief had been trained to fight, and she had been very much alive. No, Gonmer thought sourly, it was the protocol, the rules and regulations of the Fire Queen and her Silean court that smothered the fighter's spirit like a damp blanket over a fire. They were no more than warrior puppets waiting, always waiting, for the Fire Queen to pull the strings.

Quite suddenly Gonmer was seized with anger. She glared at Lais, Lais stared back, eyes opaque, unwavering. Gonmer approached closer, her eyes boring into the expressionless face, waiting to see some spark of emotion. There, for an instant the lips parted in surprise. Then Gonmer's fury doubled as she watched Lais exert self-control, withdraw emotionally, straining to be as Gonmer had taught her. Gonmer pulled her sword and the steel shimmered like a strand of water. Lais's eyes widened, but she held to her stance. Gonmer brought the blade up, the edge close to Lais's neck. I could cut it off, she thought, amazement riding her fury. I have trained her so well that she would never, not even to protect her own life, break with discipline.

Gonmer brought the sword down and returned it silently to its scabbard. As she did, her gaze fell on Lais's knees. They were trembling. She exhaled, exhausted suddenly by her anger and frustration. What in Zorah's name was she doing terrorizing her own page? She looked up again at Lais and saw where sweat beaded her forehead.

"Come on," Gonmer said hoarsely. "You and I know the city better than most of the Guard. I'm not going to sit here and wait while they follow their arses. Get your cloak, we're going out ourselves." She turned away then and busied herself with her own cloak. Behind her she heard the muffled sounds of Lais dressing. Without turning around she asked, "Ready?"

"Yes, Firstwatch," came the reply.

Gonmer nodded and led the way out the door. "We'll look around Market Square first, and then later I want to go to Crier's Forge again," she said as they left the room. "I have a feeling Master Donal hasn't told us everything he knows."

Behind Gonmer's retreating figure, Lais let out a long, slow breath, hoping not to be heard. Little orbs of yellow light danced at the edges of her vision. Fear made her light-headed. She concentrated on walking smoothly, one foot before the other, as she followed the Firstwatch. She wished she could stop her hands from shaking.

What was that all about? Lais flinched, the hairs on the nape of her neck rising as she thought on the steel's edge a mere whisper from her skin. Had the Firstwatch been testing her? Had she passed? she wondered as they left through the main gate and into the cool spring night.

Lais looked up at the blue-green stars twinkling in the sky. The yellow spots faded as she sucked in the fresh air. Lais stared down at the spreading city, hearing the distant murmur of Fire-faire celebrations. In one black rectangle hundreds of small fires burned like a field of orange flowers. The Hiring Fields sending up prayers and hopes with the smoke of their fires. Lais watched a wisp of smoke curl and reach like a thread to the sky. She hoped she had done the right thing.

• • •

Kai jerked her body flat against a door, the hard wood thudding painfully against her shoulders. She was almost certain the Upright Man hadn't seen her, but she wasn't so sure about Bonesnip. She peered around doorways, ready at the same time to jerk her head back in case she should be spotted.

She had followed close behind the Upright Man. As he traveled through the city, he stopped briefly here and there to give messages to street snitches and beggars. Now at the docks she watched puzzled as the Upright Man laid a heavy hand on Bonesnip's shoulder, leaning down close to speak in his ear. Bonesnip had looked up, and just before she hid herself in the doorway, Kai had seen the look of surprise flash across his craggy face. But no alarm had been sounded and she ventured another peek. The Upright Man was moving again, his cloak flapping down another street. Bonesnip was rousing his Flock, sending them scattering through the alleys. Kai swore and running close to the shadows picked up his trail again.

It had been that way for the better part of an hour. She'd been trying to use her Reader's sight on him, but he had never remained in one place long enough. He was in a hurry all right, she cursed, wondering what urged him with such haste. She followed down one alley and at the end of it stopped, confused. He had disappeared. She stood in the empty alley searching in both directions. Nothing. Angrily she stamped her foot. Then a door creaked open, the light trickling into the street. Kai saw the toe of one black boot, and without waiting to see the rest, she flung herself behind a pair of fishing nets laid out to dry. She crouched as close to the wall as she could, hearing the rapid banging of her heart. He passed her, and his step slowed, hesitating. Kai held her breath, slouching her frame into a tighter ball.

The Upright Man stopped and turned, his head cocked as if listening. Kai cursed her pounding heart, certain that somehow the Upright Man could hear it in the dark. He took one step in her direction and then froze as the shrill cry of the Silean alarm whistle distracted him. He looked around, his head raised like a wolf scenting the air. Without another pause, he turned and fled down the alley, while behind him Kai moaned softly with relief. Scrambling to her feet once more, she followed.

The Upright Man doubled back from the docks and now strode quickly up Blessing Street. From the doorway of the Raven a young whore appeared and clung to his arm. Kai watched as the woman spoke to the Upright Man, her glance darting fearfully around the street. The Upright Man reached into his cloak and handed the clinging woman some coins. She grabbed them and ducked back into the tavern. Kai frowned. For what had he paid the whore?

Business on Blessing Street was lively, and Kai had an easier time of hiding amid the crowded streets, though a man tried to stop her, thinking she was there to whore. She ignored him, and when he insisted, she shoved him away angrily, her eyes fixed on the black cloak of the Upright Man. He veered suddenly down a small alley that Kai guessed ran behind the taverns of Blessing Street. Maybe he was meeting the whore there, she thought with mixed emotions. While she didn't much want to watch the Upright Man with his whore, she reasoned at least he'd stay in one place long enough for her to Read him.

The Upright Man stopped near the back door of the Raven, and a moment later the whore appeared. She handed him something wrapped in a white cloth and disappeared inside again. The Upright Man took the bundle, sniffing it. Then he tucked it under his arm and continued down the alley.

He turned once more down a narrow flight of steps that led to a small passageway burrowed beneath two old buildings, their upper reaches bricked together. Kai knew the place and shivered. It was a short length of dark tunnel running beneath the old buildings, smelling dankly of wet stone. Two whores had been murdered there recently, and despite their screams, each time the killer had escaped through the passageway and out again into the busy streets. Now at each end of the passageway a torch spluttered, casting ovals of light into the dark tunnel.

Kai hesitated. If she followed him into the passageway, there would be no place to hide. She waited on the steps, listening to his footsteps echoing faintly in the passageway. They stopped abruptly, and there was a moment of silence. And then Kai heard the raspy mewling of an infant.

Realization touched her with an icy hand, and her skin was pricked with horror. She reached into her pocket for the knife. Adrenaline spread the cold fear in her veins, and her heart beat furiously. The infant gave a shrill cry, and Kai bolted down the stairs to the entrance of the passageway.

She stepped silently into the passageway and saw the broad blackness of the Upright Man's back, his head bent over something in his arms. Without waiting, she Read him. The colors boiled over his shoulders, flaring out in a wild erratic pattern: deep blue shifting into shades of green along his legs and arms; white light limning the edges of his bowed head. Only the red flame of the fire element was missing. She stared, her eyes straining at the seething light that curled away from him. All those colors. All those elements. Kai knew that he had done it: stolen the magic in their blood.

Rage sharpened her fear to a knife point as she released her Reader's vision. She drew her dagger from her pocket and approached him. "Bastard!" she hissed. "Blood-sucking bastard!"

The Upright Man looked up startled, peering over his shoulder at her. Beneath the white brow, his black eyes shone like obsidian, his pupils two sparks of red. He stood swaying, blood speckled on his opened mouth. His teeth gleamed in the black beard. He ran his tongue over his lips, and dropped the bundled infant. Kai eyes darted to it, seeing only a small upraised fist amidst the swaddling.

She wrenched her eyes back to the Upright Man and bared her teeth. Mist thickened in the air, spiraling upward from around his feet. He replaced the black scarf over his mouth and nose and turned to face her. He threw back one edge of his cloak and reached for his sword.

With a shriek Kai flung herself at him. She held the dagger in her hand, casting overhand to stab his heart. He twisted, knocking her arm away. But she rammed her body into him, latching her fingers around his scarf and yanking it free.

"Frigging bastard," she screamed at him, staring into his eyes, "I'll turn the screw to you. I'll kill you for what you done."

He roared and she heard the rumbling of cobblestones in the passageway. The ground beneath her feet buckled. He shoved her to one side, backhanding her as she stumbled. The dagger skittered free across the passageway. She staggered with the pain, shaking her head as the world rocked with waves, unbalancing her stance. She saw through the mist the snarling lips still touched with blood and the pinpoints of red in the black eyes. Then the glint of steel as the edge of the sword swung toward her. Screaming, Kai rolled to one side and heard the sword clang against the stone. Bricks on the wall rattled and then burst, the powdery red mortar coloring the mist. The sword rose again, and she rolled desperately to the other side, ducking her head.

But she moved too slowly, and the sword sliced an opening along one shoulder. Kai cried out as the blade scraped the bone and a fiery pain screeched down her arm. She slumped to the ground, air heaving from her chest, each breath exploding with fresh pain. Her hair clung wetly to the sides of her face, and blood from her wounded shoulder streamed across her throat and down her arm. She dragged herself away from the wall, expecting the final stroke of the Upright Man's sword against her neck. Through the rippling mist she saw the little dagger where it lay unused a short way off on the cobblestones.

Then Kai heard a gurgling noise, the sound of someone strangling. She lifted her head and saw the Upright Man, his body taut and shaking, his arms outstretched and rigid. The sword was still poised in his clenched fist but he seemed unable to move it. His black eyes rolled glaring white, his head arched back and a low howl issued from his throat.

"Z'blood," Kai gasped and wrenched herself along the ground away from him. She rolled her body, crying out as the gash on her shoulder pressed against the ground. With an outflung arm, she scrabbled to find the dagger. Her hand closed on the hilt and she drew it back.

She struggled to her feet, her good arm clutching the dagger as she rose unsteadily from the ground. Her shoulder throbbed with a loud, angry pain, but rage pushed her upward. She raised her head to the Upright Man, seeing in the pink and pearl glow of the mist his features. Within the black matt of his beard, his lips curled back over his teeth, stretched tight in a grimace. His eyes still glared unseeing. The howl was deepening in his throat, becoming louder and more visceral. His body shook violently, and Kai stared transfixed as his head craned farther backward.

She raised her dagger, weaving on her feet. But the Upright Man's body snapped forward. His head lunged toward Kai, his mouth open and gagging. The sword clattered to the ground and his hands flailed, grabbing her blindly. Kai screamed with new panic as the Upright Man vomited with a loud retching growl, blood spewing over her chest and splattering across her face.

She screamed again at the thick pulpy stench of blood, sour as rust. She plunged her dagger wildly, thinking only to free herself from his grasp, to flee from the blood that stung her face like a tanner's acid. Her dagger raked across his bearded cheek, and he bellowed in rage. His hands tightened on her shoulders, and he shoved her hard into the wall, slamming her repeatedly. Light flared in her eyes, blinding and white, and she gasped in terror.

Then the Upright Man released her and staggered away. She slid down along the wall, falling heavily to the ground. Dimly she saw him lurching down the passageway. One hand reached out against the wall to steady himself as he leaned down to retrieve his sword. Red light crowded her vision, but she saw him look around as if he missed something. He turned to look at her,

**163**

touched his cheek and then turning away again he stumbled out of the passageway.

Kai closed her eyes, the lids swollen with dirt. His scarf, she thought. She had his scarf. And she'd winked him good. No matter how he hid himself in respectability, she'd never forget his face.

Kai rested on the damp cobblestones, letting the throbbing ache in her skull duet with the fierce pain of her shoulder. At last she resolved to pull herself up into a sitting position. She moved slowly, moaning softly. Her head swam and she swallowed thickly, catching against the stench of the Upright Man's vomit.

She reached out, wincing as the movement seemed to drive nails into her skull, and grabbed the black scarf on the ground. Balling it up she tucked it into the torn remains of her dress to staunch the blood of her wound.

Exhausted, she looked over to where the bundle lay. There was no sound, and she knew without looking that the child was dead. Why'd the whore do it? she thought angrily. And then she shrugged sadly. Every child born with power was born with a death sentence. What difference would it make to the whore who did it? That brought her thoughts round to the Waterlings. She wanted them out of the city. Away from Beldan at least until the Upright Man was cocking up his toes.

And after that? she asked herself, using the wall as a support while she tried to stand. And after that, well she'd just have to see what could be done. There was that offer from Finch's Reader. Perhaps there was some use in it.

Kai walked slowly toward the child. Grunting with the sharp pain of her shoulder, she knelt just far enough to cover the child's face and gather it to her arms. She didn't want to see its face.

She looked up and down the passageway, pain and the fatigue of fighting making her feel light-headed. She needed help from someone who'd not ask too many questions and who wasn't afraid to take her in despite the way she must look covered in blood. Zeenia, Kai thought, seeing in her mind the image of the grinning bird over the lintel of the door. Only Crazy Zeenia would do all that. And the teahouse was mercifully nearby. Kai drew a deep breath and set out, trying not to stagger beneath the weight of her swaddled bundle and the throbbing ache of her wound.

# 15

"Where are we going?" Lirrel asked, rushing to keep up with Jobber's long-legged stride.

"Cloth House," Jobber answered, walking along a road that ran parallel to Hamader River. Light from the torches stippled the black water breaking upon the current into tiny orange fragments. Jobber cast an eye to the water. "Kai's probably up there with her Waterlings. She and her Flock scavenge the river. That there is Grap's Bridge, Kai's usual resting place."

Lirrel looked out over the water. "There's no one there."

Jobber stared at her and frowned. "You sure? I mean it's dark and all."

"Not too dark for me. And I don't see anything except an opening in the wall."

Jobber nodded, convinced Lirrel spoke the truth. "Tunnels. Beneath the city. Don't ever let yourself down there. Not unless you got a Waterling with you. Won't never find your way up again."

Lirrel nodded. "I don't much like closed-in spaces."

"Nor I wet ones," Jobber added with a shiver.

Jobber led Lirrel through a maze of backstreets on the riverside. They could hear the faint roar of noisy celebrations and see the orange glow of bonfires in the Pleasure district more than a few streets over. But in the riverside alleys, the torches spluttered with desultory smoke; crates, empty barrows and garbage competed for space in the narrow streets. Water trickled everywhere between the loose cobblestones, and the air was thick and damp. Lirrel sneezed as a pungent stench flooded her mouth and nose.

"Tanneries," Jobber murmured, pointing to the black husk of a building. The doors were opened, light from the vat fires outlining several men sitting on barrels taking their ease. They wore long leather aprons and wooden clogs. They smoked pipes, the bowls glowing with tiny red flares. Someone laughed and it turned into a long drawn cough. Jobber looked at Lirrel. "Hear that sound, Lirrel, that rattle in the throat?" Jobber said, her chin pointed toward the door of the tanneries, "that's a tune sung by all Beldan laborers."

In Beater's Alley they passed an old man hunkered near a small brazier. A wire cage filled with nuts was heating over the coals. "Give us a few coins," Jobber demanded of Lirrel, holding out her hand.

Silently, Lirrel gave her a string. Jobber removed three coins, handing the rest back to Lirrel. Jobber nodded to herself; Lirrel wasn't the stingy sort to bawl the first time Jobber asked for money to spend. Jobber turned to the old man and spoke in a loud voice.

"Oy, Old Duff, three bags."

The man jumped as if startled by a distant noise. A long scar ran the width of his forehead from his eyebrow into his scalp, giving his face a lopsided slant. He cocked a hand to his ear, and Jobber yelled her request a little louder. "Deaf as a brick," she muttered to Lirrel. "Sileans done it, by giving that crack over his noggin one night." The old man reached out with rough, soot-covered fingers, scooping the hot nuts from the wire cage into three small paper cones. Steam drifted from his fingers. He blew a quick breath on his hand before he took Jobber's coins.

Jobber handed a bag to Lirrel and took the other two. "They ain't for us," she said. Jobber began walking toward a tall building squeezed between storehouses with boarded-over windows. "Up here," Jobber motioned, and she slipped into the door and began to climb up the dark stairs.

At the top of a landing Jobber pushed open a door and ushered Lirrel into a long room with only one window at the end. Paint peeled from the walls, and along the edges of the ceiling water stains spread mildewed patterns. Lamps hung over the room, the light uneven.

"Oy, you cutters!" Jobber called out cheerfully. "Who's on for the Faire?

Weary faces lifted sharply at Jobber's words. Twenty children, all between five and ten years old, were sitting before upright rug looms, piles of colored threads scattered in baskets around them, small sharp shears poised in their hands. In contrast to the room's ugly dullness, elaborate and richly colored rugs appeared on the warp threads of the looms. Lirrel's eyes began to water, irritated by the dust of wool threads constantly being tied, cut and beat into proper place.

"Jobber," called back a little girl with black braids and deep violet shadows beneath her brown eyes. "Did you bring us anything?"

Jobber smiled. "Silly pin, Raer," she chided. "It's Firefaire, ain't it?"

"How'd we know, stuck in here?" answered a boy glumly from the back.

"Master giving you tomorrow off?" Jobber asked casually.

"Depends on whether we finish enough. You know him," Raer said with a shrug of her thin shoulders. "Greedy gaffer."

"Yeah, I know," Jobber said, moving through the children, handing out the warm nuts.

Lirrel followed behind, her lips parted in wonder at the beauty of the rugs, each with its own intricate pattern of tiny wool knots. Some had animals peeking shyly between the branches of imagined forests, others scrolls of vivid flowers and birds intertwined with lattices. Some of the children glanced up at her, and Lirrel grew shy beneath the bold stares, their eyes made larger by the narrowness of their pinched faces. They said nothing to her, but returned to their work, their heads bent to the rug frame and the little piles of threads. Their small hands were swift, taking a thread, wrapping and knotting it around the warp threads and then cutting the nap to the right length, before beating it into place to join the thousand other knots. Lirrel wiped her eyes and sniffed. She coughed, her throat irritated. Jobber tapped a finger to her ear. Around her Lirrel became aware of the steady sound of coughing that formed a part of the constant noise of the room along with the clip of the scissors and the soft scratch of wool combed into place.

"These are naffy, Jobber," Raer said, peeling back the hull of the nut. Her mouth full, she leaned up to smile. "Where's yer skin, Jobber?" she asked, pointing to Jobber's head.

Jobber shrugged. "I give it to a Silean. Asked for it in a way I couldn't refuse."

"Nah, really?" Raer asked, screwing her face in disbelief.

"What else did you give him?" the boy in back asked without taking his eyes from the rug he was working on.

"A kick up the arse."

The room erupted with snickers and giggles.

"You gonna teach me how to do that?" asked the boy, his eyes glaring, his cheeks flushed with two red circles.

"Maybe," Jobber answered evasively.

"I'm ready."

"Sure, sure. Later, maybe. But I'm off now," Jobber said,

**167**

backing out of the room quickly. Jobber caught Lirrel's arm and pushed her through the door. Lirrel's brown face had paled, her eyes watering. Lirrel needed fresh air, and Jobber needed to get away from the look of disappointment on the boy's face.

On the street again, Lirrel started coughing. Tears streamed down the sides of her face as she inhaled the chilly air. "How do they stand it?" she asked Jobber.

Jobber shook her head. "They don't. See, this here is the Pirate Cloth House. The real Cloth House that used to protect the weaving trades is over there," she waved her hand toward the tops of the buildings, "up in the Guild district. Under the Fire Queen, the old Guild laws don't mean much anymore, and the Sileans turn a faster coin in their houses than using the Guilds. Poor farmers with too many mouths to feed hire out their own children, selling them to rug merchants, stockingeers, knitters or whatever for a seven-year contract. They get Named, get their working papers and then work like dogs until they drop dead. Sileans use the children 'cause their hands is quick, their eyes good for the work. And mostly 'cause they don't argue and they're cheap."

"But that's—"

"That's the way it is here," Jobber said with finality. "All along here, you can find 'em, working in cutter houses, strangling themselves slowly in warp threads. Sometimes it seems all they weave are shrouds for each other."

Lirrel gazed up the dark street, her face troubled. Jobber wondered why she had thought to bring Lirrel to the Pirate Cloth House. She shrugged to herself. Maybe it had to do with Lirrel's talk of being a witness and her boast about Ghazali peacekeepers. Some disputes could never be solved just by standing around and playing a flute. Growler had taught Jobber to fight and that had always been her road to peace.

Jobber turned away from the weaving houses and led Lirrel down Pike Row. Here the air thickened with the haze of smoke. It smelled sharp and metallic. Jobber turned and smiled at Lirrel. "Listen," she said and held a finger to her ear.

Lirrel stood still, her head bent to hear the sound.

Someone was singing in a hoarse voice accompanied it seemed by a whirling, scrapping sound.

Jobber approached the thrown-open doors. Inside a man was bent over a grindstone, sharpening knives. Near his feet, a boy polished a kitchen knife on a wet stone. The boy's nose was running, and he wiped it away on his sleeve, though it left a track of gray dust on his face.

"Oy, Neman," Jobber called out to the older man. "Darbin," she said to the boy, who looked up long enough to flash a bright smile at her.

The older man stopped singing and looked up from the wheel, gray bushy eyebrows raised in surprise over the squinting eyes. Soot streaked his gray-stubbled cheeks and collected in the corners of his eyes.

"Jobber, my lad, what brings you to the Grinder's house?" Neman asked and then began coughing, a deep heavy hack that rattled in his lungs.

Jobber waited until he stopped. "Sounds worse, old man," she said.

He shrugged and wiped his mouth with a dirty cloth. "Drinking steel dust does that. Comes with the trade."

"What are you doing, Neman," Jobber asked, coming to look at the knives he was sharpening. "You're a pike maker, not a kitchen carver."

"Sileans'll pay three strings for the lot of this steel if I can hurry and get it done for the ships going back to Silea after Firefaire.

"Three strings ain't much, Neman. Time was you could ask for a siller for a well-made pike."

"Time was, Jobber lad. But time is now and it's a string for kitchen carvers they're paying. Ain't the Guilds setting prices no more. You know that. 'Sides, it makes the Sileans feel a bit nervy, us making the old pikes and all," he winked at Jobber. Neman went back to turning his wheel, the knife in his hand scrapping against the stone.

Jobber crossed to where a bucket stood beside an open fire. She reached in with the ladle and, after first stirring the steel dust that coated the surface, withdrew water. She filled a small cup and handed it to the grinder, who stopped his wheel and took the cup gratefully.

"Your dell?" Darbin asked, casting a sly glance over to Lirrel.

Beneath the cap, Jobber blushed. "Nah, just a friend that wanted to see the sights of Beldan."

"Neman's grindstone maybe ain't what she had in mind, Jobber," the old man started to chuckle and ended coughing. He took another sip of the water.

"Maybe not," Jobber agreed, looking at Lirrel. She was standing in the doorway, her white eyes reflecting the glow of the fire, her arms pressed close to her body. Her brown skin seemed sallow, her expression miserable.

"She blind?" Neman asked in a husky whisper.

"She was," Jobber answered, "but I think now she sees better."

She left Neman and Darbin puzzling this remark and, after nudging Lirrel out the door, waved a quick farewell.

Once outside, they heard Neman's hoarse cough just before he started singing again to the scraping of the grindstone.

"That sound, that frigging sound," Jobber said softly.

Lirrel walked, her head bowed deep in thought. At last she sighed deeply, and when she raised her head Jobber saw the twist of a sad smile. "I should have known you would shame me."

"Not shame you, Lirrel. You said that Ghazalis were witnesses to misery and trouble. So I showed you how things are in Beldan. But it'll take a whole lot more than music to change things here."

"I am a peacekeeper, Jobber," Lirrel said, shaking her head. "I don't believe in violence as a solution. But I have no music for what I have seen, no way to answer these injustices."

"It ain't you who has to answer for them, Lirrel. It ain't your fault," Jobber answered.

"Not my fault, but I feel, my responsibility," Lirrel replied, her voice tinged with anguish. "My duty to ease their suffering."

Jobber shrugged angrily. "Do what you like. All that matters to me is that I survive each day as it comes."

"That's all?" Lirrel asked.

"Yeah," Jobber answered irritably. "That's all."

"And what of those people back there? Those children," Lirrel insisted. "If you could help them somehow, wouldn't you?"

"But I can't help them," Jobber replied testily.

"You mean you won't. There are things you can do, Jobber."

"I don't know what you expect me to do about it," Jobber snapped. She started walking more quickly, not caring that Lirrel had to run to keep pace. Jobber swerved close to a lighterman reaching up to trim a dying torch. She bumped his elbow, sending a shower of sparks raining down on their heads.

"Watch yerself," the lighterman growled, ducking beneath the scattering of sparks.

"I intend to," Jobber replied angrily, adding to herself, and that's all I'll do. What right had this Ghazali flute player to demand anything more of her? Wasn't it hard enough to keep her own skin whole but that she should be putting out for others?

Hadn't she given enough already? Growler was dead, Jobber figured she had no more to spare than that.

"Jobber," Lirrel called, her voice pleading, apologetic.

Jobber saw a group of men huddled in a circle outside a tavern. The torch overhead showed the excitement on their faces, the eyes staring eagerly at something within the circle. Jobber leaned over the back of a squatting waterman, his blue river cap turned backward, the brim slanting down the nape of his neck.

"Give us yer coppers, lads," he was saying. "Lay it down."

"A string to the Gray," someone shouted, tossing a string of bright coppers over the circle to the waterman. He caught it and settled it on a pile.

"Any others?" he called.

Jobber turned quickly to Lirrel. "Give us a string."

"What is it?" Lirrel asked, frowning.

"Quick," Jobber hissed, rifling her fingers in the air.

Lirrel dug into her pocket and gave her a string. Jobber nudged the waterman and handed him the string. "To the Black," she said.

A farmer near the waterman swore at Jobber. "Bah, you've lost, Beldanite."

"Have I, dirt-twirler?" she taunted. "The Gray's big, but he ain't got the eye for it."

"What do you know of cocks?"

"Yours ain't much."

"And that goes for the one in the circle as well," a burly man in a journeyman's coat said. Jobber looked over at him and grinned.

"Watch now," Jobber said to Lirrel and leaned to one side so that she could see over the bent backs of the men and into the circle.

Two fighting cocks were held to either side of the circle, their heads of shining feathers bobbing rapidly. They reached and stretched with taloned feet, crowing with agitation.

"At it, lads," called the waterman and the two cocks were released. The large gray cock flew to the black, slashing across the gleaming black breast. The Black jumped back, his head stretched, his beady eyes showing white and red. Blood sprouted on the black feathers, and he flapped his wings furiously.

"You've lost," shouted the farmer, leaning eagerly forward.

"Ain't over," Jobber answered as the Black rallied and attacked the huge Gray cock. Talons raked across its eyes, blinding it.

**171**

"No," Lirrel shouted in sudden outrage. She pulled at Jobber's shoulder, trying to drag her away from the circle of cheering and swearing men. Jobber pushed Lirrel off, annoyed at being disturbed. The Black was terrorizing the half-blinded Gray cock, leaping at it and digging into its back with its sharp beak. "No, it's wrong," Lirrel continued to tug at Jobber's arm. "Come away, please don't do this."

"The Gray's lost," the waterman shouted, calling the match to an end. The farmer scrambled to recover his injured bird. One broken wing fanned out over the bloodied dirt. "Here you go, lad," the waterman turned to Jobber and handed him back the string of coppers plus a share of the winnings. Jobber grinned.

"I know my fighting cocks."

"But not yer dells, I'd say," the man replied, pointing to Lirrel who stood huddled against the wall. "You won't be winning anything with that one tonight."

Jobber eased up to a standing position, dusting off her trousers with one hand. Her anger was spent, lost in the excitement of the cock fight. But now she felt vaguely embarrassed and guilty. She had deliberately punished Lirrel, picked out the one sport that she knew would upset her. Jobber closed her hand over the coins and shuffled to Lirrel. Afterall, she thought, Lirrel hadn't set out to insult her. Z'blood, by all accounts Jobber still owed Lirrel for hiding her.

"You owe me nothing," Lirrel said in a cool voice that didn't match the trembling of her hands. "You've already paid me."

Jobber looked at her, shocked to hear her unspoken thoughts answered.

Lirrel started to walk past Jobber, but Jobber caught her by the arm. "Let me go," Lirrel said. "You can keep your winnings, but let me go."

"Look," Jobber tried to answer. "I'm sorry, all right? I didn't mean to . . . to . . ."

"To rub my face into it? Force me to see what an ignorant and foolish person I must be because I believe in peace?"

Jobber scratched the brim of her woolen cap and sighed. Lirrel's eyes stayed on her, angry and accusing.

"Violence is all I know, Lirrel," Jobber answered softly. "I wake up to it every day and I lay down every night with it. My hands are always in a fist." Jobber sighed and weighed the string of coppers in her palm.

"But why?" Lirrel asked. "Why does it have to be like that?"

"Have you seen how they hang them after Firefaire? The ones

the Readers finger during the Naming?" Jobber asked Lirrel.

Lirrel shook her head.

"Happens about a week after Firefaire. The dust settles, folks go back to where they came from. And in the old ashes of the Great Bonfire, they set up the scaffolds. You can see them when they haul them out of the prison wagons. Little 'uns most of them, hung right there along with all the other cutthroats and thieves. Most of them piss all over themselves they're so frigging scared. And then that hood goes 'round their head, just before they collar them with the noose..." Jobber stopped, her face frozen like ice. She shivered. "Every year I watch, and every year I feel the itch of the rope coming that much closer. I'm like that black cock back there, just fighting to stay alive. That's all I care about."

"That's not true," Lirrel said, one small hand circling Jobber's arm. Jobber was surprised to find her grip so firm. "You care about Beldan. About the weavers, the grinders and all those like us born with Oran's gift of magic. You care about your dead, Jobber. You mourn for them—"

Jobber jerked her arm free.

"Wait," Lirrel said. "Wait, don't deny those feelings, Jobber. I can hear them in your thoughts."

"Stop listening, then," Jobber replied gruffly.

"I can't," Lirrel said with a smile. "I can close out the others. I have to close them out, otherwise I'd go mad. But I can't shut you out. It is as if I am forced to listen, like a Ghazali child learning the old songs is forced to listen and repeat until they understand it."

"What's to understand?" Jobber asked.

"That we need each other, Jobber."

Jobber made a rude noise and walked away.

"Jobber wait," Lirrel called, running to catch up. Jobber stopped and waited. "We need each other," Lirrel repeated.

Jobber stared at the crystal eyes, the smooth oval face and the slim shoulders. "What do you need from me? she asked. "You got your family, your life. What do you want from me?"

Lirrel smiled. "You have shown me things tonight I needed to see. I would be a poor witness if I ignored the true sufferings of others. But far from feeling despair, it has strengthened my resolve. I cannot fight like you, Jobber. I must learn how to use my faith. No one else could have made me realize that better. But that's not all," Lirrel said.

"What else," Jobber asked.

"You need me to show you that compassion, too, has its strengths and will not weaken you as a fighter. We can be friends, Jobber. Good friends."

Jobber was silent as Lirrel's words cast her thoughts into a gnarled turmoil. It brought fresh pain, but like a wound that is lanced, it also brought a measure of relief. Jobber steadied herself, not trusting her emotions.

"I'll think about it," Jobber answered, and Lirrel smiled at her, accepting that much as enough.

"Jobber," she said tentatively as they continued to walk toward the lights of the Pleasure district, "there is a place in your mind that I saw for a moment. A garden—"

Jobber stopped walking and turned gruffly. "Frigging shit, Lirrel, you make me feel like a window. Can you hear and see everything I think?" she asked indignantly.

"No," Lirrel hurried to reply. "Just strong images. Ones I think you would like to share with someone."

"How 'bout now?" Jobber asked, a grin lighting up her face.

Lirrel burst out in a peal of laughter. "Very creative," she said. "Not physically possible, but very amusing the way you imagine it."

"Imagine nothing, I seen this dell and her fancy man go at it like that once—"

"Jobber," Lirrel interrupted.

"What?"

"The garden," Lirrel reminded her. "Can we go to the garden?"

"All right," Jobber consented. "As long as you listen to my story about this here dell and her man."

Lirrel sighed. "If I must. But stop shouting."

"I ain't shouting."

"You are. You're also drooling."

"Well if you'd a seen how much food they messed with, you'd be drooling, too."

"I'm going to be ill, I know it," Lirrel groaned.

"Wait, it gets better."

Jobber swung close to Lirrel, taking her the long way through the Guild district and up to big houses, her story growing more ingenious and impossible with every step. And as Jobber's willing captive, Lirrel listened with one ear, while her face blushed scarlet every time a passerby's head swiveled in their direction, catching a fragment of Jobber's story.

•  •  •

174

"Pretty out here, ain't it?" Jobber said softly as she rested for a moment in the middle of small square of grass. Around the square was a garden that had been carefully cultivated and shaped into a complex, interlocking pattern. None of the low growing shrubs were yet in full leaf, but even in the wood Jobber could see their differences: slim gray stalks light against the darker shades of woody shrubs. She followed the twisting turns of the pattern in and out as they wove around the garden; as always she never found where the pattern started and where it ended, each strand of the pattern dependent on the other for its design. "Hasn't changed much in five years," she murmured, thinking of when she was last here with Growler, the moon casting their shadows as they sparred in the middle of this patch of cut grass.

"It's calming," Lirrel said, walking slowly around the four sides of the square, smiling at the pattern.

"Yeah, Growler thought so, too. We used to come here at night to practice."

"Here!" Lirrel asked, incredulous. "Wasn't that dangerous, to be so close to the Sileans?" She glanced nervously out over the top of the wall they had just climbed. She could see the lights in the windows of nearby Silean houses.

Jobber laughed. "Yeah, it was pretty snarky of him. But he always said this place brought him a sense of balance he never found anywhere else in Beldan."

"He was right," Lirrel agreed. "This garden represents a Queens' quarter knot. It must have been here since before the Burning. Sileans don't know how to make one."

"What's so important about a knot?" Jobber asked and then swore silently to herself at the concerned expression on Lirrel's face that meant a lecture was imminent.

"Didn't Growler teach you anything?" she asked.

"Yeah," Jobber answered gruffly. "How to stay alive. Ain't that enough?"

"Of course. That's basic to the body. But this," Lirrel turned slowly in the square, a hand outstretched as if to touch all four sides of the pattern, "this is basic to the spirit."

"Vagger blow," Jobber said under her breath.

"*Ahal*, it is. But everyone in Oran was a vagger once. Well, not quite a vagger. We weren't vagrants and mendicants. We were scholars in magic and things of the spirit. Four houses of learning, each to represent an element, a thread in the Queens' quarter knot. The Ghazali were one house, our element, air. Beldan Guilds were another," she looked over at Jobber, head cocked to one side at her reluctant pupil. "Can you guess what element?"

Jobber shook her head and then blurted out, "Fire," surprised at the sudden logic of it.

"Yes," Lirrel said. "The Guild of Forges was the most important. Fire was the heart of their craft. Oran's farmers were the third house—"

"Earth," added Jobber.

"Yes," Lirrel nodded, "and Islanders were the fourth house, water elements. And with them, the Namire."

"I always thought the Namire were monster stories, to keep docksiders' brats from straying to the water."

"No, not at all. The Namire were human once, but changed their bodies so as to live in the sea. They harvested shellfish and pearls and spun the gold threads gathered from mussels. Well, they weren't really gold, but the color was similar and when spun..." Lirrel stopped, seeing the sour expression on Jobber's face. She shrugged apologetically and then finished quickly. "Sileans hunted the Namire after the Burning. Now all that is left of their schools are stories, and none of them nice."

"And this garden," Jobber pointed her chin at the pattern, "this was to show how the four houses worked together?"

"Yes." Lirrel said. "Look, Jobber," and she drew from her shawl a long string from the fringe. She tied the two ends together so that it made a circle and then wrapped it around her hands, stretching them apart. Her fingers dipped into the center, catching threads around her fingers until between her hands a pattern appeared in the string.

"I know this game," Jobber said excitedly. "Growler showed it to me."

"At least he thought to teach you something other than fighting," Lirrel grumbled.

Jobber reached her hands into the patterned string, and hooking a finger here and there, she lifted the old pattern off Lirrel's hands. She pulled her hands apart, and the string opened into a new configuration. "Queen's cradle, ain't it?" she said proudly.

"Queens' quarter knot, actually," answered Lirrel. "Though it comes from the image of a cradle, that's true."

Jobber sighed. "Lirrel, how come with you an answer is never simple?"

"You never ask simple questions, Jobber," Lirrel replied and reached her hands back into the patterned string to make yet another configuration.

When it was back on her hands, she looked over at Jobber. "When Amasortoran first conceived the world—"

"Oh no, not religion, please Lirrel, this stuff gives me a headache."

"Tcha, Jobber, be quiet and listen. It's a good story," and she added with a wink, "I'll make it quick." Jobber groaned but said nothing further.

"As I was saying, when Amasortoran first conceived the world, she made a little child she called Oran." In the center of Lirrel's hands the string configured into a star. "Oran was a son."

"Why not a girl?"

"Amasortoran was creative. She wanted to make something other than Herself. She let Him play in the chaos that was the world then. But this beloved Son was unhappy. He was tossed back and forth and had no quiet resting place." Lirrel dipped her hands into the center and changed the pattern once more. The center star was a small knot surrounded on either side by four smaller knots. "So, she made a cradle of four points to hold Oran firm against the chaos. And like all beloved children, safe within the cradle He was happy. But after a time, He became lonely."

"Yeah, well it does get a bit boring bouncing around in chaos, you know," Jobber scoffed, but her gaze was trapped by the string between Lirrel's hands.

Lirrel laughed. "Indeed. So She pulled four threads from the chaos and made four guardians, four queens, to amuse Him and see to all His needs. Fire, water, earth and air. Oran was happy for a time. There was light and warmth when He needed it, water to drink and earth to shape into figures like Himself and His mother. But as Oran grew, so did His ambition."

"How long can you live in a cradle?" Jobber asked sarcastically.

Lirrel ignored her. "He began to make more and more figures. Breathing on them to give them life. Amasortoran warned Him there was danger in doing this, but He ignored her advice, finding it pleasing to Himself to make His own world within the cradle."

Lirrel dipped her fingers again into the center of the pattern, and when they straightened out again, the pattern had twisted more deeply, the threads weaving in and out in a tighter knot. "But His world grew too heavy for the cradle, and His little figures in turn began to create themselves."

"Randy little buggers," Jobber smirked.

"His creations drew on the strengths of the elemental queens and shaped the world to their own needs. And the cradle grew heavier still. Oran called to His mother for help. Amasortoran sent Him death so that His figures would not break the cradle with their growing numbers. But the threads of the cradle frayed against the weight of so much life pressing within and the raging force of chaos without. Oran was afraid His figures would be crushed or swept away by the chaos. So He climbed out of His cradle and, standing in the chaos, held His hands beneath the cradle to shelter and protect His world." Lirrel shook her head sadly. "But ah, the knots of the cradle entangled Him in its design, drawing Him into its pattern until He became inseparable from the world He had made. When Amasortoran looked and saw what had happened, She cried. Tears became stars. Oran had given His world a resting place, and the four queens remained the points of the cradle, protecting Oran from the surrounding chaos. Every generation has had its Queens' quarter knot, four threads, four elements, four queens, bound together that Oran and all His people may continue to exist. Balance and harmony within the sea of chaos."

Lirrel held up her hands to show Jobber the final pattern in the string. Looking at it closely, Jobber saw the similarity between it and the flowing, intricate lines of the garden.

"Nice story, I guess."

"You don't believe it?"

Jobber laughed. "Well look now, we've got only one Queen, one element, and it looks like we're going to have her forever, and I don't see us breaking apart into the chaos. Do you?" Jobber scratched her head where the wool of her cap itched.

"Perhaps. But as I travel the roads it is hard to imagine the world as having balance. Oran magic cursed. Oran ways forgotten. Doesn't it seem wrong to you?"

Jobber shrugged. "You know me, I don't think about it. The world is as it is, that's all. Who am I to say it should be different?"

"Given that story you tortured me with on the way here, I should have thought someone as creative as yourself could have come up with a plan for a better world. At least one that would insure your continued existence, not to mention others." Lirrel stood, her fists on her hips, her face a friendly scowl.

Jobber laughed. "All right then. In my world there would be no shortage of things to eat and drink. Especially beer. Come on then. I've someone waiting to meet me at the Hungry Owl."

Lirrel lingered to gaze at the garden. The wind carried the

fragrance of damp earth and the woody scent of the shrubs. Above the arched edge of the wall, the new moon rested like a sickle above the wheat.

"Come on," Jobber whispered loudly, "don't want to be late." Lirrel sighed and joined Jobber in scrambling over the wall and out into the broad tree-lined streets again.

# 16

Kai winced as Zeenia cut away the sleeve of her dress. "Z'blood it hurts," she growled, and stinks, she thought, wanting to forget the memory of the Upright Man's yawning face. Her stomach lurched and the blood drained from her face, leaving her feeling suddenly clammy. She shuddered.

"Lie down," Zeenia ordered, "you've gone all green on me."

"But my dress . . . it's filthy," Kai said vaguely.

"My sheets will wash," Zeenia answered matter-of-factly, pushing aside the red coverlet and the rumpled linen sheets of the bed.

Moaning curses, Kai allowed herself to be lowered to the bed.

Zeenia kept cutting away at the fabric of the bodice until Kai was clad only in her blood-soaked shift. Zeenia cut this away, too, and Kai shivered, pimples raised on her white skin. Then Zeenia stood and gently pulled off the skirts, casting the mess of soiled clothing into the far corner of the room.

With a small basin of warm water, Zeenia carefully started to wash Kai's blood-stained torso and wound.

"At least it was a clean cut," she murmured. "Won't be hard to fix." She smiled encouraging, but Kai saw the way Zeenia's freckles blazed against her ashen complexion. It had to look awful, Z'blood it felt awful. "Here," Zeenia said, and lifting Kai's head she gave Kai a drink of something bitter tasting in a cup. "Ought to take the edge off things."

The liquid was hot, but its burn was soothing. Kai sipped it as Zeenia gazed back at her over the rim of the cup. Almost immediately Kai felt woozy, her focus blurred and her tongue thickened. The pain in her shoulder fragmented into smaller pieces, muffled by a hazy warmth seeping through her limbs.

"Better?" Zeenia asked with a knowing smile.

"Much," Kai answered, surprised to hear her voice sounding like syrup.

"Good, then, I'll start. Now don't move," Zeenia warned.

Through slowly blinking eyes, Kai saw Zeenia's hand rise and fall to the injured shoulder, a length of silk trailing after it. Sewing something, she thought absently, and then Kai giggled realizing that it was her torn skin. Sewn up like an old Firefaire dolly, she thought.

"What happened?" Zeenia asked.

"Not fair," Kai answered in her slurred voice.

"What's not fair?" Zeenia asked, arching her brows to a puzzled point over her nose.

"Not fair to ask when I'm so, so, whatever I am." It seemed a tremendous effort to find the right words to Zeenia's questions.

"All right then," Zeenia said and fell quiet.

A drop of sweat stung Kai's eye, and she realized it came from Zeenia's forehead, bending over her to cut the thread of silk.

"Frigging bastard," Kai said, as much to herself as to the face deep in concentration above her. "I got him good though."

"Really?" Zeenia replied. She started dressing the wound, wrapping clean white bandages around Kai's shoulder.

"Bastard Upright Man! I'll turn the screw to him for what he done."

"Were you fighting with him?" Zeenia asked with a sudden start.

"Frigging right! Nearly scaffered the puking bastard, too!"

Zeenia gave a low whistle. "You bit the bulldog himself. I'm surprised there's anything left of you to stitch at all."

Kai leaned up in the bed with sudden urgency, grabbing Zeenia's sleeve. "I had to. It's my Flock you see. He wants to kill them." Her words came quickly now, chased by the terror of what she had seen. "He drinks their blood to steal away their magic. I saw him do it to the baby." Kai blinked through a wash of hot tears, and she started to tremble, her teeth chattering as if icy cold.

"The one you brought here?" Zeenia asked as she gently pushed Kai down and spread a thick blanket over her.

"Yes," Kai said miserably. "He'll kill all of them if he can. I got to get to my Flock, to warn them."

"Hush now," Zeenia said. "You need to rest."

"But—"

"Rest!" Zeenia said more sharply. "Where are they?"

"I sent them to the Ribbons."

"Sensible," Zeenia answered, sounding to Kai not at all like the scatterbrained woman she had assumed Zeenia to be. "I'll go

**181**

to the Ribbons myself if you like. What do you want me to tell them?"

Kai tried to gather her thoughts as they scurried away from her. The warmth of the blankets and her exhaustion was making it hard to think. "Talk only to Slipper. Tell him to take the Flock, he'll know which ones, to Market Square tunnel and wait for me. Tell him, it's the Upright Man. He'll know the rest."

"All right, then," Zeenia replied. "I'm off." She started for the door but a cry from Kai stopped her. "What is it?" Zeenia hurried back to the bedside.

"What have I done?" Kai said, gasping. "What have I done?" she asked again, shaking her head. The bitter liquid that Zeenia had given her to drink had done more than dull the pain. It had dulled her caution as well and loosened her tongue. "I squealled on my own people," she moaned, shocked at how easily the truth had parted from her. Supposing Zeenia—

Zeenia leaned down close to the bed and ran a hand over Kai's forehead. She smelled like tea spice and sweat. "You've trusted me with an important secret, Kai. And I'm not the one to betray that trust." She gave Kai a lopsided smile. "The Grinning Bird has been home to more secrets and more fugitives than I can count. I'll see your Slipper and warn him. And when I get back we can talk about what to do with the Upright Man. You're going to need help with that one. But, for now, rest."

Kai nodded slowly, reassured by the gentle firmness of Zeenia's voice.

"I'll take care of the Flock for you," Zeenia repeated, but her voice sounded distant to Kai. The ache in her shoulder was a slow burn that heated her body, drawing her into sleep.

"That's right," she heard Zeenia's whisper as she closed her eyes and surrendered to the fatigue, "just rest. I'll be back as soon as I can."

Kai turned over, curling herself into a knot, and slept soundly. She cried out only once as she saw the fleeting image of his face, unmasked, two black eyes with pinpricks of red gleaming at her.

When Kai next woke the room was dark and stuffy with silence. The effects of Zeenia's tea had worn off, and though her head had cleared, the ache in her shoulder was more pronounced. She sat up slowly, not certain she could trust the feathery lightness of her head.

The room whirled lazily and then settled. Kai gave a parched swallow, wiped a hand across her face and tried to take stock of her situation. The bandage on her shoulder was smudged with a dark patch of blood but otherwise seemed clean, which meant the bleeding at least had stopped. As she threw off the blankets and stood up, Kai realized she was naked.

"Z'blood," she swore looking down at her thin shanks and bony ankles. An old knife scar snaked across one jutting hipbone. With her good arm raised protectively across her chest, Kai started scrounging the corner for her clothes. Her hand went to her skirts and then recoiled from the sodden fabric. She couldn't put those on again. Kai went to Zeenia's wooden chest and, after routing through it, found an Islander's shift made of scratchy linen and embroidered with a black band of fish around the neck. A second look netted her a brown wool skirt, and last she found a blue bodice, the sleeves attached by ribbons at the shoulder. Sweating with the effort and pain, Kai dressed herself in the shift and skirt. She untied the sleeve from the one arm and was able to slip her injured arm, bandage and all, through the armhole of the bodice. But it was impossible to tie the bodice, and she had to make do with pulling the laces tight with one hand and hoping that they wouldn't loosen.

As she was about to leave, Kai grabbed one of two black shawls hanging on a peg on the back of Zeenia's door. Wrapping it over her head, she slipped quietly through the door and into the kitchens of the Grinning Bird. Zeenia had closed the shop, but the stove still burned with a low, steady heat beneath the brass urns in accordance with Zeenia's rule that there was always tea to be had at the shop as long as she was in the city. The room seemed to sigh with the moisture as steam condensed on the windows.

Kai headed for the backdoor, undid the latch and stepped cautiously into the alley. Her shoulder was throbbing, so she cradled the arm in her shawl, trying to give it more support. To have rested longer in Zeenia's warm bed would have been a blessing. But Kai was impatient and anxious. She couldn't wait any longer. She had already told Zeenia too much about the Waterlings. There was nothing to be done about that now, however, except to hope that Zeenia was true to her word. But one thing was clear to Kai as she walked, gritting her teeth against the jarring pain of her shoulder: she had to see her Flock, touch them and reassure herself they were alive. And then she had to get them out of Beldan.

She threaded the shadows of High Street, traveling in the direction of Crier's Forge. She had made up her mind to chance that Finch's Reader had made her an honest offer. If she could safely smuggle the Waterlings out of Beldan for the time being at least, she'd be able to concentrate on settling the score with the Upright Man. The ache in Kai's shoulder reminded her that the Upright Man was only the beginning of their troubles. She was going to have to figure out how to save the Waterlings from the Readers, too. One step at a time, she cautioned herself, as in her haste her foot stumbled on a loose cobblestone, one step at a time.

The main room of Master Donal's living quarters was crowded. Around the wooden table faces earnestly studied the spread papers and maps, scratching notes for themselves after pushing aside cups of strong tea. A small fire burned in the grate casting long thin shadows on the white plaster walls.

"We can't wait for Zeenia any longer," Master Donal said. "It's too dangerous for us all to be here as it is. Begin without her. Who's first to report?"

"I will," said Pedar, the Masterweaver of Cloth House. He was a gaunt-looking man with a sallow complexion above the blue neck scarf. He laid his long hands on the table, the blue veins rising like threads on the backs. "So far we've been lucky. The Sileans have been careful when it comes to searching the incoming wagons, but they have left alone those merchants and journeymen traveling out of Beldan. We've been able to smuggle out a fair number of swords wrapped in bolts of linen. There's a grinder that says he'll give us the pike heads if the New Moon can provide the wood shafts."

"Aye," answered Farnon. "The vaggers have promised us all the wood we need from the forests of Avadares." Farnon was a laborer, his hands thick from years of plowing fields, dirt etching lines around his nails. He spoke slowly, carefully, as if he were slow of thought as well. But beneath a rugged brow of leathery skin his eyes were keen and beetle black and his ear quick to hear deceit. Ten years a laborer had callused his spirit as well as his hands.

"And the children?" Alwir asked. "Have many come through here?"

Osa, Pedar's wife, nodded. "Yes. We have been able to send small groups out with the Ghazali. Also, some of Zeenia's vagger's have been helpful. Three more are boarded in the cargo hold of the *Rising Star*." Osa put her arm around her son seated next to her. Soltar was a boy of about fourteen with his father's

**184**

sallow color but the round face of his mother. He tensed at his mother's arm, shrugging it off. She released him with a rueful smile. At times like these, she knew, young men didn't want the circle of their mother's arm.

"Any luck finding Jobber?" Donal asked.

"No," Soltar answered with a quick shake of his head. "Cutter lads and I have been searching ever since you gave out the word. I heard rumor she was over at the Pirate House, but she'd left by the time I got there."

"Hard to think of her as a female," Wyer said softly, staring out the window. "I keep picturing that boastful swagger and those knobby knuckles of hers." He kept watch at the window, searching for signs of Zeenia.

"Do you think she has the power?" Alwir asked.

Donal nodded slowly, taking a long-stemmed pipe from his vest pocket and tapping the ash into the grate. "A vagger named Growler came once to the forge wanting to make a deal. I would keep an eye out for his student, give the lad a place to sleep if needed, and in exchange he'd teach me a lost bit of the old craft."

Alwir leaned forward. "And did he?"

Donal lighted the pipe and sucked deeply on the stem before answering. "Yes. At first I thought he weren't much to look at, skinny even in them brown robes. But when he stripped to the waist, I could see the muscles on him like an iron chain roped around his arms. Z'blood, how he made the anvil ring with a clear, sweet sound. In his hands, the fire danced. He sent the flames licking the edge of a sword until the blade was pure and white."

"What happened to him" Alwir asked.

"He was killed by the butcherboys. But the boy—Jobber—escaped. She's been coming round here ever since, and I've let her work the bellows, still thinking all the while she was a lad. But you should have seen it today when the hat come off and that red hair burst into flames." Donal shook his head and tapped out the charred tobacco of his pipe into the grate. "There wasn't a man or woman there at that moment who didn't know the girl had power."

"We need to find her," Alwir said.

"We will," spoke up Soltar proudly. "I know most everyone that lives on the street. And with the Cutters, we'll find her faster than the butcherboys anyday."

Alwir smiled at him, thinking of Finch and all the other strays like her living on Beldan streets, all of them in need of such a rescue. He wondered if she had come to the forge. "I hope so," he said aloud, thinking of Finch as well as Jobber. "Z'blood, I hope so."

"All right then," Farnon said, shifting nervously in his seat. "We must settle the question of tomorrow." His glance jerked to the window, only slightly reassured to find Wyer still staring out at the street. "Let's finish and be off." He turned back to Donal. "Are you on for it?"

"I say it's too risky to try anything now," Pedar answered the laborer. "Beldan is unorganized. There are over a hundred trades, some of them loyal to the Queen, some of them not. We don't know who we can trust. The New Moon asks too much from us too soon."

Farnon gave a dry, cackling laugh. "For a long time it's been too much on our backs. The New Moon is fighting already in the west country. Not big battles, mind you, but enough small ones to make it count for something. The time's come to show us where the Guilds stand. Will you compromise with the Silean bastards, or will you help us to sweep them into the sea?"

"What do you want from us?" Donal asked.

"Beldan," answered Farnon simply. "This city organized from within and ready to join us when the time comes."

"But first we have to bloody our nose, is that it?" Donal asked.

"Aye," said Farnon, locking his arms over his chest, "that's the way of it. You'll have to prove to us and mayhap yerselves that you're ready to fight."

"But the reprisals? The Sileans are sure to retaliate. They will kill innocent people for our acts," said Osa, her face paling and her arm reaching for Soltar's shoulder to draw him close to her side. For once he let it rest there.

Farnon stared at her hard, the angular shape of his face collecting the shadows in dark planes along his cheeks. "You know now't of reprisals in Beldan. Maybe a bread tax, maybe an insult fine, maybe a hanging or two. Well then, I've seen entire villages burned, livestock run off and not a person left alive to weep for the loss. I've seen a whole family hung for the crime of gathering fallen wood from a Silean's forest that once was common land. I worked for a Master who wore on his belt a string of dried ears that he'd sheared from the heads of Oran shepherd boys he didn't like. We bleed and die every day from reprisals, but there's not one who would turn their back on the New Moon." Farnon spread his wide hands on the edge of the table, gripping it tightly.

186

"We have few enough people to spare, not enough weapons either," Master Donal answered, leaning forward, his elbows propped on the table. He raked his fingers through the sides of his beard, pulling it thoughtfully.

Farnon shrugged. "You have to start somewhere. Take a bold step and show them the way. And if there are reprisals, you can be certain of gaining a faster recruitment. Nothing moves a man to greater courage than the fear of being next on the noody-noose." Farnon closed one hand into a fist. "Hit the butcherboys hard and often. Smash holes in their ships; steal from their warehouses, arsenals and graneries; kill them by ones and twos. Put rocks in the hands of your children. Anything," he said savagely. "Force your people into the fire and forge them as you would the sword."

"You ask too much," Donal insisted, shaking his head.

Farnon drew himself up preparing to leave. He gave the gathering a look of disdain. "You give o'er little. Must be you aren't desperate enough for freedom. I've already given you proof of our commitment. It cost me the lives of two of my people last night, not to mention a sword. I'll go then," he said angrily and made for the door.

"Wait," Donal said, "Sit. I've not said we won't help. I've only spoken my doubts for our success."

"I can tell you this," Farnon said as he leaned his bulky frame over the table and held each one of them with his keen gaze, "the doubts will never leave you. Nor will the fear of death, your own and the people who follow you. But you must bury your doubts with a greater faith. Faith that we will succeed against the Sileans where our fathers before us failed."

"What of the Fire Queen?" Donal asked. A candle spluttered, sending a spray of hot wax across the papers.

Farnon shook his head. "The New Moon cares only in freeing Oran from the Silean tyranny. It's vaggers who will settle the Fire Queen's fate."

"There's a rumor the vaggers want to form a new Queens' quarter knot, to challenge Zorah."

"And more luck to them," Farnon answered. "But I've also heard rumor that they won't find the threads they need; that there aren't those with enough of the old magic left among Orans who could form such a knot."

"Jobber?" asked Alwir, looking at Donal rather than Farnon. Donal smiled slightly and shrugged. How could he know for certain? How could any of them know?

"Whether or not the vaggers can do as they want is of no interest to those like myself," Farnon continued. "The New Moon wants only to boot out every last Silean bastard and take back the land stolen from us. Now I'll ask you again, Master Donal, are you on for it?"

Donal looked at his companions, and though he read the reluctance in Pedar's and Osa's face, he saw, too, the eager readiness in Soltar's and Alwir's expression. A young man's foolishness, he decided, to see glory and valor in the promise of violence. Wyer by the window gave him a nod of encouragement. He would accept whatever his father decided in this matter.

"We're on," Donal said, with a sinking heart, despairing the deaths that would follow whatever course of violence they now set themselves on. He would have to harden himself to it, he thought wearily. There would be a lot of death before it was over.

"Good then," Farnon answered, returning to his seat. He pulled a rolled map out of a deep pocket sewn on the inside of his smock. He laid it flat on the table.

"It's Fire Circle," Alwir said, recognizing the huge circular plaza not far from Market Square. Smaller sidestreets like the rays of a star radiated from the center of the plaza. A mark in the northern arc of the circle designated the Great Bonfire and around it the stands that would hold the Readers and other Silean dignitaries. Dotting the map were numbers scratched in red and blue circles.

"I don't like the place you've chosen," said Donal pointing to Fire Circle, "it's too damn tight. The place will be crowded with fairefolk."

"Which is why you'll hit the Sileans here, in Hayman's Street," Farnon's finger traced a line from Fire Circle down the street marked on the map. "You'll have to be quick about it."

"Are you sure the procession will pass through here?" Alwir asked, looking up from the map.

"Aye. Vaggers told us. Said they could tell where the procession was going to be by how the butcherboys have been going over the routes, cleaning up the streets. How many of your people can you pull together?"

"Fifty," Pedar said.

"It's enough. Divide them into three groups. Spaced along Hayman's Street, between here at River's Edge and Bell's Point."

"Why there?" Alwir asked.

Farnon smiled. "Street is narrow, the shops and storefronts many. Ought to give you the best cover."

"For what?" Donal asked.

Farnon smiled again, his lip curling back over square front teeth. "Choose a target, Mastersmith. But make it a good one. If you hit the procession along three points at the same time, you'll create enough confusion to get your people in and make good the kill. So who's it to be? A Silean merchant well hated by your fellow Beldans? Maybe the Firstwatch, to settle the score for my lost people."

Donal scowled at the red squares and lines plotting the movement of a small army on the map. On paper it looked easy. "It doesn't matter who?" he said with a slight mocking in his voice.

Farnon's answer was smooth and cool. "Not a wit to me, Mastersmith. But it should matter to Beldan."

Donal leaned back in his chair and reached for the cold pipe. "That settles it then. Silwa Re Familia, Regent to the Queen," he said gruffly, shocked to hear himself so easily pronounce a death sentence on another.

"Good choice, Mastersmith," said Farnon.

"What are the blue circles here for?" Alwir asked, his gaze still centered on the map.

"Bowmen," Farnon said. "We'll guard your back from up here." He looked over at Donal and smiled at the look of surprise. "I didn't mean that you should go it alone, Mastersmith. We'll be there in case you've need of us."

"How will you know not to shoot our people?"

"Wear a bit of blue. It doesn't matter where, but it should be easy to see; a ribbon tied round yer arm or a scrap of it pinned to a cap. We'll be looking for it."

"And in a sea of folk dressed in orange and red for Firefaire, it should be easy to spot," Alwir said, looking up from the map at last and grinning.

"Oy," Wyer said sharply and the room tensed. "Thought I saw something moving in the street." He strained his eyes to pierce the darkness. There had been something there a moment ago. There! Suddenly he could see the edge of a gray sleeve where the wearer had crossed too close to the torches. "Guards," he warned.

"How many?" Donal asked amid the flurry of regathering papers.

"Can't tell," Wyer answered.

"Is there a back way?" Farnon asked, scooping up the papers and tucking them into his smock again.

Pedar tapped Soltar on the shoulder and the boy jumped in alarm. "Out through the roof. Go on, Soltar, take him round to Greffen's."

Osa clung to the boy, her face tight with worry.

"Let him go, Osa, before it's too late," Pedar said.

"Hist, lad, and hurry. Show me the way," Farnon growled, hurrying the boy through the door to the kitchens.

"Are they coming here?" Alwir asked, crossing to Wyer.

"No, they seemed to be waiting."

"For what?"

The door of the room burst open, the wood splintering where it had torn from the lock. Osa screamed and ran for the kitchens. The Firstwatch Gonmer and a squad of Silean Guards spilled into the room, their swords drawn.

"After her," Gonmer ordered, pointing to the fleeting figure of Osa. "I want them all." A heavyset Guard detached himself from the group and barreled through the hallway after the screaming woman. They heard him as he crashed through the kitchens, knocking plates and crockery to the floor. They heard Osa's shrill voice, and the Guard cursing loudly. Then abruptly it was silent again. Pedar's face grew haggard and white in the silence.

The Guard reappeared, holding a bleeding arm that had been slashed open across the forearm.

"My wife," Pedar whispered hoarsely as he saw the blood dripping from the Guard's drawn sword. He started for the kitchens.

"Stop him!" Gonmer shouted and two Guards blocked the entrance.

"But my wife—" Pedar said, giving Gonmer a frantic stare.

"Is beyond your help," Gonmer finished. The wounded Guard continued to stand holding his arm, the blood splattering in little drops on the clean floor. Gonmer swore under her breath. "Get him a cloth for a bandage," she barked to Lais. "Tie it up, so he doesn't bleed to death." Slowly she resheathed her sword and then looked up at Donal, a grim smile on her lips.

"You've distinguished guests tonight, Master Donal. Alwir Re Aston, are you not?" Gonmer asked.

Alwir tried to quiet the rapid beat of his pulse. The use of the Re honorific stung him like a slap on his face. He drew himself up, reassembling his expression into the likeness of an outraged noble.

"What's the meaning of this? Breaking into Crier's Forge and murdering people."

Gonmer laughed. "Murdering people," she mocked. She plucked at the papers on the table, noting their contents and nodded. "Chance brought me here tonight, but it would seem Re Aston that murder and treason brought you."

"Ridiculous. I am here to purchase a sword. Since when has that become treasonous for a noble?"

"Not one sword, Re Aston," said Gonmer tapping a finger on the papers, "but many, I'd say. Enough in fact for a small band of ruffians. You see, I've been listening to your conversation for quite some time now."

"Ear to the keyhole, Firstwatch," jibed Donal. "That doesn't seem very dignified of you."

"Ah, but duty demands it of me. If I thought examining your shit was worth the trouble to send you to the hangman, Mastersmith, I'd have it on a plate."

"Eat it, too, would you?"

Gonmer laughed. "Why bother when it would be more enjoyable to force you to that task." Gonmer pulled up a chair and sat down graceful as a cat. The sword rested at her side within easy reach. "It has been an interesting evening, gentlemen, though admittedly tragic for some of you," she waved a hand toward the kitchen. "Sit," she commanded. "Before we leave here for your new accommodations, I would like to hear more from you, while my Guards do a little looking around. I want to know all about your plans."

The Silean Guard spread out through the house, some of them lining the walls. Pedar sat down looking like a lost and frightened child. He kept turning his face toward the kitchen, as if expecting Osa to call out to him. Wyer came and sat between Donal and Alwir, his broad legs curled beneath the stool and his arms crossed over his chest. Alwir glanced from the elder smith to the younger as their expressions hardened like cold iron. Then he stared at the floor and allowed the silence to fall heavily in the room.

In Shipper's Alley, Lirrel stopped walking. She stood in the road gazing out at the street and frowning.

"Come on," Jobber said impatiently. She could see the amber light streaming from the windows of the Hungry Owl, and she could almost taste the froth on Fran's brown ale. "We're just there. What's holding you up?"

"Something's wrong," Lirrel answered.

Jobber looked the street over quickly. The crowd seemed as usual, three men gambling knucklebones in a doorway, a whore farther down the street plying her trade for a prospective customer. "There ain't no Guards. Just some waterman having a turn at the bones. It's safe enough here."

"Still, there's something wrong. Something that doesn't feel right," Lirrel insisted.

"What doesn't feel right is my throat. I need a drink. Now are you coming or not?"

"I'm coming. But I don't like it. Why does it have to be this place?"

"'Cause I have to say good-bye to someone here. That is if he waited for me. Z'blood, I'm late enough." Jobber hurried her steps, and behind her Lirrel followed reluctantly.

They entered the inn, edging through the crowd along the far wall toward the kitchen. A quick check told Jobber that there was mostly countrymen and merchants staying in the inn. Fran was working behind the bar, draining tall pitchers of ale into tankards and pouring out neat measures of Oran brandy. He laughed at something a customer said and pocketed the coins. Jobber looked around again, spooked by Lirrel's warning. But there were no Guards and for that matter no Sileans. Jobber relaxed. This was going to be naffy. No one here would be interested much in her.

"Come on. Just nip out in back and see if he's there. Mind you, don't get in the Mistress's way. She's a wicked shrew," Jobber warned as they slipped around the bar past the kitchen entrance.

Maise came out, arms ladened with plates of food and Talia's shrill voice screeching after her. "Raving bitch," Maise was muttering to plates of stew. Her greasy hair hung in tired locks around her reddened face. Her eyes were puffy and bloodshot. She looked up and saw Jobber. Her mouth gaped open in surprise and then shut again quickly. She cast a furtive look about before sidling close to Jobber.

"Oy, Jobber, haven't you heard?"

"Heard what?"

"Z'blood, you are a hard nut ain't you?" she said looking Jobber up and down with an impressed expression on her bland face. "Butcherboys is out looking for you, you know."

"Anyone else?" Jobber asked.

"Yeah, a boy out back. Been hanging around most of the day

waiting on you. Scruffy lad. Mistress nearly scaffered him with a pot."

"Thanks," Jobber called and, pulling Lirrel along by the sleeve, headed for the back door.

Jobber paused in the doorway of the Hungry Owl limned by the gold light of the hallway. She peered into the dark alley not seeing anything at first but the bulky shapes of crates and netting hung to dry.

"Oy, Dogsbody, you out there?" she called.

"Over here, Jobber," came the quiet answer.

"Where?" Jobber continued to peer in the blackness.

"There," Lirrel pointed over Jobber's shoulder to a stack of piled crates on the far wall.

Jobber gave Lirrel a sidelong glance and for a second time wondered how much she could really see with those white eyes of hers.

"Come on out and have a drink with us," Jobber called.

"Nah, I can't."

"Bah, don't mind the Mistress. We're paying guests tonight. She won't hurt you."

"I only came to tell you something important, Jobber."

"Come out of there, you half-wit. I can't even see you in this dark."

"No, you come over here, Jobber. It's safer that way."

Jobber scowled, annoyed, but started toward the crates, leaving Lirrel to wait by the door. Why was Dogsbody being so cagey? Jobber passed into the shadows, the dark suddenly cloaking her.

"How come you're hiding?" she asked.

"Huh," snorted Dogsbody. "You ought to be, you know." He leaned against the wall and rubbed his thin arms. "Jobber, where you been all day that you don't know what's going on? Everyone's out looking for you."

"Yeah, what for?"

"Queens," the boy answered flatly. "Lots of them, too. There's a price out for you. Knackerman herself made the offer. And then to top it off, Upright Man come around and doubled the amount to the Flocks if they could find you first."

"Popular, ain't I?" Jobber laughed to mask the growing unease she felt. No one offered gold for a pickpocket. And now the Upright Man wanted in on it, too. It was her damnable hair. Had to be. Too many people had seen it bristling with sparks at Crier's Forge. Zorah's tits! Jobber swore angrily. She'd spent most of her

193

life hiding her sex and shielding her power. And now in one single afternoon the entire city knew of it, and she hadn't even had to pass the Readers.

"It ain't so funny, Jobber," Dogsbody answered, sounding hurt. "I done give Ratcatcher the slip so's I could come and warn you."

Jobber's face became serious. "Thanks," she said more gently. "Thanks a lot. Times like this I seem to count on very few friends."

Jobber could see the question in his eyes before he asked it. He was studying her, staring at her body.

"Jobber?" His voice was soft and tinged with awe.

"What?"

"Is it true?"

"Is what true?"

"Are you a dell?"

Jobber laughed and shrugged her shoulders. "I guess so. At least what's under these clothes looks more like a dell than anything else."

"Z'blood," he whispered. "Fooled me all right." He started giggling and one hand scratched through his matted hair. "You know that shitting Ratcatcher was telling us how he always knew a dell just by the way she smelled. Said it had to do with blood an' all, and that's why he'd have no dealings with them."

"What does Ratcatcher know anyway?" Jobber said scornfully.

"Enough to find you," replied a smug voice.

Jobber wheeled around and saw a black hulking shape making its way slowly up the alley. It was too dark to see clearly, but Jobber knew the husky voice well enough. Dogsbody pressed closer to the wall as if trying to disappear within it.

"Jobber," Lirrel called out a warning. "Three men."

"Is that all?" Jobber asked, sounding more confident than she felt.

"A dog, also."

Jobber nodded. There could be no doubt about its being Ratcatcher. But what mattered more was which bullyboys he'd brought with him. Jobber settled her shoulders and shook her arms to loosen the tension that coiled in her neck.

Ratcatcher sauntered into the light, his hands tucked into the pockets of his trousers. He stopped and, pushing back the black hat, grinned at her, exposing the pair of long front teeth that earned him his name. At his heels the dirty white bulldog sat

**194**

down on its squat haunches and growled. To Ratcatcher's left, Nicker appeared, his red hat pulled down over one eye and his lips twisted in a sneer. In his hand he held a length of rope. Jobber nodded to herself. She could handle Nicker; he wasn't as good at the old style as he thought.

Then Jobber's stomach squeezed into a knot as the second man approached the light and stood at Ratcatcher's right hand. He was an ugly snitch named Skull. Despite the skeletal nature of his name, the man was solidly built, with a thick neck that sloped into humped shoulders. He'd no hair, but shaved his scalp regularly with an old razor that left a trail of nicks and cuts across the stubbled scalp. His face was passive, blank as badly cut stone, and his eyes two black holes. Jobber knew how fast he could move in a fight and just how deadly he was when he used his razor as a weapon.

"Jobber, Jobber, please," Dogsbody was whispering frantically. "I didn't have nothing to do with this, honest I didn't."

"I know that," Jobber answered. She pulled the boy roughly from the wall and shoved him across the alley toward Lirrel. She wanted him out of the way and to have the comfort of the wall at her back. "Get him out of here," she snapped to Lirrel.

"No!" the boy answered. "I ain't leaving you, Jobber."

"Then stay out of my way," Jobber said, keeping her eyes on Ratcatcher's bullyboys.

"It don't matter what you do, Dogsbody," Ratcatcher said, pointing a finger at the frightened child. "I'll get you later. Nobody cheats Ratcatcher and gets away with it."

"Everybody cheats on you Ratcatcher, from your snitches to your whores. But you're so frigging stupid you don't even know it," Jobber said angrily to draw Ratcatcher's attention away from the boy.

"Like you, Jobber?" Ratcatcher said with a pout. "You should have owned up sooner you was a dell. I'd have given you protection."

"You'd have given me a disease."

"Ah now, is that any way to talk to someone come to make you a proposition?" Ratcatcher moved in closer, his hands held out to show he'd no weapon. Behind him Jobber noted how Nicker clutched the rope with anticipation. "The Upright Man wants to offer you a flash deal, Jobber. If you come quiet now, could be worth it to you."

"And if I don't come quiet?" Jobber asked, beginning to understand Nicker's intent with the rope. They wanted to take her

195

alive. That was to her advantage. At least Skull would have to keep his razor quiet.

Ratcatcher shrugged. "You'll come, willing or not."

"Bugger yourself," Jobber spat.

"Oh, if only I could," Ratcatcher answered, rolling his eyes in mock delight. Then, with a snarl, Ratcatcher flicked his hand. "Take her," he said, and Skull and Nicker sprang like two cast spears.

Nicker reached Jobber first, his leg swinging out in a high arced kick aimed at her head. Jobber ducked the kick and thrust herself forward beneath the raised leg. She swiveled around and slammed a double punch into his unprotected kidneys. Nicker groaned and doubled over, arms flung out. The rope dropped from his grasp. With the rigid edge of her hand, Jobber struck the back of Nicker's neck, sending him crashing into a stack of crates that toppled down over his falling body.

Jobber turned on her heel, blood coursing wildly but her body poised and ready. Skull was circling slowly, cautiously, as he kicked the rope to Ratcatcher. The wool cap Jobber wore itched and was distracting. She pulled the cap off and shoved it into her vest with a quick motion. The fiery hair tumbled down her shoulders with a scatter of sparks. As she wove back and forth, keeping the distance constant between herself and Skull, she passed from the shadows to the bright edge of light spilling from the inn door. Her face was stark, caught between the darkness and light. The amber light from the inn turned her hair the color of rust.

Skull was laughing softly, a deep rumbling sound. "Come on, pretty-pretty. Ain't you a flash thing. Give us a lock." He pulled his razor from a pocket and opened it. He held it up by its wooden handle, and Jobber saw the spark of light glance off the edge of the blade.

"Oy, Skull, remember what I said," Ratcatcher warned.

"I remember," Skull answered, mesmerized by the coppery glint of Jobber's hair. "Just hold still, pretty-pretty, and ain't no one gonna get hurt."

Jobber watched him steadily as he passed the blade from hand to hand, trying to scare her into surrender. Jobber shifted quickly to the left, feinting with a swift jab as she went. Skull lunged for her, and she shifted right again, seeking an opening in his defenses. But as quickly Skull passed the blade to his other hand and swung up. Jobber jerked her head, twisting her neck. She felt a lick of cold air as the blade swished past, just missing her throat.

"Watch it, Skull, or Upright Man will be peeling both our skins!" Ratcatcher called in alarm.

Skull laughed, and the impassive face sparkled to life with the deadly dance. Jobber chanced an attack, bolting upward, her crossed hands catching Skull's wrist in a lock. The razor waved in the air.

Skull reached with his other hand and grabbed a handful of hair at the base of Jobber's neck, wrenching her head to one side. She could see the razor, the edge hovering above her face. She was afraid to use her feet to kick him, afraid she wouldn't be able to control the razor if Skull fell down on to her.

"Get the rope, Ratcatcher!" Skull shouted.

"Jobber!" Dogsbody cried and darted forward away from the door to help her. Over Skull's shoulder Jobber saw him run, saw Lirrel try to stop him. Ratcatcher heaved himself forward and shoved Lirrel sideways, knocking her hard against the wall as he lunged for the boy. Lirrel crumpled to the ground, a hand reaching to her temple.

"No," Jobber roared, but it was too late. Ratcatcher collared Dogsbody by the scruff of his shirt. Dogsbody's arms flayed as he struggled to free himself, but Ratcatcher held him fast, swearing angrily. Jobber could only watch helpless as she fought with Skull, trying to wrestle away from the razor. She saw the sudden flash of Ratcatcher's dagger raised high. The steel glinted for an instant before Ratcatcher plunged it into Dogsbody's chest. The boy screamed in pain, and his arms lifted with terror. Ratcatcher stabbed him again, leaving the knife buried in his chest. Blood appeared, soaking through the ragged shirt. Dogsbody shuddered and then went limp, his shoulders folding and his arms dangling at his sides. Ratcatcher released him, thrusting his body away.

To Jobber it seemed the world moved with an infinite slowness and silence. As she watched, Dogsbody fell, drifting downward, red and gold like an autumn leaf. She saw Lirrel lift her head, a small stream of blood cutting a line along the edge of her cheek; then Ratcatcher's triumphant smile as he wiped his bloodied hand on his trousers. As if from far away Jobber could hear the scuffling of feet and the rasping sound of Skull's breath in her ear as he fought to keep his grip on her hair. At last, Dogsbody landed on the cobblestones and rolled slowly to one side. Jobber saw his face, soft like a sleeper, his mouth opened slightly.

Within the silence, Jobber heard the roaring of her blood, rage gusting like the wind sucked through the bellows to ignite the coal beds. Jobber's thin veneer of control bubbled away like scorched paint as she let the magic of her element shape itself into a fire that could match the heat of her rage. The coppery hair glowed hot, crackling and shimmering with orange and yellow sparks. Around her face, the fine hairs gleamed an iridescent blue. Skull bellowed a curse and pulled away his hand from her neck, the palms crisscrossed with livid, steaming stripes. The air tasted metallic and reeked of burnt flesh.

Distracted by the searing pain, Skull ignored the struggle for the razor. Jobber snapped his wrist around, the joints grinding, and with a shriek she forced the razor's edge across Skull's throat. Blood spattered on her hair and evaporated into trails of hissing mist. Skull reeled back from her, choking and gagging. His eyes rolled white with alarm, and he tried to turn his head toward Ratcatcher. He tumbled instead, falling heavily into the street, his body jerking in rhythm to the slowing pulse.

Jobber beggared one glance for him before she directed her fury to the retreating figure of Ratcatcher. She rushed him, her shoulder shoving into his back and knocking him down in the street. He turned, scrambling to his feet, and swung a punch to her face, the fist connecting hard to her chin. Her head snapped to one side, and the fiery hair sent a shower of sparks into the street. Pain flared along her cheek to be answered by a surge of fiery rage. Jobber wrenched her head back, and her shoulder lowered as she drove her own fist upward, burying it in Ratcatcher's gut. His heels lifted off the ground, and he lay poised for an instant over the point of her hard-driving fist. She freed him and he buckled over, gasping hard as the air was forced from him. He wheezed, his mouth opened like a gaping fish seeking air.  •

"Frigging bastard," Jobber screamed at him and grabbed him around the neck, jerking him upright. Jobber squeezed her hands tighter around Ratcatcher's neck, digging her thumbs into his flesh. He struggled to free himself, his hands raking at hers, trying to pry back her fingers.

But rage and magic together made her stronger, and Jobber refused to let go of him. Jobber smiled, feeling the sharp prickle of heat on her skin. She looked at her hands and saw the skin glowing white. She wouldn't have to strangle Ratcatcher; she'd merely hold him fast and make him share the fire of her rage. She drew in a long dry breath and tasted the rank odor of Ratcatcher's fear.

Ratcatcher's face flushed red, sweat beading his forehead and trickling down the sides of his temples. Jobber's hair continued to snap, throwing off sparks like splatters of molten metal. Ratcatcher gave a hoarse scream. His face began to erupt in blisters as water and blood boiled beneath the surface of his skin. The blisters swelled and burst, their contents turning to steam.

"Bastards," Jobber whispered to him. "Frigging bastards."

Ratcatcher howled again as his hair flashed with fire. It sizzled with pungent, gray smoke, scorching his scalp.

"Jobber!" Lirrel's voice called weakly. "Jobber," she cried again.

The sound of her voice penetrated through Jobber's fury. Jobber's gaze shifted slightly from Ratcatcher's scalded face, and she saw Lirrel leaning heavily against the wall of the inn. In the shadow her eyes glowed like two round moons. "Jobber, don't," Lirrel implored. Jobber ignored the words but couldn't turn away from the silver eyes. Lirrel pulled herself upright with effort and reached out a hand to Jobber.

"Don't touch me!" Jobber snapped.

"Release him."

"When he's dead."

"Now!"

Jobber forced her eyes away from the seductive dazzle of Lirrel's eyes and fixed her attention again on Ratcatcher. His face was barely recognizable from the seething mass of burning skin. He was blind, tears steaming in the empty sockets. His cries were growing weak, his voice a rattle. Only the two long front teeth gleaming white against the red and blackened mass of burned face reminded Jobber that it was Ratcatcher she held. Soon now, she thought, satisfaction sending ripples of heat along her arms to her hands.

Then suddenly Jobber heard the keening of a flute. A hollow, mournful sound that swept a chill across her fiery rage. Her hands softened their grip. Jobber looked around and saw Lirrel standing in the alley, the bone flute pressed to her lips. The music spiraled, gathering notes in a whirlwind. A wind gusted through the alley sweeping up the loose trash and tossing it over and over. A shutter banged open and shut. The dust rose in a fine cloud and stung Jobber's eyes.

Jobber ducked her head, her eyes tearing and blurred with the blown dirt. Red-gold hair blew across her face shrouding her. The wind continued to gust and keen, its notes driving cold air over her fury. The wooden crates skittered across the narrow alley, smashing into the walls and splintering, refuse scattering into the streets.

Through the thickening dust Jobber looked up.

Lirrel stood alone, untouched by the spiral of wind and dust. Her face was calm as she played, her eyes clouded as a winter moon. The keening music plucked at different sorrows in Jobber's heart and sent them fluttering like ragged flags. Jobber felt the rage in her abate, felt the heat cool beneath Lirrel's chilling wind. Jobber lowered her head and pried loose her fingers from the furrows in Ratcatcher's neck.

He crumpled to the ground and fell into the rectangle of light cast from the inn's open door. Jobber saw him now in the light; his face black, white teeth jutting stubbornly above the charred flesh.

"Enough," cried Jobber to Lirrel as the wind continued to gust fitfully and the hollow cry of the flute dug into her skin. "Enough," she choked out.

Lirrel lowered the flute and the wind died down, blown debris settling on the upturned crates.

"Z'blood," Jobber moaned, weariness stabbing her bones. She felt stretched thin like old parchment.

A shadow crossed the rectangle of light, and Jobber heard Talia's piercing scream slice through the mournful silence. "Murderers! Murderers! Get the Guards!" she wailed and slammed the door to the inn shut.

"Come, Jobber, we must go," Lirrel said, her voice sounding thick in the near dark of the alley.

Jobber shook her head sadly as she crossed to where Dogsbody lay. She bent down and grabbed the hilt of the dagger in his chest. It resisted, and she pulled harder until it finally slid out reluctant to part from Dogsbody's flesh. The child's body seemed to shrink then as the blood seeped from the wound and etched the spaces between the cobblestones. Jobber brushed the speckle of dirt from his face.

"Why'd he do that?" Jobber asked softly.

The shrill caw of the Guard's alarm sounded near to the alley.

"The mistress has sounded the alarm, Jobber. We must go now," Lirrel insisted.

"Well, I won't leave him here," Jobber answered.

"He doesn't know anything, Jobber. He's one with the chaos now."

"All the same, I won't leave him here," she said with finality and picked up the small body. Even in death he weighed less than she had imagined.

The alarm cawed again, closer, and now they could hear the stamp of boots and the cries of the Guards.

"This way," Jobber said, and clutching Dogsbody close to her chest, she began running down the dark alley. Close at her heels, Lirrel followed like a shadow.

# 17

Lirrel became frightened as Jobber led her running through narrow alleys where even her own sight could not penetrate the thick blackness. Jobber ran on instinct, trusting the twist and turns of Beldan's maze to hide her. Close behind, Lirrel followed the warm, metallic scent of Jobber's hair left hovering in the wake of her flight.

The air was cool and moist in the alleys, smelling pungently of the docks. Water splashed from muddy puddles soaking through the soft leather of Lirrel's shoes. Jobber turned a sharp corner, and Lirrel, running blindly, scraped her shoulder against the rough corner of the wall.

Lirrel stopped with a sudden cry as her eyes were bathed in stinging tears and the breath was snatched from her lungs. She coughed and blinked furiously, seeing the cluttered street shrouded in a dense veil of gray smoke. She took a shallow breath, fearful of its acrid taste. The smoke reeked of overly sweet incense, and beneath the perfumed aroma was the underlying stench of burning corpses.

Lirrel walked slowly, her steps halting. Jobber waited for her, shifting the burden of Dogsbody higher in her arms. She looked haggard. Smoke circled her face, but Lirrel could see the green eyes still lit from within by scraps of yellow flame. Lirrel covered her mouth with her shawl to keep from breathing in the bitter smoke and drifting ash.

"Where are we?" she asked.

"Scroggles," Jobber answered. "Where the poor hide their dead in the smoke."

Stepping from the shelter of the street, they crossed a small square and stopped before the opened doors of the public crematorium. The high wooden doors were thrown back, and inside pyres blazed bright against the soot-black walls, golden arms of fire reaching to the wide-mouthed chimney in the roof of the building. Dense smoke lifted from the pyres, teasing free flecks of ash and then carrying them aloft to the sky. Between the pyres lay the dead, wrapped in white shrouds, waiting alongside stacks of wood. Lirrel saw the bellowlads, dressed in their black coats and black neck scarves, hooking the wood over the bodies and pumping the bellows beneath the fires. A Sweeper's child in a black vest and ragged sleeved shirt, raked through the ashes of cold pyres, searching for the little trinkets and bones left behind by the dead. His face and hair were dusted white with the powdery ash. As they approached, Lirrel heard the rhythmic sound of the creaking bellows, their deep exhalations gusting through the flames.

A stout workman approached them, stepping out from the glowing light of the fires to stand at the door. Whisps of gray smoke eddied around his shoulders. Ash creased his face, and his shirt showed rings of sweat down the front. The sleeves of his black jacket were cropped short above his wrists.

"How much, Keeper?" Jobber asked, clutching Dogsbody closer as if unwilling to relinquish him to the man, and the place.

"Two strings," the Keeper answered.

"One. He's only a child."

"Give us a wink."

Jobber held out the body, and Dogsbody's head rolled to one side, white and lifeless in the orange glow. The man grunted and nodded in agreement.

"One then, and an extra copper for a scent stick. Lay him here."

From a hook on the side of the building, the Keeper took down a sheet of coarse, white cloth and spread it on the ground. Jobber laid the body down gently. She saw Trina's earring pinned to Dogsbody's chest, an ivory heart in a bloody stain. It would belong to the Sweeper's child before the night's end, she thought. The Keeper quickly folded the cloth over Dogsbody and secured the bundle with long, loose stitches, pushing the needle through with the callused pad of his thumb.

Lirrel took out a string of coppers and one extra and gave it to the Keeper. As he took it, she saw the gnarled web of scars on his hands and the charred fringe of his coat sleeves eaten away by the fire. It reminded Lirrel of Ratcatcher's blackened face, and she shuddered as she handed him the coins.

The Keeper gave Jobber a thin taper which he lit from a torch above the door. She held it, watching the sweet smoke escape in a fine blue haze. The Keeper grunted softly as he bent to pick up the bundle. Then he carried it over one shoulder and laid it along a stack of wood.

Jobber stepped closer, and Lirrel joined her when they saw the Keeper add the body to a funeral pyre. A bellowboy wiped his face with a corner of his scarf and rocked his foot on the bellow's handles. The pyre burst into a gout of new flame nurtured by the bellow's breath. Lirrel glanced at Jobber and saw her sharp features dissolve into the blunted curves of sorrow. The fine skin was slack, her eyes staring helplessly as they committed Dogsbody to the flames. The white shroud ignited, and Jobber's lips parted with a silent cry. In that unguarded moment, Lirrel had a vision of Jobber as a child, this same miserable face washed with remorse, peering with frightened eyes. Loneliness and anguish clung to her like ash, turning her pale. Tears brimmed in Lirrel's eyes, blurring the vision. She laid a comforting hand on Jobber's arm and drew back, startled by the scalding emotions of rage that entwined the grief.

The flames encircling the shroud were deep blue edged with gold and red. The shroud vanished in the fire, and the shape of the body suddenly emerged stark as a black shadow against the brilliance of the fire. It stayed a moment as if to resist the flame in this final farewell. Then it crumbled, falling inward on itself and, sinking into the heart of the pyre, commingled with the ash and fragments of the other dead.

"Let's go," Jobber said, dropping the scent stick. Absently, Jobber brushed at the blood drying on her vest. Remembering something, she reached into the vest and withdrew the blue cap. Her hair disappeared beneath the blue knitted brim and with it the metallic scent of copper. They walked back through darkened alleys, avoiding the lighted streets and merrymaking crowds. Lirrel looked up, hoping to catch sight of the night sky with its stars and saw only the pall of smoke drifting along the buildings.

Without warning, Jobber veered down an alley and entered once again into High Street. She walked quickly, her long legs reaching for the cobblestones.

"Where are we going?" Lirrel asked, stunned by the noise and gaiety of the crowded street. Drunk and boisterous fair-goers collided aimiably into her as she forced her way up High Street trying to catch up to Jobber. Jobber edged through the crowds, her arms pressed tight against her sides as if to avoid being touched.

"Where are we going?" Lirrel repeated.

Jobber halted and spun on her heel. "I'm going to Crier's Forge," she answered, her voice crisp and taut. "Master Donal will hold me over for a day or two until I can figure this out. You should run home to your people."

"No," Lirrel said, surprised by her own vehemence.

"I don't want your comfort, Lirrel."

"I know that, Jobber," Lirrel answered. "But you must realize that you won't be able to escape this thing so easily. It's not like before. With Growler."

"Why not?"

"You can't hide anymore. All of Beldan knows you exist."

"Bah," Jobber scoffed and shook her head disbelieving.

Lirrel threw her hands up in frustration. "Tcha, you are stubborn. You still believe you are like the black cock, just scratching in one circle to stay alive."

"That's right."

"You're not."

"Then what am I?" Jobber asked in a hoarse whisper.

Lirrel was quiet, hearing in the question not belligerence, but desperation. Lirrel sensed that it was an old question, one that turned over and over in Jobber's mind, seeking an answer. Deep in her pocket, Lirrel held her flute, as she thought wearily to herself, you won't like the answer, Jobber.

Lirrel looked away, her eyes resting on the sight of two countrywomen settled down before a small campfire on a street corner. Skirts tucked beneath their haunches, they leaned companionably toward the fire's warmth, its glow illuminating festival happiness on their rugged faces. Lirrel smiled sadly at them. This was the fire she had known; the peace of the hearth, a fire embraced by stones. But when Jobber's power unleashed itself in the alley without warning, Lirrel had been cast into the fire's roar. There had been no way she could avoid the intimacy of its violent grasp. She had tried to close her mind and her senses to its shattering blast, but she had not succeeded. Lirrel, who believed only in the solid strength of peace, was seized by the fire of Jobber's destructive rage and every nerve of her being had cried out in horror. While she had lain there trembling, Lirrel felt the fierce rocking of Oran's cradle and heard the howling of chaos.

And in the midst of the inferno, there had come a moment of prescience, a diamond-hard fragment of knowledge that rose untouched by Jobber's rage. At once Lirrel knew that Jobber's power came from the fiery core of Oran's cradle; not in one of the many small threads of magic that marked most of Oran's people, but as an elemental thread in the Queens' quarter knot itself.

Lirrel confronted Jobber's fire, opened her terrified senses to all its tumultuous power and peered into its white heart. It gleamed pure, not tainted by rancor or violence, but only with the desire to be shaped and used. Jobber's rage had pulled but a tiny spark out of its vast heart.

"What am I?" Jobber asked again, the yellow sparks igniting in her green eyes.

"Beldan's fire," Lirrel answered, catching the words as they hung in the air between them, understanding their meaning where Jobber did not.

"What does it mean?"

"That you, and not the Fire Queen Zorah, are the elemental guardian of Oran. You are like the cornerstone of a forge; the magical source of fire. From you, all the fire in Beldan is derived, whether in the tavern kitchens or the coal beds of Crier's Forge. And without you, Jobber, Beldan and all of Oran would be so much cold ash." Lirrel looked at Jobber, amazed even as Jobber was, hearing the truth pronounced in words.

Jobber stared stunned and then she rolled her eyes upward and gave a harsh, barking laugh. "And you're frigging crazy. I'm a street snitch with a bad temper that turns to sparks, and I don't give a rat's shit for all that vagger blow." Then she smiled as if she'd brushed aside some unpleasant duty.

"You can't escape it," Lirrel said simply.

"Watch me," Jobber answered.

"*Ahal*, I intend to."

Jobber scowled angrily and, stuffing her hands in her pockets, started up High Street again. She moved quickly, not looking back to see if Lirrel followed. Perhaps, Lirrel thought, Jobber meant to shake her loose, abandon her in the crowded city streets. Lirrel smiled ruefully. That was impossible now, no matter what Jobber did, no matter where Jobber went. Lirrel could hear her thoughts, loud and strident, crackling like the fire over the paler whispers of the others. She could see her, a slender wave radiating through the air, carrying with it the scent of copper. Knowledge was responsibility, Lirrel told herself. Sooner or later Jobber would accept that. And Lirrel wanted to be there at Jobber's side when it happened. She started walking, slowly but with determination, drawn on by Jobber's invisible trail and the angry buzzing of Jobber's thoughts.

Jobber slowed her steps at the entrance to the Iron Block. She forced herself to concentrate, raising a protective shield around her aura. She had to calm down, she warned herself. Save your neck from the noody noose, Jobbernowl. And what about the rest of it? she asked herself irritably. Lirrel's words had scraped a hole in her world, changing the dimensions of Jobber's self-image. Jobber didn't like it, she wanted things simple. It was easier to run that way.

Jobber resisted the temptation to turn around and see if Lirrel still followed. No, she murmured fiercely, it was too dangerous. Lirrel would only get her into trouble with all that talk. Jobber cracked her knuckles and told herself that Lirrel's warning didn't mean much; she would manage, just as she always had in the past. And then without wanting to, Jobber turned abruptly and stared down the dark street, tracing back the way she had come.

There were fewer people in the streets here, and most of the shops were dark and closed. A few torches sputtered greasily, shedding daubs of light on the street. In the upper balcony of a building Jobber heard the strains of dance music and singing. A woman laughed with a high-pitched whinny that grated on Jobber's spine. Jobber searched the shadows, watched each face as it passed beneath the dappled torchlight. But none of the faces except for a corner beggar, holding out his hand with its stubbed fingers, was familiar. She swallowed her disappointment, feeling it harden in her stomach. Who cares anyway, she muttered, it's what you want, ain't it? To be left alone. No ties to anyone. Z'blood, she swore, thinking of Dogsbody, it was just too painful.

"Jobber," a voice called softly.

Jobber's head jerked up, and she gasped in surprise as Lirrel emerged from a doorway close to where Jobber was standing.

"Frigging shit, don't do that!" Jobber yelled. "'Bout peeled my skin with fright."

"I knew you would wait for me," Lirrel said without arrogance, and Jobber saw the silvery gleam from her eyes.

"Who says I was waiting for you?" Jobber replied gruffly. "I was just having a wink around the street and then up you pops."

Lirrel was silent but the smile on her face told Jobber that she wasn't very convincing.

"You can't lie to me, Jobber."

"Can't escape, neither," Jobber growled. Jobber scratched her head, the knitted cap itching her skin again. She swore softly, as if exasperated, but she could not entirely hide the grateful expression. "Z'blood, do what you want then. But remember," she warned, "if anything happens to you, it's your game. I ain't here

**207**

to look after you, you know," Jobber said, annoyed with herself for sounding so petty.

"*Ahal*," Lirrel agreed, inclining her head. "I can take care of myself, Jobber. I did before I met you."

"Yeah, sure you can," Jobber answered, pointing to the bloody scrape on the side of Lirrel's head.

Lirrel touched it and winced with pain. "Violence is not the only coin that pays," she answered, squaring her shoulders.

"I wouldn't know," Jobber replied. "It's the only coin I've ever had to spend."

As they walked deeper into the Iron Block, the street sounds grew quieter and more subdued. The smaller stithies and forges were closed up tight, though occasionally they saw the dull orange of a coal bed through the bars of an opened window.

Jobber slowed her steps and lifted a finger. "Over there, that's Crier's Forge."

Lirrel opened her mouth to speak, her hand held out in caution, when from the darkened recess of a doorway a figure darted out and roughly jerked her backward. Hearing the scuffle, Jobber turned and saw Lirrel struggling with someone in the doorway.

Forgetting her own warnings, Jobber lunged, grabbing the figure with one hand on its shoulder, her other hand cocked in a fist ready to punch.

"No, Jobber," Lirrel cried loudly.

"Whose brangle is this?" Jobber shouted, suddenly confused by the feel of the frail shoulder collapsing beneath her grasp and Lirrel's unexpected cry.

"Shut up, Jobber," a familiar voice hissed, "shut up or you'll bring the butcherboys on us!"

"Where?"

"In the forge," the voice insisted. "I saw them go in awhile ago. Two squads, led by the Knackerman."

Jobber swore and stepped back swiftly to hide in the doorway next to Lirrel. Jobber glanced to her right and saw Kai's gaunt face near her shoulder.

"Now that's a frigging turn of the screw," Kai said drily.

"What are you doing here?" Jobber asked. "This ain't your usual territory."

"Same as you, I guess," she answered, pointing her chin toward the forge by way of explanation. "Funny that the old power should have brought us together. We ain't ones for sharing a plate are we?" Kai said.

"Yeah," Jobber said, her eyes averted. That was true enough.

They could never seem to be anywhere together but she and Kai fought. Jobber knew Kai resented her because she had refused to join the Waterlings. She'd wanted Jobber as a strong arm. Huh, what did Kai know anyway? And then Jobber heard again the words she'd just spoken... "that the old power should have brought us together..."

Jobber's head reared up, the back of her skull hitting the wooden door with a thud. Until then she hadn't believed Dogsbody. "Z'blood, does everyone on the street know I got the old power?" she demanded angrily.

Kai's eyes widened with surprise, the arched brows lifting. "I didn't know," she said slowly. "I only figured you was doing what I was doing," and she jerked her thumb toward Lirrel, "bringing her here. You know..." Kai's voice trailed off, as if having heard Jobber blurt out secrets Kai feared exposing herself in the same fashion.

"Zorah's tits," Jobber cursed, realizing her mistake. She squeezed her eyes shut, and her hands balled into fists. "I'm killing myself, that's what I'm doing. I'm frigging killing myself everywhere I go. What's the point of it all then?" she snarled, ripping off the cap and throwing it down in the street. "I might just as well strip naked for the Readers and get it over with."

"Z'blood," Kai whispered in awe, her eyes raking the length of hair that even in the dark glimmered with a faint red light. She touched it, drawing her hand away in surprise.

Jobber scowled at Kai's stunned face. "Didn't know I was dell neither, did you?"

Kai shook her head.

"Tcha, Jobber," Lirrel's voice warned, "they're coming out."

Swiftly Jobber scooped up the hat and shoved it on her head. They waited in the darkened doorway, watching as the Knackerman emerged, followed by Guards. Flanked on either side by the Guard, were Master Donal, Wyer, Pedar and Alwir, wrists bound and tied before them. They shuffled uncertainly, their steps plodding and heavy. Master Donal stumbled and Wyer stopped, awkwardly helping him to his feet again. In the torchlight, Jobber saw Donal's face, misshapen with swelling bruises and a bleeding cut over one eye.

"Frigging shit," she whispered angrily.

Last to leave the forge were two Guards, dragging between them by the hands and feet Osa's limp body. Her head arched back, the eyes staring at the retreating door. Her long braids swept along the ground, brushing a pattern in the trail of blood.

Another squad of Guards appeared at the corner and moving quietly occupied Crier's Forge. They shut the doors, and a face peered for an instant at the window before disappearing again. To anyone coming late to the forge, all would seem normal.

Kai groaned and slumped in the doorway.

"Jobber, help me," Lirrel said worriedly. "She's hurt."

Jobber leaned down and started to pull Kai up by the arm.

"Let go," Kai shrieked in pain. "Frigging . . . don't touch me!"

Jobber dropped her arm rapidly and squatted down beside the huddled figure.

"What happened to you?" she asked, now seeing Kai's face white and sweating with pain.

"Took a slice, in the arm," Kai grunted.

"Z'blood, Kai, that ain't your style," Jobber said more softly, this time wrapping an arm around Kai's waist and hoisting her gently.

"You don't know much about me," Kai said spitting out her answer between clenched teeth.

"Seems I don't know much about anyone these days," Jobber said, staring down the street where they had taken Master Donal. "I know I made some trouble for Master Donal today, but that don't explain why they'd take him and Wyer in like this. And Pedar and that other skinny one. And why, why did they scaffer Osa? And where's Soltar? I didn't see him." Jobber shook her head, confused and angry.

"We must leave here," Lirrel said, uneasily nudging Kai away from the wall.

"No," Kai replied with a sharp intake of breath. She cradled her injured arm. "We've got to warn the others. If they come, the Guard will take them, too."

"What others?" Lirrel asked.

"The others like yourself," Kai insisted, annoyed. Her eyes squeezed shut, and she licked her parched lips. She opened her eyes slowly and saw the soft moonlit eyes staring back, puzzled. "You really don't know what's going on here, do you?" she said surprised, looking from Lirrel's to Jobber's face.

"What is it then?" Jobber asked, growing impatient.

"New Moon," Kai said.

"Nah, I don't believe it," Jobber snapped. "Master Donal would never hold with the New Moon."

"That's straight-fingered, Jobber. The New Moon has been giving safe passage out of Beldan for those with the old power. I was told to come here if interested."

"But you ain't one of those. You've been Named," Jobber answered, pointing to the mark on Kai's hand.

"We must go," Lirrel interrupted, watching the street nervously. "It is dangerous to remain. No others will be coming here tonight."

"How can you be sure?" Kai asked.

"Someone else knows what has happened," Lirrel stared up at the rooftops, searching the black edges of the buildings. "Someone else is watching."

Kai hesitated and then her shoulders sagged with weariness. "If you're sure."

"I am certain of it," Lirrel said gently.

"Let's go then."

"Where?" Jobber asked harshly. "Where is it safe anymore?"

"The Grinning Bird. Zeenia's place," Kai said.

"You'd trust a crazy dell like her?"

Kai nodded. "I don't think she's so crazy. Fact is, I'm willing to lay sillers she's got some secrets of her own. Like us." Kai bowed her head, her crow's hair shading her cheeks and hiding her face. The bandage on her shoulder was stained with fresh blood. She covered it with her shawl and hugged the arm close to her body. "Seems like we've all got our secrets," she murmured angrily to the cobblestones.

They walked back through the quiet streets of the Iron Block, avoiding the noisy avenues and streets that led into High Street. Through back alleys they stumbled over sprawled figures of drunken sleepers and the occasional clutch of street children, huddled together for warmth and security. Kai looked them over as they walked past, her step slowing.

"Looking for someone?" Jobber asked when Kai stopped in an alley where two children were curled in a bed of rags.

"Always," Kai answered curtly and continued walking.

They walked on in stony silence, Jobber chewing on a ragged fingernail. She could hear Lirrel's warning echoing in the streets. It's not like last time, Jobber. It's not like last time. Perhaps Lirrel was right, she conceded. But what was the answer then? Where should she go? With a sudden rush of sorrow, Jobber wished that Growler were still alive. That he would tell her what to do. Jobber could see his face, hear the gravely sound of his voice. Life was dangerous with him, but never as fearful as it was now. It was the loneliness, she decided, that made it so terrible.

"You never answered me, Kai," Jobber said, breaking the si-

**211**

lence. "What were you doing at Crier's Forge if you ain't got the old power?"

"I'll answer yours, Jobber, if you answer one of mine," Kai replied.

Jobber scowled, not certain what secrets she had left anymore that would be of interest to Kai. "Fair enough, then."

Kai pursed her lips and then spoke. "I'm a Reader."

"Z'blood!" Jobber spit reflexively.

Kai glared at her but continued talking. "I'm bastard got, wrong side of the bed from a big house. My ma hid out with me out on the Ribbons. When I was old enough to be on my own, I formed a Flock. Most of the Waterlings are children I found, left to die because they had the old power."

"That's how you knew about me, isn't it?" Lirrel said softly.

"Yeah. I was waiting near the forge, just Reading people as they passed to see if the offer of help was a good one. I figured if I saw anyone with the old stuff go into the place, I'd know it to be safe. So I seen you coming and Read you. Air, ain't you?"

Lirrel smiled in agreement. "*Ahal*, you are right."

"If you're a Reader, what are you doing down here?" Jobber asked suspiciously. "You could be living up at a big house, 'stead of trawling the tunnels."

Kai's lips twisted with disgust. "I'm street born and bred. I'll have nothing to do with them. They sell us out, year after murderous year. I know where my loyalties lie, and it ain't with those boot-licking bastards."

"Fair enough," Jobber answered.

"And what about you, Jobber?"

"What do you mean?" Jobber snapped, hearing the accusation in Kai's question.

"Where do your loyalties lie?"

"How can you ask such a stupid question. There's a price out for me now. Knackerman's offering up queens, and to make it worse, even the Upright Man's got his bullyboys hunting me. So why should I have any love for the lot of them, eh? I got more reason than you to hate them, don't I? I'm staring up at the noodynoose."

"No you ain't," said Kai slowly. She stopped walking and turned to face Jobber. She pulled out her knife from her pocket and held it up. Her black eyes sparkled with hate. "I Read you, too, when you were coming up the street. You didn't give off no aura. You're black, just like me, just like ordinary folks. So what's your lay, Jobber?"

212

Jobber stepped back from the knife. Kai shoved herself between Jobber and Lirrel as if to protect Lirrel from Jobber. Jobber's mouth gaped open in surprise. "Zorah's tits!" Jobber spat and moved to knock the knife from Kai's grasp.

"No!" Lirrel shouted, reaching out a hand to stop Kai from thrusting the knife. "No," she cried again, pleading to Jobber as she held Kai's knife hand. Jobber backed off, her face tight with fury. "Kai, listen to me," Lirrel said quickly. "It's true what Jobber said. She does have the old power, and she is being hunted. She's a fire elemental."

Lirrel released Kai's arm, and stiffly Kai lowered it to her side, her eyes never leaving Jobber's face. "If that's true, then why don't you cast an aura? Why couldn't I Read it?"

"An old vagger trick," Jobber replied, her voice hoarse and constricted as she struggled to contain her temper. "Growler taught it to me when I was little and he first give me the leather cap. It was to protect me."

"And it worked."

"Not always."

"But usually," Kai pressed, leaning forward. "Like tonight."

Jobber shrugged. "Tonight it did. Though it's too late to do me any good," she added sourly.

Kai shrieked like the caw of a riled crow and flew at Jobber, the knife raised in an attack. Jobber stumbled back, startled by Kai's fury. But her reflexes snapped to life and she easily blocked Kai's wild swing. She slammed Kai's wrist down on the hard crest of her knee. Kai's shrieks changed to cries of pain. The knife clattered to the street.

Jobber yanked Kai's arm upright again, and twisting her wrist, locked the wrist joints firmly. Any movement would cause Kai pain as the joints ground together.

"No wonder you got yourself sliced," Jobber's voice rasped out next to Kai's ear. "I told you this ain't your style of work."

"At least I care enough about something to try," Kai answered bitterly. "But not you, you selfish little bastard. But for the know-how of a trick, a stupid vagger trick, half of my Flock would still be alive."

"That ain't got nothing to do with me," Jobber hissed and thrust Kai away. Kai's words stung, and Jobber wasn't certain why.

"Yeah it does," Kai said. "You could have shown them. You could have taught the others. But not you. You never wanted a Flock. Your precious Growler turned your head into thinking you was so special that you had no need for anybody."

"How was I supposed to know the Waterlings had power. You're the Reader, not me," Jobber argued back.

"It didn't have to be the Waterlings. You knew there were others with magic. Some of them boasted about it. Like Shrike, who never made no secret of his power and went to his hanging without a hood so all could see his scorn for the Sileans' fear of him. What about them? Were you too good for all of them?"

"That weren't it and you know it," Jobber said, her shoulders hunched with anger. She felt cornered. "I did what I could." Jobber heard the hollowness of her own words as the memory of Dogsbody's death stabbed her with remorse. He had tried to help her, and he had been killed. It was the same with Growler. It was the same with anyone she allowed too close. She did them all a favor sticking to herself. Why couldn't Kai understand that?

"You did only what suited you," Kai said sourly. "Never took anyone's side but your own. You could have helped them," she insisted. "You could have taught them."

"What the frigging shit good would any of it done?" Jobber cried out angrily. "What good would it have been? It don't always work and ain't no way it would work against a crowd of Readers—"

"It might have. It worked against me, and I'm as good a Reader as any on the hill." Kai sat down heavily on a storefront stoop, her expression crumbling. The windows behind her showed an array of ribbons and hand-knitted lace. Kai bowed her head and tucked it into the corner of her elbow. Her shoulders shook with silent weeping. Jobber shoved her hands into her pockets, waiting uncomfortably and wishing Kai would stop. Out of the corner of her eyes, Jobber saw Lirrel standing as if uncertain who first to give comfort.

Finally Kai's shoulders heaved with a ragged sob and slowly she raised her head. She sniffed hard and wiped a hand across her eyes, dragging the tears off her face. She showed Jobber a weary face, the large dark eyes puffed and swollen. When she spoke, her voice was cracked. "If even one of them knowing your trick had made it past the Readers, it would have given the rest something to hope on." Kai shook her head. "There ain't nothing left I can do for them. The New Moon was my last hope. Between the Readers and the Upright Man, they ain't got much chance."

Jobber frowned. "What's the Upright Man got to do with any of it?"

Kai twisted her hair into a knot. "Someone's fingering those with power," she said dully, "then the Upright Man murders them by sucking the living blood right out of their bodies."

Lirrel gasped in horror, one hand flying up to cover her mouth.

"Why would he do that?" Jobber asked, eyes narrowing.

"To steal their power. Take it into himself. He's got an aura of all different colors, though like you he must have a vagger trick or two to keep the Readers from finding out about it."

"It can't be true," Jobber denied flatly.

"I seen it with my own eyes," Kai replied coldly. "Caught him murdering a whore's babe in Knacker's Alley. I tried to stop him, and he give me this." She lifted her injured arm.

Jobber's stomach churned with nausea. She felt encased by helpless anger and revulsion. Heat flared in her cheeks, igniting the flames in her eyes.

Jobber saw that Kai studied her, stared at her with those large black eyes, the gaze unfocused. Jobber knew that she was being Read, and the fire in her veins bubbled hotter.

But for once, she felt suffocated by the fiery rage, as if its blatant presence betrayed her selfishness. Kai gave a startled cry, her weary expression replaced by wonderment. Kai's face glowed with a faint yellow light, and Jobber realized it was the reflection of firelight from her own eyes. Jobber stumbled, hands pushing back the crush of remorse.

"I never hurt anyone that didn't deserve it," Jobber said thickly, her eyes averted from Kai's piercing gaze. "There's nothing I could have done for any of them," she exclaimed, the words wrung from her throat as she struggled not to shout. Her heart was pounding; and she heard again the steady clamor of nails being hammered into the scaffolds. The fire roared in her heart, but not loud enough to obliterate the dry wailing of children perched like birds on the scaffolds shoved from the ledge into a final flight. And as the fire crackled in her joints and yellow sparks burst before her eyes, Jobber recalled Shrike as he was standing, the winds ruffling his black hair with its braided lock of white. He smiled contemptuously at the gathered crowd as if enjoying himself, and just before they sprung the traps, he threw back his head to howl with laughter. Standing here now, Jobber could have believed the bitter smile was for her alone.

"Jobber," Lirrel's whisper called to her.

Jobber looked at Lirrel and then recoiled, seeing the look of sadness mingled with pity. It was far worse than Lirrel accusing her of betrayal; it was a gesture of forgiveness for something not even Jobber was willing to forgive herself.

"Leave me alone. Frigging leave me alone, all of you," she shouted. And turning sharply on her heel, she began to run, fleeing in a shower of sparks. She turned a corner and disappeared in the darkness.

Lirrel watched her go, wanting desperately to cry out to her to stop. But she heard the anguish in Jobber's thoughts, sensed the fury that drove its point like a dagger into Jobber's heart. She won't listen to me, Lirrel told herself. Not yet.

Lirrel reached into her pocket and withdrew her flute. If the words wouldn't reach, perhaps the music could.

She played a tune on the flute, offering its sweet voice like balm over the city. Lirrel knew it would do little to heal the wounds in Jobber's troubled heart. That Jobber would have to do for herself. But Lirrel hoped that the music would at least let Jobber know that she was not alone.

# 18

Candles burned with thick smoke in the state room as servants hurried to bring trays of food and wine. The mood however was not celebrant but tense. Regent Silwa wore an outraged expression, his skin flushed a ruddy color as he paced angrily. Queen Zorah watched him, thinking to herself that strong men had such a weakness for the scent of battle. He must have been waiting for this moment, she thought, for even at this hour he wore his sword strapped at his hips as if anticipating attack.

"We should make a show of power tomorrow," Regent Silwa was speaking forcefully, one hand hitting against the other palm.

"I say we wait until after the Festival," the Queen disagreed. "We must preserve the integrity, the spiritual nature of the Naming ceremony." Roused from sleep, Zorah looked tousled, her face tired. She had braided her hair loosely and it was coming unraveled.

"If you wait until then, it may be too late," Silwa insisted. "We need to crush this New Moon now like vermin before they infect others with their ideas."

"These papers indicate that they are planning an assault from Sadar, but not until after harvest. We have plenty of time to clear them out and do so away from the city."

"Madam, why are you hesitating?"

"Why are you in such a hurry to persecute my people!" Zorah flared.

"Because they are in a hurry to destroy you."

"Nonsense. These plans show they mean to rid Oran of Silean influence. They say nothing about me. Silwa, listen to me," she said as if speaking to calm an excitable child. "I have seen this sort of thing before. It will be over before it starts."

"Nonetheless it is a bold course they have entered on. Joining with the Guildmasters," Adviser Antoni said softly as he slipped into the room. "Can you be certain they have not found a way to remove you and preserve Oran? That red-haired thief perhaps. She seems to have disappeared."

Zorah stared angrily as he turned to close the doors. "Impossible," she answered, plucking at her skirts in agitation. When he faced the room again, Zorah frowned at the sudden chill skittering up her back. Antoni looked different, his dark eyes opaque. He swayed slightly when he walked, and Zorah wondered if he was drunk. As she watched, he laid a hand self-consciously to his beard, smoothing it down.

"Either way, Madam," Silwa called her attention again, "either way it could prove disastrous if the New Moon is allowed any more time in which to acquire further strength. There is enough trouble with vaggers and laborers without adding Guildmasters to the ranks of the New Moon. Give them room to grow and there will be bloodshed and a return to the horrors of the Burning. We must crush it now."

Zorah lowered her eyes, and her teeth raked her lower lip. She lifted her head and looked to Gonmer.

"What do you think, Firstwatch?"

"I am concerned that they have netted a Reader among their numbers. Readers have always been loyal to you."

"They know who cuts their meat," Silwa said.

"But I agree with you, Madam," Gonmer continued in spite of Silwa's remark, "it could be more imprudent to do anything here and now—"

"There is no better time than now," Silwa insisted.

"Beldan is full of people, many who have nothing to do with the New Moon. If we make much of them, word will spread. These rebels will be martyrs, and the New Moon will spring up everywhere. I say we keep them locked until the fair is over and then quietly set about undoing their work," Gonmer said with finality.

"No. It cannot be like that," Silwa argued. "When you train a horse you show on the first mounting who is the master. Give them too much lead and they will throw you off."

"The people of Oran are not a horse."

"But they will be ridden like one, Firstwatch. They need to be guided, directed, and that can only be done by a firm hand," Silwa answered.

"What are you proposing, Regent?" Zorah asked.

"Tomorrow at the Great Bonfire we commit the rebels to the flames."

"You forget where you are, Regent Silwa," Zorah answered coolly. "In Oran we do not taint the fire with execution."

"And in Silea we do. I will admit we have a difference of

opinion," Silwa squared his jaw. "But think on it, Madam. Perhaps what is needed is a new policy. These are people bent on destruction. Burning them will not taint the fire. Regard their execution as a cleansing, a purging of Oran of the threat of another Burning. Is that not the significance of the Great Bonfire?" he asked, hands clasped behind his back.

Zorah was silent, her arms crossed over her chest. What did he know of Burning? This man standing here, inflated by his self-importance and his foreign ideas. What did he know of fire? Zorah's head dipped, her chin resting above her chest. Only she knew what the Burning was. She had been there, seen the blackening of Beldan's sky, heard the screams as people died and felt the earth buckle and split angrily beneath their feet. It had been the end of time. To Silwa it was history, a battle he never saw. To her it had been the end of time.

"Madam," Silwa's voice called to her and she looked at him dimly seeing him through the mist of remembered images. He was bent, hands leaning on the wooden table, his face dark as he stared attentively. A strong face, she thought, the black hair and beard like coal. "Madam, give us your answer."

"I have no wish to return to the Burning," she said evenly. "But you will hang them, and when they are dead, their bodies will be sent to Scroggles."

Silwa nodded, his expression triumphant, even eager. He's going to enjoy this, Zorah thought grimly. Flexing his power over the Oran people.

"Agreed then. It shouldn't be too difficult to raise the scaffolds in the time remaining before the procession at Fire Circle."

Gonmer nodded. "I shall prepare for an additional squad of Guards to handle the prisoners—"

"No," Silwa interrupted her. Gonmer's mouth tightened in a wordless reply. "No, Firstwatch. I shall handle it."

"With all respect, Regent Silwa, the protection of the city is my responsibility."

"Not when it becomes a military matter. Then it is my responsibility."

"Are you declaring war?"

"On the contrary, I am preventing one."

"I must protest. This is a breach of protocol." Gonmer turned to the Queen, waiting for her to confirm her status.

Instead Zorah pursed her lips. "You haven't found the red-haired girl yet, Firstwatch."

"No, Madam, but surely this—"

"Leave this matter to the Regent Silwa. I am more interested in the girl."

"But, Madam," Gonmer insisted, trying to keep her anger under control. She moved closer to Zorah, her voice lowered. "I am not a common blade, Madam, to be removed from my duties with such dispatch."

"Firstwatch Gonmer," Zorah added more firmly, "your duty is to me. And I say I wish you to find the girl. She is the real threat. Not the New Moon."

Gonmer nodded stiffly. "Madam," she replied, consenting against her will.

"I will speak with you again, Firstwatch, in the morning," Silwa added, with a look of satisfaction at her face clouded with fury as she left the room, one hand clasped on the hilt of her sword.

"Madam, I will need your assistance tomorrow as well," Silwa said to Zorah.

"In what manner?" she asked. Reluctance was easily read on her face.

"I need you to speak to the people. The judgment against these rebels must come from you."

"So as not to be seen as an arbitrary act of Silean justice?" Zorah said without humor.

"Let them know, Madam," Silwa said, irritation flickering in his eyes, "that following the path of the New Moon will lead them to bloodshed. At all accounts you will not be lying to them."

"I shall do that, Regent Silwa. My people will trust me to give them the truth."

"Good. It will make the task of executing these rebels that much easier and quicker."

Zorah studied him uncertainly. Silwa had settled himself before a table, his manner full of purpose. "Are you sure you know what you are doing, Regent Silwa?"

He looked at her surprised. "Of course, Madam. Don't worry. I want what is best for all of us."

She nodded slowly. "I hope so." Zorah shivered suddenly as if caught in a cold draft. "I'll return to my rooms then and prepare tomorrow's speech."

Silwa crossed to Zorah and laid an arm over her shoulder. It felt warm and comforting. Beneath its grasp she could feel the tremor of excitement in his body. *He finally has what he wants,* she thought, feeling weary. She stepped away from his embrace and headed for the door.

When she had left, Silwa turned back to the state room and motioned Antoni over to the table. He spared Antoni a quick glance and then frowned.

"Who cut you?" he asked.

Antoni's hand rose to his face, the long slender fingers grazing the cut on his cheek. He shook his head slightly, a sardonic smile playing on his lips. "A woman. A minor disagreement."

Silwa shrugged his shoulders. "I never figured you for that sort of game, Antoni." Then he forgot the matter as his attention was drawn to the papers on the table. An idea had formed itself, and he wanted to take action on it quickly. "I need you to take a message to Secondwatch Fabrian. He's a good man, and I think I can trust him for this job."

"What's the message?" Antoni asked, eyebrows lifted in interest.

"I want every available Guard ready to mount up. I intend to use the cavalry tomorrow."

"What do you really have in mind, Silwa? Are you expecting trouble?"

"No, merely anticipating in case there is. Look here at this drawing of Fire Circle. Only five narrow roads lead out. We will have the cavalry wait here on each road. From there it will be easy enough to ring the crowd, contain them should that become necessary."

"Yes, I see what you're getting at." Antoni tapped a finger along the line of narrow roads. "It will be a massacre, Silwa, if you run the cavalry through there."

"Merely a stern reminder of who is in power. They are peasants, Antoni, and they need occasionally to have the fact pointed out to them."

"A word of caution, however, as your Adviser. They are stubborn peasants. If you act too harshly now, you may have to do worse before it's finished."

"I'm prepared for that," Silwa answered. "This cavalry is only my insurance against a restless crowd. I don't particularly like the idea of sitting up there with a mob of Oran peasants at my feet getting angry because we swing some of their rebels from the noose."

"I shall be there, too, remember," Antoni smiled. "May I suggest clappers to help sway the crowd to our point of view."

221

"As you wish. Pay them well to shout the Queen's praises."

Antoni stroked the sides of his beard with one hand, then asked, "Do you think the Queen is as invincible as she claims?"

Silwa's head jerked up. "Is that what you're after?" he asked sharply. "I've often wondered what kept you in Oran all these years."

Antoni gave a coarse laugh and waved the suggestion away with his hand. "Curiosity, that's all it is. It raises my hackles to see her in power and to think that it may be for an eternity. Imagine what we could do if we had a free hand?"

Silwa smiled. Hadn't he wondered that himself?

Antoni continued talking. "What has kept me in Oran all these years is a secured and wealthy life. Much harder to come by in Silea. Although noble, my father's holdings were precious little to be pared among three sons."

"Indeed," Silwa replied. "I'm not certain anymore whether I would return to Silea or remain here in comfortable exile. I have begun purchasing vineyards in the west country to that purpose."

Antoni laughed again. "You're a soldier, Silwa. I'd give you a year in the country before you roused the ire of the local peasants just so as to have an opportunity to batter them down."

"And you, Antoni?" Silwa asked. "What will you do if the next Regent does not want your advice and selects someone else?"

"I shall retire."

Now it was Silwa's turn to laugh. "And return in a year's time, no doubt, after your replacement has suffered some terrible misfortune. Don't think I didn't know about you before I requested you as Adviser, Antoni. One doesn't keep this position for as long as you have without stealth and perhaps a bit of low dealing."

"You give me too much credit as schemer, Silwa. I don't know whether to be flattered or insulted."

"Let us just say we understand each other."

"Fair enough." Antoni looked amused as he prepared to leave. Silwa finished writing his orders and handed them to the Adviser.

"Tomorrow should prove very interesting," Silwa said rubbing his hands together.

"And, I trust, successful," Antoni added.

He headed for the door, leaving the Regent Silwa behind musing over the maps of Fire Circle and breathing in the anticipated dust and sweat of battle.

# 19

Ener Re Aston walked nervously down the dark corridors of the dungeons following the Guard he had bribed. They were hidden deep beneath the Keep, carved out of the bedrock that formed the promontory on which the Keep rested above the city. He remembered his grandfather telling him that these caverns were once storage holds intended to store seed grain in the event of a harsh season. But the dusty scent of grain was gone, replaced by the stench of decay. The holds were now filled with prisoners, lost to the light and air of the world above. Light from the Guard's torch flickered through the heavy bars of the prison cells and Ener watched in horror as men scattered from the light like rats. A few did not scatter but lay still, shoved against the bars of the gates, and he knew as he covered his nose and mouth with his sleeve that they were dead.

"Z'blood," he murmured, and the Guard in front of him turned around and smiled unpleasantly.

"Get's a bit thick, don't it?" Then he shrugged. "They clear out the stiffs once a fiveday, but with Firefaire it could be longer."

They passed another crowded cell, and a child appeared briefly, her eyes staring unblinking at the light. Ener stumbled, seeing the chalk white face and the hollow eyes. Papery fingers reached for the light. She started to wail as the Guard passed and the light faded. The sound of her keening followed him down the corridors.

How could my son have done this? Ener asked himself angrily. How could Alwir have done this to the family. To me. Ener's face grew hot with indignation, and he wiped away the clammy sweat that had gathered on his forehead. It was hard enough for the Reader families to maintain their position in the Silean regime. Ener was constantly on his guard against any such attacks on his family that might endanger their delicate status. And now this, he thought savagely. His own son in a rash moment of thoughtless idealism had doomed them all. He was convinced that a Silean judgment would go hard against the family. Their lands and holdings would be confiscated, their titles stripped from them. Maybe even this damnation, he thought anxiously, eyeing the prison cells.

No, no, Ener thought adamantly, they would not. He would see to that. Alwir would not be allowed to ruin their lives. He would order Alwir to renounce the New Moon and convince him to beg for mercy from the Queen. He had already decided to humiliate himself and plead for clemency, claiming his youngest son's former illness made him weaken to the false promises of the New Moon. And then he would bribe as many Sileans as was necessary to insure the judgments against them would not be too severe. All this he would do to save the honor and position of the Re Aston family.

And, he hoped as the Guard's torch waved over the contorted face of a corpse, perhaps one night in this dark hole would be enough to bend Alwir back to the straighter course.

"Here we are," the Guard said, noisily rifling through a set of keys. He looked worriedly at the keys. "Can't seem to find the right one. Pity, too, this is the last gate." He looked up expectantly and without hesitation, Ener pulled a small bag of coins from beneath his vest and gave it to the Guard.

The man weighed it and smiled. "Here it is," he said, producing the key, "got his own special cell he does. Lucky lad." Then, pausing before opening the door, he added. "Don't stay long, or I'll lock you up with him."

Ener Re Aston kept his face composed as the Guard glanced at him, but inwardly his guts twisted with a sharp stab of fear. It was possible he would do that. With the Silean Guard, anything was possible.

"I shall be brief," he answered.

"I'll call you once and once only, and you'll come here to the gate," the Guard said.

"Leave the torch."

The Guard hesitated and then shrugged, placing the torch in a rusted stanchion. The old man stepped inside the cell and the Guard locked the gate behind him.

The cell was small and dark, the light from the torch sputtering weakly and casting only a narrow smear of light. From the gate it seemed unoccupied.

"Alwir," he called uncertainly. Fear spasmed again as he wondered if the Guard had locked him in an empty cell.

"Over here, father," came the reply.

Ener heard scuffling sounds as Alwir stood and slowly moved into the light. All thoughts of anger and outrage at his son's betrayal faltered as he gazed on the gaunt face, the long hands bound together at the wrists. Looking at the slender frame, he remembered that whatever else he thought about Alwir, this man was his youngest son, a child with a bright mind but a weak spirit. Alwir was as different from Balder and Renn as the moon to the sun, but he was still a child of his own flesh.

Alwir stared at him steadily. "I had not thought to see you here, father."

"Alwir, my son," the old man replied, stung by the bitter tone in Alwir's words. "We may argue, but I am not indifferent to your fate."

Alwir smiled thinly. "How are my brothers?"

"Worried."

"About themselves, no doubt."

"Alwir, surely you must realize your arrest has placed us all in a dangerous position," Ener answered, the anger returning.

Alwir gave a harsh laugh, his expression suddenly twisted with pain. "All I have realized, father, is that there is no limit to cruelty. I have been here a short time, but already I've heard stories of the beatings, the rapes, the slow starvation." Alwir looked at the ceiling as if to pierce its oppressive weight. "But even in here, privilege has been served. I await my hanging alone, while in the next cell thirty or more men and women suffocate and starve in a space this size. I will be here but one night. They will be here for an eternity."

"You will not hang," Ener Re Aston seized on the words as a drowning man might a rope. "Rather, you will beg forgiveness of the Queen, and I shall see to the rest."

Alwir stared at his father with a mixture of sadness and contempt. "No, father. I will not beg the Queen for anything, except perhaps that she renounce the Sileans and stop her murdering of children with power."

"Think of the family," Ener Re Aston said urgently, gripping Alwir by the arm. "Don't be a fool, Alwir."

"I am not a fool, father," Alwir answered as he shrugged his father's hand from his arm. "And I have learned to think of the Oran people as my family. For them I am willing to make this sacrifice."

"Your sacrifice will make no difference to the common peasant. He will not care, Alwir. His life will go on exactly as before, and your death will have accounted for nothing."

Ener Re Aston studied his son's face, saw the moment of hesitation when doubt weakened the resolve. But as quickly his expression hardened and determination carved a final stamp to his face.

"You may be right, father," Alwir said softly. "My death will be one of many and perhaps go unremembered. But not so the reasons for which I chose death. Those will remain for as long as the struggle against the Queen's tyranny continues. And it will continue," he said pointedly. "That is enough for me. I will not allow you to save me, father. I will save myself by dying for the truth I believe in. A Reader's life of duplicity holds no honor for me."

Panic threaded in Ener's veins. He had been certain that a short time here would have been enough, that Alwir would have been ready to abandon his madness. Instead the boy had stood apart from him, choosing a criminal's death against all common sense and need. For Ener the choice had been one of beating the Sileans at their own game, of staying alive and prospering to spite them. His other sons, Renn and Balder, had chosen to follow behind him. Certainly it had cost lives; every Reader's life depended on the death of another. But Alwir had refused to accept the terms of the Silean game. He would play his own, even if it meant forfeiture of his life. "Alwir, you will shame us," Ener said vehemently.

"Is that all you care about, father?" Alwir burst out angrily. "The stain on your family name?" Alwir twisted away and spoke to the walls. "The Sileans will do no more to you than to slap your wrists and levy an insult fine against you. A dog after all is more dangerous when not muzzled," he turned slightly to his father. "The Queen doesn't want our kind mingling with common people. The Re Astons will be safe from punishment."

"Alwir, reconsider—"

"Time to go," the Guard shouted to Ener, and around them in the dark voices cried out, "free me, free me." "Shut up, you frigging lot. Pack it in all of you, or I'll cut your throats," the Guard yelled to the voices. "Now, Ener Re Aston," he said more firmly.

The old man reached for his son's arm, clasping it high on the forearm. In this final moment the years of angry quarreling seemed suddenly so wasteful. Alwir sighed and bowed his head. Ener circled his arms over his son's shoulders, feeling the burn of tears.

"I forgive you, father," Alwir said softly. "For though it is over for me, there is still time for *you* to reconsider your loyalties."

"Now!" came the Guard's bellow from the gate, and Ener Re Aston released his son without answering and went to the gate.

The Guard was muttering complaints as he jangled his keys in the lock. "Ought to charge you extra for keeping me waiting," he snarled. Ener chanced one final look at Alwir, standing alone in the center of his cell. Alwir looked frightened, but he was trying hard not to show it, his shoulders held straight and his head erect. The gate clanged shut, and the light faded as the Guard began moving quickly down the prison corridor.

Ener followed close behind, the putrid stench of the prison wrapping a thick cloak about him, burying him with its despair. He wanted to be out of there. To see the night sky, knowing that even now there would be the faint gray glow of dawn over the water. Suddenly, in the torchlight, a pale child appeared, heaving herself against the bars like a white moth reaching for the flame. He quickly lowered his head, his eyes avoiding hers, and stared only at the black heels of the Guard's boots moving swiftly before him.

Jobber ran until her trembling legs refused to carry her farther. She stopped at last, collapsing on a shopfront in Hayman's Street, her chest heaving desperately for more air. The blood pounded in her ears, drowning out the rasping sound of her breathing. She pulled her knees up close to her chest, and wrapping her arms around her legs, rested her forehead on her bony knees. She breathed in the coppery odor of her sweat. "I've lost them," she whispered to herself, taking a hard, dry swallow. "They won't find me here."

And then, as if to contradict her, she heard the call of Lirrel's flute, its music stretched out through the city like a hand to touch Jobber. Her head jerked up, and she stared wildly at the street afraid of suddenly seeing Lirrel standing before her, flute to her lips. There was no one but a lighterman, his long pole rigid across his shoulder. If he heard the flute, he gave no notice of it as he shuffled down the street trimming the torches.

Jobber listened and felt the sound penetrate her bones. Its voice was achingly sweet and compelling. It called to her, promising forgiveness and companionship. Jobber clamped her hands over her ears to drown out the sound. She didn't want to hear it.

She didn't deserve it, Jobber thought, hunching her shoulders miserably. Kai had been right in calling her a selfish bastard.

That's what she was. But that's how she had stayed alive, wasn't it? she asked herself defiantly, trying to shrug off the feelings of shame. Looking out for herself. And then truth crumbled her defiance into self-loathing. Looking out for yourself, Jobbernowl, she hissed, while letting others go to their deaths without so much as a thought.

Her body protesting, Jobber forced herself to stand. She couldn't sit still as anger crackled in her body. She wanted to hit something, feel the weight of her anger transfer to the knuckles of her fist and then slam into something solid. It would define the anger, shape it to something she understood. Jobber laid a hand to the brick and plaster of the building, tempted. She'd break her hand. She pushed away from the wall, not trusting herself not to hit it anyway.

Jobber walked with jerky steps, her heels landing hard on the cobblestones. People passing her were vague shadows, and she scarcely noticed them as they ambled by. Instead her eyes were filled with images of Growler and Dogsbody, seeing them bloodied in death. Her memories tormented her with doubts; there must have been something she could have done to prevent their deaths. There must have been something she should have done. She wiped a hand over her tired face, trying to rub away the memories. Her palms felt hot on her cheeks. Her heart beat rapidly.

Then Jobber lifted her head, dazed as she realized that her heart rattled in time to rapping noises coming down the street from the direction of Fire Circle. Jobber followed the sound, grateful as the noise beat against the haze of anguish.

As she walked into Fire Circle, Jobber looked up seeing the skeletal frame of the gallows. The partially built arms of the gallows reached out across the sky, and Jobber imagined the bodies that would hang at the ends like broken fingers. Workmen shouted at each other above the hammering as they labored. Silean Guards stood nearby watching the proceeding, turning every now and then to search the shadowy recesses of Fire Circle as if expecting trouble. Jobber stared at it confused, not understanding why they should be building it now on the eve of the Great Bonfire.

Then she remembered Master Donal and Wyer, Pedar and the other one being led from Crier's Forge. "Z'blood," she swore, guessing that the gallows being raised were for them.

Jobber wandered the edges of Fire Circle, not wanting to approach too closely and at the same time unable to look away.

Why had Master Donal gotten tied up with the New Moon? she asked herself. It weren't no skin off his knuckles, why'd he have to stick his neck out for them? Jobber balled her hands into fists, as the urge to hit something returned. Like Kai, she thought, the flush of shame rising hotly on her cheeks. Kai stuck her neck out for her Waterlings, even went so far as to try and scaffer the Upright Man. "Frigging stupid," Jobber muttered to the cobblestones. Then doubt twisted her face, and she clenched her teeth together. As stupid as it seemed, there had to be reasons that made it right. Growler had fought to save her, even though he must have known he would be killed. So had Dogsbody. Why had they done that for her? Jobber drew in a slow breath, feeling the remorse tighten around her chest like bands of iron.

She could have taught others how to use the shield, Jobber realized. But until Kai had attacked her, it had never occurred to Jobber that she could help others. Should help. No, Jobber shook her head violently, casting away her doubt. She could never have trusted anyone to know about her, she argued. And it would never have worked anyway.

But even as she denied it, Jobber remembered when Growler taught her to form the shield. She had been as certain then as she was now that it wouldn't work. That she couldn't do it. She got frustrated and argued with Growler. But Growler refused to argue back. Instead he walked away, and she had to follow until he stopped finally on an unknown street.

"What do you see?" he had asked her quietly, leaning a little on his vagger's staff.

"An alley," she answered.

"What else?"

Shaking her head, she answered again. "Ain't nothing but a street. Dead ender, too. See that wall over there? Nowhere to go from here."

He smiled at her, and as they proceeded down the alley, he pointed out all the narrow passageways that led to unseen courtyards. And in the courtyards, he reminded her, there were always doors that opened to other streets, other rooms. And if that was not enough, he said, looking up to the sky, there was always up, and using his staff he pointed out the handholds on the walls that would take her to the rooftops of Beldan. "There are no limits to what you can do," he said to her angry pout. "Find the way within you. The roads are there. Look for them."

And in the days that followed, Jobber had searched. She forced herself to face the challenge, accepting it not because she wanted to, but because Growler believed in her. And after hard work, it had come surprisingly easily for all her complaining. Jobber now recalled the glowing satisfaction when she had at last grasped the skill that had been there all along merely waiting for her to find it. It had been a hard lesson, one of many, but the rewards had been rich. She had learned from Growler then that life, though difficult and dangerous, could be won if not limited by fear and small-mindedness.

Jobber studied the uneven cobblestone as she walked, side-stepping a dried pile of animal excrement. Growler had died five years ago, and Jobber realized that she had stopped growing. She had stopped seeking new roads within herself. Loneliness had driven her into a corner, and she had stayed there, wanting only to preserve what she had, clinging to the scrap of existence already won. What good was growing, she had asked herself at every hanging, when it would all be over so soon anyway?

She kicked a stone, sent it skipping along the tops of the cobblestones.

"Oy, you there," a Guard shouted to her. "Get on with you!" he waved her way.

Jobber caught the insult ready on her lips. She remembered in time that there was gold being offered for her capture. She moved away, her head downcast so as not to be seen too clearly in the light.

Beldan had once been home to her, familiar and protective. But since the morning, every street had changed to become strange and menacing. The broad streets were too well lit, and she feared stares of the Silean Guard. The dark alleys that had once hidden her were dangerous as the Flocks searched every corner for her in hopes of reward. Beldan, beloved Beldan was now a trap in which Jobber wandered, trying desperately to avoid stepping on the spring. She glanced up feeling the walls close in, and it seemed to her that even the gargoyles peering down at her from the stone balconies of Fire Circle bawled their insults where she stood.

Jobber didn't want to leave Fire Circle. It seemed in some way the only refuge. She was drawn to the piled high mountain of wood that tomorrow would become Firefaire's Great Bonfire. All manner of wood had been stacked, from broken chairs and crates to the freshly cut staves of Avadares pine that bled with sticky pitch. Tomorrow when people gathered in Fire Circle they would bring with them symbols of luck, good and bad, to be burned in the Great Bonfire. Straw effigies of the Queen, a lock of hair from a faithless love, a garment from a dead loved one. All would be burned, disposing of disappointment and sorrow in the smoke, while raising to the sky the hopes for the future.

Jobber needed to be there, to feel the scorching wind of the fire, breathe its acrid reek. She wanted to lose herself in the gout of red flame and cloak her shame with the gray veil of smoke.

Jobber glanced about and, seeing that no one was watching, climbed up the sides of a building, using the roughly carved pattern in stone as hand holds. With effort she pulled herself over a low wall and onto a little balcony. Behind it on the wall of the building, the windows had been boarded over. Swallows had built little nests under eaves, and they fanned their wings objecting to her intrusion. Wearily, Jobber laid down on the stone balcony and drew her arms across her chest.

Lying on her back, she could see the faint edge of the new moon disappearing behind the building. It would be day soon. Jobber shifted on the hard surface as a small stone dug into her back. What would she do with another day, she thought unhappily. Spend it hiding? Spend it angry with herself for being such a coward and a fool? "I should have died when Growler was killed," she said harshly to the nattering swallows. They rustled their wings, frightened by her voice. Then she grunted. "You did die," she said to herself scornfully. "You ain't done nothing since Growler was scaffered," she accused. "You might just as well be dead."

As if to disagree with her, Jobber heard again the plaintive cry of Lirrel's flute. Jobber closed her tired eyes but did not deny the sound. Even through the turmoil of her own anger, Jobber heard in the music all the delicate shadings of Lirrel's emotions. There was not only joy and love, but Lirrel's fear of violence and the pain of self-doubt. Jobber grimaced, thinking herself the cause of those doubts. She had dragged Lirrel through Beldan's worst, thinking to prove to Lirrel how stupid she was to believe in peace and harmony. Jobber shook her head, amazed at her own arrogance. *"No,"* the flute protested, *"the doubts have always been there."* And for a moment, in the gentle throbbing of the music, Jobber could sense Lirrel's smile. The new moon in the night sky gleamed dully like one of the earrings Jobber had given Lirrel. Jobber stretched out her hand almost seeing the delicate face with the opal-colored eyes reflecting her own bewildered face. *"Let me help you, Jobber,"* the flute whispered with Lirrel's voice. Jobber shook her head. "I ain't worth it," she croaked to the night. *"You are Beldan's fire, Jobber,"* the flute answered more strongly. *"Deny it and we are all lost."* "What am I supposed to do?" Jobber called out, and the startled swallows flapped their wings and lifted into the sky. *"Don't run,"* the flute sang. *"Accept it."*

The flute ceased playing and in the silence Fire Circle seemed hushed with anticipation. The muscles of Jobber's shoulders coiled tightly, straining against an irresistible pull. It seemed to her that she could see the lighterman bending to ignite the Great Bonfire. She held her breath expectantly, waiting for the roar of the flames and the furious blast of hot air that would suck through the core of the Great Bonfire. And in that moment, poised on a brink she didn't understand, Jobber remembered Lirrel's tale of Oran's sacrifice. She wondered if Oran had been afraid when he left the shelter of the cradle and ventured into the raging chaos. And when he found himself entangled forever in the web of his cradle, did he cry out in despair for himself, or did he rejoice at saving his precious creations? On the edge of exhausted sleep, Jobber had no answers, only the sense of herself standing beside the lighterman, terrified as he dipped his torch to the Great Bonfire.

In the privacy of her chambers, the Fire Queen Zorah lifted her head to the sound of a flute. She frowned, straining to hear the faint sound. Wind ruffled through the quiet room, and Zorah sensed the movement of magic.

She stood in alarm, vertigo tipping the edges of the room. She leaned into the noise, trying to sense its origin. But it was impossible. The more directly she tried to hear the sound, the more elusive it became. Instead of the single voice, she heard the grinding howl of chaos. She tried again, concentrating harder on the faint sound. As if to refuse her, the keening howls grew louder, drowning out the flute's voice.

Zorah sighed and bowed her head. It was always like that now.

She waited at the center of a huge storm where no movement was possible, where the air was calm and empty, devoid of magic and time. But around her on all sides magic roiled and whirled in a raging storm, spinning so fast that she could not penetrate its flow. Time flowed with the storm, snatched into its whirlpool, and left her untouched.

There had been no other way to save herself from death, Zorah argued. If only her sisters could have understood that. Instead they had turned against her and fought. Zorah clenched her teeth thinking of Huld's wintry face, mottled gray like the granite. Huld had been the worst, raising an army against her, destroying everything.

Zorah steadied her rapid pulse and drew in a calming breath. But Huld had not succeeded, she thought fiercely. Zorah had. And though there was little magic left that Zorah could do, time had stopped and death could not threaten her with its cold hand. And that was enough for Zorah.

Zorah opened a wooden chest elaborately carved with figures of birds. Beneath the layers of silk fabric she withdrew an old sword. The scabbard was a dull black, but when she withdrew the blade, it gleamed brilliantly, red-gold light sparkling on the edge. Zorah bent her cheek to the blade and heard the low hum of magic threading through the sword.

With this sword she had killed her sisters. With this sword she had carved a hollow in the storm of magic that had followed in the wake of their deaths. And with this sword she captured time and remained immortal. The distant sound of the flute was an echo out of the past, like a long-forgotten melody that surfaces in a moment of nostalgia. Zorah shook its sound from her ears and listened only to the hum of the sword. She heard the wail of the storm spinning an eternity around her. Though it clamored and raged, Zorah sighed contentedly. The sword held her pulse constant and immortal. There was nothing strong enough to threaten it.

Zorah smiled. She laid the sword on her bed and began undressing. She threw off the linen nightdress, kicking the gossamer fabric away from her. She dug again into the chest and withdrew a pair of men's trousers and a shirt. With a spurt of excitement, she dressed, her fingers moving rapidly over the forgotten clothes.

Once dressed, she shook her head and laughed as the firehair bristled and snapped in response to her sudden joy. She caught a glimpse of herself in the mirror glowing with strength and youth. "Oh yes," she said to the beautiful image in the glass, "you are still strong. And there is no one, not even death, who can touch you." Gathering up the sword, she left her chambers and headed for the training grounds.

It was dawn when the Regent Silwa crossed the main entrance of the Keep, heading for the Guards barracks. The sun was only recently up and the slanted rays brightened the sentry towers, turning them a fallow gold. The air felt clean, just the faint suggestion of sea salt and smoke. Though tired, Silwa walked briskly, empowered by a sense of command. He would show these Oran peasants that no rebellion would be tolerated. He would tighten the leash around their throats and make them feel it. And if they struggled, well, he was not adverse to killing them. They were peasants, their labor cheap and there were always others ready to take their places.

Silwa reached the training grounds and halted. In the center of the wide circle of beaten earth, Zorah was training with a sword. The Silean Guards were standing in small clusters off to the side. No one was willing to enter the training circle while the Fire Queen practiced. Some of the Guards knelt polishing weapons as they stared, others stood arms crossed over their chests. They waited and they watched, expressions shifting from resentment to grudging admiration.

Zorah wore loose trousers tied at the ankles above her boots. She wore a man's shirt cut short at the sleeves. The shirt clung to her back, the sweat fanning out like wings across her shoulder blades. Her hair hung loose, catching up the morning sun and blazing back like threads of fire. The slim sword flickered in the air as she moved precisely and methodically through a series of attacks.

Silwa watched, fascinated by the technique. Unlike the Sileans who chose to place their attacks along a single line of advance and retreat, Zorah fought opponents from all sides. She moved in a wide circle, each arc presenting a new attack and new response. As one motion was completed, she spun into the next and then the next. Each attack bled into the other, providing a series of seamless encounters at once powerful and flowing. The sword whispered as it slashed and parried invisible ghosts. Along the edge of the blade, a pattern of steel waves glittered red, as if stained with blood from the imaginary opponents.

Silwa looked at Zorah's face, startled by the cruel expression. Last night when they had argued she had seemed soft and malleable. Now her face was smooth as white stone, the green eyes focused on the image of an attacker. Sweat streaked her neck and upper arms, and as she turned, Silwa saw the dark shadow of sweat that clung to the curves of her breasts. She held the sword firmly, striking without hesitation, each thrust finishing with a convincing snap.

Zorah drew her body up and exhaled slowly, the sword lowered to her side. Raising it a final time, she saluted the sun and then resheathed the blade. Around her, the Guards lowered their heads and averted their eyes. Zorah glanced over to where Silwa stood, nodding her head. Then she approached him, and he felt the vague stirrings of apprehension. She was changed, different from the woman he thought he knew. She moved like a wraith, cold and lethal.

"Are you ready for today, Regent Silwa?" she asked. Her eyes had not lost the intense stare, and he looked away, uncomfortable.

"It would appear *you* are," he answered, forcing himself to return her gaze.

She laughed and wiped her face with a cloth. "It's been a long time since I've practiced. I had forgotten the terrible beauty of it."

"May I see your sword?" Silwa asked.

"No," she answered curtly. "You may not. I must go now and prepare for the procession. Until later," she said and swept past him without a second glance.

"Bitch," Silwa hissed between his teeth, watching her leave. He could feel the curious stares of the Guards at his back. He clamped his jaw on the hard shell of her insult. Then he spun on his heel, crossing the training circle that was now slowly filling up with Guardsmen tackling their own weapons. Z'blood, he cursed. He'd let the cavalry do their worst today, and he'd see to it that Oran arrogance was crushed beneath his boot.

# 20

Kai circled the crowds slowly, her injured arm tucked against her chest. She searched the faces of the fair-goers, convinced that the one face she hoped to find would be there. As she moved through the crowds of Fire Circle, she became aware of the shifting mood of the crowd, like clouds across the water, both bright and somber. The usual joy of the festival was restrained by the presence of the gallows, and all eyes strayed nervously toward it. But it was more than the gallows that unsettled the crowd, Kai thought, as she studied the faces. It was a feeling hardly noticable on the surface of the crowd's general gaiety but there all the same; a brooding disquiet, and with it an anger ready to ignite if given sufficient reason. Kai watched a group of Oran laborers clustered together as they talked, voices rising and falling with anger. Some with faces as brown and weather-beaten as their smocks wore looks of resignation, while on the younger men jawlines hardened. The women hooded in black shawls walked with stolid steps, their babies perched on a jutting hip while other children followed close beside, clinging to their skirts. Beneath the smiles Kai saw a weary sadness lined their faces.

But not all were troubled. Two Beldan matrons, shopkeepers Kai judged by their clothing and the straw baskets they carried on each arm, shoved through the crowd trying to secure a place near the Great Bonfire. They had dressed for the occasion in bright yellow and red silks, and on their generous frames they looked like wind-blown poppies. A hawker, selling pennycandy shaped like the Queen, was surrounded by a noisy gang of cutters, their silvery scissors dangling on strings around their waist as they dug into their pockets for coins. A waterman strolled arm and arm with a shopgirl, her recently hennaed hair gleaming around her shoulders like a fox fur. Her skirt was torn and mended, her clogs cracked, but her face shone with happiness as she stared up at the man beside her. And pushing between the legs of the fair-goers, Kai saw the Flocks, that appeared like ravenous sparrows, their bright eyes appraising every pocket. Some of them caught her stare and winked conspiratorially.

Kai looked up from the milling throng and searched the balconies of the buildings that lined the huge circular plaza. She could see the liveried servants of the big houses setting up tables and chairs. Food was appearing along with bottles of brandy and wine. And leaning indolently against the balconies staring down at the crowd were Silean nobles. Like rare birds, the silken sheen of their clothing glittered in the afternoon sun and white plumes decked the black felt hats of the men. One woman laughed, her head tossed back, and even from the street Kai could see the amber jewels around her white neck.

Kai rubbed her tired eyes and wondered if she had been smart to come. She felt spent, drained of all but a determination to find the Upright Man. She was certain he would be here to take advantage of this crowd. But whether he would be in the streets with the rest of Beldan's ordinary, or whether he would be up in the balconies sharing a feast with the Silean nobility, Kai didn't know. Instead she looked at every face hoping and fearing to see those coal-black eyes with the pinpoints of red blazing back at her. But the constant wash of faces, the changing colors and textures of the crowd, made her nauseous.

She staggered and bumped into a teaman, his silver and brass urn strapped to his back like the body of a huge beetle. "Oy, man, a glass," she said and gave him a couple of coins.

"Bit of a show, today," he said as he opened the tap on his urn to let the tea flow into a glass. "Who do you figure they're swinging today?"

"New Moon, is the way I hear it," Kai answered, taking the glass. She took a sip, the tea scalding but sweet.

"New Moon, eh?" the teaman said. "Ain't they bold ones though? Wonder what they did?"

Kai shook her head and continued carefully sipping her tea. She watched the teaman out of the corner of her eye, noting the way he stared almost reverently at the gallows. Then he turned to her and gave a gapped-toothed smile.

"Guess I was a-hoping it might be some Silean swag about to a swing. Seeing how they built the noddynoose over where they always sits." Then he chuckled. "Some of them fine ladies is gonna get their teeth knocked in when the swingers starts kicking their legs out."

Kai laughed darkly and handed back the glass. He took it, rinsing it out with a little water from a skin strapped to his belt.

He tipped his cap to her and ambled on through the crowd again.

Kai walked toward the stalls lining the wide colonades beneath the balconies. There was shade from the sun there and more room to move. She found an upturned crate between two stalls and sat on it, savoring the taste of hot tea on her tongue. It wasn't as good as the tea Zeenia made, but it helped to revive her sagging spirits. Thinking of Zeenia reminded Kai of the Waterlings, and she frowned with unaccustomed loneliness, knowing they were gone from Beldan. But they're safe for now, she scolded herself, so you got no business complaining. With quiet amazement, she thought back on the night, trying to understand how so much could change in so short a time.

After Jobber had fled, she and Lirrel had gone on to the Grinning Bird, Kai's vision filled with the fiery brilliance of Jobber's aura. She had never seen an aura so rich in color, its hues changing from a crystalline blue near Jobber's face and fanning out like the points of a crown with golden flames tipped with orange and red. It had been like staring into the sun's corona, and as Lirrel walked with her to Zeenia's, Kai had stumbled, blinded by the sparkling after-image of Jobber's aura. "To be able to hide so much," she had said to Lirrel, shaking her head in astonishment. "Doesn't she know how powerful she is?"

"Not yet," Lirrel had answered, her eerie opal-colored eyes staring blankly ahead of her. She seemed distracted, as if listening to something Kai could not hear. Like Mole, she thought, not interested in the solid stuff of the street, but an ear always cocked to the wind, hearing its whispered messages.

Near the Grinning Bird they had parted, Lirrel joining a small band of Ghazalis. They had greeted her in Ghazali, and Kai could hear the angry scolding in their voices. A man glanced over at Kai, curious but clearly annoyed. Lirrel answered him with a low voice, her words sounding clipped. And then she was gone, swept along by the other Ghazalis that hovered protectively around her.

When Kai had entered the Grinning Bird, she had been surprised to find the Waterlings sitting around a table drinking mugs of tea. Zeenia was sitting with them, and she and Slipper were bent in serious discussion.

"What are you all doing here?" she asked angrily. "I told you to meet me at the tunnels."

Slipper glanced up apologetically. "Zeenia thought it better if we come here, Kai." Next to him, Trap looked up, her face worried. She wore a red knitted cap that Kai had never seen before, and it lent her peaked face a touch of color. Finch had on the other black shawl that Kai had seen hanging on a peg in Zeenia's bedroom. Kai felt a surge of jealous anger.

"Who's Flock leader?" Kai asked harshly.

They were silent, their eyes averted as they stared down into their mugs of tea.

"You are, Kai," Zeenia answered for them. "I don't mean to take your place. I just thought—"

"Well, you thought wrong. I can take care of my own Flock."

"Of course you can, I just thought you could use some help."

"I don't need—" Kai stopped herself from saying more. She just stood, swaying slightly as her emotions grated against her raw nerves. Why was she being so stupid? she asked herself.

"Sit down," Zeenia said softly and moved to get her a mug of tea.

Kai sat down and bowed her head. "It's been a long night," she offered by way of explanation. Her eyes itched with fatigue and her shoulder throbbed painfully. She settled her chin in her hand. "Z'blood," she said wearily. "Things just ain't been going right."

She glanced over at her Flock and saw them looking back, their expressions fierce with pride and loyalty. Of course they were hers. She was foolish to doubt them. But it made it all the harder to let them down now. "I went to see your Reader at Crier's Forge, Finch," she said. Finch glanced up expectantly, pushing back the dandelion hair from her face. "Oh yeah, the offer was good all right. Only trouble was, I got there just in time to see the Knackerman and her butcherboys leading them away."

"Crier's Forge?" Zeenia said sharply, the freckles blazing on her whitened face. Tea splashed in the cup, spilling on her hand, but she ignored it. "Any arrests?"

"Four."

"Get a wink at them?"

Kai nodded. "Two were squared bricks, must have been the smiths. Another was tall and skinny. The last wore a weaver's scarf."

"Is that all?" Zeenia asked, leaning intently over the table.

"A woman, too. Scaffered from the looks of it."

Zeenia groaned, handing the mug of tea to Kai before sitting down heavily in a chair. She laid her hands on the table and stared at them. "I was to have been there. I should have been there. Z'blood, the frigging bastards," she said softly. Then she looked up and Kai saw her struggle to regain her composure. The green eyes glistened as she fought back the tears. She sniffed quickly, wiping a hand across her nose. "Was there not another man? A laborer?" she asked.

"Nah. Just those."

Zeenia nodded, lips pursed in thought. "Sly old Farnon. He must have got away then. I'll have to warn the others." Then she stopped in surprise, one hand rising to lightly slap her forehead. "You went to the forge to get passage out for the Waterlings," she said, as if just now understanding the reason for Kai being there.

Kai nodded. "Finch here met a Reader who told her he could do it."

"Alwir," Zeenia agreed. "I should have realized—" A quick rapping at the windows made them jump. A vagger woman stuck her head in the door, the short cropped hair standing up straight from her wide brow lending her a startled expression. Zeenia waved her inside. "I just heard," Zeenia murmured to the woman.

Kai stared at the woman as she slipped quietly into the Grinning Bird. She moved with deliberate steps, her vagger's staff gripped tightly in one hand. Her almond-shaped eyes matched the deep brown of her cloak. Her facial tatooes deepened the color of her cheeks with dark swirling designs like the whorls of a tree. A small scar nicked a corner of her chin, cutting across the tattooed pattern with a sliver of white flesh.

"Orian, can you take these few with you?" Zeenia asked the woman.

She nodded quietly. "There's a ship still waiting in the harbor."

"No," said Slipper, glaring at Kai. "I ain't leaving Beldan."

"Yeah, you are," Kai answered sharply. "I want you all out of here for now."

"But Kai," he protested.

"Do as I say!" she snapped, not wanting to argue with him. It was already hard enough to think of them leaving. "Are you sure you can get them safely out?" she asked the vagger woman mistrustfully. "The butcherboys are thick tonight."

Orian gave a brief smile. She rapped her staff hard on a table, and the wooden tip broke apart to reveal a long straight blade at the end of the shaft. "I know my business," she answered simply, and Kai nodded, tyring not to look shocked, as she wondered what sort of business a vagger did that required her to travel so armed. The woman bent gracefully and retrieved the two wooden halves. They fitted together with a quiet click, concealing the blade.

After that, there had been little else to say. Kai had made her farewells short and simple. But when she had come to Slipper and had seen the stricken expression on his face, even his lighter-man's hat drooping, she had clasped him tightly before releasing him to Orian. In that embrace, she realized that Slipper wasn't a child anymore, his chest and shoulders having grown broader beneath his loose clothes. The arms that held her were wiry but strong, the hands larger than she remembered. When she pulled away she felt her cheek grazed by the slight stubble of a beard.

"Kai," he said, and she shook her head at the pleading in his voice.

"Take care of them," she had said and stepped away.

After the Waterlings were gone, Zeenia herself left, admonishing Kai once more to rest and give her shoulder a chance to heal.

Alone in the quiet shop, with only the soft hissing of the tea urns, Kai had laid her head on a table and slept, exhausted.

A sour-faced man selling straw good luck charms bawled in a loud voice near Kai's ear and startled her out of her thoughts. She shook her head, realizing that while she had dreamed, Fire Circle had grown more densely packed with spectators and fair-goers. She stood up wearily and prepared to enter the throng. They would be lighting the Great Bonfire soon. If she was to have any luck in spotting the Upright Man, it would have to be now. For once the Fire Queen and her retinue arrived, she would never be able to see above the heads of the crowd jamming Fire Circle in hopes of catching a glimpse of the Fire Queen.

In the northern arc of Fire Circle, Lirrel sat between Zia and Amer, staring out sullenly at the crowd gathered around the Ghazali acrobats. Taysir balanced his little son on his shoulders as the boy prepared to leap on the shoulders of his uncle. The crowd waited with hushed breath as the child jumped and somersaulted lightly in the air. Zia's shoulder rubbed against Lirrel's arm as she leaned forward and laughed, while on her other side, Amer draped an arm around Lirrel's shoulders. Lirrel shut her eyes, feeling suddenly trapped.

What happened? she asked herself. Am I so changed? She opened her eyes again and looked down, seeing the black fabric of her skirts merge into the black of Zia's and Amer's, flowing between them like one continuous wave. Lirrel felt the heat of their bodies pressed close to her, the constant touches like the fluttering of bird wings that were meant to be reassuring. Once they had been. Once Lirrel had been a part of this loving circle of women. But now all she wanted was to step out into a space empty of people. For the first time in her life, Lirrel wanted to be alone.

She flushed with shame, sensing in their thoughts only concern for her. It had been concern that had sent them out searching Beldan for her when she didn't return to the tent at the end of the watch. Taysir had yelled angrily at her when they found her at last, and in the company of a scrawny looking street girl. But his anger had softened quickly into relief, and all the way back to the tent, he apologized, explaining that he had been nearly beside himself with worry. At the camp, Amer had hugged her close to her breast, and Lirrel had nearly choked in the folds of her shawl with its woody perfume. When they had settled down for the night, she had slept surrounded by the other Ghazalis, as if she had been a missing bead returned at last to the string. She had tried for their sake rather than her own to feel a part of them again.

But it was too late, Lirrel thought sadly, looking out at the shifting colors of the acrobats' costumes as they tumbled like autumn leaves. She no longer felt comfortable muffled by the kindness and care of the other women. They would protect her from everything, and in so doing, Lirrel realized, they would prevent her from living as she must. She was a Ghazali, a peacekeeper and a witness. Last night with all its violence and horror had been the first time she had understood the power and the responsibility of that choice.

But more than that, Lirrel thought, there had been Jobber, with her coppery hair and the yellow flames flickering in her jade-colored eyes. In the sharp angles of her face, there had been no softness, and in the twist of her hands, there had been no gentle touches. But she crackled with life, and though Lirrel had felt herself scorched by the fiery touch, she had gained a vision of Oran's heart and had heard the howl of chaos.

Lirrel gasped, unable to breathe as though the air had grown thin. She needed to move away. She stood and gently dislodged herself from the others.

As she edged away from the circle of Ghazali women, Lirrel lifted her head to a familiar presence, warm and metallic in the dusty air. Jobber was here, somewhere in Fire Circle. Lirrel glanced back at Zia and Amer, their hands clapping together in a complex syncopated rhythm for the tumblers. She felt torn, knowing that she would leave them. Had already left them, she realized.

The winds shifted, teasing the fringe of her head scarf. She looked up, surprised by the gentle burst of air. Lirrel caught her breath as above the crowds she could see currents of air weaving into a swirling pattern, like the threads of fine lace. The threads dipped and looped, the curves forming a Queens' quarter knot. The pattern vanished, only to be reformed farther away, hovering as if to entice her to approach and study its intricacies.

Without hesitation, Lirrel stepped away from the Ghazalis, staring up at the patterns as she followed the shifting currents of air. She heard Amer call to her, but she didn't answer. Lirrel walked, an invisible wind blowing the hem of her skirt, catching her up in its breath as she followed the pattern. Jobber was here somewhere, she could see it in the flaming thread of the pattern, feel it in the now quiet hum of Jobber's thoughts. Her heart quickened, and Lirrel suppressed the urge to shout Jobber's name, call it loudly over the heads of the crowd. Instead she followed the pattern, knowing with an absolute certainty that it would lead her to Jobber.

On the stone balcony Jobber opened her eyes, suddenly awake as if wrenched from deep sleep by a shout. The dream voice lingered in her ears, distinct at first but then fading rapidly. She saw the muddy straw of a swallow's nest and blinked, confused, waiting for the strange sight to make sense. Then the rough surface of the stone and the leering face of a gargoyle reminded her of where she was.

Jobber sat up slowly and peered over the edges of the balcony. "Z'blood," she exclaimed as she saw below her the huge plaza filled with people. She had slept a long time, even through the frigging hammering, she noted dully, seeing the finished gallows. Well at least she'd not missed the hanging, she sniffed and sat up, her joints stiff and creaking. "Frigging stone," she complained as she stretched her arms out in front of her and then cracked her knuckles.

Her stomach rumbled, reminding her that she'd not eaten in a long time. She studied the wall, shaking her head as she realized that getting up here unseen last night was a lot easier than getting down. Jobber turned to the boarded window and yanked one of the boards. It squealed as she pulled at it. But it came off finally, leaving an opening just big enough for her to slip through, though she suffered a long scratch from her knee to her shin.

The window opened into an empty, dusty room. As she walked across the floor, she left footprints. The dust motes swirled around her feet, rising to form a sparkling ribbon in the shaft of light from the opened window. The room smelled faintly of mice. Jobber slipped quietly through another door which opened onto a crumbling staircase.

At the bottom of the stairs, another door led into a long corridor. Jobber followed it nervously, not liking the long dark passageway that gave no hint of opening out anywhere. She coughed in the stale air, and sweat prickled the skin of her upper lip. And just when she thought she might turn around and go back again, another door appeared in the wall. She put her shoulder to it and shoved experimentally.

Without warning, the door opened easily, and Jobber found herself squinting in brilliant sunlight. She was in the western arc of Fire Circle, standing almost directly behind the raised platforms for the Readers and Silean nobility. Above the platforms she saw the gallows arms outstretched. A lighterman scurried past her, his black coattails flapping as he carried a bundle of unlit torches beneath one arm.

"Queen's coming," he cried out to another man. "Light the torches and get 'em ready."

Jobber stepped back out of his way, excitement leaping along her spine. The Great Bonfire, she thought, imagining the rising tower of fire. She hurried past the lighterman to come around to the front of the stands. She glanced quickly up at the platform, remembering the Readers that would be sitting there, their cold gaze glaring out at the crowd. Several had already gathered there, and they regarded the gallows with hostile eyes. An older Reader with silvery hair sat straight-backed, fingering the Reader's emblem around his neck as he stared out blankly across the throng. Jobber touched the wool cap to make sure it covered her hair. She drew a calming breath and concentrated on forming the shield.

As she felt the soft numbing of the shield, she faltered, remembering Kai's shrill voice, seeing the look of hatred on her crow's face. Jobber tried to brush away the accusations, but they stayed, scraping her skin like a thorn. A cool wind brushed her face with the scent of wood stacked before the Great Bonfire. Lirrel, Jobber thought, with regret. Lirrel was gone. She'd not see her again. And staring up at the Great Bonfire, Jobber knew that not even the sight of the beautiful raw flames would burn away the ashy taste of disappointment and loneliness. She glanced again at the Readers and shrugged cynically. Didn't matter much, she thought, for sooner or later it 'ud be all over anyway.

The horns blared announcing the arrival of the Fire Queen Zorah and her retinue to Fire Circle. Kai cursed, holding her hands over her ears to drown out the roar of the crowd and the brassy call of the horns.

Around her the crowd shoved and pushed in an effort to get closer to the Great Bonfire. Kai stood her ground, firmly refusing to move as she searched one final desperate time. But the faces sped past her, leaving her a blurred image of pale and dark skins, of blue eyes and brown, of hair so red it was startling and blond braids tied with red ribbons. She thought for a moment that she saw Orian but realized that was a man's face and only the short hair and tattooes had confused her.

Kai's shoulders drooped with exhaustion and she shook her head. It was impossible, like searching for a black hair on the Queen's white mount. Another shout from the crowd turned her around to watch the procession.

The Silean Guard had entered the plaza, clearing a path for the Queen. Of them, all Kai could see was the tops of their standards pointing above the heads of the crowd. A man lifted his child high in the air and placed her on his shoulders that she might be better able to see the Queen.

Behind the Silean Guard, Kai could just see the Queen approaching, her long slender form rising above the crowd as she rode in mounted on a white stallion. The horse snorted and pranced, bells jingling briskly along the length of the reins. The Fire Queen wore a dress of polished steel chain mail, the tiny links folding smoothly over the contours of her body. The red-gold hair burned brightly in the afternoon sun, washing the cream-colored skin a rosy pink. She waved to the crowds, smiling, and they roared back, waving pennants and colored scarves.

Before the brilliance of the Fire Queen, Kai felt small and dirty. Her black hair hung in a lank braid down her back, and her skin was coated with a layer of sweat and grime. She gazed at the Queen, the beautiful face radiant in the sun's light. They might have been the same age. Kai wrapped an arm across her chest, feeling her rib bones as she clung to her injured shoulder. Around her the fanfare grew louder, the cheering more insistent, as the Queen's retinue parted the crowd, processing to the raised platform.

Kai stared at the Queen, as if to steal away a thimble of her beauty to keep for herself. She held her breath, trying to imagine how it might feel to have such beauty. Her gaze slid across from the Queen to the Regent Silwa standing beside her. He was dressed in the somber black and gray of the Silean Guard. Hands clasped behind his back, she saw the shining length of his sword buckled at his hip as he stared out at the crowd.

And then she stopped and felt the chill of ice in her throat. Her whole body stiffened, and her hand on her shoulder dug into the wound. She cried out, startled not as much by the fresh pain as by the unexpected terror of seeing the Upright Man's face. He stood beside the Regent Silwa, a green silk cloak almost covering the black and gray uniform and the sword at his hip. A smile played at his lips not quite concealed by the neatly trimmed beard. He whispered a word or two in the Regent's ear and the Regent nodded grimly. From where she stood Kai could not see the small slash she knew she had given him on the cheek. But it was the eyes Kai watched; for even here in the fullness of the afternoon sun they glowed like obsidian, and when he turned to face the crowd, she flinched seeing the faint spark of red that flashed and then was gone.

"Oy," she said tugging on the coat of a journeyman in front of her. "Oy," she shouted more loudly to gain his attention. He turned around, his face bright red with excitement.

"Leave off," he growled.

"Just tell me, who's the Silean up there in the green cloak?" she asked.

"That's the Adviser to the Regent. Antoni Re Desturo." He cocked his head, looking her up and down. "Don't know much, do you?" he jeered.

Kai let go of his jacket with a shove. "More than you," she snapped. "Frigging more than you."

The man ignored her and turned away.

Kai stepped back, reeling with her discovery. It made no sense. The man was a Silean. Weren't no way he should be able to carry Oran magic. Kai pulled at her hair, twisting it up into a knot as her mind tried to sort out all the possible and then impossible explanations. He could be like herself, bastard got. The knotted hair on her neck unraveled as she shook her head. But how could a base-born Silean rise in the ranks? She glanced at him again, doubting her eyes. Yeah, she thought, it was him all right. She recognized the cut of his profile and the black eyes which now haunted her.

A hand clasped her on the arm, and she spun around terrified. Slipper pressed a hand over her mouth and started talking rapidly.

"Now look, Kai, don't start on me. The others are safe enough, but there was no way I was going to leave you here alone. So don't be mad." He waited before releasing her, trying to gauge her response. When he took his hand away she was silent, her face pale and sweating. "Well," he said at last. "Are you mad?"

Kai shrugged, her lips pressed firmly together. The sight of him was more welcomed than he knew, but she found it hard to admit in words. She pushed back his lighterman's hat and gave him a small, grudging smile. He smiled back, relieved.

"I got to thinking as we were leaving, you've done a lot for me, Kai," he started to say. He lowered his eyes, almost shyly.

"You don't owe me," she answered.

"Maybe not," he said, raising his eyes to meet hers. "But I want to help you." As he stared at her, Kai felt the color rise up her neck. "We belong together, Kai. You and me, and that's how it should be."

"All right, Slipper," she agreed. Another roar of the crowd turned her head, and she saw the Silean Guard enter with the prisoners caged in a cart. She glanced at the Upright Man, feeling her rage return at his arrogant smile and the look of disdain he gave the crowd. "Come on then," she said to Slipper, quickly taking his arm and moving along the outer edges of the crowd. Slipper's arm was reassuring, as was the faint odor of the tunnels on his skin.

"What's on?" Slipper asked close to her ear.

"I found the Upright Man, Slipper. But it ain't going to be easy to bring him down. Up there," she pointed, "the frigging Adviser to the Regent. He's our man."

Slipper swore beneath his breath and stared at her in amazement. "Are you sure?"

Kai cast him a withering look, and he relented immediately.

"What are we going to do?" he asked.

"I'll tell you soon," Kai answered. Actually she had no idea of what she intended to do. She only knew that she wanted to get close to the Upright Man, to study him unnoticed. He seemed invincible, but Kai knew that wasn't entirely true. When she had fought him in the alley, there had been a moment . . . she swore to herself, remembering. If only she hadn't been wounded. She would have gotten him then. But for now the knowledge of him was enough. He would return to the streets, and she would be there waiting for him, ready to hunt him as he had hunted her Flock.

Jobber's stomach growled more loudly demanding that she eat. She slapped her pockets hoping for a coin or two, knowing full well that there would be none. She eyed the crowd before deciding on her pigeon. He was a Silean merchant, wearing a heavy cloak even in the afternoon heat. His face was red and puffy, his beard trimmed in a style unsuited to his double chins. He took off his black felt hat, revealing a few remaining whisps of hair before wiping his sweating forehead with his sleeve and replacing the hat. Jobber wondered what he was doing down here mixing with the crowd. Then she saw the whore he was pursuing with single-minded attention, and she smiled to herself. It was one of Tinpenny's whores, a slender girl with the smooth face of a child marred only by her vulgar leer. She wore a red shift laced up tightly with orange ribbons. Her small breasts bulged over the top of her bodice as invitingly as two apples. She hooked a finger to him, and he followed her as if drawn on by an invisible string.

Jobber hustled into the crowd, positioning herself before the entranced man. As he came toward her, shoving past people, Jobber bumped into him, knocking his shoulder hard so as to draw his mind away from her hand darting in his pocket.

She muttered a vague apology, moving quickly away, but the man only grumbled an irritated curse as his head craned to follow the whore. He saw her, waiting for him near a stall selling ribbons, and any memory of Jobber fled, chased by the promise of pleasure awaiting him.

Jobber smiled at the weight of the purse in her hand and went in search of something to eat.

She bought three savories from a stall and without waiting for them to cool started eating. The grease dripped down to her elbows as she bit into them, and she had to suck in little breaths of air to cool her mouth as she chewed the hot food. Oran food, she thought chewing contentedly, overspiced to kill the taste of meat that was of questionable quality.

On a whim, she bought candysticks, knowing that she would like them at the start only to grow ill at their sickly sweet taste.

She wandered through the crowd of Firefaire feeling strangely unreal. She felt no fear, not even concern that here in this crowd there were many who could finger her and sound the alarm for her arrest. None of it seemed to matter anymore.

Jobber heard the horns and looked up to see the Fire Queen ride past. It shocked her to see that the Silean Guards at Crier's Forge had been right. On the surface they looked alike; the flaming hair and the green eyes. Jobber edged closer, fascinated by the Fire Queen as Zorah climbed the few stairs to the platform and stood erect before the crowd. Her presence was commanding, and with a collective sigh of awe, the crowd surged closer to the barricade of wood. Zorah smiled at them and raised her arms in salute. The sunlight flashed off the sleeves of her dress as dazzling as lightning.

At the corner of her vision Jobber saw the other figures herded on the platforms before the gallows. One stumbled and fell and was roughly pulled upright again. She drew her eyes away from the brilliant spectacle of the Fire Queen and saw the prisoners. Her mood of indifference was shattered as she recognized Master Donal's battered face and beside him Wyer, his cheek crushed and swelling like a bruised plum. Behind them stood the Silean Guard, and in their hands Jobber saw the black hoods with which they would cover the prisoners' faces before they hanged them. Without warning, Jobber was seized by the terrible sense of anticipation of the night before. Fear scratched the skin of her arms, made her hair itch beneath the cap. She wanted to flee Fire Circle, and yet her steps dragged her forward, closer to the gallows.

Lirrel gasped as she felt the fierce stab of pain between her shoulder blades. She stared down at herself in shock, half-expecting to see a blade's tip protruding between her breasts. But there was nothing there except the searing pain of an invisible wound. The pain gouged deeper, seeming to snap the backbones from her spine as it traveled the length of her body. Lirrel reeled in silent agony, knocked from side to side as people pushed past her, each stranger's touch like another blade cutting into her side. She hunched over, her hands pressed against her breastbone as pain drummed in her chest.

And then as quickly, the pain was gone, wrenched from her like a sword freed from its target. Lirrel stared, seeing the shuffling legs of the crowd, realizing she was crouched like a frightened animal. She straightened slowly, every joint in her body vibrating with the memory of pain.

Dazed, she looked around, seeing the crowds of Fire Circle, hearing the horns announcing the arrival of the Fire Queen. A vision, she decided slowly. But whether of the past or future, she didn't know. Cautiously, Lirrel opened her senses to the crowd, afraid at first of the cacophony of so many thoughts and emotions gathered in one place. Her shoulders tensed, her fingers curled into fists. But the thoughts of the crowd rose to her senses with a dull murmur, like that of waves pounding the shore. She sensed fragments of individual thoughts, like sparkling points of light across the water. They shimmered for an instant and then dispersed, returned to the constant din. Lirrel breathed in deeply, growing more confident as she experienced the tumultuous emotions of the crowd. Almost without realizing it, she started humming, and discovered that within the music she could balance the discordant voices into a semblance of order; and each sound, each emotion whether harsh or gentle found a place within the chorus.

And then Lirrel cried out, struck by a wall of hate. It surrounded her like a fist, strangling the music in her throat. She heard the snorting of horses, smelled the oil of weapons and felt the touch of gloved hands gripping the reins. Involuntarily, she lifted her hands to her chest as the stabbing pain returned.

Jobber forced herself through the thick crowd to stand in front of the gallows. A barricade of wood separated her from the gallows. She leaned against it and stared up. The prisoners stood proudly, their faces grim and battered. The younger man, still wearing a Silean coat, had not been beaten, though his expression was flat. He craned his neck to look at the Readers sitting close behind the gallows. His eyes glanced up briefly, seeing the rope that dangled above and then quickly returned his gaze to the crowd.

"Master Donal!" Jobber cried out, but the smith couldn't hear her, for the crowd had begun shouting for the Fire Queen, calling on her to light the Great Bonfire.

The Fire Queen walked with slow, measured steps toward the Great Bonfire, letting the voices of the crowd urge her on. She waited, her arms folded in front, one long pale hand resting atop the other. She raised her hand for silence, and the crowd responded by cheering. They pressed forward, and Jobber had to cling to the wooden barricade to keep from being swept up in the crush. In mounting fury, Jobber rammed an elbow into the ribs of a man pushing her. He fell back a bit, clutching his injured side and gasping.

The Fire Queen raised her hand again, and this time the crowd silenced itself, faces upturned and expectant. Jobber caught her breath, feeling the irresistible pull as the lightermen gathered behind the Queen.

"Let the fire be lit," the Fire Queen commanded.

The lightermen dipped their torches to the mountain of wood and stepped back quickly before casting their torches into the flames.

The crowd waited, hushed as the whoosh of flames sucked through the dry wood. Almost at once Fire Circle was permeated with the sharp odor of smoke and the loud crackle and snap of burning wood. Smoke uncurled like a serpent from the Great Bonfire and then spread out to shroud the tops of the buildings in a gray mist. Spires cut the smoke into ragged streamers that trailed off into the sky.

"People of Oran," the Fire Queen began in a loud, clear voice. "My people," she called and opened her arms widely. "On this day of Firefaire have we come to celebrate the passing of the old year. On this day shall we rejoice in the fire and see within the burning flames our ill-luck and troubles destroyed. And from these ashes we welcome the promise of spring and the New Year."

The crowd began its cheering again. Next to Jobber a man waved a flag vigorously, and it hit her in the face. She batted it away, recognizing the man as snitch from Tinpenny's Flock. Frigging clappers, she swore under her breath. Wonder how much they were getting paid to cheer the Queen, she thought angrily. She looked around again, recognizing more of the clappers. A lot of them, she thought. Silean bastards ain't taking no chances today. She looked back at the Queen, feeling uneasy. Above on the platform the Fire Queen smiled and waited for the crowd to settle down again.

"But people of Oran, in this our time of celebration, let us not forget the true meaning of Firefaire. Let us not forget that it came to us as a symbol of hope—"

"and oppression," a gravely voice said bitterly near Jobber's ear. She turned sharply to see who had spoken, but every face she looked at seemed intent on the Queen.

"We will not forget," the Queen was saying, "that Firefaire serves as a symbol of our will to survive, even beyond the bloody nightmare of the Burning. When Huld betrayed the Queens' quarter knot and murdered my sisters, she split our land apart, burying it in an avalanche of civil war. Then did Oran tumble to the edge of oblivion." Zorah spit the words out in defiance, a fist raised against the nightmare of the past. "But we held fast against

251

Huld's armies. I held fast, strengthened by my love of the land and my love of the people."

"Lies!" another voiced hissed, this one a woman's, "all frigging lies!" the voice insisted. Jobber didn't look this time, but turned her ear to the sound of dissent being whispered through the crowd. Looks like the clappers ain't the only ones with opinions, she thought.

"And so we survived the time of the Burning," Zorah said looking out over the crowd as if to draw them in closer. "And now each year as we build the flame anew that the people of Oran can thrust light into the dark well of our past . . ."

Zorah paused a moment as if struggling to contain her emotions. Her hand reached out to the crowd, trembling. Her face shone white as alabaster. Over her shoulders the red and orange flames billowed as more of the Great Bonfire was consumed. The air rippled with heat, and coppery strands of Zorah's hair floated on the hot currents.

"But, my people, the Burning is not over. There is among you a conspiracy that would lead you to the dark days again, to the horrors of a new Burning."

All around Jobber, she heard cries of "Never!" and "To the Queen!" Frigging clappers, she swore. She caught the motion of an arm swung back and heard the soft pulpy sound of rotten food splatting against Master Donal's shoulder. The smith turned slightly as more food was pitched onto the gallows. Something green oozed down his back, staining it.

Zorah held up her hands again to the crowd, commanding their attention. They waited, restless. Angry murmurs rumbled like distant thunder.

Zorah continued to speak. "My heart recoils with horror when I contemplate the new chaos into which these conspirators, the New Moon, would lead us. It is a road made bloody with war. And why? They seek to unleash a new Burning and will not rest content until the roaring flames have consumed us all. They care nothing for the human price paid for their ambitions. Their goal is one of greed and deceit: to divide the spoils snatched from fires that they themselves have kindled!"

"NO!" came roars from within the crowd, drowning out the sounds of the Great Bonfire. "NO!" they chanted, and as Jobber looked up she saw the Silean nobles standing on the balconies, their swords raised skyward. In the circle of their lips, she could see the single word shouted out over the heads of the crowd. The sound of it reverberated, growing louder as it echoed in the colonades.

"Wait!" Alwir shouted in reply from the gallows. "I demand the right of the condemned to speak." Sweat darkened his brow. "I demand the right to speak!" he shouted again.

"The condemned have no rights!" Zorah shouted back. She waved a hand at the chanting crowd. "They speak for you!"

"Are you afraid?" Alwir taunted the Queen, refusing to back away from the pelting of rotten food. "Are you afraid of the truth?" He turned to the crowd. "Hear me! Hear me, people of Oran, citizens of Beldan! Let me speak of the Burning and of the horrors that await us if we do nothing to stop the Sileans!"

The Regent Silwa motioned several of the Guards closer. They began covering the prisoners' heads with the black hoods, but Alwir writhed away, furiously refusing. Two Guards wrestled him into a headlock as a third stuffed the black cloth sack over his head, muffling his shouts.

The mood of the crowd altered as if jarred by the sudden sight of an old enemy once hidden and now seen. A scuffle broke out as a journeyman attacked a clapper. Silwa motioned for more Guards, and the platform became mottled with the black and gray uniforms of the Guards. Even the Queen was no longer as clearly visible to the crowd.

"No!" Zorah protested, "not yet!" But the Guards facing the crowds didn't hear her.

The nooses were placed over the prisoners' necks, the knots given an extra tug for good measure. On Alwir's covered face the black cloth sucked in and out around the mouth as he gasped for air. Within the crowd disagreement was growing, and Jobber felt around her smoldering anger ignite into outrage. While the clappers still chanted for the prisoners to swing, an increasing number of voices cried out to hear Alwir speak.

"It ain't right," someone said close to Jobber, and she saw the cutters, their pennycandy forgotten, as they folded their hands around their scissors. "Frigging butcherboys, always ready to scaffer one of ours," grumbled another.

"Let him speak!" roared out a man. Jobber craned her head to see who shouted the words and caught sight of Tremare, the Mastersmith of Ironheart, a rival forge. Around him, the other apprentice smiths began shouting and waving their fists in the air.

The cry was taken up through the crowd, and here and there Jobber could see the colored neck scarves of the Guilds raised high in protests. Fire Circle was ablaze with a mosaic of colors:

253

brilliant red and yellows of the metal workers and smiths flickered between the blues and greens of the weavers and dyers. Woodwrights and plasters shook the white dust from their aprons, and even the lightermen snapped their coal-black scarves as they shouted. Between two young whores, Jobber saw Neman, the old Beldan grinder, his neck scarf soiled a pewter gray from the steel dust, while on either side of him the whores raised their orange ribbons like candle flames amidst smoke. A teaman banged a metal cup on the side of his urn, and it rattled like a drum. Laborers and farmers without guilds waved flags and hats as they joined in proclaiming Alwir's right to speak. The clappers were silenced, and when Jobber looked she couldn't see them anywhere. Along the balconies, Silean nobles stood stark and ready.

"Wait!" Zorah shouted and pushed her way between the Guards. "I command you to wait until *I* give the order!"

The Guards hesitated, turning uncertainly between Zorah and Silwa.

"I give him the right to speak!" Zorah commanded.

Silwa glared at her. But he could not refuse her order in public. With an angry jerk of his arm, he motioned the Guards to fall back, and they stepped away from the prisoners.

The crowd cheered, knowing it for a victory.

"Gently, my Regent," Antoni said to Silwa as he sat down again. "You are moving too fast for the rabble. The Queen knows what she is doing."

"Fuck the Queen," Silwa responded savagely.

"I would like to, however the honor has been reserved for yourself," he said giving Silwa a sardonic smile.

Silwa failed to be humored. Instead he watched tight lipped as the Guards freed Alwir's head from its black covering. To his Adviser, the Regent Silwa said in a cool, flat voice; "Let the Queen command as she will for now. But I will give the last order here today. The cavalry shall answer my call," he finished.

Alwir stepped close to the edge of the platform. He was pale and sweating, the skin of his face stretched tight. His chest heaved and he gulped in hurried breaths of air. The crowd quieted, shifting restively as they waited for Alwir to speak. Jobber licked her dry lips. Her hair itched beneath her cap, and with a tentative hand she pushed back the brim. Strands near her face fell free in the wind. She saw them, but for once it didn't matter.

Alwir drew a deep breath and smiled. Jobber thought of

Shrike, but it wasn't the same. There was no contempt in Alwir's defiance, but pride.

"People of Oran!" he began in a strong, steady voice. "My people. The Queens' quarter knot twists into infinity and the strength of Oran is undying!"

The crowd cheered with a single roar of agreement. In one arc of Fire Circle, Ghazali women ululated in high shrill voices, their voices echoing from behind their cupped hands.

"The Fire Queen has charged the New Moon with the crime of conspiracy. Conspiracy is the act of a few whose greed and ambition would threaten the welfare of all. Look around you, here in Fire Circle. And look at us of the New Moon. Are we not people like yourselves? Are we not a part of you?" There was a murmured assent through the crowd. Jobber saw a farmer in a faded smock nod his head in quiet agreement as he thoughtfully rubbed the gnarled calluses of his hands.

Alwir's voice gathered volume, the cords of his neck straining as he shouted to the far reaches of Fire Circle. "Who then are the conspirators in our future destruction? I charge that it is the Sileans, a conspiracy of thieves and murderers, who hang the shadow of death over the Oran people."

"No!" Zorah shouted in protest. "The Sileans have brought us peace. It is you and your kind that would tear the Oran people apart with civil wars. You would return Oran to the Burning."

Alwir bared his teeth, flecks of spit at the corners of his mouth. "Your Sileans have not brought peace. They have sown instead the seeds of Oran destruction. And we must learn the bitterness of our harvest. Can you not see that?" Alwir demanded of Zorah, turning to confront her squarely. "The Oran world is dying; our children are murdered on the gallows or starved slowly in the countryside and on Beldan's streets. We are denied our rights, our land—"

"Enough of your poison!" shouted Zorah, fire exploding along the strands of red-gold hair. "Silence him, now!" The Guards moved quickly, jerking Alwir back from the edge of the platform.

The flames of the Great Bonfire lifted higher, wood popping and cracking. "No!" Jobber shouted. "No," she cried out again, her voice blending with the cries of protest from the crowd. The crowd drew closer. Jobber glanced around, shocked to discover herself a part of them, one with the sea of faces rising like a foaming tide to the edge of the barricade.

"Do not think that with our deaths it is over," Alwir continued to shout as the Guards dragged him back to stand beneath the rope. "The conspiracy against you remains. Silean steel will flash again, gathering its own harvest of death among you. Better we should die on our feet than live on our knees!"

Throughout Fire Circle the crowd exploded with angry cries, their voices joined to the booming roar of the Great Bonfire. Flags and scarves waved as people pressed against the barricades demanding the release of the prisoners. Zorah tried to speak to them, tried to call them back under her control, but they would have none of her, hearing only the harsh warning of Alwir's words.

The Regent Silwa snatched a horn and blew a single note. Its voice carried the alarm over the noise of the crowd. He blew it again, and the sound slashed the thickened dust of the stamping crowd like the blade of a sword falling from the sky.

The surge of people halted, stunned by the piercing cry of the horn. Wary faces turned, searching. A shudder ran through the body of the crowd as in the dreadful silence they heard the distant cry of an answering horn. The horns neared, and now could be heard the drumming of hooves. In the densely packed plaza the smoke of the Great Bonfire was laced with the sudden reek of fear.

Jobber's face blazed with heat. She snatched the cap from her head and threw it on the ground. Her hair bristled with a shower of sparks. She was surrounded on all sides by the people of Beldan. Her red-gold hair lifted like a banner, and the coppery strands sailed over the heads of the people nearest her.

From behind, nearly crushed in the dense press of the crowd, Lirrel saw the fiery hair burning like a raised torch. At the same moment the pain in her chest exploded and her ears were deafened by the sounds of the screams.

"Jobber!" she wailed and began frantically pushing her way through the crowd. People parted as if thrust aside by the sheer magnitude of her panic. "Jobber!" she shrieked again, this time her voice drowned in the collective cry of terror that started along the edges of Fire Circle moving inwardly as the cavalry filled the narrow streets and converged on the crowd of Fire Circle.

Jobber spun around hearing Lirrel's voice. But she couldn't see her among the rocking of the crowd as it swept back and forth like waves dodging the swords of the mounted horsemen.

"Jobber!" Lirrel cried again, and this time Jobber saw her, an arm outstretched above the crowd, her fingers splayed. Terrified people streamed around her, knocking her from side to side.

Jobber started after her, forcing her way through the crush of bodies and the stifling dust that swirled in a brown cloud. A woman fell in front of her and Jobber had but an instant to yank her up to keep her from being trampled underfoot. Jobber was knocked back by a laborer diving for a mounted Guard with a scythe in his hands. Jobber turned away, hearing Lirrel cry her name. She choked as a gout of smoke and dust blinded her. A hand reached through the haze and gripped her hard. Lirrel's face emerged from the dusty cloud, the brown skin ashen, her eyes a bright white with crystal tears.

"They intend to slaughter us," Lirrel sobbed, her words escaping with painful gasps.

"Have you been hurt?" Jobber demanded, drawing Lirrel close to her side.

"Not in the way you think," she replied. "It was a vision . . ."

"Later," Jobber barked, quickly pulling Lirrel out of the way of two cutters fleeing with their hands over their heads. Jobber turned and halted. A woman ran toward them screaming, a child clutched in her arms. Behind her a cavalryman pursued her on horseback. The muscles of his horse bunched as it drew close to the fleeing woman. She saw it too late and crouched to protect her child from the blow. The sword slashed across her back opening a gaping wound down her spine. Blood gushed in a ruby fountain spraying the horse's chest. As Jobber watched horrified, the woman toppled forward and the child tumbled from her arms, rolling beneath the hooves of the horse.

"Come on," Jobber shouted to Lirrel. "To the Bonfire."

Arm around her waist, Jobber dragged Lirrel, forcing her way through the pandemonium of the massacre. People were jammed close together as the cavalry trampled through their numbers, as through a field of dried corn. They fell, dying in bunches, one atop the other, slashed and broken bodies piling into stacks of corpses. Between them the cavalry horses pranced, their eyes rolling white at the rusty odor of blood that thickened the rising dust.

Jobber scrambled over the barricade of stacked wood, dragging Lirrel up with her by one hand. On the barricade, Jobber saw that there were those who had chosen to fight rather than be slaughtered trying to escape. They had stormed the barricades wielding staves of wood as clubs against the swords. Someone had removed Master Donal's black hood before getting killed by a Guard's sword. Jobber recognized Zeenia by her green and orange hair as she bent behind Wyer to cut him free from his bonds. At her back a young boy with a kitchen knife defended her. A Guard swung his sword at the boy's head. The boy jumped back screaming as the blade caught him across the arm. He fell to one side, and the Guard drove his sword into Zeenia's back. Jobber cried out as she saw Zeenia's back arch with the blow, her face shocked and angry. She wheeled around unsteadily, the small dagger in her hands. The Guard raised his sword again intending to finish her off.

Instead an arrow streaked through the smoky air and caught him from behind. He toppled forward, the force of the arrow driving him to the ground. Zeenia fell slowly to her knees and crawled away.

"Where are they coming from?" Jobber shouted to Lirrel as more arrows hummed in the air, striking the Guards that fought near the gallows.

"Up there, on the rooftops," Lirrel shouted and pointed.

Jobber looked, but not for long, feeling the stacked wood beginning to give way beneath her feet. So much had been pulled out that the pile no longer offered a firm footing.

"Z'blood, I hope they know who's on their side! Come on, quick," Jobber shouted to Lirrel as they jumped from the barricade to the platform. Her feet landed squarely, and she crouched to get her bearings. Out of the corner of her eye, she saw Lirrel run toward Wyer. Jobber ran quickly toward Master Donal. Arrows buzzed like angry wasps over the platform.

Jobber ducked as a Guard attacked her. She kicked out her leg, driving it into his midsection. He folded with the strike, and she rushed him, her palm striking upward into his face just under his nose. She could sense the shattered cartilage as it was shoved higher into his skull, killing him. He wavered and then fell back. She stole the sword from him, turning once to look for Lirrel. She saw her, the little mirrors of her head scarf sparkling as she bent to cut the ropes from Wyer's hands with the fallen kitchen knife.

Jobber kept moving, the sword heavy and unfamiliar in her hand. She reached Master Donal and began cutting the ropes that bound his hands. The ropes frayed and then snapped as the smith drove his hands apart.

He turned quickly to her, his eyes raking her face with questions. "Jobber?" he asked.

"In the flesh," she answered.

His face creased with emotions as the weary eyes studied the bright flaming hair. Then as abruptly his manner became brisk.

"Over there," he said, pointing to where rope ladders had been lowered from the rooftops of the nearby building. They dangled hopefully just above the backend of the curved platform. Lirrel was already there, clinging to Wyer's arm. A Guard tried to stop them, but Wyer caught the man before he could raise his sword and squeezed him in a bear hug. He lifted the struggling man off his feet and flung him down into the crumbling barricade of wood. That done, he lifted Lirrel on to the ladder and urged her to hurry.

"Farnon stayed to help us," Donal said, pushing Jobber forward. "We have done more than bloody our nose this day!"

As Jobber darted across the platform, she saw Zorah standing on a small stone ledge amidst the flames of the Great Bonfire. The flames curled around her like the petals of a huge flower. She shimmered like the soft steel of a sword newly drawn from the coal bed. Her hair was a white gold, and the black chain mail dress gleamed a silvery blue.

Zorah stared back at Jobber with an expression of rage and terror. She emerged from the flames, her body rippling with heat, flames trapped in the flowing hair. Her skin glowed a coppery color, her cheeks burnished red-gold. Zorah raised her hand to stop Jobber and the colors of the chain mail dress shifted, becoming verdigris in the cooling air.

"How dare you!" she cried indignantly to Jobber. "How dare you!" she said again, her mouth twisted with hate. She lunged for Jobber, but Jobber jumped back in alarm.

"Go!" shouted Master Donal as he thrust himself between them. He grabbed Zorah and then howled, head thrown back and mouth opened wide, as the searing heat of her arms burned him. Jobber smelled the sharp stench as steam issued between Zorah's fingers and the smith's flesh was scorched black. Zorah shoved him hard, and he stumbled at the edge of the platform, the looming flames of the Great Bonfire rising to meet him. The hair of his beard ignited with small puffs of smoke as he teetered toward the fire. Then he fell, arms outstretched as if to embrace the fire.

"No!" Jobber cried. She reached out for him, catching only air as he toppled into the Great Bonfire. She heard the last fragments of a scream as the fire exhaled with a loud roar engulfing him.

Then Zorah grabbed Jobber, and the hands of fire closed in a taloned grip around her arms. "I shall burn you," she hissed, drawing Jobber closer to her. Jobber tried to resist but found she could not; the green eyes bore into Jobber's face, and she felt helpless against the riveting stare. "You are but a spark of the past sent to haunt me. But I shall extinguish your pathetic fire."

Zorah's face seemed to fade in a circle of white light. Jobber closed her eyes to the brightness, but the fierce light burned behind her eyes. She opened her mouth to breathe and sucked in the hot dry air of the fire.

"I shall make you join with me. Become one with my element," she heard Zorah's voice whisper.

Jobber groaned as she felt herself compressed like a bar of cold iron and lowered into a crucible of molten metal that bubbled smooth as quicksilver. The velvety liquid brushed against her skin, and she screamed in agony. She was dipped deeper, and the metal glimmered red as it rose higher, traveling over her thighs and stomach, the skin peeling back. She struggled weakly as the molten liquid folded opaquely overhead, drowning her. Immersed in the crucible of fire, Jobber held her breath, afraid to draw the searing metal into her lungs.

Jobber felt her body disintegrate within the crucible, becoming liquid to join the pool of blazing metal. Her limbs drifted away from her, transformed into swirls of color. Her hair became a mat of fine white threads floating on the surface of the crucible. She exhaled slowly, a final breath that streaked the molten metal with a tongue of bright orange.

As form and memory escaped in steam, Jobber heard a name, lodged like an unyielding scrap of carbon ash between her teeth. "Beldan's fire," she murmured, hearing the words rise and break on the surface like thick-skinned bubbles.

And as she spoke the words, she felt a shifting of power. A core of her remained intact, denying the blasting heat of Zorah's crucible. Jobber clung to it, slowly feeling herself reshaped, molded by the fire. Her heart leapt violently, and she felt it slam against a cage of iron ribs. From within the rigid core, fire opened like a rose, the points of the flame reaching out to describe the edges of her body. She moved her fingers and felt the molten contents of Zorah's crucible move between the webs like cooling water.

Jobber smiled as she recognized the source of her power. Each fiery petal drew its strength from outside the confinement of Zorah's crucible. Jobber tasted the smoke of the Anvil, the sweet and bitter coal ash of Crier's Forge, the resin flames of the Great Bonfire burning Avadares pines, even the thick ash of Scroggles. Each one defined her, contributed in shaping her anew. The walls of Zorah's crucible weakened as Jobber's core called to the fires of Beldan to answer her need.

Jobber gasped at the sharp sensation of air cooler than her

body brushing against her face. She opened her eyes, seeing the flames around her and the jade-colored eyes of the Queen staring back at her in terror. Jobber sensed her own power doubled and redoubled as the rose of fire cast another bloom. It burst open with brilliant streams of white. And Jobber knew that it was not just the fires of Beldan that answered her. Power surged in her veins, carried along arteries of fire from deep within the core of Oran's flesh. Jobber became whole, solid once more as she was remade in the fire. The crucible bubbled over, unable to contain the fullness of Jobber's power. It splashed out, and spatters of molten fire were sucked away in the whirlpool of infinity that surrounded it.

Jobber saw the flames, caught like gems in her hair. She stared back at Zorah in mute amazement. Zorah's face was livid with envy and fear. But she leaned toward Jobber, as if to kiss her. Jobber felt Zorah's warm exhale close to her lips and smelled the odor of copper and roses on her breath.

An arrow sang a brief note and buried itself in the Fire Queen's shoulder where the chain mail did not cover the burnished skin. So close to her own face, Jobber saw the delicate eyebrows lift in surprise. Through the shared sense of fire, she felt the pain like a stick stirring the molten metal in Zorah's crucible.

Startled, Zorah released Jobber and spun around. Then a second and third arrow pierced her in the neck, and she stumbled back. Her hand reached to her shoulder as blood began streaming down her neck.

She wavered on the platform, her eyes half-shuttered, her hands uplifted but not quite touching the protruding arrows. Throughout Fire Circle a low rumbling sounded. The ground vibrated, carrying the ominous noise into the center of Fire Circle.

The cobblestones of Fire Circle began to tremble and dance. The ground swayed and undulated like a slow rolling sea, each wave riding on a crest of the rumbling noise. Buildings shivered and people were cast from the balconies. The Great Bonfire leapt higher, flaming arms reaching into the sky and belching thick black smoke. Zorah turned slowly, her feet dragging, her head arched back. The rumbling quake grew louder, and as the platform lifted, forced upward by the buckling ground, Jobber turned and ran.

Behind her Zorah fell, landing hard on the platform, for there was no one to catch her fiery body.

Jobber darted to the end of the buckling platform. She looked

**261**

up and saw Wyer climbing the last rungs of a rope ladder. At the top, Alwir and Lirrel called to her.

Jobber reached for the rope ladder just as another tremor cracked the platform beneath her feet. She began climbing, cursing as she saw the rope smoke and fray at her touch. She kept climbing, hand over hand, desperately trying to outclimb the smoldering ladder. Near the top, the ropes began to give way. Glowing red and black, the fire snaked along the rope, snapping one side of the ladder. Jobber clung to the remains of the other side, trying to hoist herself up farther. Smoke appeared between the cracks of her fingers. She made a wild grab for a ledge that might hold her weight. Her legs scrabbled against the sides of the building, kicking free bits of white plaster as she frantically searched for a foothold.

"Oy, Jobber," Wyer called.

She looked up and saw him lean down, one hand extended.

"I'm afire!" she answered.

"Take my hand," he yelled, "before it's too late."

She thrust her hand upward, and he clasped it in the same moment the burning rope snapped and crumbled into ash.

Wyer groaned as the heat of her palm burned him. Jobber hung in the air, hearing his cries of agony, wanting to let go but unable to release him. Terror made her grip hard and firm. She twirled in the air, her legs dangling uselessly. Beneath her she saw the ground of Fire Circle had buckled and across the plaza cracks had opened in the earth. Steam hissed between the sliding cracks and showered the trampled bodies of the dead. Fire erupted from a window, exploding with a shower of glass. The sounded reverberated, and more windows exploded as buildings around Fire Circle bloomed with fire and smoke. The Fire Queen lay on her back, the arrows dipping with the slow draw of her breath. She stared vacantly up at the sky, her lips moving as if she spoke words.

Wyer, grimacing with pain, pulled Jobber slowly upward. His other hand clasped her by the shoulder, and he hauled her over the edge of the roof.

Jobber lay on her back breathing heavily and trembling. She closed her eyes, hearing the screaming and rumbling earth from the plaza below. She was exhausted, horrified by the violence she had escaped and terrified by the power that had come boiling so easily to the surface. And what did it mean? Without form, fire was an all-devourer, making no distinctions as it engulfed everything in its maw. It was possible, she whispered to herself, that

262

the fire that erupted in the plaza below was her own doing. Lying there, still feeling the fire that raged seemingly just beneath the surface of her skin, Jobber feared herself a frail object to contain and control such power. Too much. It was too much.

"Jobber, are you all right?" Lirrel asked.

"Don't touch me," she answered. "I'm burning."

"We must go. Can you walk?"

"Beldan is burning," Jobber answered weakly, not wanting to move but to share its destruction.

"Look at me," Lirrel demanded, and Jobber opened her eyes reluctantly. Eyes like moons dusted with smoke stared back, commanding. "Let's go," Lirrel said, and she held out a hand wrapped around with her head scarf. "Alwir knows of a ship that will take us away from here," Lirrel said, holding tightly to Jobber's arm.

"I ain't never left Beldan," Jobber said, pulling back. Lirrel's hand tugged at her.

"You must."

"Where?"

"It doesn't matter," Lirrel said. "Anywhere will be safer than here." She gave Jobber a small, encouraging smile. "I'm coming with you."

"Somehow I figured that," Jobber answered, shaking her head.

Another tremor shook the building, and the roof began to open. A section caved in, crashing to the floors below and raising a huge cloud of plaster dust.

"Let's go," Alwir shouted, "while there is still time."

A flock of swallows screeched in the air as Jobber and Lirrel started running across the rooftops of Beldan.

"Slipper, are you all right?" Kai asked as she emerged from beneath a pile of fallen rubble. Her black hair was coated with dust and streaked with blood from a cut on her forehead. She looked around and saw the black shape of the lighterman's hat.

"Slipper!" she shouted and started clawing at the pile of brick and lumber. She choked back the coughs and wiped her teary eyes as more dust rose in the air. With effort she pulled off a heavy beam of wood, recognizing it with a shudder as a gallows arm. A hand wriggled out from beneath an opening in the pile, and Kai heard Slipper call her name.

Relief at finding him alive flooded her with new-found strength. She tore into the pile of wood, and after removing two

**263**

more sections of beam, Slipper's head and shoulders appeared.

"Frigging shit, Kai," he sputtered. "I thought we were done for sure."

Kai continued to dig him out, sweat beading on her upper lip.

"Ain't over yet," she responded grimly.

"Think we can take to the tunnels?" he asked hopefully. Kai stopped digging as another rumble answered and set the ground moving again. Steam hissed in a nearby crack. Kai looked at Slipper and frowned.

"You tell me," she said and gave him her uninjured arm with which to pull himself free of the pile.

Slipper slapped at the dust on his trousers, but Kai saw on his face an absent expression. She knew he was concentrating on the water, listening.

He shook his head finally. "No. Too dangerous. Many of the tunnels are filled with water now coming in from cracks in the seawall. We'll have to go aboveground."

"And soon, I'd say," Kai said, looking up at the remains of the platform. When the cavalry had first arrived, Kai and Slipper had followed the instincts of all Waterlings and hid in the nearest hole they could find. They had jumped the barricade of wood and found an opening in which to burrow beneath the platform. From their hidey-hole below, Kai had heard the heavy tramping of the Guards' boots as they fought and the thud of bodies falling lifelessly to the boards. She saw through the cracks in the wood, the soles of the Silean nobles and Readers fleeing the platform, and she thought she knew which ones belonged to the Upright Man. Kai and Slipper had huddled close together as if to close out the shrill neighing of the horses and the screams of people dying.

And then the rumbling earth had buckled, and the platform over their heads caved in, burying them. Kai had been saved from serious injury by a crosshatching of beams that fell first, acting almost as a cage to take the weight of the heavier pieces that fell after. But now as she looked up at the gaping hole, she saw the ragged spars of wood teetering, threatening to collapse further.

"Out of here," she ordered. Slipper followed, helping her to push aside more of the fallen wood so they might escape.

Once out of the shelter of the platform, Kai stopped like a cat in a doorway. She quickly scanned the street, seeing a group of cavalry horses disappear down a sidestreet. People were lying in the street, looking like piles of discarded rags. From the wounded came weak groans and curses, while the dead lay with their faces pressed to the stones.

"Come on," she said motioning to Slipper, and cautiously they entered the street and started running. Kai tried not to look at the crushed bodies, tried not to see anything but the road before them that would lead to their escape.

She passed an abandoned barrow tipped on its side so that its contents had spilled across the street. Straw effigies of the Queen were scattered, the gold straw broken and muddied. Near the barrow a woman sat propped against a doorway. Her hands rested quietly on the ground as a small pool of blood collected around her. Kai glanced at her face and stopped, recognizing the pale skin even whiter against the dark speckling of freckles.

"Zeenia," Kai said, bending down beside her. She touched her cheek, and the eyes opened slowly.

"So, Waterling, you made it out of there in one piece," she said softly.

"Let me help you," Kai said, preparing to lift Zeenia up.

"No!" Zeenia barked. And then more softly, "No, it's no good."

Slipper appeared at Kai's shoulder, and Zeenia smiled up at him. "Two Waterlings!" she said with light humor. "Even better," she murmured to herself. Then she coughed, a small trickle of blood appearing at the corners of her mouth. Her eyes closed, the lids drawing heavily over her eyes.

Zeenia's breathing became shallow and noisy. Then suddenly her eyes opened wide, the green startling in the pale face. "Kai, do something for me," she demanded.

"Anything," Kai answered, leaning closer.

"There's two keys in my pocket. The large one opens the doors to the Grinning Bird. The smaller one is for the box hidden beneath the floorboards of my bedroom under the rug." Zeenia struggled to speak. Kai wiped away the blood at her mouth. "In the box is the deed to the shop and some money. They're yours."

"Ah no, Zeenia," Kai protested.

"Yes. But in return you must do something for me."

"Anything."

Zeenia gave a weak smile. "Keep the Grinning Bird open and help the vaggers that come to you. You're the right person for it. You know Beldan from beneath. Slipper told me about the tunnels. That information will be useful."

"I know who the Upright Man is," Kai said, wanting to share the knowledge with Zeenia.

265

But Zeenia didn't hear her, the last threads of her existence concentrated on the final words she wanted to speak. "Form an army," she whispered. "An army of Waterlings. The vaggers will help you." Then a smile parted her lips. "Z'blood," she swore through clenched teeth. Her body slumped, and her head rolled softly to one side.

Kai leaned back on her haunches, silenced by Zeenia's words. "An army of Waterlings," she repeated and looked across to Slipper to see what he would make of it. The drumming of hooves sent them clamoring over Zeenia's lifeless body to hide behind the fallen barrow. They heard the horses snort, a Guard shouting orders, and then they were gone, disappearing down another street.

"She's right," Slipper growled softly. "Build us a frigging army of Waterlings and scaffer the butcherboys once and for all."

"Yeah," Kai nodded in agreement, another possibility forming in her head. "And with an army we can take the Upright Man."

Kai rifled through Zeenia's pocket and withdrew a ring with two keys. And then as an afterthought, she said to Slipper: "Here now, fix that barrow."

Without question, he righted it to a standing position. Together they lifted Zeenia's body onto it, Slipper supporting most of the burden. Once on the barrow, Kai straightened the body and drew Zeenia's arms over her chest. She looked at the heart-shaped face, the features strangely quiet for a woman who had been so animated in life. "Sorry it can't be more, Zeenia," she said.

"We have to go," Slipper warned. "I hear the horses again."

"Right then, follow me," Kai said, her feet already beginning to run down the cobblestone street.

"Where to, Kai?" Slipper asked trailing behind her.

"Home. To the Grinning Bird," she answered, and her skirts flapped wildly around her legs as she ran.

Jobber tried not to look down as she flung herself from one rooftop across the narrow expanse of air and onto another rooftop. Far in the distance, she saw the ocean dotted white with the sails of packet ships. Each time she jumped, arms reaching desperately for the opposite side, her stomach squeezed into a knot. And each time her body collided with the hard tile of the opposite roof, the air was kicked out of her with startled gasps. Crossing Merry's Row, she lost her footing and nearly went scrambling down the steep pitch of a tiled rooftop. Shards of tile clattered to

266

the street below, breaking apart on the cobblestones. As she clung precariously to the eaves, Jobber glanced below and saw the cavalry riding down fleeing peasants. After Lirrel and Alwir carefully edged down and helped her reclimb the slope, Jobber sat next to a chimney, her whole body shaking.

"I can't do this," Jobber protested, her hands slippery with sweat.

"Not much farther," Alwir urged. "There's an alley just over there that will bring us near to the docks. Once in the street, we'll have to make a quick run for it."

Alwir turned, running nimbly along the ridged back of the roof. Lirrel held out her hand and waited for Jobber to uncurl herself from the protection of the chimney.

"Your hand is no longer hot," she said.

"Frigging iced with fear!" Jobber grumbled. "Z'blood, I hate high ups."

"Hurry!" Wyer called from the next roof. Lirrel tugged at Jobber's hand, and still muttering angrily, she rose and followed.

They reached Beakner's Lane, a narrow, damp alley lined with fishmongers barrows. She sighed with relief seeing the piled crates and barrels that had been intended to look like they were simply stored there but in fact acted as a makeshift staircase down from the rooftops.

Once on the street, Jobber felt her confidence return. The ground was solid beneath her feet, the cobblestones mercifully flat. Alwir led the way through the barrels of salted fish and fishing nets draped to dry. Cats hissed at their approach and arched their backs from behind the barrels. A damp breeze cooled Jobber's sweating face, bringing with it the clean ocean smell of the harbor.

Between two fishmonger shops, they spilled out from the alley and onto the docks. On one side were the storefronts, dingy sailors inns, the dusty windows of shipping offices and the locked doors of the merchant houses. Cargo stacked on pallets of wood waited to be loaded.

Along the dockside ships were being hastily prepared for voyage. Every rumble of Fire Circle reverberated along the docks, and rising swells lifted the ships, heaving them into the stone dockwall. The water had turned from blue-green to a muddy brown as the quakes stirred the silty soil of the harbor. High in the riggings of the packet ships sailors clung like wrack to the spars. Sails were unfurled and luffed fitfully, cut to close the wind as captains ordered faster escapes from the seething waters of the harbor.

"Where's the *Rising Star*?" Alwir called out to a captain barking orders to a crewman waiting on the dock to tie off the last bight that would free the ship.

"Gone! As will we all be in a moment! The harbor's too dangerous!"

Alwir swore but the words were lost in the sudden screaming as a knot of people burst from a street and scattered along the docks, pursued by the cavalry. The Silean Cavalry made no distinctions among their vicitms, assaulting anyone close enough to strike. A woman selling fish from a barrow ran into a shop, leaving a trail of silvery scales. A Guard followed her into the shop and returned a moment later, reeling into the street as an oyster knife protruded from his throat. More of the cavalry joined those already swarming the docks. The air was filled with their jeering shouts and the shrill neighing of their horses. Dockworkers abandoned their cargoes and began escaping into warehouses, bolting doors behind them. Those remaining in the streets hid behind the crates, while others leapt into the churning waters of the harbor. Sailors took to the safety of their ships, pulling in boarding planks.

Jobber bounded up the docks, followed in a close cluster by the others. From the corner of her eye, she could see Lirrel's black hair streaming behind her straining face. Terror moved her, sent her scurrying like a pitched stone up the wide promenade. Then Jobber remembered a name. It had seemed a silly thing once, but now it held the possibility of escape.

"Alwir," she shouted above the screams and din of the horsemen approaching fast behind them. "Look for the *Marigold*." Faul's ship. Maybe, thought Jobber wildly, maybe she'd give them refuge.

Alwir stopped running as he rapidly scanned the names of the few remaining ships. "There," he cried, pointing near the end of the dock. They began running again heading for a packet ship, its name painted in red and yellow letters on its stern. The mainsail was filled with wind, tugging at the remaining bights that held it fast to the harbor. Jobber could hear the anchor chain tapping as link by link it creeped through the hawsepipe, the pawls catching in measured cadence. A crewman hurried to the dock, one fearful eye on the Guard as he prepared to cast off.

Jobber ducked her head and demanded more speed from her legs. They responded, tearing at the distance between herself and the straining ship.

She came to the gangplank and shouted out.

"Faul! Faul Verran, are you within?" Jobber ventured a glance over her shoulder. Some of the Guard had dismounted their lathered horses, the better to attack people wedged between stacks of cargo. A dockworker fought back using a monger's fishhook. Behind him a woman shrieked obscenities as she cast stones at the advancing Guards. All along the docks, the black and gray uniforms were splattered with the muddied brown of blood.

Faul appeared on deck, her eyes bleary and dazed. She was as Jobber had seen her last, dressed in the black uniform of the Knackerman, the sword belted at her hip. Jobber swore, seeing the bottle of brandy she carried in her hand.

"Who calls?" Faul asked, annoyed at being disturbed.

Jobber couldn't answer, for a group of Guards closed in on them. Jobber turned to confront their drawn swords. Wyer and Alwir carried broken slates from a smashed crate, intending to wield them against the Guards. Jobber bent to pick up a loose cobblestone. Lirrel screamed suddenly and clung to Jobber's arm. Jobber glanced up from the street and saw the upraised sword. With a hard jerk, she yanked Lirrel out of the way as the sword hissed downward. Jobber kicked out, her heel slamming into the Guard's knee, and he toppled, his body curled over the injured leg.

"It's me, Faul. Help!" Jobber cried out again, throwing a stone at another Guard and pulling Lirrel behind her. The stone glanced off the Guard's shoulder, and he pressed forward to attack again.

Faul frowned, not recognizing the strange collection of faces, nor understanding the reason the Guards were attacking. Then her gaze fell on Jobber, the flaming red-gold hair bristling as she ducked and swerved away from the attacking Guard. Faul's face hardened, she tossed the bottle over the side and came swiftly down the narrow plank.

"Madam," she yelled to Jobber, "get on board immediately. All of you fall back." Jobber jumped away from the Guard, dragging Lirrel by the hand as they turned to run. She was afraid to look over her shoulder, afraid to see the sword coming down across her neck. Wyer joined them running for the ship, and together they swept past Faul, who had not yet drawn her sword. Alwir, clutching his makeshift weapon, remained, but Faul yelled at him to get out of her way. He dropped the broken slat and sprinted for the ship.

The Guards shouted and pressed their advantage forward until they saw Faul waiting for them. One by one, as they recognized her, they drew themselves up short and stopped, surprised. They glanced at each another, hesitating to see who would move

269

against her first. Coolly, Faul stepped toward them, her body like a razor's edge, thin but sharp. The Guard rattled their swords as if embarrassed by their sudden mood of caution. They sneered encouragingly to each other and fanned out into a circle around her. Together they attacked her.

Faul's sword suddenly flashed into motion. Grabbing the hilt with the left hand instead of the right, she jerked the sword free and thrust straight backward with it, killing the Guard behind her. The man buckled, his hands clutching at his torn gut. In that moment Faul switched the blade into her right hand and with one continuous sweep slashed through the bodies of the two attacking Guardsmen on her right. Their battle cries rose into squeals of pain. Extending forward on bended knee, Faul killed two more with the return sweep of her blade. They fell heavily, as thick red lines of blood scored their uniforms. Once more, Faul shifted her stance to face the opposite side, changing to a two-handed grip on the hilt. The Guard tried to defend himself, bringing his sword up for an attack. But she was faster than him. With a whiplike slash, she cut upward, severing his arm and cutting his throat. The man whirled in an explosion of blood and then fell. There was a flash as she turned the edge of the blade and swung it again, this time catching a Guard across the ribs and belly as he tried to swing his sword. With a final slashing stroke, she drove the blade downward across the neck and back of the last Guard as he turned to flee the carnage.

It had lasted for a moment, scarcely long enough for Jobber to blink. The slain Guards lay around her, the cobblestones turning wet and slick. Faul never looked at them, her eyes staring straight ahead. With a precise motion, Faul wiped her sword clean and then returned it to the scabbard.

Aboard the ship, Jobber shuddered. Never had she seen anyone kill so quickly, so effortlessly as Faul had dispatched the Guards. Faul stepped over the bodies and came briskly toward them. Up the plank, she shouted to a crewman to cast off. He unknotted the last bight and leapt aboard as the ship scraped against the dockwall and then bounced freely on the current. The sails turned to the wind and carried the ship into the open harbor. Spray splashed over the sides, and Jobber clutched the rails awkwardly as the ship heeled to one side.

Faul was still shouting orders to her crew, taking the wheel to guide the *Marigold* through the rough waters of the harbor. At the mouth of the harbor, the ocean opening out before them, Faul gave the wheel to the first mate and came quickly toward Jobber.

"Madam," Faul said respectfully and bent her head.

Jobber frowned at Faul, confused, and then an inkling of understanding penetrated.

"Z'blood, you think I'm the Queen," she said, a queasy feeling starting in her stomach.

Faul's head jerked up and genuine surprise softened the edges of her angular face. She stared at Jobber and her eyes narrowed.

"You're not the Queen," Faul said slowly.

Jobber shook her head.

"Who are you?"

"Jobber. Remember, we drank together at the Anvil—" Jobber was speaking quickly, afraid of the cold gray eyes.

Faul's lips parted with a groan, and she looked back to the disappearing dock. "What have I done? What in the frigging whore's shit have I done?" She stared back at Jobber. "All I saw was your hair. That color, and I took you for the Queen." She turned from Jobber, looking closely now at all of them. Her lips formed a thin line of displeasure.

"Why were you running away?"

"The butcherboys was after us, you saw that," Jobber said simply. She knew Faul wasn't going to like the rest of it.

"That part I know. Why?"

"It started at Firefaire. See, the Queen was going to string Alwir and Wyer up by the noddynoose and—"

Faul breathed in sharply, interrupting Jobber's rapid explanation.

"Why were they going to be hanged?"

"Because they're New Moon," Jobber answered in a low voice.

"Ah no," Faul groaned again and lowered her head, shaking it. "That's all I need. A charge of killing Silean Guards while defending the likes of the New Moon and street brats." She lifted her gaze to Jobber suddenly. "You were a boy the last time I saw you," she said sharply.

Jobber gave a thin smile and shrugged.

"I should toss the whole lot of you overboard for the frigging mess you've put me in."

"But you won't, will you?" answered Jobber boldly. "'Cause you know, even if we was the worst sort, we ain't nearly as bad as those butcherboys you knackered back there. Look here, Faul," Jobber started earnestly, "it was a frigging massacre. It wasn't just the New Moon who stood to get scaffered. Fire Circle was packed with all sorts, and out of nowhere the cavalry rides in and just started killing everyone they could get their swords into—"

"I need a drink," Faul said sourly. Looking at all of them, she shook her head and reconsidered. "I need a bottle." She turned and left them, heading down the tiny staircase beneath the poop deck to her cabin.

"She's drunk fair enough already, I'll wager," Jobber said, watching Faul lurch across the deck.

"Drunk?" Alwir repeated and paled. "She can fight like that even drunk?"

"Probably how she fights best," replied Jobber, remembering that night in the Anvil when Faul had baited the Guard.

Jobber shivered with the moist wind and turned back to stare over the ship's railing at the city. Beldan was burning. Smoke hovered above it like a malevolent cloud, and she could see that fire had spread throughout the city. Jobber fell silent, her mouth drawn into a tight frown. Lirrel came and stood next to her and touched her lightly on the arm. Jobber's hands curled into angry fists.

"It hurts to think of all those people back there..." Jobber started to say. She stopped speaking, having no words that could express her fury. Trapped in the whirlwind of the butcherboys' swords, seeing women and children slaughtered in Fire Circle, fleeing people hunted through Beldan's streets, all sense and reason disappeared, crushed beneath hatred.

"*Ahal*," Lirrel agreed. She reached for the flute in her pocket and brought it to her lips. Accompanied by the creaking sounds of the ship, she played a hollow-voiced tune, the notes lifting out over the water. It was a discordant song, filled with the horrors of Fire Circle; the clamoring of fleeing people pursued by the cavalry. Through her anger Jobber heard it, and her shoulders sagged as the music exposed the ache of grief. Dogsbody and Donal dead. Beldan in flames. Herself cut adrift. Then Lirrel stopped playing as if the anguished voice of the flute had become unbearable.

In the silence, broken only by the rushing of waves against the hull, Jobber thought of Alwir's words as he spoke from the platform. "A bitter harvest," she whispered softly to the burning city.

# 21

With a loud bang, Faul threw open the door of her cabin and stormed on deck. Her eyes were no longer bleary but a deadly cold gray.

"Oy," she shouted. "All of you, come here." She pointed in front of her with one rigid finger and then waited, her feet well apart to balance her stance on the rolling deck.

Jobber released her grip on the ship's railing, realizing suddenly how tightly she had been clinging. She stumbled across the deck, unaccustomed to the swaying and pitching of the ship. She glanced up and saw the swinging masts of the *Marigold* high above her head. At once, her stomach tightened, and the blood seemed to rush away from her head down to her unsteady feet. The greasy hot savories had settled in a solid lump in her stomach and now seemed to roll from side to side with the motion of the ship.

"You're not in Beldan anymore," Faul was saying. "And if you're taking passage on my ship, you'll work."

Jobber sat up and licked her dry lips. Her mouth was flooded with a sour-tasting saliva. Looking out over the opposite railing of the ship, she saw the horizon rise and fall at a slant. "Frigging shit," Jobber groaned as a wave of nausea rippled through her.

"None of that on this ship," Faul snapped. "The only one permitted an opinion is the Old Man."

"Old Man?" Jobber turned a questioning face to Faul.

"The Old Man is the captain and that's me."

"If you ain't a Knackerman, then you're an Old Man. When are you gonna get a job that's fitting for a woman, Faul?"

Faul pursed her lips in an expression of annoyance. "Think I'll wait for the world to come around instead."

A sudden swell lifted the ship. Jobber lurched forward, her flailing arms grabbing at ropes lashed around the mast. She looked across the bow of the ship and saw again the horizon dip and sway, rise up and drop at an angle. Above her the halyards slapped against the mast in the brisk wind. Her face paled and the savories weighed heavily in her stomach.

"Ah, Faul," she said meekly. "Give me a moment will you?"

Faul stared at Jobber's greening face and smiled drily. "Not much of a seahand are you? You'll get over it. But standing still won't help you much."

"What about brandy, eh? Just a drop or two?"

"Rations are given out at day's end. And not before."

"Z'blood, Faul," Jobber swore as another wave of nausea forced its way up her throat. Her tongue felt glued to the roof of her mouth.

"You there," she pointed to Alwir, "get a bucket and join with Rikel swabbing the deck. Later he can show you how to climb the riggings and work the sails. And you," she turned to Wyer. But Wyer held up his two burned hands apologetically. Faul swore under her breath and then said: "Get the Ghazali girl to bandage those hands up. Afterward, you learn to coil ropes and sail mending. Tige here will show you," and she motioned to an older man sitting near the railing, a sail draped across his lap as he pushed a needle through the coarse fabric. He grinned at Wyer out of one side of his mouth, a pipe nestled firmly in the other side. "And you, girl," Faul said to Lirrel, "when you're done with him, go to the galley and help the cook. Now off with you," Faul motioned with her head, and they left, Lirrel casting anxious glances behind to Jobber.

Faul gave a dry smile and sauntered close to Jobber. "And now for you," she said. She motioned the first mate over, and Jobber saw a burly man with a thick chest and short bowlegs approach. "A bucket of slush, Harral," Faul ordered.

"Look here, Faul, I ain't feeling so good," Jobber said.

"Really?" said Faul with mock concern. "How's that?"

"Sick. Kind of squirmy."

"Like a bucket of eels?"

Jobber's stomach flopped violently, and she gagged at the savories that came crowding up her throat. "Z'blood, Faul," she said through gritted teeth, trying not to vomit, "you're making me pay, ain't you?"

"Oh no," Faul shook her head, "I haven't begun to make you pay for the trouble you've caused me."

Jobber was still swallowing at the lump in her throat when Harral came bustling up to her, a pot of thick yellow grease in one hand. He smiled knowingly at Faul and then wickedly at Jobber.

"Ever been aloft before?" he asked in his gruff voice.

Jobber shook her head.

"Come on then. First time for everything. Get that hair out of the way though. You'll want to see where your putting yourself up there." He handed Jobber a length of leather cord, and she tied her hair back with it. Harral took her by the arm to give her assistance, but she shook off the gnarled hand with an insult.

He lifted a bushy eyebrow at her. "Right little pisser, ain't you? Make no mind though. If you're thinking you belong with a higher quality, then higher you'll go."

Jobber followed, wobbling unsteadily behind him. He stopped before the rigging.

"Here you are," Harral said jovially and slung the bucket over Jobber's arm and the rope handles to a small board seat over the other arm. "When you get to the crosstree just shackle the chair to the topsail halyard block—"

"The what?" asked Jobber, not liking the sound of this.

"That bit up there, like a platform, that's the crosstree. The rope over there lying across it is the topsail halyard block. Shackle this here bos'un's chair to the block, then sit. We'll hoist you the rest of the way to the topmast. Once you're up there, just slap this grease on thick over the topmast. It's been newly scraped and it needs a layer of this to protect it."

"No. I won't go up there," Jobber said, panic rising in her voice.

"Growl you may, but go you must if the Old Man orders it."

Jobber looked back at Faul, who was staring out to sea. The wind was ruffling her graying hair.

"No," she said again more vehemently. "I'll be sick."

"There's worse things needing doing," Harral answered. "This one ain't half so bad, and at least you'll get hauled up instead of climbing the way on your own feet. Come on, don't delay then. Can't be that you're scared, is it?"

"I ain't never scared," Jobber said furiously.

"Up you go then." He placed a heavy hand on her shoulder and steered her to the masthead.

Looking up into the riggings, Jobber stared worriedly at the lattice of ropes. High overhead the blue sky was stippled with fine clouds spread out like fleece.

"Frigging bastard," she swore at Faul and started up the rigging, moving slowly and cautiously. The ropes tore at her hands, the coarse fiber prickling like tiny splinters. Reaching the crosstree she shackled the bos'un's chair to the topsail halyard block and gave the signal to hoist away.

The ropes lurched and bumped as she was lifted higher and higher up the mast. In the distance she could just make out the deep blue shoreline etched against the horizon. The ground swells were rolling the boat heavily, and from her vantage point in the sky, the spars swung in a wide arc over the gray-green water.

The ropes stopped pulling, and Jobber clutched the mast, trying not to look down at the deck below as it rocked in the rough sea. Her hair unworked itself from the leather tie and fluttered around her head. From below she looked like a red tassel tied to the top of the mast.

"Start slushing down the mast!" the mate called in a voice that seemed to be carried up from a long way.

"Z'blood!" she mumbled and groped with a trembling hand for the brush in the pot. Holding fast to the ropes with one arm, she began slapping grease on the bare top mast. The slush was a thick yellow grease that reeked of animal fat. Jobber squeezed her eyes shut. Between the rancid odor of the slush and the black rolling deck beneath her, she knew she was going to be sick.

"Get me down!" she screamed to Harral watching from below.

Faul looked up, like a small doll tied to the wheel. "You'll not come down 'til the job is done," she shouted back.

"It's going to be done awfully quick if you don't get me down right now!" Jobber called. But the wind blew her words away, and Faul merely glowered up at her and shook her head. "Faul, get me down from here, you frigging bastard!"

A sudden swell lifted the ship's prow out of the water and set it down again with a hard slap. A shudder traveled through the length of the ship, and as the mast on which Jobber clung swayed deeply with the motion, Jobber's stomach gave a savage heave.

The contents of Jobber's angry stomach spilled down the belly of the mainsail, some of it spattering Faul standing below at the wheel.

Faul bellowed with rage, and dimly through the haze of retching, Jobber heard the obscenities that Faul screamed up to her. After listening to the continuous stream of searing insults, Jobber decided it was probably safer to stay just where she was until Faul calmed down. She ventured a peek down below and saw Faul's fist raised, the mate wiping her shoulders off with a wet cloth. Faul's face contorted with fury as the angry words blasted out of her. From her perch high aloft the *Marigold*, Jobber smiled, discovering that of the two of them, Faul had the distinction of being cruder and more inventive when it came to obscenities.

Feeling somewhat better now that her stomach was emptied and that she had managed to sidetrack Faul's attempt at revenge, Jobber settled down on the hard bos'un's chair to wait.

The afternoon dragged on, the sun making its passage around the masts. It glittered on the sea, broken into a million shards of bouncing light. In the far distance Jobber saw long dark shadows appear on the surface of the water. They rose slightly like narrow islands and then slid again into the sea, disappearing from the water's surface. Slowly, Jobber became accustomed to the rolling of the ship and the swaying of the ship's spars. The wind gusted strongly aloft, and the sea smelled sharp and cold. On one side she could see the gray edge of the coast. On the other side was the sea, meeting the sky with a fine line of purple. Birds wheeled and screeched above her attracted by her hair.

And as she waited, Jobber found herself with time to think. It struck her as odd that while she had lived within the crowded streets of Beldan, she had never known how sheltered her life had been. Beldan was a city of walls. And though she roamed freely in the streets, she remained always hidden in its shadows. She had teased the Waterlings once for preferring the tunnels to the light and air of the streets. But now perched high above a vast expanse of blue-green ocean, Jobber saw that she had lived in a maze of her own, tracing and retracing her steps through its narrow corridors. It was like her life, each day passing but she going nowhere, only clinging more tightly to old habits.

Jobber breathed in deeply savoring the cold air. In these last two days everything had been torn apart. The common ordinariness of her life, even Beldan itself, was changed. And Jobber realized that she had survived so far only because she had not been alone. Faul had killed the Guards and given her the gift of flight. Donal and Dogsbody had died for her, their sacrifice a painful gift. And Jobber realized that Kai, too, in her own way, had given Jobber a valuable gift. Jobber had accepted the world, accepted the inevitability of being found and hanged for having power. Though she despised it, feared it, she never dared to believe that anything else was possible. Kai was different. She fought back, defying the laws that oppressed all of them. In the continual night of Beldan's tunnels, Kai had seen much farther than Jobber, believing with a blind faith that not only she would survive, but her Waterlings as well.

Jobber's fiery hair billowed around her, reminding her of yet another more dubious gift: that of self knowledge. The Fire Queen Zorah had tried to destroy her, absorb her like a candle flame in a burning house. They had both been terrified when Jobber's elemental power roared its reply, cracking the edges of Zorah's control. She was Beldan's fire; and now that Jobber knew the true substance of that calling, she could no longer avoid the need to confront herself. "To have so much power," she breathed to the wind, warming it with her exhalation. "And to be little more than a half-witted, bad-tempered snitch," she added, the scorn of her voice revealing also the fear. "What do I do with it all?"

"*Accept it*," Jobber heard, not knowing whether it was a memory of Lirrel's voice or whether she spoke to her now. Jobber looked down to the deck of the *Marigold*. She caught sight of Lirrel's black hair and saw the upturned oval face. In the late afternoon, Lirrel's eyes reflected the golden light like two setting suns. Jobber waved tentatively at first and then more vigorously as she saw Lirrel wave back.

Hugging the mast again, Jobber smiled, resolution surfacing like the black shapes out of the water. She wouldn't be limited by fear. And though she fled into exile now, she promised herself that somehow she would return to Beldan. On the far horizon the sun began to set, the fiery ball dipping gracefully into the water.

"Oy, Jobber!" someone called from below. Jobber looked and saw Harral, his hands cupped over his mouth as he shouted. "Prepare to come down!"

She just had time to clutch the ropes tightly before she felt the ropes under the bos'un's chair lurch and then drop her down a few inches at a time. She peeked down between her legs and saw Faul staring up intently as they lowered her down slowly.

Faul was no longer dressed in the black uniform of the First-watch but now wore a loose white shirt, tucked into brick-red trousers. Over that she wore a leather vest tooled with a scroll pattern of waves. Still slim, the clothes did much to hide the sharp angles of Faul's body. The brown hue of the vest lightened Faul's usually sallow complexion.

"You look better that way, you know," Jobber observed honestly as she gingerly stepped onto the deck again. Her legs trembled, unused to the solid feel of wood. "Like a real person and not some walking stick."

Faul glared. Jobber held the steely gaze, chin pointing up. Then Faul sighed, and Jobber heard the soft chuckle in her throat.

On Faul's face a crooked smile lifted her cheeks, and her eyes turned a light gray.

"You are the most piss-annoying little bastard—"

"Oy, no need for insult," said Jobber.

"Like spit on the wind that comes back to hit me in the face."

"I didn't get it on your face. Only that uniform, which you're better off without anyway."

"Which is the only reason you're still standing here in one piece."

"You know, Faul," Jobber said and leaned back to take a better look at the woman, "you know, I'd say I'd done you a favor. I hope you've tossed that black thing overboard."

"That's none of your business," Faul answered shortly.

Jobber shrugged, unable to hide her amusement.

"I'll make an agreement with you," Faul said.

"What?" Jobber asked.

"I won't make life too miserable for you aboard ship, and you in turn will give me no trouble. No trouble whatsoever."

"Sounds fair," Jobber nodded.

"I expect work from you," Faul continued.

"As long as it ain't washing your uniform."

"No, but you will swab decks, help with the sails and do everything else I order."

Jobber pretended to think it over. Inwardly she was relieved to be getting off with so light a sentence. "Done," she blurted out.

Then she spit into her palm and extended it to Faul to seal the bargain. Faul looked at the wet palm, and her mouth curled with disgust.

"I'll take your word for it," she replied. "It's a short voyage, Jobber. Just try not to make it any longer than necessary," she warned.

Faul left and Jobber grinned as she wiped the spit off her palm on her trouser leg.

Jobber walked slowly up the rolling deck of the *Marigold*, hearing the sound of Lirrel's flute. She found Lirrel sitting amidst coils of rope in the pointed angle of the ship's prow. Lirrel's eyes were shut as she played, her brow furrowed in concentration. Her long black hair streamed over her shoulders damp with the ocean's salt spray. Jobber sat beside her drawing her knees up close to her chest as the music revived her grief. It was a song of Beldan again and the nightmare of Fire Circle. The music seemed awkward, almost tentative, as Lirrel struggled to find a melody within the discordant threads of the song. Then gradually Jobber heard it change, grow stronger and more lyrical as Lirrel searched for understanding, and even forgiveness. The song became a requiem for Beldan's dead and a promise of hope for the survivors. The flute's hollow voice seemed to float on the surface of the water as fragile as the lacy foam. Sighing, Jobber rested her chin on her knees and let the mournful sound of Lirrel's flute shape her sorrow.